VERNON F. ANDERSON was b[illegible] in 1900. After displaying an early aptitude [illegible] interest in medicine, he was sent to London to train as a doctor, and studied at Kings College, University of London and Westminster Hospital Medical School. In 1928, he applied for a post in the British Colonial Civil Service and was sent as a medical officer to British Honduras, where he went on to head the medical division. To diversify, he also studied public health and tropical medicine, and spent time in Greece and Albania, examining how the respective governments coped with malaria.

In 1946, Dr Anderson represented the Belize government in his home country, helping to plan the University of the West Indies. On retirement from government services in Belize, he was awarded an OBE in recognition of his work. He returned to Jamaica and set up a private practice, in which he continued working until 1971.

Sudden Glory is his only novel, inspired by his work in medicine, his growing interest in the literature signifying the 'coming of age' of Jamaica, and a quote by the seventeenth century English philosopher, Thomas Hobbes, 'Laughter is a passion without name, it is a *Sudden Glory*.'

Dr Anderson now lives with his family in Ontario, Canada.

VERNON F. ANDERSON

SUDDEN GLORY

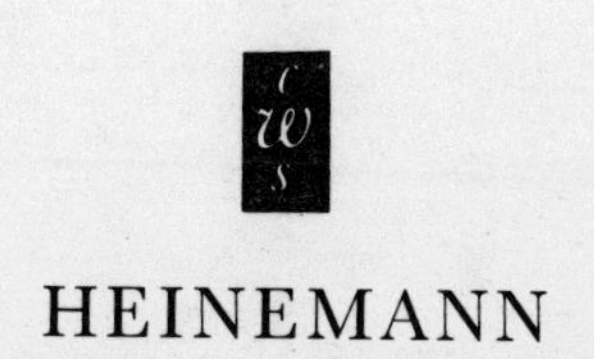

HEINEMANN

Heinemann Educational Books Ltd.
22 Bedford Square, London WC1B 3HH

Heinemann Educational Books (Nigeria) Ltd.
PMB 5205, Ibadan
Heinemann Educational Books (Kenya) Ltd.
Kijabe Street, PO Box 45314, Nairobi
Heinemann Educational Books Inc.
70 Court Street, Portsmouth, New Hampshire, 03801, USA
Heinemann Educational Books (Caribbean) Ltd.
175 Mountain View Avenue, Kingston 6, Jamaica

EDINBURGH MELBOURNE AUCKLAND
SINGAPORE KUALA LUMPUR NEW DELHI GABORONE

British Library Cataloguing in Publication Data

Anderson, Vernon F.
Sudden glory.—(Caribbean writers series).
I. Title II. Series
813[F] PR9280.9.A5

ISBN 0–435–98808–5
ISBN 0–435–98809–3 export pbk

Typeset by Activity Limited, Salisbury, Wiltshire, England.
Printed and bound in Great Britain

Laughter is a passion without name ...
it is a Sudden Glory.
Thomas Hobbes 1588–1659

PART ONE

ELUTERIO'S EARS: 1932

'Now, Eluterio,' Captain Medina began, riding his mule with his muscles slack and his body responding to the animal's jolting pace with experienced ease, 'Eluterio, before he had his vision, was generally esteemed as a *chiclero* of exemplary habits. He was a diligent worker in the bush, unusually temperate when "at rest" in the dry season and not given to coarse or boastful play even in his infrequent and reticent cups. It was true he had a keen eye for a toothsome girl and was not too particular whether some other man had a prior claim. But in his wooing Eluterio was speedy, smooth and dexterous and his tactful, even tearful, departure from the wooed and won left little room for dramatic beating of forsaken breasts or gnashing of jealous teeth.

'Then Eluterio had his vision. He saw the wealth of the world at his feet. Instead of being a *chiclero* he would become a chicle-contractor. To this end he used the good offices of a former female friend, who was now in an advantageous position, to get him a concession to bleed chicle in a small area of the forest, difficult of access, where it was said the sapodilla trees, which give gum, grew but sparsely. His friend, drawing on her tender memories of Eluterio, got him his concession.'

Captain Medina was telling his tale to Dr. Ephraim Cutbush who bestrode a mule beside him but sat on it stiffly and uncomfortably with the result that it was not long before he felt that his body had been enshrouded in an ill-fitting carapace which chafed his flesh and made his bones ache.

They had, earlier that morning, accompanied by a band of *chicleros* and baggage mules, crossed the border between Guatemala and British Honduras, at El Cayo. They were on their way to Shoonantonich which was the headquarters of the U.S. Consolidated Chicle Company and the location of an archaeological expedition funded by the Nethersole Foundation. Dr. Cutbush was the President of the latter and was making his first visit to the almost empty forest lands of Petén where, once, a peaceful Mayan civilization had flourished.

'Having become a chicle contractor Eluterio was on his way to wealth and power,' Medina continued. 'Of course he had to borrow money to feed himself and his few *chicleros* for the season, to buy the mules to bring out the chicle and to take in food and equipment. He also had to borrow money to give his *chicleros* their "advance". With this purpose in mind he approached the fabulous Mr. Gaskin ... the contractor of chicle contractors ... who even went to New York every year to bargain on the price of the gum. Mr. Gaskin lent him the money and Eluterio worked on his remote concession like a demon, and saw to it that his men worked with him just as diligently. The result was that his mules appeared at Mr. Gaskin's warehouses in El Cayo laden with prime chicle and Eluterio saw that his vision had not been vain.'

The straggle of laden mules and *chicleros*, led by Medina, reached a part of the trail where they had to proceed in single file and Dr. Cutbush was forced to fall behind the Captain with nothing to attract his attention but the dense walls of the forest on each side of him. Had he been in the mood he might have found observation of the botanical wonderland which flanked him on each side a rewarding occupation. However, the subject he had in mind was one he could not relinquish easily. It was labelled 'Eluterio's Ears: 1932.' It had been the starting point for Captain Medina's story and while, perforce, Dr. Cutbush waited for the opportunity to ride beside the Captain again he thought back to his brief sojourn in Belize, to the hospitality he had received there from the District Commissioner, to his impressions of the small British colony, to the news he had heard on the D.C.'s 'wireless set' and to his visit with the local M.O., Hastings.

The hospitality had been exemplary. His impressions of Belize, his first visit to a British colony, he had noted in his diary. There he had described British Honduras as a place where it seemed the mental and physical life was spent in a shady afternoon with occasional disturbances caused by the Guatemaltecan Government which, every now and then, used the border problem for a kind of 'bread and circuses' diversion. As a further comment on that subject the District Commissioner had suggested that the turbulent appetite of the Guatemaltecan people needed something to feed on between revolutions. While the *golpes de estado*, the frequent *coups d'états*, formed the bulk of their diet the frontier question of 'Belize the Lost Province' was something for them to chew between meals, though the satisfaction it gave was small and therefore very little came of it. It was, to change the metaphor, the peacetime neurosis of the Guatemaltecans.

The news he had heard on the D.C.'s 'wireless' was that Mussolini's forces had invaded Ethiopia and, he thought, another colony was, thus, in throes of birth. It was a conquest that did not, however, involve any stout Cortez and 500 men, but rather army corps, squadrons of bombers and bloodshed raised to the nth degree of frightfulness.

Finally, there had been Doctor Hastings, a man of medicine after Cutbush's own heart, who found the isolation of the town of El Cayo a purgatory of futility. He had, in fact, expressed himself by saying that the trouble with living in a bankrupt and stagnant backwater of the far-flung British Empire was that it 'could not, nor could it ever have been, flung far enough.'

Hastings was keen on pathology but his small hospital, with its dozen beds, offered him little scope to practise this discipline. So, he tried to occupy his time by doing a little elementary natural history and had a bottled collection of the smaller snakes from the region. Cutbush had been impressed by how well the snakes had been preserved and mounted but he had been even more intrigued by a bottle containing a pair of human ears. Each had been damaged. Through one there was a neat hole. The other was crumpled and had ragged edges. When he had asked Hastings for an explanation the doctor said that the story was a long one that would have to wait until he had plenty of time to tell it. Such an occasion had not arisen and only now, when Captain Medina had volunteered to recount it, did Cutbush get an opportunity to hear a tale that would probably soon become a part of the local folklore.

After a few minutes the trail they were following widened and

Cutbush was again able to take up his position beside his Mexican companion.

'Of course,' Medina continued at once, 'one season's work could not completely pay off all Eluterio's debts but he now owned mules and equipment. He borrowed more money, hired more men and went back to the bush the next season.

'His results, at the end of his second season, were as encouraging as at the first. During his third season, however, he began to have problems. He found it difficult to get his former *chicleros* to go back to the bush with him. He had worked them too hard. Setting the example he would be climbing and tapping the tall sapodilla when but the tip of their topmost leaves shone in the morning sun. Besides, it was not right, it did not march with chicle morals that the contractor should be there in the bush overseeing the tapping, the collecting, the boiling, the moulding and then emphatically and personally conveying the chicle-blocks from bush to warehouse. So he had to collect other *chicleros* ... not a particularly creditable lot ... and, as he had decided to finish bleeding all the available trees in the concession this season and negotiate for a bigger and better area next season, he had to accept *chicleros* whom he feared would be lazy and difficult. Mr. Gaskin lent him more money and Eluterio bought more mules in spite of the fact that Mr. Gaskin explained to him that the market was now very uncertain. He could not, he said, agree to pay Eluterio a firm price per pound at the end of the season. He could only pay the current price as offered in Belize minus ten cents per pound. Eluterio did not think it mattered. He went back to the bush with men and mules.

'As ever he drove himself, his men and his mules mercilessly. Mules, however, will not be driven beyond a certain point. Thereafter they are apt to sicken and die. Eluterio had much sickness amongst his mules. Then he had to shoot the gun out of the hand of a mutinous *chiclero*. After this several more mules died, mules which had not been sick. But he brought in his chicle, though his men and mules arrived back in El Cayo worn out. El Cayo was not sympathetic. The market had crashed. The "golden twenties" had finished.

'Then Mr. Gaskin discussed matters with Eluterio ... item by item ... and the visionary found he owed Mr. Gaskin money ... a great deal of money ... more than it could ever be conceived that a man who could only sign his name could ever owe anyone.

'Eluterio was appalled. His dream of power and wealth had betrayed him. Now, his mules were not his, his house was not his, his few acres were not his and he even appeared to breathe at the pleasure of Mr. Gaskin. The final straw which made Eluterio take a despairing view of matters, had no relation to book-keeping. It was the affair of "moisture content". In the midst of this piling of horror upon despair one of Mr. Gaskin's young men came in to announce that the chicle had been weighed and was now being tested. There followed a quick display of glass tubes and chemicals.

'"You see," said Mr. Gaskin a few moments later, "the moisture content is too high so the penalty clause is now applicable."

'Then another of Mr. Gaskin's men appeared. He was not so slim nor so dexterous but quieter, slower, smoother, and altogether more deadly. He read the total sum of the indebtedness in a purring murmur ... so many dollars.

'"There are not so many stars in heaven," thought Eluterio.

'In the turmoil of his soul he turned for comfort to the friend who had got him his concession. She had already heard the bad news from an unimpeachable source and would not listen to him. Besides, she told him, his affairs with Zena and Claudia and Miranda had, as it were, worn the obligation of friendship thin.

'So Eluterio took to drink, drowning himself in it between bouts of deadly sickness. Then he saddled his horse and left El Cayo.

'Since that moment Mr. Gaskin had not crossed the frontier into Petén for several years. And even then his sojourn in El Cayo did not extend for more than a few days at any one time. He always came and went quietly without fanfare though now and again, while in El Cayo, he would take some exercise. He loved riding a spirited horse and would ride to some of the neighbouring farms or "ranchos" where he had still one or two friends.

'It was while returning from such a visit that Mr. Gaskin, who was holding the reins in his left hand and had swayed his body to adjust himself to the sudden movement of the horse, was struck by a bullet that tore through his left hand, smashed the adjacent rib and sped on, but not through. Blood spattered the left side of his shirt and he fell into the grass.

'Eluterio came to look curiously at him, was satisfied at the widening patch of blood on the shirt and rode away without a second shot. He was a man who was proud of his marksmanship. One bullet was usually enough. Though that was before he became a confirmed drunkard and made the mistake of speaking of his deed without knowing that Mr. Gaskin was still very much alive.

'Whether he then, returned across the frontier to complete the job, or to get some of the goods he still claimed were his, or to visit his friends is not known. He was, however, seen by a policeman on night duty in a village. The latter was armed with a revolver and a truncheon, though all the world knew that the cartridges in the revolver were so old that one could never tell which would fire until the trigger was pulled. The policeman was found mortally wounded, his truncheon by his side, the revolver still buttoned in its holster. What had taken place no one ever knew with certainty. The dying man was able to gasp out "Eluterio – him" – and to mumble something else before departing this world. Some folk concluded that he had tried to apprehend Eluterio depending only on the majesty of the law and a truncheon.

'Now, public opinion said, Eluterio had done something foolish. To shoot Mr. Gaskin was a crime. To kill a policeman armed with no more than a stick was the height of folly. So that was his first blunder.

'His second blunder was when he avenged himself on Major Jaime Peat-Patterson.

'Jaime's offence was that he had saved Mr. Gaskin's life and a few minutes later saved Eluterio's life. The first was accidental but the second was quite deliberate. At that time Jaime Peat-Patterson was one of Mr. Gaskin's "slim young men". But there was something about this young man, no longer so young and much too thin, which marked him off from most of the other young men. For one thing Jaime could never quite make Mr. Gaskin feel that he, the master, was the sum and substance of his being and that to be in his service was a reward in itself. Those who gave Gaskin good service were well paid but he was the final judge of what counted as "good service".

'Jaime worked for him for several years and served him well

though mostly in the mahogany section of Gaskin's enterprises. The business practices of the mahogany trade differed greatly from those of the chicle business. There was never that flavour of "illicit diamond buying" in the mahogany business which pervaded chicle. So there grew up a curious relationship between Jaime and Gaskin. The latter knew, without being told, that there were certain things which though strictly within the law should not be asked of Jaime.

'Amongst the qualities that made Jaime valuable to his master was an excellent memory for detail. Gaskin called it a "fly-paper" memory. And Jaime could remember such details for quite a time, sometimes for a long time. It was something which Gaskin appreciated because, as he said, he was surrounded by people "whose brains were sieves who could not even remember their own name from last week to this". Good as Jaime's memory was, however, it was a poor thing compared to Gaskin's which was self-winnowing. No fact, figure nor feature of the smallest value escaped it, provided any one of them would be useful in his business interests. "Asleep or awake" it was said, "he was thinking of his affairs." Why Gaskin, who until he educated himself, had had only that limited education which Belize could give, should have been a millionaire while Jaime Peat-Patterson should have been merely his clerk was more than a question of memory and more than a matter of cataloguing and filing.

'Jaime was sent to Quintana Roo in Mexico to work in Mr. Gaskin's mahogany operations there for the cutting of this timber had declined sharply in British Honduras. The forests near the rivers had been cut out and it was now too expensive for a weak market to haul mahogany timber from the distant forests to the rivers.

'So Gaskin closed down his mahogany works in the Colony, but extended his holdings in the adjacent territory of Quintana Roo for the forests of the Mexican Territory could still be worked at a profit. Curiously Jaime, singularly efficient in the mahogany operations in the Colony, was a failure in Quintana Roo. For one thing, he became involved in a tortuous and fetid quarrel involving his mother's relatives there. The relatives were many, influential and vicious. Gaskin recalled him to the Colony and put him in the real estate section of his affairs. Here he wilted – but the cause was not connected with his occupation.

'He was not happy and started getting attacks of the "flu". Gaskin made him accountant in the business of his cinema theatre. The only one in the Colony. The "flu" became "influenza". Gaskin uttered no word of exasperation. He knew men and he knew this man. He often staved off outbreaks of "influenza" by taking Jaime with him on his travels about the Colony - part secretary - part companion - part guard. But there was one weakness to which Gaskin confessed, one which wasted much time, one that he actually read books about and he hadn't read a book on any other subject for years. He played chess and that bound him to Jaime. Gaskin was a resolute chess player; he played chess with passion, with a consuming, a tenacious zeal. Why, on his journey to New York to discuss chicle prices, he had actually delayed two whole days in Havana to see Capablanca, the world champion, play. His precise memory, his instinctive knowledge of an opponent's weakness made him a formidable opponent. He could, he confessed, smell recklessness in an adversary in the first two moves. The cautious, the cunning, the erudite, or those who trusted to native genius and daring took him but a few moves longer. If his opponent was obviously not of his mettle Gaskin became bored and developed a consuming distaste for any ass who only pretended to understand the divine pastime. Lest he should dishonour the game by losing his temper, a thing which hardly any man had seen him do, he allowed himself obviously to be check-mated speedily and aggravatingly. Then a game with Jaime became necessary to take the bad taste out of his mouth. Jaime at his best was his master, but he was not always, not even very often, at his best.

'For he got struck with sudden delicious ideas, he experimented, he developed involved gambits, so involved that after the game not even Gaskin could follow the rationale of the gambit, nor appreciate the subtlety of the ideas involved. They compared notes and worked out problems together. It was no uncommon sight for his mahogany labourers to see Mr. "Peat" and Mr. Gaskin poring over a chess-board hour after hour. Darkness came, lamps were lit, the silence of sleep fell on the camp. Master and man sat on through the night. The labourers swore that they had known the camp to wake, the day's work to start and only then did the master stop the play.

'Gaskin was a very courageous man but not foolishly so. As long as Eluterio was alive or until he was seen dead and buried by unimpeachable witnesses Gaskin did not visit El Cayo. It was too near the frontier. It is true that the British Government had applied for the extradition of Eluterio Sosa. The authorities in Guatemala City in their own good time replied that if and when Eluterio Sosa was apprehended they would be happy to hand over the ex-*chiclero*.

'Now, no *chiclero* loved Gaskin. *Chiclero* contractors might value him, but the *chiclero* ... that lowest common denominator of the chicle trade, only one step in value, according to circumstances, above or below that of a mule ... had no reason to love Gaskin.

'Whether true or not they thought that somehow Gaskin and men like him made their lives more difficult and their trade more hazardous. So Gaskin took no chances. Jaime was sent to El Cayo as general factotum. He was not, of course, allowed to make decisions at high level but he ran the business there and did it well. There were very, very few attacks of "flu". He seemed to be able to keep away from the bottle.

'Gaskin remained on the river, but took no chances. He sent for Jaime to meet him about a score of miles below El Cayo. Jaime obeyed and reported, received praise, blame, reproof, encouragement and commendation, each in the measure Gaskin knew to be suitable to his man. He gave him instructions as to the future but only the near future, for he was somewhat perturbed about his clerk, secretary, factotum and chess opponent. Jaime seemed distrait, maybe, "getting ready for the mother-and-father of a drunk only more so", thought Gaskin, and as usual he was correct, but only in a measure.

'Jaime was "bored", he found no savour in the substance of his life. He was sick of his job. He was sick of El Cayo. He was sick of himself. He had tried women, but his sickness was aggravated by that medicine, aggravated to compelling nausea. He was afraid, now, of drink. He loathed it. In his sober senses the sight of a bottle revolted him. He thought he would leave the Colony, he had after all worked in other Central American countries, but he knew with a terrifying certainty that he could never flee from himself and from the memory of his mother.

'One day Gaskin and Jaime were in a small house not far from the river with the nearest house about 100 yards away, for the village straggled down a path which followed the river bank. One of the boatmen was, technically, on guard outside the house. Gaskin took no chances. They had finished business and the evening meal. Gaskin suggested a little game, a short one, he had to leave at midnight. He delighted in sudden departures and quiet inconvenient arrivals. So they began their last game of chess together. But Gaskin was inspired. He felt, as the game slowly progressed, that never had his opponent played with such devilish foreknowledge and never had he, Gaskin, forestalled him with such god-like power and prescience. He brooded over the board, his body relaxed, his forearms crossed on his lap in a characteristic posture.

'Physically, he was relaxed to the utmost, recuperating his unusual energy while his mind, with heightened enjoyment, grappled with the problems on the board in front of him. Thus, Francis Gaskin was at peace.

'Then Jaime laughed, spluttered suddenly, howled with laughter and rushed out onto the verandah. He ran with such sudden force, pushing wide the slightly open door with such abrupt energy that he upset Eluterio was was leaning gently against it while he pointed his rifle carefully at Mr. Gaskin. Before he could recover Jaime had knocked it from his hands and grappled with him. Struggling furiously they fell together into the lighted room.

'Gaskin recognized Eluterio and lost his temper. He pulled his automatic pistol from its holster and fired at the battling men. He continued to fire purposefully, savagely. Jaime tore himself from Eluterio, leaped up and struck Gaskin's arm with the water bottle. Eluterio bled on the floor. Gaskin leaned against the table supporting himself with his left arm, the right was paralysed from the blow.

'"Give me the pistol – let me finish him."

'"No," said Jaime, "you deliberately fired at *us*, not at him … at *us* … even if you killed me though you meant to kill him. You didn't mind killing me."

'"Yes, yes, kill him," shrieked Gaskin.

'Eluterio sat up, his right ear bled furiously. He saw Jaime with the pistol in his hand. He stumbled to his feet and rushed into the darkness. The boatmen arrived and stood on the verandah outside and watched Gaskin and Jaime who threw the pistol to the floor.

'"Why did you laugh?," asked Gaskin.

'"You were prepared to kill me so long as you killed him. You wanted him even if it cost my life."

'"Why did you laugh?", asked Gaskin again.

'"The hands, the hands, the crossed hands. The one with the wound mark in the palm. The crossed hands. The sign of St. Francis of Assisi and of St. Francis Gaskin!".

'Then Francis Gaskin lost his temper again. He knew what Jaime Peat-Patterson meant him to know. The life of St. Francis of Assisi was taught to all the children of Belize whose parents insisted that they attend Sunday School at the Roman Catholic Cathedral. They knew that St. Francis bore the stigma of the scars in both palms. But his followers, lest the portrait of the Saint be confused with that of his Master, instructed that all portraits of the Saint should show only one palm, with the scar, the other palm normal.

'To make the lesson the more obvious, the paintings would show the forearms crossed so that the difference in each palm could be readily seen, and the identity of the Saint unmistakable.

'Twice within the hour Gaskin had lost his temper. A thing which had never happened before. He cursed Peat-Patterson – cursed his as "a nincompoop, a failure, educated in your fine school, officer and gentleman, my toady and footstool" – and so on. The boatmen crept away because the boss might turn on them, too. But Jaime was unmoved. He looked at Gaskin with pity. Gaskin was no fool; insane temporarily, but still no fool. Jaime was escaping him. So he cursed Jaime's mother, relating incidents and events, calling names and numbers, quoting chapter and verse. He finished saying, "So I married her to my chauffeur who taught her to drink. Then I used her as my procuress, my cheap bawd, till she became useless to me. After that she went on with the trade getting cheaper and cheaper and that is why you never stay in Belize unless I order you to. That is why her relations in Quintana Roo despise her and you … she and you". But Jaime, like Eluterio, had rushed into the darkness.

'For Jaime Peat-Patterson's world began and ended, quite certainly ended, with his mother. He could remember her so beautiful, so tender, so understanding, so sympathetic. He could remember peeping at the world from the shelter of her arms at the threatening, scolding, painful world then compressed into one form – the form of his mother's mother.'

'Jaime's mother, Isabella, was the only child of Carmen Munoz. The family was one with justifiable pride of lineage both in their own eyes and in those of most of their contemporaries. They could trace their ancestry back for over three centuries to a Munoz who was with the conquistador Francisco de Montejo when he conquered Yucatan. A Munoz was also one of the founders of the city of Bacalat in the remote south of Quintana Roo. Then, when Bacalat was overrun in 1847 by the Santa Cruz Indians, a Munoz had fled to the colony of British Honduras where the family prospered and another Francisco Munoz became a Justice of the Peace, married Carmen and fathered Isabella.

'When the last named was eighteen the colony received a visit from a certain Captain James MacDonald Peat-Patterson of the Highland Light Infantry.

'There was no British Army Garrison at the time since the colony was of no strategic importance and the young Scots Captain's task was to help to train the locally raised British Honduras Militia.

'The date was 1898 and inevitably the handsome and vigorous young Highlander met the exquisite Isabella, as it happened, at a party given by the Governor and both of them blessed their luck thus offering a challenge to Destiny who rudely took up the challenge.

'Britain became involved in a war with the Boers in South Africa and James Peat-Patterson, the first, was recalled to his regiment. That was in 1899.

'There followed an inevitable call at the home of Señor Munoz to say "good-bye".

'The Señora was out visiting a sick relative. Señor Munoz was at choir practice at the Cathedral. The aunt, who was a born chaperone, had migraine and was in bed being attended by the maid servant.

'So, Isabella opened the door to the man who had won her heart. She apologized for the absence of the other members of the family. Normally, as a well brought up young lady Isabella was heavily chaperoned, even at Mass. On this occasion, however, they were free of the frowning aunt, free, that is, to ride their ardours unbridled and unattended and they found that Romain Rolland was right when he said, "Passion is like a genius; a miracle."

'Broken-heartedly they parted, the Captain left the Colony then, and only then, but of course a little later, Isabella came to understand what he had left behind him and nearly lost her reason.

'Now began a period of purgatory. The proud Munoz was humbled. In an excess of abasement her father resigned his Commission as Justice of the Peace. This hurt him more than Isabella's downfall and for a while he heaped the ashes of humiliation on his own head. Nothing that Isabella would or could ever do, would make her other in his eyes and in his heart than his lovely, loving daughter, his joy and pride, his solace and comfort. He did, however, rather overdo his public penance and appeared to lose his zest in his business. He no longer played the organ in the Cathedral. He shrank into himself. His doctor murmured some words to his wife which sounded like, "Pernicious anaemia – there is no cure". After three years he left the sorrows of the clan to his widow.

'The widow, the redoubtable Carmen, lived on to chastise Isabella with every breath she drew. Because of their straitened circumstances they had to rent half their house but Carmen Munoz was careful, very careful, whom she took in as tenants. The most satisfactory ... and they remained there for years ... was a family of Syrians with several small children. They did not object to the solitary little James, now Jaime, playing with their children and, in fact, the lonely little boy found himself absorbing from his playmates a third language. He understood much and could actually speak a few words in Arabic. But never,

never did he speak anything but Spanish to his grandmother. The birth of the child had redoubled the venom with which she had greeted the news of his pending arrival. For twelve years she made her daughter's life a never-ending penance. Her malice was alive, sensuous, pervading; her bitterness surrounded her like an aura.

'When the child was about twelve years old Señora Munoz received a letter from a local firm of lawyers. It begged Señora Munoz and Miss Munoz to call at their convenience to discuss a matter of some importance. They called, learnt of the matter and Señora Munoz was so overcome that she fainted. She came to herself to find that she was stretched out on the sofa in the lawyer's office while the latter fanned her zealously and offered her sips of water. The lawyer could afford to be zealous for Isabella had signed the paper before he had groped for the fan.

'To explain the commitment which Isabella made when she signed that document in the lawyer's office it is necessary to cast back a little way in time.

'The Governor, a compassionate man, who had seen his old friend Munoz fail and die owing to his young Scot's compulsive passion for Isabella, felt strongly that the innocent offspring of their union deserved a better fate than that of being withered in the bud by his grandmother's endless and bitter scolding. So he wrote a well-phrased letter to this effect to Jaime's father who had been matured by his experiences in battle at Magersfontein, Colenso and Spion Kop.

'Now a Colonel, James MacDonald Peat-Patterson was shocked when he heard the Governor's news and wrote for an independent report on the boy immediately, to the lawyer in whose office Isabella had signed that important document. Shortly, Colonel Peat-Patterson received a reply which read, "The master of the boy's class at his school gives him a good name. He works well, behaves well and has an excellent memory. He is also a reader. His grandfather, Munoz, had many books of prose and poetry in both English and Spanish. They are all, or mostly, classics and the boy is steadily reading through them. His master is a Jesuit priest so you may trust his opinion when he says the boy is definitely University material."

'To Colonel Peat-Patterson the fact that he had brought ruin and degradation to the lovely Isabella, had maimed, bankrupted and killed her father ... he had no thought for the mother ... caused him great concern and he decided to do something for the child. So he wrote to the lawyer asking for Isabella's compliance in the plan he put forward in his letter. It meant that Jaime would have to leave the Munoz home and get the rest of his education in England.

'However, the boy did not go to his father's school but one that, though it was small and in a remote part of Scotland, gave him a first-class education.

'Jaime, of course, had no visitors though once or twice, in the holidays at different holiday homes arranged by a scholastic agency, he would be visited by an imposing person who never alluded to himself as his father but who asked after his welfare.

'When his school career was over the all-knowing and well-paid scholastic agency received the last of their instructions from his father and got Jaime an introduction to a Bank.

'After two years in a provincial city in England Jaime wrote to the manager of the Belize Bank and returned there as a clerk.

'His mother's letters had never been very informative about herself in all the years of his absence. For his part, he wrote regularly, as fully as his painfully reticent nature would allow, of his apprenticeship in the Bank. She replied promptly and always in the same uninformative way filling the pages with encouragement but otherwise with trivia. In a way these letters forced him back onto fervent memories of her. As the years passed they became more roseate, her beauty was enhanced, her gentle lovingness more angelic, her understanding love more limitless. By contrast he found her, when he returned to Belize early in 1914, a vigorous, shrill and overwhelming personality. He bowed before the torrent of her joyous pride. She no more understood his British understatements and reticences than he understood her change from the shrinking, tender and very young woman of his early childhood to this positive and full-bosomed worthy. His world shrank into a tight bitter knot in his heart. He did his work well, but mechanically and without zest. He made few friends. The young women he met bored him. The outbreak of the World War came as his release. He had saved his pay and took the first available ship for England to enlist in Kitchener's Army. He was a good soldier and he was wounded in a very creditable action. However, it was only when his skill as a rifle shot developed with practise and he had his chance as a sniper that he felt he was face to face with the enemy, man to man.

'He became the sniper's sniper, finding his targets with speed and accuracy. He had unlimited patience and outsat the enemy, body relaxed, as unwinking as a cat at a rat-hole. The enemy sniper made a move but it was seldom enough for Jaime's first and final shot. The enemy fired and a man on his own side fell, or not. Jaime sat on. In time the enemy moved again, Jaime fired; it was all over.

'Major-General Peat-Patterson saw his son's name in the honours list, no other British soldier could have the name of Jaime Higenio Munoz Peat-Patterson, none but he would have that outlandish list of Christian names attached to his Patronymic. Jaime found himself detached from his regiment. A commission came his way and he sat out the rest of the war in a quartermaster's office in Alexandria. He did his work in the office sufficiently well to escape notice. He called it his morning recreation. It took him a couple of hours per day then he got down to his real business which was playing chess. He wrote to his mother quite often and she replied promptly. He hardly read these responses; satisfied simply to receive them. She had only slightly varied their style or content since she wrote her first letter to her schoolboy son. She was the great mystery of Jaime's life, the prime engima of his world. The thought did not occur to him, that when, to get him an education, she had sent him away as a child, the original Isabella, his own Isabella, his angel mother had died.

'With, as it were, her son set aside, Isabella contracted not into the concentrate of malice which was her mother but into a steely and devious selfishness. She did not want much for she knew little but she did know enough, now, to put her mother in her proper place. The old woman shrivelled before this unfamiliar Isabella while Francis Gaskin liked her ... for a time. Then, she, like all his women, bored him. However they remained friends in a very special Gaskin kind of friendship.

'At the end of the war Jaime continued his two recreations, soldiering and playing chess, in Alexandria for many more months. Finally demobilization caught up with him and he returned to Central America but not to Belize. However he could not keep away. After working in various banana ports in several republics he returned to British Honduras in the employ of Mr. Gaskin. None the less he kept away from Belize as much as possible although his mother was now more respectable and even married.'

'After the incident when he laughed at the idea of Francis Gaskin having the gesture and stigma in his hand like St. Francis, and when within the next few moments he saved not only Gaskin's life but also the life of Eluterio, Jaime became an alcoholic. He remained in El Cayo, without employment, living on his savings and at times drank himself silly.

'He became a not infrequent lodger in the deep and, during the dry season, "comfortable" gutters. Eluterio in one of his daring forays into El Cayo found him drunk and asleep in such a gutter.

'Eluterio was and always had been a roguish fool, a painful creature. Eluterio thought not that Jaime had saved his life but that he had left his game of chess a second too soon and had thus caused Mr. Gaskin to live and Eluterio to have a mutilated ear. So he decided to avenge himself and what could be funnier than botching Jaime's ear.

'The doctor, the medical officer of the District, Dr. Hastings, was the only person who did not think this an unnecessary stupidity. He thoroughly enjoyed himself and unbotched the ear most beautifully. When the doctor had ceased his almost proprietary care of Jaime's ear his patient disappeared into the bush though he would reappear for provisions now and again. Occasionally he was seen deep in the forests of Petén and he even crossed the other frontier to Chiapas. Men knew he was hunting Eluterio. He had saved the roguish fool's life when Gaskin had the man at his mercy and Jaime had been repaid by mutilation wreaked on him when defenceless and unconscious.

'The chase was an epic in which men gave information to hunter and hunted of each other. Jaime was sober now. Dr. Hastings took almost a proprietary interest in Jaime because he carried an ear so enchantingly debotched. He once suggested to

Jaime during one of his rare visits to El Cayo that it was a waste of time to chase so stupid a ruffian. Jaime replied that when a man has earned his gutter he should be allowed to keep it. "I am striking a blow for the freedom of the gutter," he said. He then asked the doctor to receive a small parcel of a special twine and certain small pulleys which would come to him by post.

'In time, Jaime called for his twine and his pulleys. At last Eluterio decided to end it for it seemed that Jaime was now, sometimes, laggard as if he did not intend to overtake him but to break his nerve by just being behind him and just beyond rifle shot. Then Eluterio turned back. The battle in that deep forest lasted for seven hours of unfathomable silence. Finally, Eluterio took careful aim at the hat which, had he not been desperately vigilant, he might have missed seeing, so skilfully was it hidden by the friendly leaves. But it had moved, so slightly, as if the head it covered had slowly, cautiously moved. The careful aim at the hat was slightly lowered so that the bullet would blow the head beneath it to bits. Eluterio fired, then stood up to make assurance certain. Jaime also fired.

'The rifle fell from Eluterio's hand. The hat was, with the pulleys and the twine, but a trick of a sniper's craft. Eluterio was not a coward but as he looked into the barrel of Jaime's rifle the dew of death moistened his forehead. He had heard much of Jaime's ruthlessness as a soldier but he could not know nor understand that Jaime was civilized enough to be incapable of taking the life of another man in a personal quarrel and that vengeance by violence offended him. So Jaime aimed carefully at Eluterio, fired and drilled his remaining "normal" ear. Then Jaime told his quarry that he was finished with him. And that truly finished Eluterio. A man with both ears damaged, one in rags and the other with a neat hole through it, cannot go far without being recognized. And recognition brought a smirk and a snicker for he was no longer a hero. Jaime's contemptuous dismissal of him had, as it were, put him in a proper perspective in other men's eyes. He was no longer a "character" but a sorry buffoon and girls would no longer allow themselves to be "kidnapped" by him.

'One day word came to the police that he would be in such a place at such a time. He saw the ambush set, then came cantering into it, firing as he came. He died as he had hoped and arranged. Dr. Hastings did the post-mortem and, as an afterthought, had cut off both ears.

'He put them in a jar of rum on the shelf amongst his snakes. There was a label on the jar. It read, as Cutbush had discovered, "Eluterio's Ears; 1932". There were also two arrows on the label. One arrow marked "Jaime" pointed to the ear with the neat hole. The other marked "Gaskin" pointed to the very ragged ear.

'Jaime's prowess with a gun became a legend. His war record was remembered and added to with compound interest. He was never seen to fire a rifle but that did not prevent people saying that he could hit the swiftest bird on the wing. He existed between bouts of drunkenness by doing sundry bits of auditing for chicle contractors in El Cayo. He became more hopelessly, helplessly futile.

'Then, one day, Fatima Birbari rescued him from a gutter which was no longer comfortable, but wet and in fact rapidly becoming a torrent during a sudden rainstorm. Fatima was a careful housekeeper of an economical turn of mind. She was also a business woman in so far as she managed her husband Fuad Birbari's many affairs in his absence with discretion and tact. She had the good housewife's distaste for waste, furthermore she thought she remembered Jaime as being a little boy playing with her cousin's little children in the house of Señora Munoz. She watched the water rising in the gutter, looked long and seriously at the half-drowned waster, then called for help.

'He was taken at her orders to a room in her house. The next day she sent for the doctor. Jaime recovered at last from his pneumonia. He crept out into the sunlight, four weeks later, a shadow of his former self. But the shadow lived on. He occupied a stool in Fatima's office gradually releasing her from those details of the business she was pleased to delegate. He became her henchman, and more, he became her loyal and understanding friend who never intruded. When she wished to be quiet Jaime receded into shadow. When she needed diversion Jaime told her tales of his life and the life of his comrades in Flanders and the Near East. He also told other tales; tales in which, as hero, he had a person he called "a friend of mine". This mythical friend became involved in mythical adventures. Fatima knew Jaime had passed out of the realm of dull truth. She did not mind. In fact she preferred it. She did not need to feel a retroactive sympathy for a "friend of mine". And when Jaime felt the compulsion on him he did not need to go elsewhere for his rum. He went to his room complaining of a "sickness" and she sent the required medicine. But it was milk liberally diluted with rum. He had merely to stretch out his hand; there was the jug never empty. By the fourth day, however, it was plain milk ... then milk and eggs.

'Jaime's "sickness" was now a kind of "cure"!

'And Fatima's two youngest boys worshipped him when they came home, during the holidays, from their boarding school in Belize. It was she who reminded her sons that he was a famous war hero; that the most terrible German snipers feared him; that finally to save his life after so many brave deeds he was promoted and taken away from the front. And then she brought to their notice things about him which were different from the men with whom they had hitherto been in contact. The first was that he had stopped drinking. Not even on a social occasion would he take a sip. Again, he was always polite, always considerate, he could refuse another cup of coffee with such charming manners that one almost regretted when he left the table. He was quiet, he never forced his opinion on anyone but would argue a point tactfully, intelligently, patiently and at the moment of triumph say something which, as it were, gave the other party the victory. He was neat in his person and considerate to others. She pointed out to the boys how, after a time, even the servants adored him. The very same who had nursed him, during his former "sickness", like a baby. The business of the "milk" was no joke to them, then, or now. Jaime had had a good education in a very good school. It did not seem to have helped him much but long after he was ashamed to mention his school what it had taught him influenced two tough young Syrians.

'Fuad saw the difference when Fatima pointed it out to him. "You are right," he said, "they have manners like Mr. Wilberforce."

'Mr. Wilberforce was an English gentleman and scholar interested in Syrian and Lebanese emigrants and what they did in their new countries, who had once stopped at Fatima's house when he visited El Cayo on the trail of his studies. So Fuad approved of Jaime. Jaime was not, however, only a private entertainer and clerk to Fatima. He became the trusted confidante of both husband and wife and, above all, their go-between, Fatima's messenger to Fuad. They had other messengers but when Jaime went to Fuad he took with him two letters. One letter was the letter of any affectionate wife to doting husband and father. Quite often there were in it references to business deals, the price of chicle, the arrival of a mule-team laden with so many pounds of chicle, the fact that a henchman from rival chicle contractors had said so-and-so and done this and thus. Jaime took these letters from the British side of the line into Petén. Fuad might be anywhere in those vast forests but Jaime found him and delivered the letter. The letter was read and Fuad carefully folded it and secured it in its appropriate bundle. Then Jaime began to recite the letter which contained what Fatima meant Fuad to know.

'This was more, far more, than was safe to put on paper in a region where even Jaime might be waylaid and where Fuad's papers might be "lost" or be confiscated while he wrestled with some sudden legal whim of any of sundry *commandantes*. Jaime related the gossip of Belize as it affected the movements and actions of Mr. Gaskin and of other chicle potentates. For instance, he told of a certain batch of mules that had been imported from Texas by one firm and sold to another firm, sight unseen. However, the whole transaction had been tied up in insurance clauses dealing with animals being sound in wind and limb. They were sound in wind and limb but there was another clause dealing with minimum height in which no mention was made of maximum height. And that was the trick. The rival firm found themselves with a magnificent batch of mules, sound of wind and limb, and every one of them useless for the chicle trade because they were too big. A very big mule laden with chicle was a nuisance in the bush. The chicle bales were scraped off its back by overhanging branches in the forest. Jaime also knew that such and such Guatemaltecan officials had passed through Belize to or from Petén. He knew what he had said when he lived at the hotel and what were his habits. He received word from agents in Guatemala City as to how far this official had been indoctrinated by the austere financial morals of President Graña. He received the addresses of relatives of the official who lived outside Guatemala to whom largess could be paid to the credit of the official. He knew the complexion of affairs in the Guatemala Treasury, the goings and comings of officers of the Forestry Department, the extent of the outbreak of a disease in a neighbouring country which would affect the supply of mules and much else that was of value to an ambitious businessman. For Fuad was no longer a Syrian pedlar. As he grew older it seemed to Fuad that his patriarchal role as family provider was the most acceptable that a man of vision and energy could desire and he worked to that end. He left Fatima with the children in El Cayo where the latter went to the village school, received private lessons and were prepared for the Jesuit High School and the Convent School in Belize. In due time they were to graduate from these schools and go to Universities in America. His eldest son was now a doctor, a resident in one of the most prestigious clinics in America, after a most creditable sojourn as a medical student; the other children were to follow other professions. But Fuad did not think the shape of things in the chicle business in Petén could continue indefinitely.

'"The world is changing," he had said to Fatima. "I won't be in Petén much longer. Things that used to be done can't be done any more or, at least, not much longer. Now when a man is found dead a few folk, there, are apt to say, 'What is Dato doing – why does he still allow these things?' And more and more folk say it every time. When a place is cleaned up the big profits go." Dato was the nickname of the formidable President of Guatemala. His name was Deodato Graña but he was spoken of as "Dato" – on both sides of the frontier. Fuad did not say aloud, "Well, I hope I live long enough to get out with the profits I have made," but he said it to himself and Fatima said it about him to herself. Fuad had to have correct information, enough reliable information for him to make his profits. In the transport of this information Jaime was invaluable.

'And that is the end of Eluterio's story – but not of Jaime,' Medina concluded and then dismissed the two *chicleros* who had been riding with them as guards. And it was but a few minutes after Cutbush and Medina had taken leave of the two *chicleros* that they were overtaken by a solitary rider. It was clear that the meeting was prearranged, though it was some days later that Cutbush learned why he had been asked to carry a rifle and why Medina was so obviously glad to be overtaken and be accompanied by Major Jaime Peat-Patterson. For Medina was a marked man and knew it, as he also knew that his remaining days in the chicle business were few. He asked but to be allowed to live till the end of this season.

He had been too brilliant a '*contrabandista*', too good a hijacker of chicle destined for other contractors. He had played his hand too greedily this season and confessed that he might have over-reached the bounds of prudence once or twice. However, he had intended, in any case, not to come back into the bush next season. He was a fairly important member of the field-force of the Chicle Company but he never deceived himself. He knew that every man of that force was expendable. If every man had had a fatal accident or had been killed as a 'job' they could easily be replaced next season. The labour market in 1936 was saturated with men who would be glad to go to Petén even if it meant the risk of being considered 'expendable'. Medina wondered what he was rated at. The price of murder varied. An assassin had been known to do a job for a friend as a favour but he was, obviously and literally, an amateur. Medina thought that he would probably be rated as 'a hundred dollar job'. Clean. No bungling about 'severely wounded but likely to recover' and no effort spared to make it look other than what it was, a 'job'. So he welcomed Jaime who, deep in the bush arrived at a certain place in the road exactly to the minute, just five minutes after Medina had sent off the *chicleros*.

Medina was now safe for that journey. The Jaime legend would protect him.

He introduced his friend the Major to Dr. Cutbush. The arrival of this thin, drooping old-young man to the party enlivened the doctor's spirit. He tried to assess Jaime as hero of the legend though he certainly looked anything but a hero. He sat his mule, as it were, negligently, or trustingly rather, knowing that it would not take any awkward step, would make no capricious hop or skip but would continue on its journey with a proper respect for the rider along the path it chose to tread for itself.

After making contact they rode in single file for an hour or so and then, as the path widened enough, Cutbush rode up alongside Jaime. The latter smiled but said nothing. He left it to his mule to keep pace with Cutbush's animal, indicating, as it were, that companionship was its own reward, given that the path was wide enough.

Cutbush contained his curiosity as long as he could but no more than a few minutes had passed before he said, 'Captain Medina and I had a very pleasant meal with Doctor Hastings a couple of days ago and I noticed some interesting books on his bookshelf. There were a couple belonging to Harkness, the botanist, whom I have not yet met. He is based at Shoonanto-nitch, isn't he?'

'Yes,' said Jaime, thawing slightly. 'One of the most interesting of Harkness' books is *Phantastica*, by Lewin. I don't read German but when it was put into English last year I pounced on it. You probably know all about it of course; it's in your line'.

Cutbush said it rang a faint bell. He did not know the book in English and asked Jaime to tell him what it was about.

'It is historic in two senses,' said Jaime. 'The first sense, the one with which you are probably familiar is that Lewin was the man who persuaded Freud to leave psycho-pharmacology alone and to concentrate on psychology. That was in about 1890. Meanwhile, Lewin himself, went on with pharmacology and extracted the active principle from the Mexican Cactus which is used to make their national drink. He called the chemical Mescaline. It is a book which interests Mrs. Farr very much.' Cutbush was soon to learn a lot more about Mrs. Farr and her interests.

At that point the mules decided that the path was once again for solo rumination, so Cutbush ruminated. For *Phantastica* was not the only interesting book on those shelves. Dr. Hastings showed him several which he said were Jaime's. He had left them with the doctor for he knew they were in safe-keeping and quite often lived a second life because the doctor read them. A few were books of poetry and Cutbush noted that Jaime had the habit of underlining passages, poem or prose, which pleased him.

For the remainder of that day the whim of the mules kept

Cutbush from confidential chats with Jaime. That night, however, after they had finished their supper, Cutbush tried again. In the course of the conversation that developed Jaime asked, 'Did Doctor Hastings tell you how he was offered a massive bribe or, rather, not a bribe but a tip of hundreds of dollars?'

'A tip to a doctor,' Cutbush exclaimed.

'As you know,' Jaime told him, 'Belize is a busy port, busy in that a sizeable fleet of diesel-engined schooners are based there. They have one purpose, rum running. The liquor is brought by cargo steamers, landed and the legal duty is paid. Sundry merchants present the correct papers to the Government warehouse and the liquor is released and loaded aboard the rum-runners. They then have to clear for a foreign port by declaring their point of destination to the Customs. They all declare their destination to be Ruatan, a microscopic island in the Bay of Honduras, a speck under the Sovereignty of the Republic of Spanish Honduras. When they return they have to show papers as to the port from which they departed. You can be sure that their papers always show they are from Ruatan. All the world knows, of course, that somewhere else the cargo is trans-shipped, but the law is the law and if the paper says Ruatan then the law reads Ruatan. To make it even more idiotic, every vessel entering the port of Belize from a foreign land has to hoist a yellow flag and a doctor has to board the vessel, see papers and, if he thinks fit, the crew. He then declares the ship in good health and orders the yellow flag to be lowered. Only after the flag has been pulled down can any person other than the doctor and the customs officer leave or board the vessel. Dr. Hastings was, a few years ago, attached to the Belize Hospital and being port health officer was a small and irritatingly futile part of his duties. He would often have to leave a very busy clinic to take part in the legal idiocy by examining the health certificate from Ruatan while knowing that on board that very vessel were a dozen such certificates lacking only the date which was duly filled in by the rum-runner. On this particular day he and the Customs Officer, as junior in the service as he was himself, boarded a rum-runner. The Captain was in good humour. 'Here you are, boys,' said he, putting his hand into a box the size of a shoe box – 'here is something for you'. His hand came up full of dollar bills, not one-dollar bills but tens and fifties.

'The young Customs Officer and the Doctor looked at them without interest. "No thank you," they both said and gathering their papers together without haste, or dudgeon, left. "His face – I can still remember the man's face and his expression," the Doctor said when he told the story, adding more ominously, "and I can remember his name. It is an uncommon one, Delfosse."' Then both Medina and Jaime exchanged sideways glances as if they were sharing a secret.

'You mean,' Cutbush asked, 'that he is the man who is now the manager of the Consolidated Chicle Company in Shoonantonich?'

Jaime's and Medina's expressions widened into grins but neither of them would say any more on the subject though, after a moment, Jaime did respond. Rather impishly he covered first his ears, then his eyes and then his mouth with his cupped hands. They were gestures which left Cutbush a little uneasy about what he might find when he arrived at his destination the next day.

PART TWO

SHE OF THE SLEEPING FACE

For a few minutes after his arrival at Shoonantonitch camp, Dr. Cutbush felt lost, anxious and out of place. No member of the Archaeological team was there to greet him but he was informed that Dr. Gibberd, the leader, had received the message he had sent the day before leaving El Cayo and that a house had been put at his disposal. Furthermore, Dr. Gibberd had sent word that he could be expected not later than mid-afternoon, though he had not yet arrived. Nor was the manager of the Chicle Company in the camp. So Cutbush was made welcome by other members of the company staff as soon as Medina reported his arrival.

Hardly had this welcome reassured Cutbush, when the blessed news was brought that a hot bath was ready for him. In it he soaked away his fatigue and his anxiety. He changed his clothes and relaxed, his *amour-propre* again intact, while he took stock of his surroundings.

The place was decidedly more than a camp for there were women and children about. Nor did it have the air of a barracks. The houses were in general palm-thatched and arranged around an open square. 'The eternal plaza', thought Cutbush. However, the other houses had been built in orderly rows parallel to three sides of the square. At a distance of about two hundred yards there were the stables and corrals. At one side of the square was the most ambitious building of the camp. It was roofed with galvanized metal sheets and its size and generally forbidding aspect marked it as the Company's warehouse. Chicle was stored in it until convoys of mule-teams could be arranged to take the blocks across the border. Two of the palm-thatched houses were larger than the others, one being a dining-room plus common room for the senior staff while the other was the manager's house. Another smaller metal-roofed building was Fuad Birbari's office and store-room. Finally, two rooms attached to the store-room were occupied by Mrs. Farr and Miss Quinn.

Cutbush had taken this cursory glance around the camp when Medina returned bringing reassuring messages. Gibberd would be here soon.

He had received Medina's message and had sent on a muleteer in charge of two mules laden with potsherds early that morning. The muleteer had arrived and said he had been ordered to report that Gibberd and Mrs. Farr would be about an hour behind him. Medina also brought a message from Mr. Delfosse, Field Manager of the Chicle Company's operations in Petén, who regretted he would not be in camp to welcome their distinguished guest because there had been an emergency in the bush which needed his personal attention. He would, however, look forward to meeting the Doctor at supper. In the meantime Cutbush was to be informed that all the conveniences and amenities, such as they were, of a forest camp were his to command. Medina concluded his report with the words, 'And Doctor, as it is still two hours from supper, I have taken the liberty of ordering some tea for you. Our cook is bringing it immediately. Now I must leave you for there are a few things I shall have to do immediately because tomorrow I start for my section of the forest. I shall, however, be back in two days.'

Cutbush accepted the pot of tea from the cook and, sipping the beverage with relish, he decided he had much to be thankful for.

As he relaxed in the hammock Cutbush considered himself a fortunate man but was afraid to express any self-satisfaction too emphatically because he feared the vengeance of the gods on any frail human who puffed himself up with pride of vainglory at his achievements or his conquests. Cutbush in his secret heart knew, and was not afraid to confess it to himself, that his only creative work had been in abnormal psychology. Thus, he would always consider himself a psychiatrist who by the accident of success and some rather unusual qualities had been seduced away from that discipline. A seduction that had come at the proper time with the phenomenal success of his book, *Nociception as Destiny*.

He was a man who found it easy to write of psychology so that the moderately-instructed layman could understand him and his ideas could be easily summarized and digested. Consequently he found himself invited to lecture to many large audiences with many different interests. He had, however, always been careful to be, regretfully, too busy to lecture to any audience who could not give a reasonably close attention and understanding to his thoughts. This moderation on his part to swallow the bait of the lecture tour, paid off handsomely by his being accorded the supreme honour of being asked to lecture to the National Convention of the Industrialists of America. As an honest man he had said to himself from the beginning, 'I have one note only to blow in the symphony of abnormal psychology. It comes in the latter part of the first movement. I am not capable of carrying a major part of the music. It is not in me. There are giants in Vienna, in Zurich, perhaps in America, but I am not a giant.' He had been wise in his timing and correct, if modest, in his appraisal.

Shortly after the success of his book, and the blaze of publicity it generated, his lectures and his withdrawal to academic shades, a great work of psychology emanated from the Zurich school. In it Cutbush found that his ideas had antedated by very little the Zurich hypothesis. What, however, was most important was that his ideas, his particular hypothesis, had been integrated into and had become a part, a small but essential part, of the massive edifice reared by that school of Psychology.

Seen from this perspective, and too near to the time of publication for any charge of plagiarism to be made or acknowledgements given, Cutbush realized to the full how correct had been his own diagnosis of his own potentialities. He had blown his one note and it was a sweet little note, true in pitch, correct in emphasis and placement but there was no other note on his piccolo. 'I will creep out,' he had promised himself, 'between the first and second movements and never write another line except clinical stuff for psychiatry journals.'

He had, however, to his surprise been invited to be the Professor of Abnormal Psychology at a University. He had accepted and it soon became clear that however good he was as a professor, and of course he had his detractors especially amongst those whose books never could be boiled down to a 'Monthly Digest', it was as a committee-man that he shone. Success bred success and he had been invited to serve on other committees. It had been a new experience for him. It had forced him to examine dispassionately the qualities needed to be a good chairman of committee and he had soon become chairman of many with his success based on the simple discovery that committees loved a chairman who did the work by marshalling the valuable, discarding the unlikely, leaving no suggestion untouched and thanking each committee-man for his 'valuable' contribution.

Secretaries, of course, wrote the minutes but Cutbush, immediately after a meeting, wrote his own 'minutes' for his own information. That being done, he wrote what he called his 'seconds' which were for no eyes but his. He wrote of the atmosphere of the meeting, the clash of temperaments, the origin of suggestions. He described how suggestions were taken up and thrown from man to man, each man showing not so much what was right with the idea but what was askew in the man. For in his 'seconds' a man's attitude was not 'wrong' it was 'askew'. These 'seconds' excited Cutbush. They were as revealing to him as his clinical notes on his schizophrenics. So he became a first-class committee-man and quite soon an executive and then President of the University. There, unfortunately, he found himself unhappy. The President's first duty was to get, somehow, anyhow, money for the university. 'Somehow' meant wheedling money from Alumni and others who, for one reason or the other, might find it valuable to endow higher education. He was not a good 'wheedler' though he could perhaps have learnt the trade if he had not been offered and had accepted the invitation to become President of the Nethersole Foundation.

In his new capacity his job was not to get money but to spend it. The money had been earned by the late Macon Nethersole, founder of 'Transport and Express, from Atlantic to Pacific'. Where the last tendril of the railroad left off, 'NETHERSOLE' began with his 'Express' organization. Then came roads and road haulage. The old order changed and Macon Nethersole found that every mile of road from Atlantic to Pacific became his private cash register. Soon he was known as 'Atlantic to Pacific' Nethersole, or A.P. for short. He left an enormous sum of money and stocks and shares in all forms of transport in America to the Nethersole Foundation. The purpose of this creation was established without the remotest possibility of paraphrase or reinterpretation. It was, 'The Study of American Customs and Institutions and the encouragement of such Customs and Institutions as in the opinion of the trustees, would redound to the greatest good of the greatest number of Americans'. Old A.P. had been a man of strong beliefs, both able and far-seeing, but he did not foresee that his own beliefs would develop that sclerosis which hardens into chalky prejudices.

Acting on these fossilized concepts he had drawn up a long list of institutions and customs which could not be considered eligible for his bounty. His was a chauvinistic yard-stick. He could 'smell' the foreign influence even in so native an American custom as Thanksgiving. For was not the indubitably indigenous table-bird named a '*Turkey*'. At this stage of his career that old A.P. became known as 'Abana and Pharpar' Nethersole. He retorted that the nickname was a compliment picturing him as a Prince who, riding in a chariot, had stood up for the virtues of his own country, his own state.

When old A.P. at last made his habitation in a narrow cleft of his own beloved landscape the Foundation had come into being.

From the beginning Dr. Cutbush had had no qualms about carrying out Nethersole's ideas, up to a point. Only gradually did he move his tongue into his cheek; so gradually, in fact, that the other trustees did not take fright. Besides, since he worked all the time and they only occasionally, they could leave things to him. When he suggested that the study of American prehistory would have met with A.P.'s approval they did not strenuously demur. He pointed out that there was then a hiatus in the study of Mid-America Archaeology. The Chicago museum which had had several famous teams working in Yucatan, in Vera Cruz and in British Honduras had had to suspend operations because of the abrupt dislocation of their assets following the stock-market crash of 1930.

The British Museum team had also been disbanded. Cutbush proposed that Old A.P. would have been pleased to have had an ancient American City discovered and uncovered in his name's sake. The trustees thought that it was a wonderful idea. It would tread on no toes ... for they were mortally scared of another Thanksgiving Day Rumpus ... and if Old A.P. had never heard of an ancient American race called Maya, that was all to the good. It meant that he had not and could not antagonize either the pro-Maya, or the anti-Maya factions.

So Cutbush set to work and the work was not difficult. The most important instrument was ready at hand in the person of an old acquaintance, the expert Horatio Gibberd. Long, long ago Cutbush had helped Gibberd's family in a very difficult situation. The wealthy and aristocratic Gibberds had an unfortunate skeleton in their cupboard, a skeleton who was nearly as difficult when he was legally sane as when he was undoubtedly and very actively insane. It was Cutbush who arranged everything in the last, protracted and very boisterous bout of the skeleton's insanity. The late lamented Mr. Byron Gibberd, formerly Governor of his state, had had a long and tedious illness, patiently borne so said the obituaries when he was, finally, gathered into the long line of his distinguished forebears with decorum and gentility.

The family were everlastingly grateful to that able young psychiatrist who, although suddenly a world-famous man because of his recently published book, had handled the affair so that not even the nearest neighbours knew, really knew, more than they could guess. The nephew and heir of the former Governor was Horatio Gibberd. Doctor and heir saw much of each other, became friendly and the acquaintance would doubtless have become warmer if varied interests had not taken them into wider fields. Cutbush left psychiatry for higher education and deserted that, too, to become the great executive. Gibberd took advantage of the wealth that had come to him to live the social life of a man of his caste. He was well born, well educated, wealthy and when he chose to apply it, possessed of a first-rate brain. So far he had found nothing worthy of his application. Of archaeology he knew no more than one would expect for his education and background. He was not strongly addicted to women; but in the pursuit of one of his infrequent *amours* he became inoculated with an interest in the forbidding subject which afterwards became the passion of his life. The girl he met in Paris had enraptured him. Nor had her response to his ardour been too chilling. Alas, she had had to leave for Egypt because she was the ward of an aunt whose husband was an Egyptologist.

They lived in Cairo where he had a post on the staff of the Museum of Egyptology. Gibberd, therefore, decided to continue his world tour and to spend some time in Egypt. In his later years he gave grateful thanks to the fate that had made him follow her. For one thing he realized that she had snatched him from adolescence though not because she had encouraged his passion. She suggested it would make matters easier if he flattered her uncle by simulating an interest in the only subject which the uncle considered worth his attention.

That subject was History, by which Uncle Ephraim meant the impact of man on events and vice versa, in the past, the present and the future. His trade was, in fact, to decipher Egyptian historical records though he considered this occupation of value only if it were related to other records of other times and peoples. Gibberd heard for the first time that American pre-history might have as powerful a tale to tell as that of ancient Egypt. He heard of the mathematicians and their calendar and how their records seem to be monuments to the passage of time, of the seasons, of astronomical and perhaps of astrological lore. There were no monuments to conquerors, no Maya statues to compare with that of Ozymandias. So it appeared that the Maya sense of the meaning of time was so immediate and pervading that to commemorate a 'great man' was a piece of irrelevance.

And there was no mystery so tantalizing as the desertion of their fabulous cities. No one knew why their civilization had declined, indeed was almost moribund when Columbus sighted their shores. But Gibberd had listened to Uncle Ephraim with polite attention and but half-an-ear. He was still obsessed with his love and continued thus until she let him know that he had served his purpose. He had been a dupe in that she had used his attentions and his interest to force the hand of another lover who had hitherto been too circumspect. She was a decisive female and the lover had hardly given this tardy assent when the marriage took place under Gibberd's very nose. To hasten the withdrawal of the latter from the scene she let him know, in such a manner that he was never sure whether it had been true or not, that she had been mistress before she had become wife. Gibberd realized that he had been much younger than his years and, what was worse, he had been innocent. Curiously enough he retained for the aunt and uncle, especially the latter, a deep respect and Uncle Ephraim, at their last meeting had spoken to him not to commiserate or to sympathize but as one man to another, as one man who knew the devious ways of the human heart and the powers it had to harm and to hurt. He also spoke of the sublime conjunction of mind and heart where man could neither give nor receive harm nor hurt in the study, for instance, of archaeology. Gibberd had been touched and, when he returned to America, the influence of the uncle's passion for history was strong enough for him to try to fill his idle days with American pre-history. Soon it was no effort and, soon, the day was not long enough to satisfy what had become an overriding passion.

Gibberd was no longer an idle rich young man. He was too modest, too genuinely a scholar, too aware of his ignorance yet to fit out and support expeditions but, as he felt more certain of his grasp of Maya archaeology, he spent more time with others more experienced and more learned than himself in the field of exploration and research. His war service, in World War I, he counted as an interruption to be endured but he was scarcely out of uniform before he was in Central America. His family fortune had grown, abstemious personal habits having increased his wealth and for several seasons he fitted out and led his own expeditions.

Thus Gibberd had found himself, and he was not yet of middle age, when his writings on American pre-history and his discoveries and decipherings made him famous in that narrow corner of learning.

He married. His wife spent a season in the bush with him. She was unutterably bored. He was sorry, wishing it could be otherwise. But of course it was impossible for him to change the shape of his labours. He was dedicated to a life of grubbing on little hills deep in dismal forests for potsherds; or of making of rocks and stones a story of high history of vanished might. When she proposed divorce he facilitated her release. The alimony she demanded and got interfered considerably with his plans for further exploration. To make things more difficult she persuaded him that the alimony should not be paid from the dividends of his stocks and shares but from a separate fund of U.S. Government securities. She said her lawyer told her that the stock-market was too good to last. Hardly had the settlement been completed and the fund put in her name than the stock market crash of 1930 almost completely wiped out Gibberd's fortune.

He was no longer a wealthy man. His ex-wife was, however, in very handsome circumstances.

Then Gibberd knew consternation though it was not so much for his daily bread as for those who depended on him. For now he had dependants. In Central America there had been men who had been 'his', who had depended on him for a livelihood. There had been muleteers, labourers, research workers, secretaries and all the worthy camp followers of archaeological research. They had now had to fend for themselves and had departed with regret on both sides. He had, then, spent several years in a museum, his days full of classifying, arranging, cataloguing. At night he had put together the notes from which he had written many published papers. A book had fallen into shape, had written itself and he had realized that the years away from the forest and the diggings had been just what he had needed. He had published a major work and had become an established authority with a doctorate, *honoris causa* from his *Alma Mater* as only one evidence of his standing amongst scholars. Then Cutbush contacted him and he went once again into the bush under the aegis of the Nethersole Foundation. Now, however, his personal prestige was such that it added to rather than received lustre from the Foundation. As an explorer and scholar he had become an international figure.

He had taken with him to Petén a small team. The objectives were now rather specialized. It was not so much exploration but rather to work on the ruins of the Ancient City called Caracol which he had visited years before. The team had consisted of an eager neophyte Samuels, now sick in Honduras, Mrs. Karen Farr, a mathematician who specialised in numbers as these applied to archaeology. A second archaeologist, Aguilar, had been seconded from the Museum in Mexico City but he had had to leave quite early in the season owing to internecine uncertainty in his Museum staff at home. The final member of the depleted team was Miss Quinn who was an artist and acted as secretary.

The proposed visit of Cutbush was welcome to Gibberd. His team did not need extraneous encouragement but he was sure so receptive a mind as Cutbush had would kindle at seeing the fabulous relics of the past being patiently and skilfully revealed and interpreted. And Cutbush's enthusiasm would react on the team. He was very disappointed, however, that the abrupt cessation of the rains had closed down operations so that when Cutbush visited Caracol he would not see his team at work but would have to be satisfied with a conducted tour of the site. Work was no longer possible because there was no water at the ancient city during the dry season.

Late on the evening of his first day at Shoonantonitch Cutbush returned to his house and his hammock. He was healthily tired but sleep would not come to him. Almost automatically, by force of habit, he began to arrange in his mind the people he had met at supper. He categorized them as though he had finished writing the 'minutes' of a committee meeting and was arranging them for his 'seconds'. The minutes of that particular meeting would have been brief and would run thus:

'Delfosse, Field Manager of the Consolidated Chicle Company's operations in Petén, Guatemala, had welcomed Dr. Cutbush to the Company's Shoonantonitch Camp. He said that collectively and individually the members of the Company's staff were glad to welcome him and all the members of his archaeological expedition not only as visitors, or as neighbours, but as 'folk'. He and his staff liked to be reminded that life did not begin and end with chewing gum. He had personally introduced several members of his staff to Dr. Cutbush, after which drinks were served and there had been general conversation.

'Mrs. Karen Farr arrived during the proceedings. She reported that Gibberd, herself and a muleteer with a team of several mules heavily laden with baggage, with potsherds and other articles of archaeological interest had set out early enough to reach Shoonantonitch well before dark. They were hurrying so as to arrive before Dr. Cutbush, for Captain Medina's message had told them the hour his party expected to reach the camp.

Misfortune, however, overtook them. The bell-mare leading the team of mules had been bitten by a snake and had dashed off the trail into the bush. The other mules had raced after her. She had galloped panic-stricken until she fell. The mules, losing the guiding note of the bell, separated and wandered about the bush while the loads of precious artefacts were scraped from their backs by the trees and some of them of course had been smashed. Mrs. Farr had helped as much as possible but it was clear that even if they had had several more muleteers it would have been improbable that they could have found all their burdens, repacked them and got the team started again on the trail before nightfall. Some *chicleros* on their way to the camp had come to their aid and Gibberd had decided to send on Mrs. Farr with one of them as guide to bring this information to Dr. Cutbush.

'The latter was reassured by the experienced Chicle Company field staff that in time all the mules would be found though it was highly unlikely that Gibberd and the mule team would arrive before the afternoon of the next day, if not later.

'After further general conversation mostly dealing with the geography of Petén and its isolation, some discussion on the more unusual aspects of the character of the President of the Republic of Guatemala and on the recrudescence of the claim of the territory of British Honduras, Dr. Cutbush had bade the party good-night.'

Thus ran the 'minutes' but as sleep still seemed far from him he began to compose his 'seconds'.

First in his 'seconds' came Harkness, the Chicle Company botanist who came to his mind not so much by reason of force of character but because he had interested Cutbush by a remark about the savouring of sensation 'in reverse'. It being a gala evening, Harkness explained, the drinks served would be worthy of the name. They would not be one-year-old British Honduran 'firewater', even if it had the blessing of an excise stamp on the label and was called 'Rum'. No, they were having the genuinely noble aristocrat of the sugar cane, they were having Bacardi Rum of an excellent vintage. To make the welcome really memorable Mr. Copius the chemist had prepared, as a special treat, a 'chaser' for the Bacardi. He had prepared 'soft' distilled water. Harkness had suggested that the rum was good enough to be sipped neat, as one would a brandy, but that then one should follow it with the chaser. Since the water from the wells and lagoons of the limestone plain of Petén was very hard, after several months, the palate became grateful for the innocent smoothness of Copius' soft water.

'We have that advantage of you Dr. Cutbush,' Harkness had said, 'your palate not having a calcareous groundwork cannot appreciate that the soft water is as exciting as the Bacardi. It has not got the smooth, ominous, brassy overtone of the rum but it has its own timbre, that, perhaps of kettle drums and fifes.'

'Yours must be a rare palate that can get so definite a thrill out of soft water,' had replied Cutbush.

'Hardly a rare palate. It has little to do with the temper of the palate as such. It is more a matter of contrast. Isn't it amusing to savour sensation in reverse, '*au rebours*'?

'You know there ought to be another book written, a second *Against the Grain*, not the imaginings of an aesthete but a description of actual experiments on all possible apprehensions of our full and jaded senses to discover, describe, experiment and record for others a widened horizon of sense-experience. Were I to establish a Foundation like yours, Doctor, do you know what I would do? I would finance two teams of adepts to sample, describe and record two sources of sensation which I fear the life of our times make so dull, so drab. I know, of course, your Nethersole Foundation has strings tied to its activities but, perhaps, if I get a chance later on to tell you of my two sources you might be able to stretch a string or two.'

Harkness was a little man, neat in an absent-minded fashion with a thin face, a wide, mobile mouth and deep brown eyes. Later in the evening Cutbush learnt that he was a Londoner who had taught botany in a boys' school for a few years.

'I then learned,' he had told Cutbush 'why Jesuits insist on a period of teaching in a boys' school as part of the training for their priests. It gives the teacher, in vaccination doses, knowledge of all sins. You get doses just big enough for your soul to develop its protective mechanisms, of understanding and pity, against the evils of mankind. You learn to recognize foetal evils in your pupils and that often the arrows they playfully shoot against you are tipped with these evils. You also learn to recognize, however clumsy in expression, stumbling and inept they may be, the virtues which in the years to come become wisdom, tolerance, patience, integrity, charity and a sense of responsibility to all mankind. However, I was no Jesuit, I was no dedicated priest. I thought of specializing in some branch of botany. Then I became interested in sauces ... sensation again you see. And, ultimately in one sauce, a Chinese Soya Bean sauce. An idle question in a Chinese restaurant in London about the sauce which as students we called "frog's blood" led to the knowledge that it was made by a process of fermentation with a fungus. So I found myself involved in that third world of living matter, the fungi. You see, I divide living matter into animal, vegetable and fungi?'

Cutbush understood that, although he was on the books of the Chicle Company as botanist to study the latex-bearing plants and any other plants whose products could be processed into gum, he was above all a student of the fungi of the forests of Mid-America.

So, in his 'second', Cutbush summed up Harkness as a man of deep sympathies and few convictions, tolerant of knavery as long as it was 'amusing' and with an engrossing love for fungi. However common, however rare, they excited in him a tender respect. The green misty growth on damp boots, the yeast of bread that quite incidentally made alcohol as it made the loaf to rise, the great tree fungi of the tropical forests were to him different aspects of nature at her most intriguing.

'Decidedly,' thought Cutbush, 'Harkness is not quite the usual scientist.'

Nor for that matter could Owen Copius the chemist be classed as quite usual. He was also on the staff of the Chicle Company but he had completed the work on which he had been assigned so he had taken advantage of being on the spot to investigate a latex of another species, not for the purpose of making chewing gum, but to isolate an enzyme that had the power of making tough meat tender. Copius had said that there was a tradition in the bush that if the bruised or crushed leaves of a certain species of Ficus were tied up with a tough steak for a few hours that steak became tender. The difficulty he had encountered was that there were no cattle in that part of Petén so he could not try out his enzyme on a beef steak but he had tried it on venison and on tapir-meat.

He had indeed isolated several substances from the leaf and the latex of the Ficus and was now in the process of separating them into pure substances. Copius was American by birth with an accent that was noticeably German. It became apparent that he had lived many years in Germany, had been trained there and had returned to work there in 1920. He had many relatives in that country which was to him a second home and he spoke feelingly of his friends there. He seemed to have read widely outside his subject, particularly on matters relating to philosophy. Cutbush wondered whether the relatives and friends were all in comfortable positions now that Hitler had started to put his racial laws into rigorous effect, but he asked no questions and refrained from following up a remark which might have led the conversation into European politics and the ideas of Nazism.

After Karen Farr arrived the conversation became fragmented and Cutbush had had little opportunity to gather reliable material for writing 'seconds' on other men that he met at supper. He noticed that Copius and Mrs. Farr appeared to be very friendly or, rather, that they had much to speak of but pursued no particular line for very long. There seemed to be some common interest in a chemical experiment that Copius was doing, or had promised to do.

Cutbush had met Mrs. Farr before and she was a character worthy of a long 'second'. They had met once in Chicago and again when the expedition was about to sail from New York. On both occasions their acquaintance had been very slight. He had left the choice of personnel to Gibberd but he had, before his written order was given, caused as thorough an investigation as was possible to be made in the short time at his disposal and without letting any candidate for inclusion in the expedition know that he, or she, was being investigated. He had not thought it necessary to single out Karen Farr for more critical attention of his investigations than any other member of the team but he had learnt quite a lot about her. Academically she had a formidable record. She was Anglo-Irish, had been schooled at a French convent school in Cairo and wrote and spoke Arabic though, since she hardly had occasion to use it, she never mentioned it.

Her father had been a British official stationed for years in Khartoum; her mother had died whilst she was an infant; her father had married again and after he had retired had lived in England until his death. She had early shown an aptitude for mathematics and an interest in folk-ways. She had taken a first-class degree in mathematics in Dublin, had worked on that subject for a semester in Grenoble and had gone to London. There she had deliberately chosen to teach her subject in a 'cram' school so as to allow herself time to develop her interests in past customs and habits.

At that time the influence of a famous Egyptologist was still at its zenith in a London college and his School of Ethnology and Anthropology had much to do with the shaping of Karen's next move. She had accepted an appointment to teach Mathematics in Cairo so as to give herself a better opportunity to study one particular brand of prehistory and then she married and gave up her position as a teacher. At that point Dr. Cutbush's investigator lost track of her because he had not had the time to probe more closely into all her movements. Her husband had been a prisoner of the Turks, having been captured at the fall of the town in Mesopotamia where a besieged British force had capitulated. He was a musician.

The Farrs had appeared again in Mexico where they had lived for a few years in various places in the country. By the time his investigator caught up with Mrs. Farr again she was already spoken of with respect by the officials of the Archaeological Museum in Mexico City. She had concentrated her energies on the study of the Zapotec civilization, being delighted by the beautifully sensitive art of these vanished people of the Mountains of Oaxaca. There was one theory that this art owed much to Maya civilization. Mrs. Farr had so far had no direct contact with Maya archaeology but the fact that the Mayas were superb mathematicians would sooner or later have directed her attention to them.

She was next heard of at an American University without her husband or, at least, there was no record of his being with her. She was now a serious student of Mid-American archaeology. There she met Dr. Gibberd, profited by the proximity to concentrate on the study of the Mayas and, when the opportunity was given, applied for a post in his expedition. With hardly any doubts or reservations he welcomed her as a colleague. She was then in her late thirties, a woman who could be silent without offence and amiable when occasion demanded.

She was unusually tall though otherwise her figure would have been termed 'passable'. Her greenish-blue eyes veiled with long dark lashes at times lit up her face, with its well-formed nose and full mouth, with an almost incandescent glow. At these times her dark shoulder-length hair acted as a back-drop to a sudden revelation of genuine beauty. After the cause of the revelation had passed, or could no longer be sustained, she relapsed again into a well-poised, well-mannered, well but not too painfully groomed woman, easy to engage in any conversation however trivial or abstruse. However, she was not, herself, given to opening a subject.

The investigator, who obviously relished his task, had been told that she had been called, by a Zapotec maid-servant, 'She of the sleeping face'. Not that she was 'poker-faced', for she was capable of quick and resolute changes of expression, but one felt that she had been born with a mask. It was neither the mask of comedy or tragedy, but the mask of a sleeper, one who had awakened before dawn and had drifted off to sleep again. Of her family background Cutbush knew a little. They had been Catholics in Northern Ireland, in the professions and she had had an aunt who had married a shipbuilding fortune, and had left much of it to her niece and nephews.

Of her husband, the musician, little was known. A quartet by a certain Hislop Farr had been played at a musical festival in Arizona; a concerto in Amsterdam and a suite 'Ixthaxihuatle' had been played to esteemed success in Mexico City. The success in Mexico City was apparently his first and last. The critiques of the other pieces had been reserved though one man had been intemperately flattering of the concerto. Nothing of Farr's had been played, in public at any rate, for several years but that did not mean that he had ceased to be a composer. Mrs. Farr never spoke of him but if deliberate enquiry was made of her she would say clearly and with finality, 'Oh yes, he still works at his music and he likes to travel.'

With all this information in mind Cutbush had sat and looked at Karen as she sipped her Bacardi at the party and again the Zapotec maid-servant's description of her repeated itself in his memory, 'She of the sleeping face'. And Cutbush wondered what the mask concealed, what private purgatory drove this clever and, in her own way, beautiful woman to hide from the world behind an expression which seemed so to shut her out from her surroundings that he, for one, was tempted to force the issue with her. To demand 'Why?'. As he drifted off to sleep he promised himself it was a question he would ask quite soon unless the answer was vouchsafed in some other way.

Dr. Cutbush rose early. He had slept well after mulling over his 'seconds' to find that the aches and pains brought on by his journey were subsiding rapidly. So now he looked forward to a day which might be full of interest and pleasure. Doubtless Gibberd would arrive with his precious sherds and there would be the man's burning enthusiasm for his trade to heighten his greeting for his friend, Cutbush, who had snatched him from dim museums and put him where he really came alive, in the Maya forests. Karen Farr, Copius and Harkness were already at breakfast when he went to the 'dining hall'.

The talk was amiable because all agreed that weighty subjects at a lazy breakfast were out of place. Karen, as Cutbush came to call her in his mind, confessed that she had been awake a long time before dawn and had gone over all the most important aspects of her work in the clear light of dawn and therefore she was resolved, now, to take a day off. Copius approved of her idea enthusiastically and proposed a stroll through the bush to examine a discovery that had been made by Harkness. It was a very rare orchid flowering about a mile from the Camp which closely resembled the fabulous 'White Nun' orchid of the Guatemala highlands. On the front of that variety there were reddish streaks which, when viewed in the oblique rays of the morning-light, and with a macabre touch of imagination, appeared to be 'tears of blood'.

They started shortly after breakfast and in the course of the walk Copius revealed that he was considering starting, quite soon, on the long road back to America. There were family difficulties and as his work in Shoonantonitch was finished it seemed appropriate that he should leave. He had originally thought of extending his stay for some considerable time because he had an idea that was an offshoot of his 'tenderizing' experiments which he wanted to work on. But, he added, watching Mrs. Farr rather closely, the work could wait and might even be better for some incubation.

As for Harkness, in the bush he was like a hunting-dog, swift yet cautious though, unlike a dog, he hunted everything *except* animals. As he walked he pointed out to Cutbush the Ficus tree from which Copius had isolated his 'tenderizing' system of enzymes. 'And there', said Harkness a little later, 'is Polyporus.' The name was new to Cutbush and following the direction Harkness indicated with his forefinger he saw a beautiful tree. It had shed its leaves but the bare branches were covered by a profusion of flowers of a bright, declamatory crimson. In the prevailing greenish gloom of the forest it had the aspect of an apparition as the light caught the upper branches 30 feet above ground and made the flowers glow like long pendant rubies.

'So,' said Cutbush, 'that is a Polyporus. It is certainly a beautiful tree, a magnificent spectacle with those blood-red flowers.'

'No, no,' corrected Harkness, 'the tree is not Polyporus, that is an Erythryna. It is the fungus, the epiphyte, that is the Polyporus.'

He pointed to a flattened semicircle of woody growth which protruded from the trunk of the Erythryna like a shelf about ten feet above ground.

'That is the sporophore of the fungus. We three have been rather exercised in our minds about Polyporus recently. It has helped us to keep our wits alive during our exile in this green sea. But let Mrs. Farr tell you about it.'

So Karen reminded Cutbush how often, in widely separated civilizations, parasitic plants had had religious significance. There was the ready example of the mistletoe. It was the recollection of this fact that had led to a theory of the significance of the Polyporus in Mid-American prehistory. It is true that there was no proof of its importance as a religious symbol and also true that in only one small part of Mid-America, amongst an almost completely forgotten race, was there evidence of its significance. The evidence was of the scantiest so that the use of the word 'evidence' might even be an exaggeration. However, the following facts had led to a theory.

In the lowlands of south-east Mexico there had lived, how long ago no one knew, a race which had entirely disappeared. That they lived there and indefinitely then, is known because they left three very characteristic expressions of their remarkable, if restricted, artistic gifts. The first was a flat paddle-shaped leaf of stone richly inscribed with glyphs.

The second was a stone 'horse-collar' about three feet across in the diameter of its greatest curvature and this again was inscribed with glyphs. 'The third you have seen,' said Karen.

'Have I?' asked Cutbush.

'Yes,' she replied. 'You remember that, after the lunch you gave Dr. Gibberd and myself in Chicago, we visited the Field Museum. There we showed you some of the Zapotec collection which I had found and had classified. Then, as we left that room, we turned into an alcove to look at what he called, *"the famous smiling face of the Totonacs"*. That is the third.'

'Of course, I remember,' Cutbush replied. 'Although we were hurrying out I remember the spectacle vividly. So that this is the third object of the Totonacs and it has to do with Polyporus and the Erythryna tree?'

'We don't know, you understand? We don't know and we are speculating but the Erythryna flourishes profusely at the edges of the swamps of their lands, in what is now Tabasco and part of the state of Vera Cruz. The Erythryna of those swamp edges are of the species that flower at the end of the wet season after they shed their leaves. The flowers are of a deeper, bloody red. Furthermore Polyporus, this parasitic growth, does appear to attack Erythryna for preference.

'The stone "horse-collar", of course, could not represent a real horse-collar. There were no horses in Mexico before Cortez. But presuming it had ritual significance, presuming Polyporus was to the Totonacs as mistletoe was to the Druids, would it be too much to think that their "horse-collar" was that woody, half-circular shelf cut from the trunk of the tree?'

'Well,' said Cutbush, 'I suppose if one accepts all those presumptions we might as well presume a little more and say that you could be right. Have you any ideas as to what gave rise to the paddle-shaped stone?'

'No, not yet. We do have something that is suggestive but we cannot present it, with any conviction, as evidence,' Karen replied.

'And what of the famous smiling face? That is a clay mask, isn't it?'

'Yes,' she said, 'yes, or rather heads modelled in clay. And all of them, every one, every single representation of the human form as left by the Totonacs, is only that of a head which smiles. And these forgotten artists were supremely accomplished within the limits they set themselves. They had reached that point of sophistication where they deliberately distorted the dimensions of the head to throw into greater relief the infectious humour of the face. No other emotion seemed to interest the Totonacs. They seemed to imply that no feeling was so important as the sense of the enjoyment of the ridiculous. For the smiling face of the Totonacs had no other overtones but that of pure, one might almost say, boisterous laughter. There was no trace of reserve, of cynicism, of social acceptance by private withdrawal, of pity, or of deep wisdom. It was always the smile of an enraptured child.'

They had reached a tree from which leapt, high up, a single white orchid, restrained by an inconspicuous stem. Harkness pointed to it. The slanting light gave the illusion that red drops were rolling down the gorget of the Nun's white habit. It was indeed an unusual flower. Cutbush, however, found himself allergic to orchids. Even in this most natural environment the flower looked artificial. 'It cannot help, it seems, but remind one of hot-houses and orchid fanciers. While the most sophisticated of roses never appears forced. So give me roses every time', murmured Cutbush to himself. While he looked at the orchid, however, he felt that Mrs. Farr's words about the Totonac had a common and deeper bond of interest for these three. He was professionally sensitive to atmosphere. Where two or three were gathered together Cutbush unrolled his invisible antennae to twitch and turn, gathering data, which he tested, analysed, synthesized and stored away.

He was able professionally to encourage the exudation of this data. Gently, he said, 'But there is more. You have found out something more!' The other two nodded to Copius.

Then Copius told Cutbush of a conversation which the three of them, Mrs. Farr, Harkness and himself had had some weeks ago. He repeated that he had completed the project for which, officially, he had been assigned to this forgotten forest. It was the production of a 'double-barrelled' chewing gum because, he explained to Cutbush, modern man's taste-buds have been 'circumcised'. It was thought that by treating the fresh latex a technique could be more readily discovered. So Copius had been supplied with the fresh latex. He had had a *chiclero* attached to him for that particular purpose and he had discovered how to make the 'double-barrelled gum' when the confection was freshly prepared from latex. To make a double-barrelled chewing gum, he continued, from the chicle of commerce was going to take some time but there was no doubt it could be done in the laboratories of the company in New York. The idea of having two flavours of chewing gum sprang from the ready satiation of the sense of taste because the particular taste-buds that first appreciated a flavour soon became fatigued to near anaesthesia. Copius' problem, he explained, had been to incorporate another flavour in the gum which remained dormant until after the spearmint taste had passed and the ptyalin in the saliva would then activate the dormant flavour and explode a new taste sensation in the mouth. He had found no natural flavours which would be sufficiently tractable and had had to prepare a group of synthetic esters each with a characteristic flavour. He explained to his friends that for practical purposes he had divided these esters into two categories, one of which he had called, in defiance of the austerity of chemical nomenclature, 'heavy, barbaric and cloying' and the other he had called 'pure and singular'.

It was a division of practical importance because a 'cloying' flavour would not induce the chewer quickly to take a second wad of the gum. While a 'pure and singular' flavour had not the rousing overtones to make the taste-buds remember them with pleasure. Listening to him now, Karen remembered that she had been quietly amused at the categories into which he had divided his flavours and she had wondered, privately, whether he divided people into the same classes. If so, was she 'pure and singular' – because she had no 'rousing overtones'? Certainly she was not 'barbaric and heavy' – but 'cloying' she might be to certain tastes!

Recalling the discussion which had followed Copius' revelation of his arbitrary categorization of flavours the chemist went on to describe the way the others had reacted.

First, he said, Harkness had quizzed him asking him whether he thought his concepts were worthy of the effort he had put into them.

'I replied,' Copius told Cutbush, 'that to a botanist a new species of fungus might appear to be a revelation of the Glory of God. While to me my work, chemistry, is simply a job but one that must be treated very sensitively and carefully because it can be imbued with destructive evil. For instance, so benign a work as that carried out by Pasteur on disease germs where they affect vine roots and other work carried out on silkworms or, with benign intentions on men, can end in an exquisitely precise manipulation of processes that may lead to the horrors and evils of bacteriological warfare. From clouds may come "the ghastly dew" that Tennyson foresaw. Spores of plant diseases may be created to blight crops, viruses to cause a murrain on the beasts of the fields, chemical extracts to make women frigid, and pestilential plagues to destroy men and make them pray for the happy days of innocence.' Copius sounded angry and indignant. After a pause he continued more temperately. 'I told Karen and Harkness that, as a chemist, I manipulate processes, a task that is interesting in itself, earns me a living and one from which my main reward is the pleasure I get from the work, a reward in the artistic and elegant completion of a task, whether it be a discovery that will lead to a chewing gum in which one flavour takes over when the first one stales or a new way to tenderize steak.

'At that point Karen with her usual perspicacity asked whether when I spoke of "artistic" satisfaction it included a quality that might be considered aesthetic.' Copius glanced past Cutbush to smile at the only feminine member of the party. '"Yes, indeed," I replied, "an aesthetic satisfaction of the same kind, though minimal in degree, to the satisfaction of the poet or the musician. I, too, have to make my dreams with my distorting fingers. Of course the poet escapes to dreamland where he lives his dream and may well strangle himself when he returns and tries to tell us of the dream-scapes because too few of us have ears attuned to his stutterings. What we each need is our own private trap-door to dreamland."'

Copius, Cutbush noticed, kept his eyes on Mrs. Farr watching her reactions to his words very closely.

After a moment he continued, 'I mean not only does the mass of humanity need roads to dreamland; not only are they congenitally incapable of finding the roads but they must even be given the very vehicles for the road. Poets and the other misbegotten unfortunates called, in general, artists are under a spell. Theirs is a sentence to a servitude of a different order. Their agonies and exultations have little bearing on the all-pervading dull ache of life as it is known to the mass of mankind, to the "quiet desperation" which Thoreau says is the lot of most men. Why, even to us the solace of a cigarette may be more satisfying than the comfort of a phrase of music, or the words of a sonnet.

'"But works of art are not balm and plaster," Karen objected.

'"True," I told her, "but we won't stop, now, to discuss what works of art are not. What I say is that their creators had ways of escape to that other land and, from that other dimension of the soul, could see mankind "made plausible, his purpose plain." I have never seen the plausibility nor the purpose. However, I believe that dimension exists though, alas, its existence is real only to those who can see it. Let me repeat, I am speaking of the man in street who knows nothing and believes even less of dimensions of aesthetic satisfaction; a man who prefers a cigarette to a work of art. And his need isn't something new. The history of mankind is punctuated by his attempts to escape.

'"I need but mention opium, hashish, tobacco and, of course, alcohol which has been blessed and cursed and has showered blessings and curses on humanity. In the final stock-taking, if there is ever so monstrous a procedure, surely the blessings of alcohol will be registered as having been many times greater than its curses. I, once, heard a most experienced physician say that on the aggregate, taking the long view of generations, tobacco does more harm than alcohol, if only because its effects are quiet and the habit of over-indulgence more wide spread than that of alcohol."'

'"Well," Harkness said, "why not postulate a substance that heightens and prolongs the enjoyment of the sexual act?"

'"I could," I told him, "except that perhaps by its very nature it would cause economic loss in the shortening of the life of the human machine and would interfere with graceful ageing. Most important of all, for its enjoyment it means a partnership while a man on his road to escape must escape alone.

'"I have thought a great deal about the natural pleasures which could be heightened and of the discomforts that could be reduced. But the reduction of pain is a negative blessing and we are searching for something positive. If we think of the pleasurable feelings of the body which are common to the herd, I can think of but one that meets our requirements, positive as well as negative. I can think of but one sensation, one passion the one which Hobbes called "the passion that has no name".'

'"Aha," said Karen. "A sudden conception of some eminency in ourselves for the passion of laughter is nothing else but sudden glory."

'And,' Copius told Cutbush, 'Hobbes enlarged on his concept by adding "laughter without offence must be at absurdities where all the company may laugh together; for laughing to oneself putteth all the rest to jealousy and examination of themselves." To me, above all things, mankind needs the power of the kind of laughter so as to laugh at the absurdities and infirmities of life so as to laugh and to lessen the sense of doomed futility. Laughter is here a sacrament, a sly propitiation and, finally, a provocation to swift oblivion; which must be better, far better than the bloody idiocies of history.

'Harkness asked, "Would you welcome, then, a complete wiping out of our civilization?"

'"I would welcome nothing of the sort though it appears to me inevitable, and I will not torture the dialectics of history to construct a scaffold to sustain my hopes," I replied.

'"Well – for my part," rejoined Harkness, "I do not agree with your gloomy forecast of the future. I am an evolutionist – and I believe –"

'"Yes? What do you believe?"

'"I believe," said Harkness, "that in the fullness of time – when

Mind has grown it will turn the tables on Matter. An idea will be projected from Mind, by an effort of Imagination, and Matter will move to takes its place into the pattern of the idea.

'"If the idea demands a lassoo be cast over the moon and that Sirius be moved from its orbit for the purpose then it will be done. Matter will be not matter, as we think we know it, but a symbolic protrusion of Ideas, bits of a jig-saw puzzle each piece being a part not of one pattern but an essential part of a billion patterns. Now, do not ask to what purpose. I don't know. I am not able to tell of the purpose of that Evolved Mind and I suspect Brain never will be able to tell."

'"Yes," I had to agree, "I can follow you so far. It is a possible interpretation. But don't you think we could use that drug of escape ... the drug to make us laugh. We could use it to give us surcease from the burden of our destiny, an analgesia for birth pangs?"

'Then Karen broke her silence again and told us that other people in other times had quested for relief from their burdens and their destiny.

'"Certainly," she said, "the number of vegetable extracts which have been used to give surcease and pleasure were many. Their effects were sometimes fantastic as with Mexican peyotl or bizarre, as with the Siberian agaric, which could prevent the 'morning after' by starting the debauchee off on another agaric-drunk. All he had to do was to take a few sips of his own early-morning-after-the-night-before urine. But I wonder why of all the forgotten peoples the Totonacs alone had thought it important to perpetuate one passion only, the passion of laughter."

'And then she asked the most important question that any of us had asked during our discussion. "Is it too fantastic to think that they might have discovered our Sudden Glory and so laughed themselves happily into limbo? As well as the famous Smiling Head there are the other two objects on which they lavished their skill, the Stone Leaf and the Stone Horse-Collar. Remember Aguilar, who left us so recently, has been working on the Totonac civilization at the same time that I have been working on the Art of the ancient Zapotecs. Aguilar suggested, you remember, that the Horse-Collar might have been the epiphyte Polyporus infesting as it does that particular species of Erythryna which grows so lavishly at the edges of the swamps around the Totonac area and which blossomed with blood-red flowers." She paused for a moment before adding, "But let us suppose that Totonacs had discovered that Sudden Glory came from the Polyporus and they wanted to perpetuate the memory of that fact. After all, we know that fungi are rich in alkaloids, enzymes and other potent extractives. For instance, there is the ergot of rye, used in childbirth the world over and the agaric of Siberia. While only a few years ago, a doctor in London discovered another remarkable fungus derivative, penicillin. So let us suppose Polyporus was the source of Sudden Glory."

'"My God," said Harkness, "that is a brilliant thought. And I know the species of Erythryna of Tabasco. It is rare in Petén but it can be found. Of course the Polyporus must not be too old and woody if the greatest curvature is to be at most three feet."

'"Right," said Karen. "The size of the Horse-Collars. I would never have thought of it but for Copius' admiration for Hobbes. Could you, Harkness, find the Polyporus? And you, Copius, attempt to extract from it Sudden Glory?"

'"I can and will," Harkness told her.

'"If the substance is there I can certainly try," is what I said,' Copius told Cutbush.

'So you see, Doctor Cutbush, you were right to think that we might have been looking for something more than a rare orchid.'

'And did you? Did you find Polyporus? And did you find Sudden Glory?' Cutbush demanded. 'Did you?'

'I think I did,' said Harkness.

'I got something and I am still trying,' Copius sounded less optimistic. Mrs. Farr said nothing.

'Of course, you know we all three would rather you didn't say anything about this,' said Harkness.

And Cutbush gave them his word that he would not.

Karen returned to her house after the walk to the orchid in a very depressed frame of mind. She had been distressed that Copius had said so much of their mutual interest in 'Sudden Glory'. Some two weeks ago he had given her a few grammes of greyish powder – the end result of his extractions of the specimens Harkness had given him. He had informed her that there was little doubt that the powder contained more than one alkaloid but that he was uncertain whether he could give any more time to the matter.

Copius gave her to understand that Delfosse, who as manager was technically responsible for the use the staff made of the Company's time, had asked some pointed questions of him about what he was doing. However, she had hardly expected so balanced a person as Copius to come to a precipitate decision. Another matter which puzzled her was Copius' rejection of all interest in the trial of the powder he had isolated. His manner was so final that she had almost asked him for his notes on the chemical steps on the process of the separation though at the last moment she restrained herself. A chemist's notes as to his procedures would be as sacred to him as her own notes in deciphering the glyphs of her stela. He did, however, when she put the question point blank to him say that he would like to hear the result of the trial. It was as if he was determined to leave the decision on whether to proceed with their efforts to her and this upset her because the necessity of choosing a course of action in her own affairs was, to her, the most exhausting of efforts.

She was gifted with splendid health, was capable of the severest of mental efforts in her work, could worry a problem of scholarship relentlessly hour after hour and at the end be fresh and rewarded not so much by the result as by the exhilaration of effort. On the other hand she had, recently, been faced with a distractingly important decision with regard to her own affairs and emotions. She had decided to search amongst the embers in a lacerated corner of her heart to see if there was any spark left of her nascent love for a man, a particular man, recently met. That she had to go through this painful process brought her to the edge of exasperated tears, for she had thought years ago that she had become, through suffering brought by her own guilt, immune to such feelings.

She had, a few years ago, suffered what she had then called an amputation. Her heart after that had learned to hobble with the aid of a crutch supplied by her resolution. However, she had heard that very, very rarely a nerve ending in the scar of the amputated stump would stir into futile and painful life. Then instead of gratefully accepting the scar, as the bone, skin and muscles usually did, the nerve would sprout a small, obscene bud whose only function was to hurt, to amplify and transmit pain. Doctors called it a 'neuroma'.

So she had sprouted a neuroma in her heart and it brought her no more joy that a proper neuroma in its proper place brought to a limb that had suffered amputation.

There was also another reason for her depression. The avid interest of Cutbush in the three people not so much as protagonists in a bizarre tale, but as individuals, seemed to her to be clinical. She feared that Copius had said too much and that Cutbush would think her as morbidly pessimistic as Copius was himself. She did not fear Cutbush's ill opinion of her as an employee of the Nethersole Foundation, but she detested giving anyone the opportunity of putting a label on her which might imply that she was other than dully 'normal'. She fancied she could see Cutbush summing her up as 'unsettled' or 'disturbed' or 'morbid', or some such description, anything other than 'absolutely normal'. She knew perfectly well how untrue a label 'absolutely normal' would be, but she thought her attitudes and responses were so well disciplined that she presented an urbane and impregnable front to the world. She especially abhorred the idea that she should be the subject of a clinical psychological enquiry. After all Cutbush was a psychologist and it would be second nature for him not only to weigh ideas but more importantly to assess the personalities of the people who discussed the ideas.

As a result of her own ruthless self-analysis, at one time in her life, she had confessed to herself that she was a creature gifted with splendid faculties of intellect, splendid powers of application, breeding, background and money, all advantages that would have made her an object of envy to many of her less fortunate sisters. However, with all these assets, she was without roots, had a troubled past and a future certain of sterility. She was, she had decided, possessed of pity without charity. Her husband, blundering and foredoomed genius, had first shown her to herself and she believed with precious certainty in the correctness of his estimate. 'You are', he had said, 'incapable of giving or receiving of love, of that happiness, of that joyous cleansing lightness and fullness of heart, like an unexpected blessing, which another person should get of being with you, or near you or even thinking of you. You do not get it and you cannot give it. One could esteem you, be grateful to you and take pride in you, certainly. But love, no.'

Her pity sprang not so much from an identification of herself with the person in tribulation but from a recoil at the harshness of destiny in putting on this person burdens and situations too heavy for him. She was a Greek chorus exclaiming with horror and pity though where she differed from the chorus was that she was shocked at the waste.

For Karen there was only one Devil, waste. All waste to her was evil, the waste of life, of opportunities for fuller living, of living attributes. Waste as exemplified in the sterilization of love, of gallantry, of affection and of aesthetic adventure was, she considered, worse than sin. They were, for her, aggravated and blasphemous crimes.

A forest gutted by fire caused by a lighted cigarette, a hillside eroded of living soil were to her hardly tolerable evidence of sacrilege. But the sight of the repulse of a gesture of love, or affection, or reconciliation or even comradeship, made her tremble with an aching and private expostulation, 'How long, oh Lord, how long!' Yet she did not look upon the giver nor upon the receiver of the gesture, with loving kindness. They were not sons and daughters, sisters and brothers to whom she kindled with rich warmth. They were other people. Karen Farr was an aborted saint.

Her work in the expedition had been highly satisfactory from one point of view. Officially her duties had been to study the relationship, if any, between Mayan art and Zapotec art. She had obtained material which she thought would prove that both these early American civilizations had influenced each other considerably. The influence, however, had ceased before the flowering of the first Maya Empire and had had nothing to do with the later Aztec influence of the Second Empire. Unofficially, but with the full knowledge and encouragement of Gibberd and Cutbush, she had been diligently pursuing a line of research for which her previous training and her gifts made her particularly suitable. This research was with reference to the Maya calendar. There were at least two different interpretations of Maya Chronology and the arithmetical results of the respective interpretations differed from each other by about a couple of hundred years. As long as this uncertainty existed it was impossible to be sure of the precise dates of events in Maya history and impossible correctly to interpret the numbers, the dates and the astronomical data. Indeed, the only hope of understanding what was left of their recorded writing, as presented by the glyphs on the stelae, was by correct correlation of their calendar with the Gregorian calendar. Maya enumeration was not by tens and their system of constructing their calendar was incredibly complicated. Yet complicated as it appeared it was so correct that it could record with almost absolute precision no less than 34,000 years. To make complication more complicated they themselves appeared to think that this 'long count', this recording of an eternity, was too precise an instrument and so they introduced the 'short' count of years and later even shortened the 'short count'.

Furthermore they were not content with a solar year but appeared to be possessed of a consuming doubt, if not of themselves, then of the sun. So, they had a 'second' year of 260 days. Some archaeologists had suggested that this was a statistical year, the product of their vigesimal enumeration multiplied by the number of the thirteen gods of the upper world. These difficulties and uncertainties did not daunt her. She accepted the conclusions of generations of previous scholars with caution and reserve. She was prepared to accept the evidence that the Mayas used a year of 260 days and that this 260 days could, indeed, be divided in months of twenty days each with each month, in fact, named with the name of one of the thirteen 'lords of the upper world'. She parted from other scholars in the belief that Maya time-keeping was for very practical purposes by the priests who calculated those times and seasons when the maize should be planted and reaped and, with this purpose, checked and re-checked their calendar. The cultivation of maize was the be-all of Maya culture, probably starting from the time when their forebears in the Guatemala highlands had domesticated a wild plant, the *teosinte* and had developed corn. Karen, for her part, wished to prove that this 'statistical' year of 260 days was a check on the solar year and in fact was a Venus year.

For the Mayas were astoundingly able astronomers and they made very accurate calculations dealing with several planets, amongst them the planet Venus. Long before cog wheels were put in clocks the Mayas put cogs on the time wheels of several planets and also of the sun. Then they geared them together. The Venus calendar was one of these gear wheels of the heavens. Karen hoped to prove that they knew that the 260 days was not the correct Venus year but was, to the nearest 'month' of twenty days, that period when Venus was an Evening Star plus the period in its inferior conjunction. It was a bold hypothesis but she was a student who used imagination as an angler uses his rod and reel. She could cast a dry-fly from her imagination up the stream of the subject which she studied and if there was a flurry of response, or even a ripple, she would relentlessly pursue the subject till she exhausted it or herself, or decided that the flurry was extraneous coincidence. She thought that the Mayas were quite capable of knowing that the Venus year was not absolutely accurate and, further, were capable of knowing how to make the necessary correction. She had some evidence which she thought proved that the Mayas used the coincidence of the equality between five solar years and eight Venus years for ceremonial purposes. She was elated to find that there was this Maya 'lustrum', initiated with rites and 'sacrifices'.

Furthermore she believed that she had progressed far enough in her theory to show that the Maya 'century' was sixty-five solar years, or 104 Venus years, with the proviso that at the end of every century they adjusted the two calendars by an addition of twenty-five days to the Solar Calendar. But she found that were she rigidly to adhere to either the Venus year, or the solar year, for her computation of chronology she could reconcile the Maya dates she had so far translated neither with the books of Chillam Balam, nor with the references to outstanding natural events in the Aztec calendar, nor with the Quiche calendar. She had tried to meet the problem by working on the hypothesis that for a certain number of centuries the Mayas used the solar year and then, after that, the Venus year. She had been unable to find any evidence, on any of the monuments, or in any of the codices, of this change of pace in the reckoning of the centuries. She believed she was correct, by suitable 'juggling' she could convince herself, but she knew she would discredit herself completely in the eyes of archaeologists competent to assess her work if she were to publish any 'juggling' with dates and numerations. The good opinion of this scant score of people, most of them strangers to her, good opinion formed on labours of not the slightest use to anyone, past, present or future, remained the only sanction of values, as distinct from expediency, which Karen still retained.

It was now two years since the problem of Maya chronology had absorbed her and she had decided to drop it as not capable of solution on the present data and to write off two years of labour as years wasted. Since she hated waste she conceded that, as there are degrees of evils, so there are degrees of waste and that this problem, though wasteful, had filled two years of effort. 'I owe it that amount of thanks,' she said ... it was her 'Nunc Dimittis' ... to Maya chronology. It was in the very height of this, her most fascinating season in the bush, that a letter had reached her. It came from the lawyers in Belize who handled Nethersole Foundation affairs, that is, such affairs as local law, or conditions, or emergencies needed to be handled by local lawyers. It was a matter relating to a bequest to her from her aunt's estate. She was required to swear in front of a notary public as to the facts presented by a certain document and sign the document in front of two witnesses, the notary to be one of the witnesses. So it was arranged. Gibberd had spoken to Fuad and had discovered that Jaime was leaving the next day, on urgent business for Fuad, to the Bank in Belize and would return at once. So Jaime and Mrs. Farr had left, with two muleteers to look after the animals until they reached El Cayo. There they had got on a motor boat and had arrived in Belize in about a week. Their return journey, again depending on the river, took but a day or so longer.

On the last mile of their ride into El Cayo, Doctor Hastings had overtaken them. He was returning from a call. A mother, he had explained, had been in labour about three days. 'On the third day the relatives decided I might be useful. I didn't have to do much. In fact, all I had to do was to welcome the baby into the vale of tears and to check the excessive bleeding of the mother.

That having been done, I could canter back home.'

When he had learnt of their mission, he had insisted he should be their host. 'In fact,' he had said, 'last night we heard your boat would be delayed. She was half way up the river when engine trouble began. The Captain was able to send a messenger to a village where the telegraph line had a station at the post office and sent us the news. One of our nurses is on board. So, Mrs. Farr, the Head-Nurse will put you in the absent nurse's room and Jaime will bed in my house. As for board, you are of course my guests.'

So it had been arranged. What, however, had made the interlude memorable to Karen was the relationship between the Doctor and Jaime. It had been as if they were carrying on a conversation which had no beginning and no end.

In the midst of dinner the Doctor pointed to Jaime and said, 'I found it – or rather the reference – it is from Coleridge – you know – the "Cloak of Unbelief".'

'What's this,' she had asked, 'necromancy?'

'Yes in a way,' the Doctor had replied, 'let me give you a concrete example. I was a medical student in London and during my junior years, having an almost empty afternoon, I decided to go to a theatre. I did not do Greek at school but I knew enough to know that the play was a classic which had survived a couple of thousand years. It was in English of course, the *Medea* of Euripides with Sybil Thorndike as "Medea".'

'I left the theatre not walking on air, but "purified". I had for the first time in my life been the subject of the exorcism of the dramatist as artist.'

Jaime had nodded, 'Yes, that is the word, exorcized.' So they had spoken of Coleridge who first labelled the rite 'The shedding of the Cloak of Unbelief'.

Then Jaime had said it had been said of another art, that of music, by another poet and he had recited easily and simply,

'Sweet sounds, oh, beautiful music do not cease,

Reject me not into the world again.'

He had stopped – 'Go on, go on,' Karen had said.

So he had recited the rest of the sonnet by Edna St. Vincent Millay.

Karen had slept the night soundly in the nurse's bed and

again, in the same bed, for another night. During those three days of interlude she had spoken long and often with Jaime in the Doctor's house. Then the motor boat had arrived and they went about their business in Belize and returned to Shoonantonitch where Jaime had resumed his role as Fuad's handyman.

Karen Farr had had countless things to do, to think on, to remember and some of her memories were recent.

Then Cutbush had arrived to trouble her by poking into the question of 'Sudden Glory' and, she felt, into her private affairs, an investigator, a man who liked to pry and Karen was a very troubled and private person.

However relief was at hand. When she entered her house she found a visitor waiting and they embraced warmly.

'Oh, Maria,' Karen cried, 'how good to see you. How splendid of you to come to see me. If you only knew how welcome you are. How are you and the children. Doing well at school as usual, I hope.'

PART THREE

'WHO GOES TO PICK A ROSE MUST HAVE REGARD FOR THE THORNS'

Maria Arevalo was the wife of the Commandante of the District. She was not gifted with too alarming an intelligence nor too disturbing a beauty and, had she not possessed other attributes, Karen would have thought of her as no more than the good-looking wife of a Guatemaltecan official with the obvious limitations of her upbringing and background. But Maria was as insensible of her own limitations as she was of other people's. She had a heart which warmed her countenance and instructed her mind. She liked people and would have liked more people had she not been brought up on the old Spanish tradition of ladylike reserve and seclusion.

The women of the archaeological expedition interested her first just as women and next as women who, most curiously, spent their lives in the study of stones, old stones laid long, long ago by people dead long ago, stones which she summed up satisfyingly and completely to herself as 'Ruins'. Maria felt that life itself, her life, just here and now, was so full, so exciting that for 'women' to spend their days studying dead people's dead ruins was nothing but sacrilege. It was to refuse the great gift of life of the Creator to renounce that only gift which lifted womenkind above and beyond menfolk. That gift was the creation and the nurture of life. The fact that the strikingly pretty Miss Quinn, the secretary and artist, should not find the Commandante's wife interesting or amusing did not dismay Maria. But that Karen who, on first acquaintance, was so precise, so self-contained, so impeccably mannered and who had so formidable a reputation for learning should respond to Maria's friendliness flattered her greatly. She did not dream that it was Karen who was even more flattered by Maria's interest. Nor did she realize how thrice welcome her visit was at that moment. For Karen in her ruthless appraisal of herself knew, or thought she knew, her failings as well as her virtues and no one would have been more surprised than Maria to know that this securely brilliant creature envied her anything.

The Commandante's wife had what Karen called 'loving-kindness' and she told herself, 'I have what I suppose would be called an excellent brain but Maria has much more than brains. She has an attitude, deriving from her richness of spirit, that recognizes with satisfaction, amounting to a spontaneous and communicating joy, the worth and dignity of other men. She is quite unaware of her value. She attracts because she gives a quick kindling of warmth and reassurance to others.' Maria was delighted at Karen's reception of her approach. She had come to invite her to lunch and the invitation was eagerly accepted. They were to have as the other guest a friend of Maria's from Guatemala City.

'She is a widow,' said Maria, 'she has known sorrow, much sorrow. But I have told Candellaria that you are not only very intelligent, very understanding, but *muy simpatica*.'

Karen blushed like a girl with pleasure. Maria was exaggerating, of course, but what she said was good to hear.

The word *simpatica* in Spanish does not merely mean 'sympathetic'; it has more the flavour of 'jovial, instructed interest and intuitive appreciation springing from a sympathetic mind and heart'. Maria had, with perhaps hardly conscious guile, spoken the only word which could have healed the soreness of Karen's recent struggle.

'It is not, of course, true,' she thought, quick and ruthless with herself as usual, 'though I wish it were. Oh, were I indeed "*simpatica*" how different my relationships with people would be.'

Aloud she said, 'Thank you. I shall be glad to come. I have spent too much time, lately, thinking over work done and to be done, so it will do me good to dine *en famille* again.'

They set out for the Commandante's house, Maria chatting engagingly. She was not a profound person but she realized that Karen's attention was not so much an unbending as a mood of warm almost anxious receptiveness. Maria, therefore, told the story of Candellaria Aycienena for she thought that Karen's knowledge of something of the history of the other guest at the luncheon party would, if that something were unusual and piteous, add interest and understanding to the meeting.

'She is a widow,' said Maria, 'so young and, as you will see, so beautiful. Yet already there has been calamity in her life.'

Karen wondered whether it would be improper to suggest that being a widow might not necessarily be a great misfortune. Maria, however, was obviously enjoying her role of Chorus to the tragic story of Candellaria so that flippancy would be out of place.

'Some women attract bad luck and an evil star shines but for them,' continued Maria. 'So it has been for Candellaria. She had the world at her feet. She was secure, beloved, in good health and had a lovely baby boy. Her husband was already spoken of not only as a good doctor but as a coming man of affairs. Indeed, he had been elected to the Chamber of Deputies. Then, after two or three brilliant speeches he resigned his seat. He was too conscientious to be both deputy and doctor at the same time though his influence persisted and his ideas permeated the political group to which he belonged. He was obviously a leader, a man with a great future. He decided to leave the atmosphere of politics, to get far away from political contact. He left Guatemala City to practise in Coban. He did well there and soon he had a wide practice. One day he received a call to a patient. A messenger said a certain well-known Señor was suddenly ill and needed a doctor urgently.

'Of course he went. Coban is a lonely and mountainous country. On the way he saw a man lying in the road who appeared to be ill. There were two others with him. They stopped his car. Indeed, the man was lying in such a position that the car had to stop. Then the doctor found that the man on the road was, perhaps, drunk though he got to his feet insisting that he was perfectly sober and that he would not be touched. He was waving a pistol about declaring that anyone who said he was drunk was a fool. Then the pistol went off. The doctor was mortally wounded. A traveller some minutes later heard his dying story and reported it but gave a false name and address because he could not, later, be found. Of course all three men had disappeared. Oh yes, they were eventually caught, tried and shot at the scene of their crime. It was justice certain and swift. But what is justice to Candellaria? Her man is dead and she is not quite alive any more. That was a few years ago.

'Still malign fate had another card to deal Candellaria. Quite soon her little son, her all in all, was stricken. They said it was encephalitis or some such awful thing.'

Maria paused and shook her head sadly, 'We are distant relatives, but have been friends from our convent days so she is with us for a few weeks'. She continued. 'She travels abroad a lot but she has recently come back footloose and unsettled. Poor Candellaria. She has just come from Chicken Itza where she has been painting. She is a trained artist and was taught by the finest teachers in France. She may show you some of her work though she does not gush about it.'

Maria related the story with feeling but without excessive emphasis. She knew she had a listener who could add, to the bare outlines of a history, just those lights and shadows which would give it a proper and particular value. Indeed Maria's very reticence roused in Karen a greater interest in the ill-fated Candellaria.

The luncheon party was as successful as any hostess could wish. Karen's experience of life in many parts of Mexico had given her fluent Spanish with a good vocabulary. Candellaria was gravely and gently mannered with a nicely poised sense of the ridiculous. She knew how to seize that grain of humour in a situation, or in a jest, which gave it flavour. Extensive travel had given her a metropolitan graciousness and tolerance for the foibles of others and a silent disdain for the intolerant, the narrow and the bigoted. Karen warmed to her not so much because she could tell a witty tale, or laugh at the proper place of the other person's tale, but because she bore herself with an unconscious pride and dignity. Karen thought she was worthy of her tragedies.

For although Karen thought that tragedy was an unnecessary means of proving worth, yet the reaction of the sufferer to the blows of fate was, to her, the most important factor. If the sufferer responded to tragedy by a consciously stoic acceptance she considered the gods were temporarily defeated. In the long run, of course, they always win in their game with mortals but they can, for a time, be made most uncomfortable. They choose the game, shuffle the cards in their own favour, play the cards and then cheat even when they are winning. Candellaria had, Karen felt, defeated the gods at least for a time.

They had reached the coffee stage, and Maria had made the finest Guatemala caracolia coffee, when they were interrupted. The Commandante returned home hours before he was expected and with him was a stranger, an officer whom he had been to meet. He explained to the ladies as he introduced him that Major Felipe Cibrian was a very early riser who loved to travel hard before the sun was too hot. By noon they found they had covered the greater part of the journey so they lunched in the saddle and pushed on to arrive in time for a welcome cup of coffee.

If Commandante Arevalo was worried only Maria knew. He was a quiet, precise man; he had been a school master and was often as surprised as his former friends to find himself in the administrative service of President Graña. Quite early in the latter's political career Arevalo had joined his party. The first Presidential election was one in name only and after that Graña dispensed with even this formality. There was, therefore, not a continuous crop of adherents for whom rewards in the shape of office had to be found. Furthermore, efficiency in office became necessary and for that reason promotion was slow except for those of outstanding brilliance. Soon after taking charge of his country's affairs Graña purged the civil administration of graft and at the same time he increased the pay. And the pay was paid regularly and, as regularly, some few civil servants were convicted of graft and shot. Arevalo had the rank of Captain because in this isolated region he was responsible not only for the civil administration but was the commanding officer of a platoon of gendarmerie.

Just recently he had received orders to facilitate the operations of a certain Major Cibrian who would arrive in his district on a certain day. Quarters had to be prepared and office space and personnel provided for the Major. What the newcomer's operations were to be Arevalo had absolutely no idea.

However, he obeyed the orders and, as a gesture of courtesy to a superior officer, he went to the boundary of his district to meet him. Worried though he was Arevalo thanked his stars and Maria that Cibrian should be introduced into his house just at the moment when an obviously amiable and well-bred party was taking place. It was a good omen and Major Cibrian was obviously impressed and delighted to end his ride in such pleasant company. Maria was gracious and hospitable and thus exorcized the last vestige of strain. Candellaria was beautiful and accomplished with a charming poise and dignity which, however, caused no feeling of distance. Karen was radiant. With bluish-green eyes aglow and countenance flushed, she told a very witty story which had only just begun when the officers arrived. It went well. Cibrian enjoyed it immensely and told of a similar experience but with a slightly mordant twist to his tale. Arevalo thereupon pointed out to Cibrian that great learning did not always have a desiccating effect for here was Señora Farr, a formidable mathematician and astronomer as well as an expert on American prehistory, proving herself also to have wit and with it grace and beauty. It was, perhaps, a rather heavy-handed compliment but Cibrian responded gallantly.

'Would you care to tell me, Señora,' he asked, 'how you came to develop an interest in archaeology? It seems a somewhat unusual subject for a woman. Did you begin its study by design? I know its value of course, but you must confess it has little glamour.'

He was a man who could when he chose exert an almost hypnotic charm. He was of not more than the medium height with shoulders which appeared heavy when he sat, but standing he moved as easily as a dancer. His countenance was firm and full, with a prominent nose, mobile lips and black eyes which, as he asked the question, glowed with vitality. He managed his voice well, his articulation as precise as an actor. His choice of phrasing, the turns of his speech showed him to be familiar with the classics of his language. In spite of herself Karen was flattered.

'Decidedly,' she thought, 'a personality.'

She found herself taking the question about her first approach to archaeology seriously. Without knowing it she expanded before the interest of this dynamic man. The other two women watched their witty companion and learned savant become the responsive woman flattered by the agreeable male.

'It was an accident. Shall we say an unhappy accident, which turned my thought to old beliefs and customs.' She replied. 'I am not speaking metaphorically. It was truly an accident and it kept me in bed for some days. I was then at school, a convent in Cairo of a French order of nuns and about seventeen years of age. Our family, or rather my father who was in the British civil service and whose duties caused him to travel widely in the Sudan with Khartoum as his base, thought it best to send me to a boarding school, hence Cairo. I had been finding the inactivity tedious, as who wouldn't at that age, when the Mother Superior mentioned to the doctor, an Irishman who had been many years in Egypt, that I was a serious person inclined to question things which others accepted. The doctor was, to us girls, a grubby old man with unaccountable moods; more often than not we felt that our little aches and pains and bruises bored him. Now and again after, say, irritably bandaging a sprained ankle he would take on another personality and sit down and talk to the girl. If she responded to his talk with some show not so much of intelligence but of intuition, of native awareness then that would be a fortunate girl. For he had an astringent wisdom. He appeared to have seen all things of importance and had not found them of all-absorbing importance. It also seemed that he had read everything and found but few things worthy of respect. I remember a girl telling me how, once, he washed his hands and as he shook the water from them and reached for a towel he began to speak of water.

'He told her that it was the universal solvent, the most versatile of all the mechanics of living. Then he went on to show how indestructible it was. As a puddle in the road, an ocean, a glacier, insignificant or overwhelming but whatever shape and form it took, it sooner or later became without shape or form, an invisible vapour. Next the invisible vapour took on visibility. It became clouds, like dreams constantly shaping and reshaping, ominous or benificient. From these dream-shapes came rain to fall on the just or the unjust with equal impartiality. And when the child understood that this baffling and slightly sinister old man was describing to her, in the form of a parable, the transformation and indestructibility of life, he spoilt it all by saying, "and notice that it is only when mankind uses water for our intimate purposes does it become offensively dirty."

'So, you see, he could have a disturbing effect. One day, at the time of my accident, he spoke of Irish life and aspirations and I mentioned the shamrock.' Here Karen had to describe the plant and explain to the company the almost holy esteem in which it, as a symbol, was held in Ireland. Then she went on to tell how the doctor shocked her by saying that the plant now used as a symbol of the purest and best in things Ireland was a modern misinterpretation of legend and that the 'shamrock' of, say, Tudor times, was an entirely different plant.

'When I protested, with my hackles rising, he took no more notice than to shrug his shoulders and say, "What does it matter? The past lives, if not as this plant or that plant, it lives as an idea and nothing is so indestructible as an idea, or more changeable."

'Of my teachers, some dismissed my enquiry of the shamrock as treason, some as heresy while others were bored. One of these suggested I should write to the British Museum for a judgement of Solomon. I did write to the museum and I received a charming letter in reply and an invitation to discuss the point with a certain authority on the museum staff when I came to London. But the important thing about my story is that I felt that the old doctor was very probably right.

'I did not get to London for years but then I did I follow up the invitation to visit the museum and the official was not only as charming as his letter but a fanatic on his subject. He introduced me to an enthusiatic group headed by a great man who had not only done extraordinary work in ancient Egypt but had practically re-opened Ethopia as a rich lode for the student of ancient ways. So other aspects of ancient beliefs and customs came to my knowledge. Then I went back to Egypt to work but remained there for only a short time because I really felt at home amongst the ancients only in Mexico perhaps because their descendants are, as I am, more inward turning, more introspective, less volatile, so I feel a real link with them. Anyway, whatever the motivation, from the ancient Mexicans to the ancient Mayas was only a step. And so, here I am in Petén.'

Major Cibrian thanked her for taking his question, which some might have thought to be abrupt, seriously enough to give it so clear and interesting a reply. Arevalo was pleased at Cibrian's obvious gratification. So much of his, Arevalo's, future comfort and even health might depend on Cibrian, for if Cibrian's mission should extend further and deeper than Arevalo had been informed then anything which pleased Cibrian might well be reflected in the Major's attitude to his host.

The Major then thanked his hostess not only for the delicious coffee but for the amiable and civilized environment in which he had drunk it. Without quite saying so he implied that the most agreeable part of the environment was she who made it possible, his hostess. He mentioned that he knew one of the scientists of the Chicle Company, Mr. Harkness, and thought of calling on him. As Karen was also taking her leave Arevalo suggested that they would both escort her to her house and afterwards he would conduct Major Cibrian to Mr. Harkness.

It was while walking back that Karen said, with the last of the exuberance which the enjoyment of the party had caused, that she found Candellaria beautiful and charming with a poise and dignity quite undistorted by her tragic history. Arevalo had then to explain to Cibrian the meaning of the latter phrase.

'I did not quite get her name at the introduction,' said Cibrian. 'Was it Aycinena?'

'Yes,' said Arevalo, 'Aycinena de Avila. And she lost her only child after that assassination.'

Then Arevalo continued to speak on certain aspects of that tale. He spoke of the swift hand of the law, the triple execution, the three coffins standing by the roadside at the scene of the crime, standing empty and open for a few hours only. Then the coffins were filled and stood filled for two days until, finally, the roadside was relieved of them and the kindly earth nearby received them. Arevalo was still speaking of these things when they reached Karen's house. They bade her adieu and as she entered her house she looked back and saw Cibrian's face distorted by a smile of bitter derision. As he smiled, he threw a half-formed salute towards the south in the direction of Guatemala City. What she could not read into his gesture was that the smile was for himself but the salute was to Deodato (God's gift) Graña, 'Benemerito', his Commander-in-chief.

Felipe Cibrian was an engineer, an able man, a good soldier, but first an engineer. He was a soldier by custom, an engineer by choice.

As his gifts of leadership emerged and as his reputation grew as a hard worker who drove himself and his men relentlessly, if the situation demanded, it became clear that he was a man with a future. For a few months he had been attached to the Embassy in Paris, then he was transferred to London and after a few more months ordered back to Guatemala. He had acquitted himself well on several unusual commissions after he returned home before he received orders to hold himself ready for another commission. In the meantime he was to go to the office of the Internal Security Administration and there study various aspects of certain affairs. His study was mostly of reports of the chicle trade with particular attention to the trade in Petén, its customs and the personalities of the men involved in it. One day several files were placed on his desk seemingly by accident and he read them. They were then recalled and the clerk, who had caused the file to go to the wrong desk, was reprimanded. Cibrian had read, however, in one of the files the history of the Aycinena affair. The summary was that, first, Aycinena was a man of ideas, second and worse, his ideas were infectious, much worse, he could throw out his ideas and allow them to ferment while he retired to the life of a practising physician far from Guatemala City.

His ideas, however, ran counter to Dato's ideas but Dato was careful not to make martyrs. He fully expected, one day, to be a martyr himself and he did not wish the hagiography of his regime to be cluttered with any other name but his own. Aycinena was therefore executed by those whose business it was. Dato approved of its economy and dispatch, afterwards. Those whose business it was did not worry him with details after he had reluctantly pointed out to them some certain regrettable necessity. If the necessity was well taken care of he would give brief and incidental approval afterwards, perhaps long after. Therefore three condemned criminals from various prisons far from Coban found themselves being taken, under heavy escort, hither and yon with one escort handing them over to another and so on. They saw a motor car approaching. They obeyed orders.

Then further orders included facing a firing squad by a roadside in Coban. They hardly had time to look at the three empty coffins before each man was in his own particular coffin. With this knowledge Major Cibrian had listened to Arevalo and had heard the story of Candellaria Aycinena's sorrows. As he listened he showed no sign of sympathy for, like a flash, had come the question, 'Had it been a mistake?'. Was it by accident that the file of the Aycinena affair appeared on his desk just long enough for him to read it?

His respect for 'Dato' grew when he realized that he would never know. At that moment also came the first stirring of resentment. It was a perpetual uncertainty that hurt his dignity and bruised the sense of his own completeness. He was not completely Dato's servant any more, for he was not completely himself.

Arevalo and Cibrian were constantly together for the next few days and nights. They made swift tours of inspection to the chicle-collecting depots of the district. On the day of his arrival Cibrian, accompanied by Arevalo, visited the office of the Field Manager of the Chicle Company to whom Cibrian showed his letter of authorization from the Minister in Guatemala City asking politely that his books be produced. The manager was required to state the weight of chicle already sent across the frontier for that season, the amount of chicle then in the warehouse at Shoonantonitch and to enumerate the various mule teams and supply the number of animals in each team. When the questions had been answered Cibrian reduced the replies to a formula, wrote the formula across a page of the ledger and signed it. The same formula was then committed to two letters, one addressed to the head office of the company in New York, the other to the Minister in Guatemala City. The manager was required to sign the letters as being correct. Cibrian informed him the letters would be mailed at once while Arevalo looked at the manager apologetically for he had not been able to warn him beforehand.

As the latter recovered his aplomb he realized that Cibrian's instructions did not extend to an investigation of personnel. It seemed to be basically a soldier's assessment, a reckoning in terms of logistics, of loads of chicle to be moved, of roads favourable and unfavourable, of the effect of the abnormally premature dry season on the roads and of the men and animals available for the transport of the loads. Only Cibrian knew that his present activity was a further stage in his education of that part of the chewing gum business which dealt with the gum before it crossed the frontier into British Honduras. He had been well advised in the office of the Internal Security Ministry in Guatemala City as to the 'mores' of that business. He knew something now of the life, habits and customs of the *chiclero*, the collector of the latex which became the gum of commerce. For many months of the year these men lived in a close masculine world in a small camp in the forest and their overriding anxiety was the weather, for the latex of the sapodilla tree flowed profusely only when the forests were wet and steamy. The *chiclero*, therefore, when the weather was good for production worked all day long in sodden clothes, climbing the magnificent hardwood trees with his machete and scarring them with a lacework of deep incisions around the trunk. The trees bled into canvas bags. After thorough bleeding each tree was left dying or, at least, so weakened that it could not be bled again for many years. The trees did not grow in groves but were scattered wide, singly and scantily. This meant that the camps had to be small, up to a dozen men and widely separated. Also, year by year, they had to be placed further and further into the depths of the forest, further from the villages and the homes of the *chicleros*. The journey to and from home was therefore longer, the price of food and other necessities greater, the cost of delivery of the chicle greater and the debts became more and more burdensome. Because *chicleros* worked in a system in which they were a vital part, it was necessary to fetter them to that system. And fettered they were and the fetters were their debts. They had to be induced to leave their villages for several months, to suffer aggravated discomfort, far from medical aid, a prey of the ills which they carried within them and which the forest held for them. Above all they had to be induced to forget their almost religious compulsion to plant corn at the corn-planting season. The *chicleros* were almost all of Maya and Spanish bloods but no matter how dilute their Maya blood might be it seemed that the urge to plant corn never left them.

At the beginning of the dry season the corn-planter went into the forest at a reasonable distance from his village. There he decided on the site and the size of the next corn plantation, the *milpa*, which he would cultivate. He felled the forest trees which grew on the chosen area and when, in a few weeks, the leaves and smaller branches of the fallen trees were sufficiently dry he set fire to them. As soon as the earth cooled he drilled through the light coating of ash into the hard soil with a toughened stick, dropped in the corn seeds, covered them and then waited for the end of the dry season and the beneficient rains. Months later, perhaps five, perhaps seven, he had his harvest on which his family, himself, his pigs and his hens existed until the next harvest. This cycle of destruction of forest and cultivation of corn was perhaps the only clear race-memory the Maya of Petén still retained from all the fabulously involved and incredibly rich and complicated society his ancestors had developed in that quarter of America. It reached the last of its several peaks of magnificence about the time Kubla Khan, in his magnificence at Xanadu, listened to the disputation of Buddhist and Christian, Muslim and Confucian. Unlike Kubla Khan, however, the Mayas had no doubt who was the chief in their Pantheon. He was the young Corn-god.

The *chiclero* had to be prised loose from the ritual of corn. So he was given an 'advance'. It was a lump sum which burned his pockets, gave him grandeur, ease, dignity and power as long as he could pay for the bottle which held all these god-like sensations. Were his wife circumspect and if she had a thoroughly sharp instinct for the preservation of the family then, perhaps, before all the advance went to the drink shop, she would have acquired a few pieces of equipment for her man such as a saddle, a hammock, a shotgun and a few pieces of clothing for herself and the children. But the usual *chiclero* was too oblivious of the world of tomorrow to heed his wife's prudence. He drank whole-heartedly until stupor brought about the extinction of his senses and his advance was exhausted. Thus he was committed by debt to go to the forest and to go back again at the next season and the next. He was paid a nicely calculated sum for every pound of chicle he delivered or, rather, that sum was credited to his account. Were he a hard worker, if he and his family had no more than the usual number of bouts of malaria and dysentry, had the sap flowed well and the rains not been too much too late, nor too little too soon, then perhaps he would be out of debt at the end of the season and he would then be able to bargain for a bigger advance next season.

Of all the misfortunes that beset him, however, the most characteristic of his trade was the theft of his chicle before it could be delivered to his 'patron'. The Company with their greater organization were able to take delivery from the *chicleros* at their camps. Other 'patrons' demanded that the chicle be delivered to certain collecting depots. Nor did a *chiclero* consider it much of a crime to get ready cash by selling chicle, which should have been delivered to his 'patron', to another dealer. From the circumstances of the trade, the enslavement of the *chiclero* by debt, the impossibility of policing the vast forest, the ready buying and selling anywhere in the forest at any time of anyone's chicle, the chicle business, at certain levels, was highly unethical and the immorality of the trade infected most of those who touched it.

From the *chiclero* to the 'patron', from dealer to bigger dealer the infection persisted until the mule team, with the burden of crude gum, crossed the frontier into the Colony of British Honduras. There the taint of the trade persisted not in the crude 'manifestations' of violence, or robbery, of enslavement by debt, by vice, by graft and by intimidation, but in the 'cleaner' technique of 'financing' the intimidation, the graft and the enslavement by debt and by vice.

With the first election of Deodato Graña to the presidency an unusual element had intruded into the classical order of the chicle trade. This element was the fact that it became as difficult to bribe a Guatemaltecan official as it was to bribe his opposite number on the British side of the frontier. It had not been an extraordinary thing for Guatemala to have strong presidents, or to have honest presidents, or even honest and strong presidents. To have a President who demanded and exacted the highest standards in the conduct of Government was, however, unique. Graft in the army and in the civil service was reduced to precarious and microscopic proportions. The penalty for the 'abuse of position', Dato's name for graft, was death. The Petén was well known to him. Very early in his career, when he was hardly more than a youth and a captain, he had served on the staff of the governor of that province. During his two years in the area he had actively explored this almost unknown land. In those days a few bleeders of the gum had straggled across the border from British Honduras where the chicle trade had already began to pass from its experimental nonage into its final pattern. At that stage in its history the chicle trade had given the Governor of Petén no more concern than to exact from the Honduran bleeders a small fee as licence to tap the trees.

But in the score of years between his captaincy and his first term as president, life in Petén had changed tremendously. There had been influxes of *chicleros* from the neighbouring Mexican states of Chiapas and Campeche and of criminals from the Mexican penal settlement in the territory of Quintana Roo. Their coming did not inaugurate the violence in the trade, but certainly the trade did provide great opportunities for the professional 'tough'. At one time the price of a run-of-the-mill murder was 75 dollars. If the affair had to be handled with a greater show of self-righteous justification, to satisfy the public conscience, then the price was greater. After all, the labourer who is, at the same time an artist, is much more worthy of his hire.

The Consolidated Chicle Company, which had been organized under several other names in its time, had an elaborate production and purchasing organization in Petén and in British Honduras. There were, as well, other chicle companies which had no organization in any country except in the United States. They bought chicle from any source. It is true they had agents in British Honduras but these were independent and would purchase from any source and sell to any buyer or withhold their stocks from market if they thought if profitable to wait. Since the 'industry' existed on both sides of a frontier and that frontier was merely a line on a map, with only two frontier-guards posted on either side along its whole length, it rendered the enforcement of order and decorum an impossible task. So smuggling chicle across the frontier was the rule. A man might have had a concession to bleed chicle in a small section of the forest on the

British Honduras side of the frontier but that small section of forest would produce a very remarkable output of gum. One could but conclude that this convenient concession made it an open door for the smuggling of chicle from the Guatemaltecan forests. Such chicle would not be chicle contracted to a patron. It would be chicle sold 'under the counter' by *chicleros* or chicle obtained by other methods.

From the moment that, in the depths of the forest, the boiled and thickened latex was poured into a mould and became a block of gum until it was delivered to the warehouse across the frontier it was current coin. So it was provokingly easy for any man possessed of this current coin to change it into coin of the realm, or of any of three realms, for U.S. currency was negotiable on both sides of the frontier. On the other hand the latex which was collected in a small canvas bag tied to the sapodilla tree and then transferred to a large canvas bag hanging by the *chiclero*'s hammock was not current coin. It was protected by rigid sanctions. As long as the latex remained in the bag by the *chiclero*'s hammock, and he might have to be away from the camp overnight if he were bleeding distant trees, that latex was taboo. A *chiclero* would no more steal that latex from his comrade than he would steal his blood. Day by day fresh latex would be added to the big bag. Then came the boiling. The liquid was boiled and stirred, stirred and boiled until it was thick enough to harden when poured into the wooden block. After it came out no law could protect it. Since no law could protect the latex, the formless liquid, the *chicleros* made and enforced their own laws for its protection. If a man was brought to trial by his comrades and found guilty of stealing latex then, usually, he died, 'bitten by a snake.'

Cibrian's education in the office of Internal Security in Guatemala City had not been entirely confined to the history and customs of the chicle trade. He had been required to read the résumé of the archives on the 'Belice Question'. This summary had been prepared from the complete archives and were held ready for publication when that publication seemed to Dato to be necessary and prudent.

Of course, Cibrian had read and heard the Belice Question discussed by press and radio for years. With Great Britain, always shown as the powerful bully, denying that the Province of Belice, the 'Colony of British Honduras' had even been anything but British territory. It is true that parts of it had been settled by British subjects for more than one hundred and fifty years before 1850. As late as 1859, however, its status as a part of the Republic of Guatemala was so well recognized that in that year the British signed a treaty in which they bound themselves to build a road and pay a sum of money in return for legal possession of the territory. The road had never been built. The money had never been paid. Had the road been built it would have had a tremendous effect on the development of the Republic and on the Colony.

That a road over the Alta Vera Paz mountains was incredibly difficult and fabulously expensive to construct might have had something to do with the delay in constructing it. When one remembers that the mighty Cortez in his heroic march to Honduras crossed merely the foothills of those mountains and at one period of the march in those foothills did no more than twenty miles in twelve days it is not surprising that the construction of the road was delayed. But difficulties did not daunt Dato. He had commenced the road from the Guatemala City end and it was inching its way over the Alta Vera Paz. However, it was clear that the difficulties which baffled Cortez remained difficulties even for Dato.

When Dato had gone to Petén as a young captain he had reached his post by travelling across Guatemala *away* from Petén and then he had had to double back by sea and cut across British Honduras. This tedious journey of, perhaps, six days was preferable to riding, when one could ride, over and down the Alta Vera Paz. But Cibrian had not entered Petén by this route. He journeyed in a matter of hours to Petén because Dato's second airfield (the first airfield was near Flores the capital of Petén), was now ready for service. He had been ordered to go to Petén not knowing what he should do there. He carried sealed orders which were to be opened in the presence of Commandante Arevalo on the day of his arrival at Shoonantonitch. Those orders dealt with the logistics of the chicle in the district and the writing of a formula across the chicle dealers' books. It was during this period of the examination of the books of chicle dealers that Arevalo introduced Cibrian to Fuad Birbari and the latter's henchman Jaime Peat-Patterson.

Fuad, by trade a businessman, former pedlar, now a chicle contractor, but in a minor way, and chicle dealer in any way, had insisted that his main concern in Petén was not dealing in chicle but in provisioning chicle camps. His trade was 'business man' and he was willing to show interest in whatever could be called 'business'. He would even lend money to a *chiclero* who refused to dispose of the chicle to anyone other than the patron to whom he was contracted. After all, circumstances might change and so might the attitude of that rigid *chiclero*. If a *chiclero*'s wife across the frontier had a sudden emergency such as a death or sickness in the family, and for one reason or another she did not wish to approach her husband's patron, thus adding further to the contracted debt, she would speak to Fatima Birbari. Fatima decided instantly one way or another.

If help was forthcoming then, it might be a few weeks later, Fuad would tell the *chiclero* in the bush of how Fatima had saved the situation. And no *chiclero* doubted Fuad. His word was good. Being human he had been known to make mistakes in his men and in money, but his mistakes did not tarnish his reputation for straight dealing. In an instance such as the above Fuad might decide not to buy contracted chicle from the *chiclero*. Instead he might arrange the disposal of the chicle, get his commissions from both parties and collect the debt and the interest.

In fact, he was, generally, a very useful man in the forest. He was the provision agent to the archaeological expedition and every so often Fatima would send a mule laden with little luxuries and necessities for the ladies of the expedition. He had provided the mules for the transport of the baggage and personnel into Petén although he had been unable to bind himself to do the same service when the expedition was due to leave. He explained that he had other commitments such as the transport of chicle. As his word was his bond he would not like to give an uncertain word. He also suggested that Dr. Gibberd should arrange with the company to use their animals for the transport of provisions from Shoonantonitch to Caracol. Gibberd trusted him.

It was after Major Cibrian had inspected the chicle in his warehouse and had written the formula across his books and had left, that Fuad said to Jaime, 'Tell me her letter again, amigo.' So Jaime recited word for word that other letter which Fatima had written and which she had not sent but which Jaime had committed to memory. Fuad listened with deep attention.

'Jaime,' he said, 'there may be something, must be something in it. My people say, "He who goes to pick a rose must have regard for the thorns?". We must move with care.'

So he went to the manager, Delfosse, of the Chicle Company and proposed a private deal. He pointed out to the manager that there was an ample stock of provisions in his warehouse, the goods were in first-class condition, the inventory correct to the last tin of sardines and all the papers showing customs clearance on the files. Now he, Fuad, had a sudden call for money. A cousin of his in Costa Rica was on to a good thing. He held an option on thousands of acres of prime banana land and the fruit company was going to extend the railway through the land. It was a gold mine if he could help his cousin with ready cash, at once, to close the deal. Now if the manager would buy the provision store either for the Company, or as a private deal, there would be a lot in it for him. He named terms and conditions which, fictitious as they were, made him wince. The manager would have made a tremendous profit at Fuad's expense.

Delfosse refused the offer explaining that the Company would raise difficulties for they had their own provision contractors who were shareholders. As for a private deal that was not possible because he was short of ready cash.

When he met Jaime outside the manager's office Fuad said, 'He also has heard the news. We must move fast, Jaime'.

That night he sold all his equipment and provisions in the warehouse to another big chicle contractor. To Fuad the profit on the deal was small but the advantage to the big contractor was sufficient to be obvious and gratifying. The story Fuad told was that he had information that Major Cibrian was after him for some crime which he, Fuad, was said to have committed. The big contractor hoped it was true but did not allow his hopes to blunt his business acumen. Fuad must really be on the run or he would not have sold his provisions at such a price. He put out a feeler with regard to Fuad's chicle which was met with a negative response. Fuad dared not make such a deal or Cibrian would become suspicious and seize his chicle. The contractor thereupon assumed that the crime had to do with chicle and did not pursue the subject. He enquired about the warehouse but realized he had not enough in the bank to buy the building as well as its contents.

He gave Fuad his cheque and Jaime at once started for the frontier with it and with certain instructions. He was to meet Fuad's mule team on its way back to Petén for another load of chicle. They should be but two hours away. The chief muleteer was to be ordered to return at once with his mule team to Fatima. He was to hand a letter and the mules to her. Fatima's instructions in the letter were to send the enclosed cheque to the bank in Belize by reliable messenger who should ride hard day and night. She was to keep the chief muleteer to look after the mules. Another messenger should follow two hours behind the first and he should break the telegraph line to Belize in two or three places. The line was to be broken where a falling branch or a swaying tree could have done the damage. That cheque would be cashed. As for the mules they would remain on the British side of the frontier until further orders. Jaime was to return with all speed as soon as he had seen the chief muleteer start back to cross the frontier.

Fuad did not attempt to sell his chicle. The books showed, and Cibrian had countersigned the books which showed that every ounce of chicle then in the chicle warehouse had been acquired by him in legitimate transactions.

So Fuad put his affairs in order and waited for what was to come. He thought this would be his last season in Petén. He did not regard the fact with too much regret. His life so far had been one of constant change. Since he married Fatima Zayden at the age of 25, she and the four children she bore were the only constant elements in his circumstances and thoughts. He had received his initiation in the hard school of making a living as a child in Beirut. Further education in the same school had taken him to Gibraltar, then Cadiz and next Mexico. He had gone from Vera Cruz to Campeche and there he began to deal in chicle. But

Mexico was uncomfortable after the departure of the dictator Diaz. Fuad decided to follow the chicle trade but to enter it from the safe side. He went with his family to British Honduras and so entered Petén. He was now 55 years of age and if the Petén chapter were to close he had, he believed, time for two or three more chapters elsewhere. With the capital he had accumulated he could choose to live and work either in the Spanish-speaking or in the English-speaking world. He thought carefully over the episodes of the Petén chapter. There was nothing, he was sure, for which the law could hold him permanently though, of course, one could always be held temporarily. For, as long as Dato was president, the law demanded proof.

It is true he had known of many things on which Dato's law held serious views. He often had known, for example, that such and such a load of chicle which was due to be carried from such and such a place would never arrive at its destination. The mules would be stampeded, the chicle stolen and, although someone might get hurt in the affair, he would buy the chicle. But no one could prove that he knew that the chicle was stolen and he had been careful never to appear to be an instigator of crime.

In the next few days he began quietly to arrange his affairs so that even if he did not return next season to Petén those moneys still owed to him, which he could not or did not wish to collect this season, would be working for him next season. It would be several years before he would have no interest whatever in any chicle that came out of Petén. Wherever he was for those several years, money would be working for him in those forests.

It was well towards dawn of the next day that there was a low rapping at Fuad Birbari's door. He opened it cautiously and Gil Silva fell in precipitately almost on to Fuad's pistol. Fuad held him up. His rigor, the dreadful weakness, the pallor of his face and coldness of his hands were not entirely due to terror and exhaustion. They were partly due to malaria. Fuad poured out some rum and supported the shivering wretch while he tried to drink it but he could not. Then the shivering ceased and the fever consumed him.

After the fever abated and the drenching sweats had dripped

through clothes and hammock Fuad gave him coffee and quinine. Then Gil Silva gasped out the story of how Modesto Moreno had been 'bitten by a snake'.

'Maria Santissima,' he ended his tale, 'why must the innocent be outraged? Why must we poor suffer so much? Why must our lives be bitter?'

Fuad replied, 'If a man is poor and insists on eating he must realize that his bread must be bitter.'

He had been poor for many years though it was after his bread was no longer bitter that he had dealings with the man who now sought sanctuary with him. Silva was from across the frontier. He was born on the British side of the line where his family lived and he went back to them at the end of each season. He could speak English, had been to school in the Colony and, although a British citizen by birth, in every other aspect of his life, outlook, hopes and aspirations he was Latin-American and, more narrowly, a Peténero. He was not known as a friend of Fuad's and had only once previously visited the latter, uninvited. But there was a curious relationship between the two men. As Fuad once put it, 'we are lodge brothers'.

He had become fond of Silva, as one could be fond of a rather sad, dim, moist-eyed dog whose puppyhood seemed to have been short-circuited but, now and again, showed an unnatural and puppyish friskiness. And he was very troubled by the story of how Modesto Moreno was 'bitten by a snake'.

The great mystery of Fuad Birbari's life had come to him via Gil Silva for both had loved Elenita. Fuad had met her at Shoonantonitch. He had been away many weeks from home and she was to him, then, only another woman who was accommodating. It was true that, from all he could gather, she was definitely not promiscuous but she was still very young. She was Gil Silva's woman and she was young enough and vigorous enough to come with Silva from across the border as far as Shoonantonitch for she had no children. She accepted Fuad's advances with troubled hesitation and became more agitated as he urged his proposition. The first night she came to his house he wondered if she had been drinking or had been smoking marijuana but he could smell neither. She never spoke except to answer his few questions, rather she was as if hypnotized and going through a compulsive performance.

He was bored but as she was turning to leave through the door into the darkness he noticed by the light of his discreet lamp that her eyes were large, bright and glassy as if she were about to weep. His boredom increased but he took another look at her, murmured some consoling words and he touched her gently, then Elenita woke up. The kindness, the understanding, the pity of his few words broke the troubled spell on her spirit which had made her an automaton. She turned to Fuad and did not leave his house that night.

He was alone at his warehouse one night about a month later, engrossed in the endless tasks which his energy and industry found for him, when a shadow fell across the desk and he looked up to see Gil Silva peering at him over the sights of a shotgun. Fuad knew he was a dead man. The distance was too near, only a couple of feet. No one could miss. Even if he jumped the buckshot would spread.

'I know,' he murmured, 'I know, but you also know how it is with her. She is,' he groped for words and could find none, 'you know ... ' He ended lamely.

He waited, his mind struggling to find a prayer. After a long silence he dropped his eyes to the would-be killer's trigger finger while his body tensed for the last desperate leap. He waited then lifted his gaze to Silva's face. Finally, he quietly raised a hand and moved the gun aside.

'Sit down, friend,' he said, 'we are in this together.'

They talked but Silva had little heart for discussion. After a few minutes the tears gathered and stifling sobs racked his puny body.

'Sooner or later,' he wailed, 'I knew it would happen to me, as it will to you. Then you will know that to kill is no use. For she was never mine nor is she yours.'

Fuad trembled, then his quick rush of sick apprehension and despair at the prophesy receded

'We shall see,' he said to himself. 'We shall see.'

They did not meet again for a couple of years. When they did it was Fuad who sought out Silva.

'You were right,' he told him, 'she was never mine.'

'I know. I know. I know, friend,' said Gil Silva, adding

'Blessed be her name. Wherever she is and as long as I live and as long as she lives, blessed be her name.'

'Amen,' said Fuad.

For to these two men, one an impishly ineffectual *chiclero*, the other an astute and vigorous Lebanese businessman, Elenita was the embodiment of enduring youth, of beauty, of timeless and of ageless joy.

It was not so much that she had brought to the physical expression of her love a ravishing art, unique in its changing and experimental forms. No, what was more important was that her art was spontaneous, unlearned and was embellished by a heart that was wholly innocent. For Elenita was an 'innocent'. In her relations with love there could be no place for pangs of conscience, for guilt, for a biding of time till repentance was due. She had a primal exhilaration, an amoral vigour. Fuad knew that even her very presence endowed his body and perhaps his mind with a joyous sense of well being. And she wanted nothing, not even loyalty. She took the gifts that were showered on her so lightly that they almost became an embarrassment to the giver. She had come to Silva from the house of her step-father who treated both her mother and herself with calculated cruelty. Silva had been the witness of a vicious scene and had offered her refuge. Much later, when Fuad had enquired of her how she came to remain with Silva she had laughed, 'Oh,' she had replied, '*Rainbow* is all right. He is kind. He would not hurt a fly. And he sometimes has a funny sense of humour.' She paused, then added, 'Yes, well you know, when things are gloomy and sad, he can suddenly make you laugh. Yes, he is all right.'

Fuad came to understand that this dim, 'wet' and dismal little man had moments when he brought laughter, hope, joy, and surcease of question and surmise to those he loved.

'And what do you call me – if he is *Rainbow*?' he asked and laughed.

A jealous pang caused the tone of his laugh to be heightened. He watched her with anxiety for she was given to sudden moods and reticences especially if her words or actions were questioned. If she were in doubt her anxiety might be so distracting that she became like a sleepwalker, hardly feeling or knowing. But now she laughed and touched his lip with the tip of her finger and at that contact his heart melted with a rush of devoted love.

'Do you want a name? Must you have a name? Yes, you are *Mutroos*.'

He did not know the word. She explained that it was a kind of fish which as a child she had caught from the pier at Progresso. It had the peculiarity that when it was scratched its air-bladder inflated itself. Fuad did not pursue the question. The mention of Progresso reminded him that she was Mexican. Her mother had come from Yucatan and had passed from man to man until she found herself in British Honduras and married to a *chiclero*.

Of course Fatima heard of Elenita. Of course Fuad was duly penitent and beat his breast in shame and repentance but without the least true shade of sorrow, or remorse.

'As long as I live and with my dying breath I shall thank the Good Lord for the great gift of my wife. She has been my stay and sustenance; the sun that illumined my days and promised many tomorrows. And when I have said "Amen" to that full-hearted prayer of thanksgiving, I shall continue, in my thoughts, with another prayer known only to the Bountiful Father and myself. I shall thank him with all my heart that in the vigour of my manhood I met Elenita and was loved, if only for a time, by her. The memory of her is like the memory of a velvet night when the moon is full. It is true that light is but reflected light but it is a light that softens the harsh outlines and obstructions of adult night. In the light youth and joy and innocence meet and dance a little dance, for a few paces only, but enough so that it is a dance.'

Elenita left Silva at the next chicle season. Fuad heard she was living in Chetumal over the Mexican border with a shiftless taxi-cab driver. Years later Fuad visited Chetumal. From the verandah upstairs of the hotel he had chosen, and the choice was for this particular purpose, he looked into the back-yard of the house where Elenita lived.

There were several small children playing about in the yard but motherhood had settled her endocrine constitution and brought Elenita up to the level of womankind. Her walk, her posture, her gestures were different. Even her voice as she shrieked at the children was different.

'She has become like us,' Fuad murmured to himself. 'She is lost. She endures, now, right and wrong. She knows responsibility and grief. She has gone, gone, gone.'

Fuad remembered Silva's tears, as he wept then, but he wept not for the same reason. He did not weep because he had lost her, but because Elenita, their Elenita had gone forever, from him, from herself, from all mankind.

Every now and again, more often after he had done a deal with Fuad with some chicle which was not his to sell, Gil Silva would hand a few dollars to him.

'This is for you know who!' he would say.

Then Fuad would add, perhaps, twice as many dollars to Silva's gift. Silva did not doubt that Fuad would do with the dollars what ought to be done and a letter would reach a certain woman in Chetumal containing a certain sum of dollars and a slip of paper with only two words on it, '*Rainbow* and *Mutroos*'.

Between the two men there was a relationship like a consanguinity, a brotherhood of two, who worshipped the memory of Elenita. They did not often meet, did not visit each other socially, but their business dealings were apt to be a trifle more prolonged. The way they said '*Buenos dias*' in greeting or '*Adios*' in parting had a trifle more than the usual politeness. So, when Gil Silva told of the last of Modesto Moreno, Fuad knew that Silva had come knowing he would get help. Not for a moment did Fuad argue that Silva had spared his life when Silva had had him at the muzzle of a loaded gun. Giving a life for a life did not enter into the making of his resolve. Not to aid Silva would be unthinkable. It would tarnish forever the private epic of Elenita in his heart and mind; they were 'lodge brothers'. For Silva was in deadly danger. He had killed, been forced to kill, Modesto Moreno and when Pedro Lopez, Moreno's friend, heard of it he would most certainly kill Silva. The only hope of escaping death was fleeing to British Honduras and hiding somewhere in that country. The fear of the British law, the certainty that he would be hanged when caught and that, almost certainly he would be caught, would not prevent Pedro seeking him there. But it was a country where one could hide for a long time and where with the bush at the back, the sea in front and many rivers through the bush to the sea, there were opportunities for mobility which did not exist in Petén.

For Pedro Lopez and Modesto Moreno had shared a fellowship of a different compulsion. They were 'lodge brothers' of a different order. They had come from Quintana Roo therefore there was much more than a suspicion that they had escaped from the Mexican penal colony in that territory. No one knew of their background before Quintana Roo but they appeared in Petén together and were employed in the chicle operations. Modesto was the stronger in that ultimately he could decide for himself rather than as one of a pair. But superficially it was Pedro who appeared to dominate. He was a large fat man who usually spoke in a soft voice though, when he was drunk, his voice became loud and strident. He was an expert muleteer. His touch with a team of mules was that of a rare teamster who had sufficient sympathy and imagination to be proud of his animals' temperament and patient with their sulkings. He looked on their strength and endurance as a beneficient part of the natural order of things. Pedro also had a large dog, of uncertain pedigree, determinedly amiable of disposition but useful in a foolishly good-natured way with the mules. His master showered kindness on the foolish dog, Hector. But, while he was always kind to his dog and proudly tolerant to his mules, Pedro was at times quarrelsome, impulsive and vindictive to men. Modesto however kept him in order.

But Modesto was a *chiclero* which meant they were separated sometimes for weeks at a time and then Pedro felt no restraining hand. He would have given much more concern to his friend but for the fact that he could often find solace in music and soothe the disquiet that made him quarrelsome. He played the guitar not always well enough to satisfy himself but well enough to entertain others. With guitar accompaniment he would sing in a soft, melodious, almost confidential baritone, songs which abounded in betrayal and being forsaken, in regrets and farewells. Men who wearied of his songs enough to expostulate knew that it would be wise to go away and to go quickly. Pedro Lopez was also very much in demand at dances as a player of the marimba. Not only had he a lovely touch with the deep bass hammer but he had a wide repertoire of dance music stored in his memory. It was true that this repertoire did not include the very latest hits but on visits across the frontier he would listen to gramophone records and teach what he learned to the other *marimberos*.

When Pedro was three parts drunk he was inspired and he inspired his colleagues of the keyboard which was just as well, for an exasperated Pedro had been known to lay out a player who had made a mistake by a flick of his rubber hammer at the base of the erring player's skull. When he was just drunk enough it was a joy to listen to him. The other players would toss the melody to each other, encircle each other, try urgent escapes and chuckling returns, be fierce or pleading, pliant or impetuous: but not Pedro. It was his duty and pleasure inexorably to separate the music into component parts, to bring order out of the insurrection, to establish and keep the rhythm. The melody called the dancers to the floor and there Pedro showed them that to be alone was an insufficiency, that as a couple they trod with measured pace not on space but on time, that even the floor on which they moved was a pulsing extension of their dancing feet and of their swaying bodies. Those bodies extended out into the air, enlarged, rarified, permeating all things away out to the very limits of music until that music faded and time was no longer rhythmic. The discipline that Pedro brought to the dancers was more than music to him. Made pervious by the measure of his creativity he escaped from himself and reached as far away from his unsatisfying life as a squire of mules and from the misfortune of his psychological imbalance as it was possible for him to get. Music to him was absolution.

The death of Modesto Moreno would be a crucifixion for Pedro and Fuad Birbari knew that Silva was a doomed man.

'Tell me Gil,' he asked, 'do you think anyone saw you come in here?'

'I don't think so,' answered Silva. 'I kept away from the paths, I took very good care in coming to your house and stood in the shadows for a long time without moving so as to confuse anyone who might have seen movement. It was only when I felt the malaria coming on that I moved to your door and knocked.'

'Good,' said Fuad, 'Pedro Lopez is not in the camp now but will be back soon, perhaps tonight. And he won't be far away for the next few days. He will practise his *marimberos* for the dance. It is doubtful if he will hear of Modesto's death for a couple of days or so, but if he sees you, knowing you were in the same camp as his friend, he will ask you questions about him. Now we have to wait for a mule. I haven't a mule here. All my mules, except my own riding mule, are across the frontier at the moment. As you know no one can buy a mule now since all are wanted to take out the chicle. I must, however, get one for you. I think I know where I can do that but not just at the drop of a hat. We must wait.'

Fuad had means of applying pressure, which Silva could guess at, but he did not ask who was going to furnish the mule. He was leaving all to his 'lodge brother' and asking no questions. Fuad continued to make plans.

'You know,' he said, 'since I sold the provisions in the warehouse people come to me here all day long for this reason or that. Today, you will lie on those boards laid across the ceiling timbers but be careful not to allow a hand or foot to slip over the edge of the boards. Tonight I will take you to my smaller chicle storehouse behind the house where Mrs. Farr lives. It is nearly full of chicle now. You can make yourself comfortable on top of the blocks of chicle there, the dogs will not smell you and raise a fuss and you can take your quinine. I shall bring you food and water every night. There is only one door that is chained and locked and I alone have the key. The windows are nailed up so you will be quite safe. As soon as I get the mule you start. You must have a mule and you can sell him when you reach Belize. Or, better still, if you do not wish to sell him personally, my agent will arrange it for you. I will give you a letter to him. But see him only once, by night if possible. And one thing, never afterwards try to get in touch with me here in Petén. Pedro may learn something and kill me.'

Late that night Silva made himself comfortable on top of the heap of chicle blocks. His bed was somewhat higher than the top of the window in the wall nearest him. The window was nailed shut but the top of it did not fit very well. There was a good inch of space between the top edge of the window and the frame. Through the space Silva peeped. Late though it was Mrs. Farr sat writing at a table near an open window in her house. After a time she stopped writing and sat quiet. Eventually she unlocked the drawer of her table and took out a glass tube. Whatever was in the tube interested her for she held it near the lamp and looked at it for a long time. Then she threw out some of whatever was in the tube on a bit of paper carefully corked the tube and locked it away in the box. She took up the paper and moved out of the range of Silva's vision. Soon she returned and she now had in her hand a whisky bottle.

'Ah, she has taken some medicine,' said Silva.

He knew the trade-mark on the bottle. He did not often drink whisky but he knew and linked 'White Horse' to whisky. She looked at the bottle near the lamp closely. It was nearly full. Then she put the bottle on a shelf near the window.

Silva licked his lips. 'Just enough for a few good drinks,' he said to himself.

Thus Silva passed several days.

He took the quinine and he began to feel stronger and eager to go but the sound of the marimba cooled his impatience.

'Pedro Lopez is practising for the dance and the mule is not here yet but it is coming. My man, the owner, had to make arrangements to explain the loss of a mule but leave it to me another day or so,' said Fuad on one of his visits bringing food and water.

'I leave it all to you, *amigo*,' said Silva listening to the marimba. The music seemed to sadden him.

At the camp where Silva and Modesto had worked there had been about a dozen men. The season had passed without untoward incident until news came that Pedro Lopez had been in trouble again. He had been heavily fined for this latter outrage and had been forced to sell a large part of the few goods and chattels of the partnership to keep outside prison. Modesto realized some ready cash by selling chicle, not his to sell, and refitted Pedro with gun and mule and saddle. Then he saw the pair of silver-gilt spurs. A merchant had sent one pair to show in the camp as a sample, with the announcement that the bargain could not be repeated and that a pair could be held for the purchaser until the end of the chicle season provided a substantial down payment were made at once. Modesto was overwhelmed. It would be the supreme gift to Pedro to complete the reassembly of his equipment. Such a pair of spurs would show to the world that he, Modesto, had always known that Pedro was different. These spurs would be like the little wings on the feet of the god, a symbol of something over and beyond. He had not dared to tamper any more with his own stock of chicle because it was already so low that he could not possibly meet his contract at the end of the season. The debt thus contracted plus other debts outstanding meant that the advance next season would be miserably small. He would hardly be able to eat. But the silver-gilt charro spurs, the symbol of the difference, Pedro must have them.

So, little by little, the *chicleros* began to have doubts of each other. It was Silva who caught Modesto '*in flagrante*'. He saw him stealing latex from the canvas bags by the hammocks. But Modesto, his gun near at hand, had not seen Silva. They were alone in the camp. Silva retreated silently into the bush. Ten minutes later he returned stopping to cut, lustily and noisily, a dried branch of firewood. Modesto had been suitably warned. He greeted Silva amiably. Then poor, dim, little Silva's pawky sense of humour undid him, for the more Modesto stole from the other men the more Silva stole from him.

'This,' said Silva to himself, 'is justice, justice as it ought to be administered. Surely so mean a cur as Modesto must be punished. He has outraged all honour and trust.'

Then, one day, some few weeks after he had first discovered Modesto's outrage, Silva returned to camp. There was almost a full gathering of the *chicleros* of the camp. Some were boiling chicle, others repairing gear, some preparing gum for delivery to the collecting agents who were expected in a few days with the mule teams. Silva was in an amiable mood as were most of the other men. Modesto came in bringing his latest bleeding of latex and with him came the remaining men of the camp. One man, who by common consent was leader of the camp, stopped repairing his saddle, took out his pipe, filled it, struck a match and lit it and threw down the match. At that moment Silva and Moreno found every gun in the camp pointed at them and they were on trial for their lives. Modesto had been in difficult situations before. His career before the episode of the penal settlement in Quintana Roo had been full of difficult situations. It was only the meeting with Pedro, the rounding out, the completion of his own unfinished and uncertain psyche by Pedro's competence, that made him whole. So whole, so dashingly certain that, now and again, he could decide for himself instead of as one of a pair.

The verdict had already been decided on by the other *chicleros*. Silva was not the only one to have doubts about the quantity of chicle remaining in his bag. It was not too onerous a task to find out who were the guilty parties. It was a matter of suspicion, then observation. The problem was the execution. It would be somewhat difficult to explain the sudden death of two of their comrades on the same day at the same place to Captain Arevalo. So Silva and Moreno were each handed his own rifle after certain adjustments were made to the respective weapons. The guilty men were told 'One gun has bullets the other has not'. Each convicted man had to aim at the other and, at the word, pull the trigger. The loser would be shot. The winner would be deprived of all his chicle and expelled from the camp. Silva it was who was expelled. Modesto's body was taken some distance away from the camp and dropped on the trails. It was the customary method of disposal.

PART FOUR

EL GORDO, 'THE FAT ONE'

Mr. Delfosse was in charge of the Chicle Company's affairs in Shoonantonitch. He was an American who had had wide experience of Latin America. He appeared to know Yucatan, or possibly only the city of Merida, well for he still had friendly contacts there and he also knew something of the sea ports of that part of the world. In an unguarded moment he had let slip that he had been a ship's officer.

He was a quiet man who was there when needed and not there when only needed incidentally.

He entertained guests when protocol demanded but seemed immune to the need for intimate social contact. But he was no fool for though he did not need to be intimate, he thought it wise to be appreciated. For that reason he had made a point of duty to call on the Doctor at El Cayo, on his first journey up to Shoonantonitch, for one never knew when a doctor would be useful even if he was three days by mule-back away. His foresight was timely. For almost immediately the Doctor admitted him to hospital, suffering from dysentery.

A remark the Doctor had made then, when speaking of the city of Merida, had had happy results. 'Yes,' had said the Doctor, 'there is a drug that was discovered by a German and is now on the market in Europe, even in England. I have ordered some tablets through our medical department here but it will be a year before I get them and that makes me angry because a Mexican archaeologist, who passed through here a few weeks ago, told me they could be obtained in Mexico. Of course the drug is not even purchasable in the U.S. because your Drug Department has to test it before it can be prescribed. If it can be bought in Mexico perhaps in Merida, since you say you have contacts there, you could get it for me?'

'If it is available, I will get you some in, let us say, four weeks.'

So 'Prontosil' tablets were smuggled into Honduras by Delfosse's contacts and Doctor Hastings passed some on to Delfosse giving him precise instructions on how they were to be used.

Subsequently Delfosse gave some to Señora Arevalo complete with the Doctor's instructions. Nor did the manager's benedictions to the Señora end there. He had, as he said to himself, the need to lubricate his way into the good graces of the Commandante by being, as it were absent-mindedly, gracious to the Commandante's wife. So every now and then some gifts arrived. There were new records for the gramophone; there were books, magazines and fashion papers for her. Then there were school books for the children of the school she had started. Thus in a dozen different ways Maria's housekeeping duties were lightened and made less of a bore by the ingenious Mr. Delfosse. Once when one of the children of the village fell ill, there were hurried preparations to have the child taken to Doctor Hastings. Then Delfosse reminded Maria of the tablets sent some time before by the same Doctor and the medicine helped the child immensely. Maria's gratitude was loud. Arevalo's was as sincere but somewhat quieter. Finally, there was the even more dramatic return to life of the botanist, Harkness. His recovery from 'blood poisoning' from an accidental wound was, at that time, nothing short of miraculous.

So Sulphanilamide tablets, under the patented name of 'Prontosil', the first antibiotic, began to win a name as a wonder-medicine in Shoonantonitch thanks to Delfosse.

Then, one day, while he was a patient in the hospital at El Cayo the Priest in charge of the area paid him a visit. The Priest had noted on the clinical chart hung above his bed, that at the section marked religion was the word 'None.' After the Priest had left Dr. Hastings informed Delfosse that the man was a Jesuit and that his organization did the major part of children's education in the Colony. Nor was it all that the priests and nuns did as charitable works. So it followed that quite often, when shipments were being made across the border of things which made Señora Arevalo's life more comfortable and her work in education more rewarding, a similar consignment was sent to

Dr. Hastings for him to hand over to the Jesuits for them to use as they deemed worthy and proper.

In return for all these favours it came about that, one day, Dr. Hastings received a letter from Delfosse asking him if he would kindly keep for him any letters that came by mail addressed to 'Mr. (or Snr.) Lincoln Delfosse, c/o Dr. Hastings, Government Medical Office El Cayo, British Honduras'. If such a letter was received, Delfosse said, he would be grateful if the doctor would inform him of the fact and then he, Delfosse, would come for it himself even though this might mean a delay of a week or two.

What he didn't think it necessary to tell Dr. Hastings was that ... as will be related in due course ... a fateful woman out of his, Delfosse's, past who had caused *El Gordo*, the quarter million prize in the state lottery, to escape him had repeated her murderous assault on another unsuspecting male. This time the victim was someone important, a prominent politician. Furthermore he was only half-dazed by the blow to his head. Unhappily, or perhaps fortunately, when she had her fit she fell fracturing her own skull. The politician was important enough to demand a post-mortem. He hoped to show he was not the person who had fractured her skull. The autopsy was done and the politician declared innocent in more ways than one for she was found to be *virgo intacta*.

Then her uncle the Bishop started enquiries. He wanted to hand back some money to the 'criminal' who had, several years previously, sent him a cheque. It took him months of patient enquiry until a priest, of a remote place in British Honduras, wrote to say that he thought he had found the man the Bishop was looking for. That Most Reverend Gentleman then employed lawyers who wrote to Delfosse and the letter was addressed to Shoonantonitch, Petén, Guatemala.

The letter gave the impression that they were in receipt of good news, a reimbursement of 50,000 dollars for an investment in La Ceiba, Spanish Honduras, made years ago. They wished to be told of a permanent address to which they could write since they were informed that he was only at times in Shoonantonitch. After that letter Mr. Delfosse walked warily in Petén. Indeed, he was so wary, so cautious that it irritated his colleagues and competitors and Jaime Peat-Patterson, on behalf of Fuad who liked to be in the know about everything, started making some enquiries.

Jaime's sleuthing, and he had the capability to make more contacts than a bee does with flowers when it goes searching for nectar, turned up a bizarre story.

Thanks to his reviled relatives Jaime's reach even extended as far as the Yucatan and the tale he uncovered concerned a young American officer aboard one of the steamers which sailed along a route that included most of the ports around the Caribbean from Port of Spain to New Orleans.

They were the banana boats and they collected the bananas grown on the vast farms of the banana republics for the American market.

This junior officer, so ran the tale, struck it rich with a fabulous stroke of good luck by winning *El Gordo*, 'The Fat One', the grand prize of the National Lottery of Guatemala. He collected his money, a quarter of a million dollars, in Guatemala as a cheque payable to an American bank in La Ceiba, Spanish Honduras. Then he took the regular passenger service of the airline, connecting the several Central American republics, from Guatemala to La Ceiba and there enveloped himself in secretions of prudence. He was circumspect, he was cautious; men tried to borrow money without success; women tried their wiles but he was not tempted; a large fortune, illimitable power was promised him from investments but he said he was not interested in power. To escape from sudden friends and urgent solicitations he decided to spend a few days 'incognito' in an unpretentious little town in Spanish Honduras. He gave out he was waiting for a ship to New Orleans. There relatives and friends prepared an ambush for him. In fact, he was waiting for a German ship aboard which he had reserved a passage to Hamburg, under an assumed name, intending to board at La Ceiba, Spanish Honduras, and to leave the ship at San Sebastian. From there he would go to Marseilles and then on and on. The world and all its tomorrows was now his. The second evening, in the unpretentious little town a few miles from La Ceiba in which he was waiting for the steamer he went for a walk keeping to the wider streets. As he turned back, where the town met the country, still keeping to the wider streets, he noticed a woman heavily veiled walking rapidly towards him. He turned down a side street not to escape her but because it was his route back to the hotel. She hurried after him and spoke to him. She asked to be directed to a hotel though not the one where he was staying. Her voice was very pleasant and peering through her veil he saw enough to decide that she was very lovely and young.

'This is too good,' he said to himself. 'Careful is the word.'

Soon it occurred to him that if she were a professional she was the most accomplished he had ever met and she answered non-committally, if politely, without any inviting overtones, his few remarks. They reached the hotel of which she had enquired and thanking him briefly she turned to enter.

Rather astonished at the abrupt termination of what he was sure had been a deliberate trap for him he said sarcastically, 'Now that I have seen you to your hotel, you should see me to mine.'

She turned back and accompanied him without a word. They reached his room where he became even more astonished. He wondered if this might be an amateur trying to ape a professional, or whether she was the most expert of professionals playing the part of the *ingénue*. Whatever she was she did not put him on guard by any discussion of ways and means. Nor was he on guard when she fondled the full water-carafe by his bedside.

Early next morning he recovered consciousness to find that not only he but the hotel and the neighbourhood and, it seemed, the whole town, was awake.

She had done it again. She had escaped from the private asylum again and he, a stranger, had been her victim. He was luckier than that other man from across the river who died, for Delfosse woke up. The winner of *El Gordo* heard, afterwards, that a posse of police had invaded his hotel. From previous experience the police adopted tactics which would expose them to as little harm as possible when they enjoyed the sight of the demented creature dancing over her victim.

She danced, with daemonic energy and fervour, a dance of love such as the police posse could understand and appreciate. When she had exhausted herself and fallen prostrate they waited. If she then had a fit, turned blue, stiffened, arched her body and subsided into a snoring stupor they were safe. On the last occasion one man had touched her before the fit, to smell her breath for alcohol and she had bitten through his nose, so swift, savage and purposeful was her resentment at being touched.

She was taken away in the town's Black Maria. So also was the man who had been her host and her victim. They dropped him off at the jail but delivered the dancer at an imposing mansion some distance beyond the town. Then her victim found himself in serious difficulties. It was a felony to have sexual relations with a certified lunatic. That was bad, but when the sick person was no other than the niece of a bishop, the sister-in-law of a senator, daughter of a general of division, etc., etc., then that was *very* bad.

He did not take the ship going to Hamburg for the local Chief of Police discovered that he was the winner of *El Gordo*. The story of exactly how he was relieved of all that money cost Jaime several drinks at a bar but Fuad paid 'expenses' and the winner of *El Gordo*'s name was Delfosse, so both employer and employee thought the money was well spent. It had not only been the threat of life imprisonment that had made Delfosse write so many cheques. He had also made the mistake of telling the police that he would at once call on the United States Consul in La Ceiba and explain what had happened and ask for the protection of his Consul. The Chief of Police of the town was not amused. He had acted firmly and quickly explaining to this stupid American that he, the Chief, wanted a full written confession of the crime with no nonsense about not having touched her sexually included in the text. In addition Delfosse would furnish cheques payable to Bishop ABC, to Senator XYZ, to General PQR, and the Chief of Police by name and not by rank. Thereafter he would be kept in jail and reasonably well treated until the ship for Hamburg was about to sail from La Ceiba. He would then be put in a trunk and smuggled aboard the ship as it was about to sail. At sea he could, with some luck, make enough noise to be heard after not too long a time and released from his perilous confinement. Of course he would not have any money or papers or documents on his person to help him in claiming an identity. As it happened, continued the Chief of Police, there was also another stupid man in their custody at that time. He was reported to have had something to do with the stealing of dynamite from the engineers who were building the railway line. He was being obstinate. He would not say who were his comrades and of what rebel group he was a member. What Delfosse saw being done to this 'obstinate fellow', beginning with the looping of a strong, thin rope around the prisoner's scrotum, quickly made him sign all papers as requested.

On board the German steamer he met a man whom he had known when he was a ship's officer. When the ship reached Port Liman, Costa Rica, Delfosse reported to the American Consul there. He had with him a letter from his acquaintance on the ship and the Consul helped him to get a modest job in a hotel in Merida, Yucatan. There he remained until the hotel was no longer modest and it became clear he could not only handle the people who worked for him but had other abilities. Thus he found himself invited by the American-based Chicle Company to join their organization.

With the Bishop's 50,000 dollars conscience money in the bank Delfosse soon found opportunities open to him to do thriving trade in contraband chicle. He was a fast and decided worker who protected his own private, unlicensed trade by hiding behind the public and licensed trade of the Company which he represented. He had two sets of books. One showed the Company's chicle in its correct amount while the other set showed his own and his partners' chicle as though it was also the Company's. The latter was kept posted up to date in the event of any sudden visit of any of his partners. Both were shown to Cibrian who, when he wrote his formula across their pages and required Delfosse to sign two letters showing the amount of chicle on the books as the Company's, completely ruined the season's private trading for Delfosse. With one stroke President Graña froze the chicle in the warehouse.

If any chicle belonged to the dealer whose name was on the licence well and good. If it did not belong to the dealer, so far, no one knew what would happen then.

Delfosse also had other causes of disquiet. He had sources of information in Guatemala City as good as Fuad Birbari's. When the latter came to try to sell him the provisions in his warehouse at a ridiculously low figure he surmised that the same information had also reached Fuad. He decided then to contact Arevalo and put a little pressure on him. He wanted to know if the Commandante had heard, officially or unofficially, of the matter which his information had mentioned. But however close Delfosse came to the matter Arevalo's reaction was unsatisfactory. The latter was distracted with worry. He did not, in fact, know anything. He had not the faintest idea why a soldier, who was also an engineer should be sent to Petén. Surely not to audit books and check the amount of chicle in the collecting depots and merely to write a formula across a page? And, what was worse, he was now convinced that Cibrian, himself, did not know what it was all about. What was also new in the situation was that, now, orders came by plane to the airfield and from thence by mounted courier to Shoonantonitch. So Cibrian and himself might and did get orders at any hour. A plane might even make the journey twice in 24 hours. Gone were the days of isolation for Arevalo when orders took sometimes two weeks to reach him. He had been almost childishly glad that it took the mounted courier seven hours of hard riding to reach him from the first airfield. Now it took only two hours from the nearer airfield.

Delfosse accepted the fact of Arevalo's ignorance. He reserved judgement on Cibrian. It was clear to him that Cibrian was an agent of the conspiracy of circumstances, of luck and fate of which Delfosse was morbidly afraid. He had to act and quickly. He offered a libation to fate. He called the four senior members of his staff together, told them how they had lost their cut on the season's operations and showed them Cibrian's formula across the ledger page. He reminded them that they had, some little time ago, discussed plans for a daring coup, a hijacking of a mule team laden with chicle. As he left the room, he told them that he would not be a party to the hijacking nor did he want to know anything about it. If it did take place, he wanted no profit from it. All he would do was keep his mouth shut. Captain Medina was all for proceeding with it. Since it was to be the last season for him in the bush, anyhow, the arrangements were left to him and it was Medina who bribed the head muleteer to expect the hold-up.

So it came about that Arevalo had to investigate a daring

hijacking, the first in a couple of years.

Delfosse, of course, complained in writing that this dastardly outrage had cost the Consolidated Chicle Company well over 6,000 dollars loss of chicle.

Arevalo had to do vigorous marchings and counter-marchings and much questioning of suspects but nothing came of any of his activities.

When they were interrupted by the surprise courtesy visit of a Penal Battalion Captain Arevalo saw it at first as a welcome break in his worries. Second thoughts, following on the heels of the first, only increased his worries and it occurred to him that the old fox Graña was up to something.

For a long time the Penal Battalion had been at the other end of Petén, near Flores. There they had cut down and cleared a vast square of bush and savannah and everyone thought of it as another example of the grandiose madness which afflicts all dictators, an occupational disease of their trade. Then almost overnight the cleared land became an airfield. True, only light planes could use it in the wet season. The point was, however, that *they* could use it in all seasons, wet or dry.

Then a section of the Penal Battalion began to trickle away from the Flores airfield and through Arevalo's district before he received official notification that the Penal Battalion would be working there. What their work was to be he was not told.

Soon it became clear they were going to make another airfield. It would still be about two hours ride from Shoonantonitch but something the Captain said came as another shock to Arevalo. It was that a system of airfields cannot be operated without radio communication.

'In six months,' said the Penal Captain, 'you will have a radio man in your Shoonantonitch office in contact with the other airports and of course with Guatemala City and with Puerto Barrios.'

Thus isolation was ended in Petén without any increase in the amenities of life as far as Arevalo was concerned. The immediate need to be polite to the Penal Battalion Captain forced him to put his worries aside. Not that such politeness would or could become a habit, for contact between even the officers of the Penal Battalion and other officials was discouraged.

With the general public it was totally prohibited.

Nor were the convicts of the Battalion allowed any contact with the general public because this Battalion was composed not only of criminals but of those people who had 'ideas' or of those who, for one reason or another, had earned the displeasure of President Dato Graña. Some few people on whom the misfortune of this displeasure had fallen had been allowed to leave the country. Others not so fortunate were in the Penal Battalions, others in Penitentiaries and some had been deemed too dangerous for these methods of rehabilitation.

Arevalo was now glad of the company of Cibrian who was an interesting companion and a thoughtful and courteous colleague. The ladies liked him, Maria especially, was very partial to him.

His presence also gave Arevalo a chance he had been looking for, to go on a drunk. A few drinks, followed by a few more and then some more was what his jangled nerves needed. Being an abstemious man, careful of his public dignity as a magistrate, he would have to have an obvious excuse for his intemperate outbreak. And Cibrian would help him manage the affair with tact and discretion. 'Of course,' he thought, 'it can be at the dance; I shall let myself go at the dance.' As he made this decision he gots news that another crime had been committed. An agent of a chicle contractor had been found suffering from a gunshot wound on the road beyond Pusilha. It was clear to those who knew, and all who had dealings in chicle would know, that this was not an assassination that had failed. This was merely a shot across the bows of the chicle contractor, a warning. Of course, it was unfortunate that the agent had to be hurt but that was an occupational risk. Arevalo sent a messenger to Cibrian saying he would be absent from home until probably the next evening and left for the road beyond the Pusilha.

Cibrian did not receive the message because the Major had gone on an excursion with Dr. Cutbush and Mrs. Farr to the forest.

The excursion was led by Karen taking advantage of an incredible stroke of luck. She had discovered that Major Cibrian had brought his surveying instruments with him.

Dr. Cutbush was excited by Karen's project. Her theory was

connected to the transit of Venus and a speculation about acoustics. Cutbush had visited Chicken Itza and had heard the marvellous acoustics that were the result of a most unlikely arrangement there of space and structures. From a flat roof of a house only two storeys high, built by the ancient Mayas, a speaker could be heard, if he spoke in but slightly louder than conversational tones, at a fantastic distance away in the 'arena' which was at times used by the Mayas as their ball-court. There they played their game, a kind of hand-ball, in which the captain of the losing team in certain portentous games literally lost his head. The beheading being part of the game.

Karen had a theory that when Venus reached, at a certain time of rising, a point between two structures – a window and a stela – then certain acoustics came to life. Her theory needed an expert to take measurements between the two structures she would point out to him and then further measurements would need to be made from the mid-point between the structures.

Cutbush was sceptical that acoustics could be reduced to so simple a procedure. He remembered the 'Whispering Gallery' of St. Paul's Cathedral in London. No one had ever credited the architect, great as he was, with deliberately including that phenomenon in his masterpiece. Furthermore, the construction of concert halls and the opera houses all over the world were known to be, from the point of acoustics, a gamble. There was no doubt, of course, that the Mayas had done it. By accident? Or could they have done it again?

As for Cibrian he was interested because it was his profession and he was willing to try to help with his best grace and his most punctilious exactitude.

The ruin, which Karen called the 'Priest's House' because it reminded her of the structure of that name at Chicken Itza, was about a mile from the village and as the evening star would not rise till about ten p.m. they had no need to hurry with the affair of the evening but had set out, in a leisurely way, to see the star rise from their destination.

As they walked through the growing darkness Karen explained to her companions that the Priest's House was now a ruin. The remains of the roof of the top floor were there as were most of the stone uprights bearing the roof. Two of those uprights which were part of an outside wall had the remains of a beam across them and this was, she thought, the window from which the public orator of the ancient Mayas declaimed his message. Between this Priest's House and the road, on which they were walking, was a ravine about 80 feet deep and distant about 100 feet from their road. To get to the other side of the ravine and to reach the Priest's House they would have to continue along the road for about a quarter of a mile until the road dipped gently into the ravine. After that they would mount an equally gentle slope which, because of the curvature of the ravine, led up to the backyard of the Priest's House.

There was a short cut across the ravine nearly opposite the Priest's House but she had been warned that it was dangerous. The 'Speaker' lived in the house. He had wandered into the village and, after various people who had befriended him left, he had taken over the old ruins and lived there. Maria, the Commandante's wife, had persuaded the villagers to repair one room on the ground floor for him and to attach a kitchen to it.

It was the Speaker who had taken Karen over the ruins and who had pointed out to her how a strong ladder had been built to reach the wall near the window. The top of this ladder was secured to the stone uprights while the bottom of the ladder was also tied firmly in place. To reach the ladder one walked across the lower floor of the house and emerged through a broken portion of the wall. Then it was important to mount the ladder with great care for, if a careless step was made, the result would be a fall of 80 feet to the bottom of the ravine. 'Of course,' said Karen, 'next season all this tricky bit with the ropes and ladders will have been remedied provided that, as we hope to find tonight, the evening star is an integer in the algebra of the acoustics of the Maya.'

The three made their way to their destination. Karen pointed out that she had had some hundred yards of the bush cut or burnt back from the road where it faced the Priest's House and for about the same distance along the road. Cibrian took his measurements when the star crossed the window of the Priest's House and drove pegs into the earth where Karen had had the earth lain bare. Cutbush acted as link man carrying the measuring chain here and there as Cibrian commanded and dutifully driving in the metal pegs.

When all was completed the full moon lighted them fulsomely back to their respective quarters. There Cutbush went to bed and slept well, while Karen tossed fitfully juggling complex equations in her mind and Cibrian decided, since he saw a light still burning in Arevalo's house, to pay the Commandante a visit to find out why he was burning the midnight oil. He was met by a servant who told him that neither the Señor Captain nor the Señora was in. The Señor had been called away on duty and the Señora was in the garden-house as was the Señora Aycenina.

Cibrian turned away from the house and walked slowly across the grass which Señora Arevalo hoped would some day be a lawn. The full moon was beginning to cast long shadows and Cibrian's trod toe to toe ahead of him. By walking across the lawn he would reach the gate by a more direct route than by walking along the curving path with which Maria bordered her lawn and garden. Her garden-house was nothing but a thatched booth but it had been made comfortable with benches and was shady with creepers. The latter also gave it a semblance of privacy. Cibrian walking quietly and moodily across the lawn came near the garden-house and heard the sounds of a woman weeping.

He stopped and remained rigid with surprise and embarrassment. It was a woman weeping with such an excess of grief as Cibrian had never heard before and hoped never to hear again. The sobs seemed to be torn not only from the heart of the woman who wept but wrenched also from the dark bosom of earth itself. He heard and recognized Maria Arevalo's voice and realized that the weeping woman was Candellaria. Maria begged only that she should be allowed to share her friend's grief for it was not good that one solitary soul should be grief-stricken and not share her burden.

'Ah, my dear Maria I weep, I must weep, but it is not entirely because of grief. Rather it is the end of the flood waters of grief. With this sorrow I say good-bye to sorrow for he has caused me to live again. I live again, but I do it without hope of joy or surprise. One life is dead and I do not know if the life I shall continue to live is now also a dead life. It may be so.'

'But what did he say? What could he say?' asked Maria. 'What could this ignorant old peasant say? I know they call him the "Speaker". But what does he say when he speaks?'

Candellaria replied, 'He may be a peasant but he is only ignorant sometimes. When I went into his room he was lying in the hammock apparently dozing. He looked at me for a long time. I bade him "Good-evening". He gave me back my greeting and pointed to a stool. I sat down. He asked if I was in trouble. "No," I answered, "my troubles are over." He was silent for a little then he asked me to tell him in what manner it came about that my troubles were over. So I began to speak of my baby and of the fever and the fear which catches the throat and renders the breath thin. I told him of the hope that passes little by little and then of the time when the child's life ended and so did mine.

'He was silent for a little and then he began to speak. He spoke of the burden of womankind and of the strength and endurance of woman. Then he spoke again of sorrow and of grief. He said it is not only time but life itself which takes away the corrupting power of sorrow and leaves it clean and wholesome and thus preserves its shape encasing it like an insect entrapped in amber. Life is a stream which pours over the rocks which are sorrow. And he spoke of the corrupting elements of sorrow saying there are two only that are most to be feared and avoided. They are to be lonely and to be inarticulate. To be lonely is not the same as to be alone, rather, to be lonely is to have the desire and the need for human understanding and compassion but to be denied the power to accept such compassion, even to be denied the power to give and to receive such understanding. To be inarticulate is an evil, for then the thoughts which can find no escape in words grow small, bitter and poisoned and poison the mind and the body of the sorrow-stricken. In such a way he spoke, on and on. I told him much of myself. Not of my life. He asked me nothing as to who I was or what I had been. It did not appear to occur to him to ask for it seemed to be of no importance to him. He asked instead of my thoughts and former hopes and of how with the passing of my hopes my thoughts had changed in tone and tempo. And he spoke of that forever recurring idea of the nothingness, the emptiness of all things, that nagging idea that everything was but nothing. Then, after a long silence, he began to speak of the things which I had been refusing to say to myself and by that refusal had made my sorrow more bitter and more prolonged. Thus he spoke and thus I knew that he was speaking to me and I acclaimed what he said. It was not consolation he offered: nothing could nor can console. It was showing the way to climb out of the flood of grief. For me he was making that effort. He it was who by opening my heart showed me that I was done not with sorrow but with grief. He took my hand and pulled me out of the torrent which had overborne me and by which I had hitherto been carried without resistance on my part.

'So now I weep, my friend, I weep but it is not in grief. It is in parting. I say good-bye to the best and most precious part of me and my life. The rest of life is but a thanksgiving that even for so short a time it was given to me to be so blessed amongst women.'

'Tell me, Candellaria, do you think he is a saint?' asked Maria.

'That I can't say,' she replied. 'Probably not, for he is so wise. Certainly he is no ignorant peon. He talks indistinctly at first but then his voice becomes clear and his words are of understanding and wisdom and compassion. He is indeed a "Speaker" who speaks directly and quietly to one's heart.'

PART FIVE

'... THE BELLS OF DEATH THAT HAVE NOT RUNG FOR 800 YEARS'

Cibrian at length realized his inexcusable position. He was hearing something not meant for his ears. He very stealthily retraced his steps over the lawn to the house then walked briskly and noisily down the path. He was careful not to look towards the garden-house as he passed it.

The next day he visited Arevalo's house. It was a visit late in the afternoon timed to meet the ladies when they were free of household chores and had time to entertain a visitor.

He paid courteous attention to his hostess but had to make conscious efforts to keep from gazing at Candellaria. His eyes kept turning towards her. He was quite sure that she appeared the same today as a few days ago when he had last seen her except, perhaps, he had not noticed before the true beauty and gravity of her expression. It was not the gravity of gloom. Rather it was a dignity and possession which made her a being rare and apart.

They had been talking of Arevalo's absence and of the crime which caused the absence. Maria was indignant not at the inconvenience to her husband but at the stupidity of the criminal act. For it would lead to further violence with each act being more debasing than the previous one so that in the long run no one would benefit.

Then Cibrian spoke, apropos Maria's ideas, of an accident he had witnessed years ago. It was the final scene in a sordid tragedy of betrayal and violence and of revenge.

The reason he mentioned it and inflicted a hearing on the ladies was that when the injured party had the evil-doer at his mercy he had spared him. It was not the Christian turning of the other cheek. It was a refusal to stoop to revenge even though it might be miscalled 'justice'. The renouncement had been complete and abrupt as if the idea of vengeance was nauseous.

Candellaria asked if it were possible that the avenger thought the evil-doer so debased that to touch him was debasing.

Now Cibrian was afraid of the implications of his story. He did not know how much Candellaria knew or suspected of the cause, or origin, of the assassination of her husband. He did not know if she desired or hoped for vengeance on the instigator of the crime. He did not know if she would read into his story ... one told merely to show the infinite variation of human reactions ... a warning of the futility of hate and vengeance. He did not wish to appear to be an advocate for Dato though it would also represent his own considered attitude. He admitted that he had never had the provocation, had never been the victim of betrayal and of violence.

A great surge of thankfulness came over him as Candellaria simply, but with conviction, agreed that to her, also, the idea of revenge was belittling. 'But then, of course, I have no cause for thinking of vengeance. I don't know that I have any right to speak,' she added. Cibrian took his leave.

'It appears,' he said to excuse himself, 'that the Commandante is finding the investigation of the crime needs his presence for a second night.'

He also took his leave because he had a guilty conscience having listened to a conversation not meant for his ears. He had paid his visit hoping the ladies would have mentioned seeing him pass by them the night before. If they did, depending on their manner, he could have grounds for concluding that he had not been seen eavesdropping, or even stealthily retiring on the lawn. They made no mention of the night before. They must, he thought, have seen him passing the garden-house though even when he made some comments on the brilliance of the moonlight they did not respond.

'They might have seen me and did not care to embarrass me,' he thought and he conceded that not only did he have a guilty conscience but, to be honest with himself, a consuming curiosity. Anything that affected Candellaria Aycinena now aroused his interest. He desired to know who was the old man whom Señora

Arevalo had called the 'Speaker', the one whom Candellaria had decided was probably no saint but none the less had brought her surcease from desolation and grief. He was curious but he dared not ask anyone of the 'Speaker' for his question might be discussed and reach Maria. Then she would at once, so said his guilty conscience, recall his elaborately noisy walk down the garden path of her home on the night when Candellaria related the old man's words to her. Then she could not but remember that he had not looked towards the garden-house that night though it was so near the path. It would be obvious to her that he must have overheard at least some part of the conversation. He had acted in a manner unbecoming to an officer, a gentleman and a friend.

The more Cibrian accused himself of an unworthy act, however, the more he desired to know of this person with the gift of solace. It must be an individual who was remarkably self-effacing for Cibrian had heard no mention of him in the many talks he had had with various persons of the village.

'Of course this curiosity is the penalty of idleness,' he eventually told himself.

He was accustomed to mental and physical activity and now that he had written on a dozen or so books purporting to tell of the ownership of the chicle in the warehouses and depots he had nothing to occupy his time. He was ordered to wait in Shoonantonitch and he waited, without occupation, while his idleness inflamed his curiosity.

Had he had a soldier's occupation or, better, an engineer's occupation he would have scorned to allow the chatter of women to arouse a womanish curiosity. That such a self-judgement did him less than justice was something he could, with difficulty, admit to himself for it was also clear to him that the 'old one', the 'Speaker', had a secret which Cibrian desired to possess. The secret was the ability to bring comfort to the special and particular griefs which afflicted woman. Cibrian said often that women had the strength, resilience and endurance of mules while differing from mules in that they had an infinite capacity for suffering. Their bodies and minds were so made that what would either kill a man, or leave him irrevocably a whimpering hulk, would leave them alive, perhaps, even more alive than formerly. This capacity for endurance of sorrow, thought Cibrian, is in one way a curse. If they didn't accept it as their burden so readily then they could never accept it as being in the natural order of things in such cases as the murder and mutilation of husband, or son, or brother in that barbarity that was the elaborate male game called war.

So far Cibrian could honour and appreciate the special excellencies of woman. Where they escaped him, where he found himself unnecessary, a clumsy and offensive intruder was in their sorrow. Gifted with sympathy, insight and imagination as he was he had no words to comfort and console. The sorrow of womankind seemed to him to need not so much a comforter but one who would take part in the lamentations. The only fit and proper person to intrude was a poet, some inspired singer who, joining in the sorrowing, took it over, organized and ordered it into a wild and heaven-scaling elegy which at its declamation brought surcease to tragedy and the purging of the heart by the expression of horror and pity.

'Alas, I am no such inspired poet,' Cibrian told himself. 'So I walk away and hide with my own insufficiency.'

Candellaria Aycinena had reasons for her tragic grief and here was an old man, apparently no magnificent, elegiac poet, who could bring just that solace and had just that power which Cibrian knew he so woefully lacked. He was now an idler so he decided he would fill his idleness by making the acquaintance of the old man, *el viejo*, but he could ask no one the direct question, who was he?

He heard next morning that Arevalo had arrived home late the previous evening.

On leaving the Commandante's house Cibrian went some little distance beyond the village on the road leading to the archaeologists' quarters.

A shed had been constructed to protect the marimba at some distance from the village and from the quarters so that the *marimberos* could practise their music without annoying either party. Major Cibrian knew the chief of the *marimberos*, Pedro Lopez, by sight and by repute. He knew of his passion for music, of his skill as a muleteer and of his friendship with some other unsavoury character. He knew, too, of his uncertain and dangerous temper which had caused him to fall foul of the law more than once and of his large and foolish dog. What astonished Cibrian as he passed by the open shed was to see the *marimberos* in a respectful and admiring group around Señora Farr. Pedro in particular fingered his guitar while he gazed at her with such adoration that his large brown eyes were humid with the excess of his delight.

'But once more, Señora,' he pleaded, 'but once more. I did not do you justice. Though, of course, I could never do you justice. Just once more. There are a certain few bars ... '

Cibrian watched and so engrossed were the group with the pleading of Pedro that no one saw him except the large foolish dog who wearily wagged his foolish tail.

Then Karen and Pedro began to sing while he accompanied the duet on his guitar. At the end of each verse the singers paused, the *marimberos* took up the melody on their instruments and played it softly, tenderly, heart-breakingly, for it was a song of farewell. Cibrian knew the song. It was well known. So well known as almost to be a folksong. It was '*Adios, Mariquita Linda*'.

The song ended. Pedro murmured ecstatically, '*Por Dios! Por Dios!*'

Karen smiled and thanked the marimberos with a neat compliment and then bade them good afternoon. The *marimberos* doffed their hats and replied. Pedro clutched his guitar in one hand while with the other he swept off his sombrero and bent almost double. It was good afternoon and thanks, commendation, praise, and gratitude from one artist to another.

'*Buenas tardes, Señora, buenas tardes*,' he purred.

The tone of his voice made his dog rise and again wag his foolish tail. Cibrian greeted her and walked along with her.

'A musician as well, Señora! You are an astonishing person and I notice you mix with the most humble to their delight. They accept you with acclamation because you do not patronize them.'

'Oh, don't think of Pedro as humble,' she laughingly replied, 'he has an irritable and suspicious pride. But he has a passion for music though without any training. He is a frustrated and fundamentally perverse soul and I had to flatter him to get done what we wanted. You see the night, or rather the morning, which will dawn on the dance is Dr. Gibberd's birthday and he has an exasperating habit. When he is excited or when things are going well in our work he will, often, hum a line or two from "*Adios, Mariquita Linda*". He never hums, or sings, more than two lines but when we, his colleagues, hear them we know the Chief is pleased and know we are making progress. We often ask each other if any wonderful discovery – if we discovered, say a Maya Rosetta stone or a fourth Codex – would make him sing a whole verse of "*Mariquita*". Now he has made a wonderful discovery himself. We are terribly proud and thrilled. So we have decided that at the dance, after the midnight waltz, as his birthday begins, we shall sing for him the whole of "*Mariquita*". It will be the birthday gift of his colleagues. I approached Pedro whom I know; he had done us several services and favours. He was delighted he said to accompany me on the guitar. I play that instrument a little myself but he is better at it that I am. At our first rehearsal he joined in the song. At the second the *marimberos* took part and the third you heard. I think as an interlude after the midnight waltz it ought to be rather effective. I hope the dancers and the rest of the company will think so too.'

'They will,' Cibrian assured her, 'why you are quite a singer! The whole thing will indeed be delightful.'

'Oh,' she replied, 'I am no marvel as a singer. My range is too small. I know exactly what I should not attempt. You see, I told you before, I am convent-bred and although I say it myself it was an expensive convent. We had music drilled into us and my teachers bore with me for nearly ten years. So I play a little, I sing a little and both are the amateurish end results of long, long days of drudgery at school. How many pieces haven't I had to learn by heart? And the questions with all the automatic answers at a horror of a class called, of all things, musical appreciation.'

'Indeed Señora, you make it sound like a purgatory. I won't overdo it by saying you sing like an opera star but in fact you do sing well. I am sure your duet with Pedro will be a great success. That husky confidential baritone of his goes well with your, what is it?'

'Mezzo-soprano,' she replied.

'Thank you. But tell me, before I forget, what is this wonderful discovery of Dr. Gibberd's which his colleagues desire to commemorate so tactfully and charmingly. Or is it a secret?'

'Oh, it is no secret,' she answered, 'it is the discovery of the Maya glyph for the number "eleven". We have checked and re-checked our calculations. There is little doubt that Gibberd has done it. It is an achievement, a fine reward for his patience and hard work.'

'I am dense, a numbskull. I admit it,' said Cibrian, 'but why is "eleven" exciting, why not "nine" or "seven"? And didn't I hear somewhere that the Mayas had an exquisitely simple system of enumeration, something about a bar and a dot, or bars and dots?'

'Indeed, you heard correctly,' she replied, 'but the bar and dot were, shall we say, the Arabic numerals of the Maya. In their ceremonial writings they used two systems as we would use both the Roman and Arabic numerals on an ambitious tombstone. What one might call the Roman numerals of the Maya were a series of stylized drawings of the heads of their gods of the upper world. But the head of "god eleven" was missing or, rather, it was never certain which particular head of many heads was "eleven". Gibberd has done it. It is now almost a certainty.'

'This must be one of those victories of peace as renowned as the victories of war,' Cibrian told her. 'I can understand its importance to you scholars. After all, you must know what your figures mean to do your calculations and I am delighted to know that scholars celebrate a victory with song and dance.'

Karen laughed.

'In English,' she said, 'there is a phrase which I cannot translate into Spanish. It is called "pulling a leg". I think you are "pulling my leg", mocking my enthusiasm, when you talk of song and dance and victories of peace.'

Cibrian was shocked.

'Mock you! Far from it, Señora. I am delighted, charmed. I had feared you might be so taken up with your abstruse reckonings of what the ancients may, or may not, have meant, that you had no time for anything else.'

'Why fear it, Señor?'

'Ah, indeed, why fear? Let us say, Señora that it was fear of a flaw, fear that aesthetically the whole portrait would be marred, the picture a little askew, a little astygmatic.'

Karen laughed again.

'For an engineer you make rash assessments.'

'No,' he replied gaily, 'no, not rash. Quick, yes, if you like, quick. But rash, never.'

'And experienced?' she asked.

He met her mocking glance and Cibrian realized that what had started as a polite, amiable conversation had changed in pace and pattern. He was not averse to a flirtation but a flirtation merely for the sake of keeping his technique supple bored him. He was a very experienced man. The customs of the society in which he was brought up, whereby the young ladies of his class before marriage were rigidly chaperoned and after marriage secluded, forced him to apply his arts in other social circles. But after his adolescent flounderings he was bored by women who came to him just as women. He used them, then, if necessity arose and his duties and his time and his opportunities allowed such use, without too many manoeuvrings on his part. But he enjoyed a flirtation with an intelligent woman so long as the woman realized that the flirtation was the first act of a drama of three acts. In the third act Cibrian always found himself at a disadvantage for the gift of love of a woman to him was never accepted by him as a gift however unselfish, however generous the giver. To him it was a debt which he had contracted and could never repay. The more spontaneous, joyous and grateful was the evidence of a woman's love the more she protested that to love him, to know his tenderness, his sympathy and understanding, his tact and his skill was reward over and above her hopes and her dreams, the more Cibrian found himself the debtor and not the donor.

He also knew enough of the world of men and of sentiments to realize that his attitude was unusual.

'It may be,' he thought, 'that I am vitiated by pity.'

For this surrender of woman was so utter, so complete that it was like a physiological reaction. It was more than a mere reflex it was like the 'all or none' law of physiology. Either react to the proper physiological stimulus with all available force or have no reaction whatsoever. It gave him no pleasure to see a whole personality acting like a muscle on the stimulation of a nerve. It was almost unbearably indecent to see such a capitulation to the 'all or nothing law' and its application in his affairs with his loves roused his pity for them. He did not consider that perhaps he reacted also to the same law or some other equally inflexible. It is not usual for the person who pities to consider that he, also, may be worthy of pity or an object of that enervating sentiment. As he grew older his affairs became fewer because the partings were too painful. His casual amours remained casual but when he was called upon to flirt he preferred a protagonist worthy of his skill so long as that protagonist realized that what might appear to start as a game, a thing with consequences as fleeting as a game of bridge, was to him no game. There was no such game as the 'game of love' to Cibrian.

'Señora Karen,' he said smiling, 'I do not know how experienced you believe I am but I am experienced enough to know you are a very dangerous woman. Perhaps most dangerous to none other than yourself. No, allow me please, you have poise, wit, grace, charm when you are graciously weak enough to allow it, and a remarkable intelligence. The latter does not frighten me. And yet I am frightened, or rather, am in fear and it is two-fold fear. I fear for you as I fear for myself.'

'Thank you for that overwhelming analysis but why do you fear for me?' she asked and there was an anxiety in her tone which she strove to restrain.

Though he may have heard that unwitting concern he answered, 'That I shall not tell you, yet. Perhaps the opportunity will never arise but I can tell you why I fear for myself. I fear that having analysed you I shall be tempted to synthesize you. I shall bring all these attributes of your personality into a whole. It will be you of course, only you; but I shall not be satisfied with the picture or, rather, with the statue I shall make. In the eagerness of my reconstruction I may show you things you may even prefer not to know and may fear. I, in short, may be the artist who cannot leave well enough alone. I may strive for perfection and thus bore you. Yes, to bore you, that is what I fear for myself.'

He looked deep into her eyes, took her hand, kissed it and gently dropped it. Before she could answer, he went on, 'But, to come from the sublime to the utilitarian, I would make use of you to ask a question for me. You will understand when I tell you why I cannot ask it, but you can. Perhaps your guitarist Pedro might tell you. You are interested in strange things and another question from you would be but more evidence that you are very learned and inquisitive of many curious things. When I saw how ravished Pedro was at your singing I thought of course *she* could ask him.'

Mrs. Farr realized that he had decided not to play the game. The cards had been shuffled and cut and this exasperating Major Cibrian had refused to pick up his cards. She was no wanton, nor did she consider herself a flirt but this was a disturbing man who had the power of making Karen conscious of herself as a woman. He had but to glance and smile at her and she found herself taking the posture, the attitude of a protagonist in the most ancient of all games. When she became conscious of his power she did not so much resent it as rail at herself with gentle, if bitter, mockery.

'Ah, Karen, you wretch,' she said to herself, 'you may take the part of the fencer, hold out your foil, touch blades, but does he not see that you are also armed with a poisoned dagger?'

And yet, when Cibrian deliberately refused to play, she was furious with him, with herself, with the circumstances. Then she found herself making excuses for him. 'He knows I shall be leaving in the next four or five days and that I am not one to be stormed and overwhelmed. I am sure of it. If we had time. If we were not in this goldfish bowl of a village but had world enough and time ... ' And she left the thought in the air. 'What is this important question?' she asked him. 'Perhaps I can ask it for you, or I might even be able to answer it.'

'I am afraid to ask Pedro, or anyone in the village, what they know of the man who is spoken of as the "Speaker".'

The walk had taken them to her house while the afternoon had faded into early dusk. She unlocked her door and invited him in.

'What is this, what absurdity is this of which you are afraid?' she cried.

He stood just within the door.

'He is a person,' he replied, 'an old man, she called him "*el viejo*" and he speaks to others and knows the thoughts of their overladen and inarticulate hearts. He speaks to those who are thus burdened and, I believe, he brings relief and healing. I hear he lives in this village, or near here.'

'She,' the word rang loudly in Karen's ears, 'an old man *she* called *el viejo*.' So? So, the man had not been in Shoonantonitch for more than two or three days and already ... What? Some woman had spoken of *el viejo* in front of him. No, had more than spoken of him, had poured out her heart about him. It could not be Maria. Then who? And how naïve the gallant Major was to think, since the man was lodged in an archaeological ruin that she would not know about him. What was he up to?

She was close to him in the gathering darkness and he held her hand firmly but did not pull her closer.

'So you will ask my question?' he enquired.

'Yes, I shall,' she replied. Adding slyly, 'Is there any more you can tell me about it?'

'Nothing more,' he said. 'That is all I know.'

'Yes,' said she to herself, releasing her hand, 'there is not world enough and time.'

Then aloud, 'Of course, I shall ask Pedro. Poor harassed Pedro. If he knows he will tell me. Music hath charms. Yes he will tell me, the fat, dangerous fool.'

Major Cibrian thanked her and stepped back through the door.

When Cibrian got outside he found a corporal waiting for him who approached, saluted and delivered a message.

'Captain Arevalo's compliments, Señor, and if the Major is disengaged this evening the Señora Arevalo and Commandante Arevalo would welcome him to supper. Perhaps he might be pleased to play a game of bridge later in the evening.'

'The message is received and understood. Thank you,' replied Cibrian.

The corporal came to attention, gave another salute and marched briskly away.

From the closed and darkened house behind him Cibrian heard the sound of a guitar.

Karen had heard the brisk steps of the corporal receding into the night and she had thought it was Cibrian fleeing from an uncomfortable situation. She sat down and not so much to dispel her dreariness but to fill the moment until she could take command of herself again she took up the guitar and began to play.

Cibrian was about to follow the soldier when the music made him pause. He listened. It was a theme which he knew, a song. It was not a popular song but the music followed him as he quietly and moodily set out for the Commandante's house. He was long our of earshot of Karen Farr's guitar before his memory, flogged by his resentment at not being able to name the piece of music and where he had heard it, gave him the answer. It was, of course, a song of Tchaikovsky's, 'None but the lonely heart?' The music of that composer had figured a great deal in the repertoire of a former friend of his. She had been a musician, a professional, who had come to Guatemala for a holiday and remained for him and with him until act three of this particular comedy came to its particular close. So he was very familiar with the music of Tchaikovsky.

To begin with, therefore, he was not very talkative at the Arevalo's supper party that evening being a vain enough man to know that he had interested Mrs. Farr.

It gave him an aura of assurance and of conquest that made Maria Arevalo glance at Candellaria Aycinena to see if the latter was aware of it.

It was Candellaria who had been the cause of this particular supper-party. On the day after the incident in the garden-house, which Cibrian had overheard, Candellaria had suddenly thought of his noisy march down the garden path. She had suggested to Maria that her lament might have been so fulsome that he had heard it and had even heard their conversation. Maria scoffed at the thought but Candellaria so often returned to the subject that Maria decided that it might serve a useful purpose if she invited him to supper and bridge. Then Candellaria would have the opportunity of judging from his conduct and conversation whether he had heard anything. At the supper-party, however, Candellaria forgot entirely why Cibrian was invited. To her he seemed to be endowed with an easy, quiet assurance and power while tonight there was also a pensiveness which appealed to her more softly and more insistently than naked force. The conversation was easy but Maria noticed he was at times distrait.

'May it be, Major,' she said, 'you are getting somewhat tired of the isolation. We are like fish living in a hole at the bottom of adeep green sea, the sea of the forests of Petén. Perhaps you are getting tired of this hole in the floor of the sea?'

'Indeed, Señora, I admit that I am perhaps not the best of company tonight but I assure you it has nothing to do with boredom or with Petén. I heard some music a little while ago, a few bars only, someone practising and it opened the flood-gates of memory at an event in which I played no very creditable part. I had no idea my distress was so obvious. My manners are shocking, please forgive me.'

'Oh no, no, don't apologise ... we, we like it. I mean, don't we Candellaria? We like the fact that music can have such a deep effect on you.'

'Why, Maria,' said Candellaria, 'it may have been some terrible military crime Major Cibrian committed such as falling from his horse when the band played at some portentous parade stiff with generals, all blinding with medals. Even now when he hears the music he sees those medals so shocked they hung stiff and frozen.'

He realized that she was laughing not at him but to give point to her ridiculous story and in the hope, perhaps, that it would allow him to dissolve his depression in a jest. He joined in the laughter as did Arevalo.

'Señora, señora,' said Cibrian to Candellaria, 'you are clairvoyant. How did you see the most shameful thing that ever happened to me? Why for days after my horse would not canter or trot. A funeral march was all I could get from him. I had to threaten him with transfer to the Army Service Corps before he would pull himself together. After all to be a scapegoat, yes, but when one's horse begins to take upon himself one's sins it is too much.'

'I once had a cat,' said Candellaria, 'which, I declare could sense when I was guilty of some *faux-pas.* I mean a *faux-pas* sufficiently grave to put me out of countenance with myself. The beast was an uneasy as I was and in fact the uneasiness was so conscience-stricken and lasting that it would quite often bring back to me the memory of the incident which I was hoping to forget.'

Cibrian thought, 'If it is not true, it is tactfully invented.' He liked her. She was comely.

'No,' he thought, 'she is more. She could be, indeed she is, beautiful! But hers is a beauty more than skin deep. She reflects in aspect and countenance the graciousness and fine poise of a tempered soul.'

In response to his glance of approbation and appreciation a slight colour tinged her cheeks.

A moment later, in answer to an insistent rapping at the door Maria left then returned to call Arevalo. He closed the door after them both excusing himself. 'It will be only for a moment.'

In the few moments they were alone Cibrian took the opportunity to thank Candellaria.

'That was very kind, thoughtful and skilful of you, Señora. You saved my manners and assuaged a pain. You are very perceptive.'

'There are times when all of us find it easy to be perceptive, Señor. I do not claim any high credit for inventing a silly joke. It is indeed painful enough to have memories plaguing us and they do not always choose the most tactful occasions to do so.'

'Ah, indeed they do not,' he said and asked, 'Are you thinking of remaining with us in Petén?'

'I do not know. I have been very ill for quite a time. I certainly feel much better now and I do not find the forest tedious. Perhaps I shall remain a few weeks, perhaps more.'

'Yes,' said Maria coming in to hear her last statement, 'she is so much better that we are trying to persuade her to come to the dance. Even if she does not dance her presence will grace the occasion. Do try to persuade her to come.'

Cibrian smiled at her.

'Are you easily persuaded? I doubt it but it will be a diversion. And I hear the archaeologists are honouring Dr. Gibberd with a special item of entertainment.'

'They were wise enough to ask Fuad Birbari to take charge of the ordering of the food and the catering, both liquid and otherwise,' said Arevalo. 'If we had fountains they would run with beer and there is a small cask of rum. It will be a gala affair much more ambitious than last year because, of course, the archaeologists were not here then.'

'What sort of entertainment are we to be offered?' asked Maria.

'Singing,' said Cibrian.

'Oh, who is going to sing, that new doctor? You know the one who specializes in madness, Dr. Cutbush?'

'No,' said Cibrian, 'I don't believe he will sing.' It was clear he did not wish to speak more on the subject and Maria was already chasing another idea.

'Tell me, Major Cibrian,' she said, 'do mad people or rather people who have been mad and have recovered, do they get apprehensive when they meet a mental specialist? Do you think they are afraid to meet his eye lest he should see in them some mark, some brand of Cain which he alone sees?'

'What a dreadful idea,' interjected Arevalo. 'What possessed you to think of so horrifying a thing? That's what comes of not playing bridge as we proposed.'

'I know,' said Candellaria, 'that these people have no such apprehension, or alarm. I was told so by someone who could speak with assurance from personal knowledge.'

Arevalo hastened to get away from the subject.

'It's odd having a psychologist in charge, in a sense, of an archaeological expedition and talking of archaeologists,' he continued, 'Dr. Gibberd tells me he has rigged up an apparatus to dredge Cenote Perdida, "The Lost Well". He is to try it tomorrow. It will be only a trial but if it proves interesting they will get proper apparatus to do the job next season.'

'What is Cenote Perdida? It must be near here if he is dredging tomorrow and dancing tomorrow night,' said Cibrian.

'It is the well which sometimes supplies the village and the other near the camp. They are cave-ins along the limestone surface stratum that runs from Yucatan to Petén. Beneath these surface layers are vast collections of water. You have but to experience a proper wet season to know how these underground lagoons are replenished. Many of the wells have been in existence since the days of the Maya and some of them were of religious significance. Sacrificial victims were thrown into them and other objects of propitiation. You know that when they dredged the great Cenote at Chicken Itza they found an enormous amount of votive offerings. Curiously enough many of the metal objects were bells sacred to the Death God.

'About three miles from here is a very small well, the mouth is only about six feet in diameter, hence the reason why it has been so long lost in the forest. But it is extremely deep. Gibberd tells me that from the surface of the ground to the surface of the water in the wet season is about 100 feet or so. He is particularly interested because this village and Cenote Perdida have from time immemorial been in the direct path of traffic from Belize to Petén. Traces of tin have been discovered in the Colony and Gibberd is anxious to know if the copper bells he may discover will contain tin. In other words whether the Mayas were at the threshold of their bronze age when they used Cenote Perdida. Of course if it was a sacred well he may even find some golden bells.'

'Were the golden bells so sacred to the Death God?' asked Candellaria.

'Yes,' replied Arevalo.

'How large were the bells?' asked Maria.

'Oh,' he answered, 'about the size of your thumb or a little larger. They were of the shape and general construction of sleigh-bells. It is an extraordinary thing but the Death God was the only Lord of the upper, or of the lower, World with bells on his costume. None of the other gods apparently needed to sound a warning of their coming.'

'He may not have meant it as a warning it might have been meant as encouragement,' said Cibrian, 'a gentle distraction like ritual music. But I would like to see what they do find in this forgotten well.'

'I am going nearby in the morning,' said Arevalo, 'there is some dispute about stray animals damaging a *milpa*. We could go and see what they find.'

'Let's make up a party,' said Maria. 'What do you say, Candellaria?'

'I would indeed like to see the well and possibly the bells of death that have not rung for 800 years,' she replied.

'Then we shall make up a party and take some food with us so that there will be no need to hurry back.' Maria was quite emphatic.

'Well,' said Cibrian, 'that being the case and if you ladies are going to get busy preparing refreshments I shall only be in the way. So, if you will forgive me, I shall take my leave.' He got up.

'Adios Señor, Señora and thank you for your hospitality.' As he turned to go he glanced once more at Candellaria. She was gazing straight at him. Her eyes were glowing and again his attention brought a slight flush to her cheeks.

Cibrian woke early the next morning with a start to hear himself say, 'Of course! It is he, not alone, that is not it; not only alone, but lonely! He is alone and lonely.'

He spoke as the dream began to fade but he could remember the figure of a man, a small man seen from behind. He was walking with a curious tripping gait as if he were hurrying on tiptoe. There was, however, no haste in his attitude.

As he walked the little bells which hung on his dark costume, around his neck, on the shoulders, around the cuffs of the tunic, down the seams of the trousers tinkled with a curiously inviting tone. There was neither rhythm nor melody in the tinkling. Indeed, they tinkled spasmodically as if shaken by a playful child. It gave Cibrian, for the sound of the bells filled his consciousness, the illusion that he was listening to children playing, to little children, children who for the first time became aware of tone as distinct from noise. Children who tinkled the bells again and again to recapture the pleasure of discovery. Now sound was not only sound, not only noise made agreeable, but the change, created by the alchemy of mind, giving dimensions to what had been a mere disturbance of the air. Power was overlaid upon tone; enchantment was added to sound. What had been a physical process was no longer physical and the first thin ranks of a beleaguring army had begun to march around the city. They were not yet strong enough, or confident enough; the inspired message had not yet bade them to put their trumpets to their lips, they could not yet sound chords of ecstasy. And then, as Cibrian listened to the bells, an overwhelming sense of loss submerged him. Somehow, somewhere he had heard that disjointed music, in that impossible key, before. Somehow, somewhere he had had an opportunity, a chance to play those bells and had never done so. Perhaps his infancy had been merely normal and he had discovered the proper value of rhythm and melody and their function in their proper time and season so he had never been aware of a different order of normality. Then his sense of deprivation receded. He lost sight of the figure of the small man who seemed to vanish not from, but into, the path though he left the sound of his bells, a sound which was now behind Cibrian ringing a message in invitation, still without rhythm, or melody but it spoke clearly, 'You are alone and lonely,' it said. It was an invitation which brought with it terror and such a bursting anguish of the mind, such a blinding, massively crushing terror that he stopped rigid in the path and almost with relief felt himself, like the figure that had preceded him, vanishing, shedding substance and form, diminishing and sinking into the pathway.

Then there was another figure, sitting, also in uniform but a different uniform. It was one without bells. He seemed to know that uniform and although he was seeing the figure from the front he did not see the face. There was one large medal pinned on the left breast. It hung stiffly immobile without responding to the movement of the breathing chest.

Then the figure stood up and came towards Cibrian. There was one person only who sat, who moved, who walked with that majestic sense of accepted doom, who diffused consciously and wearily, with the weariness of the leper conscious of his infirmity, that suffocating aura of power. It was his commander-in-chief, the President, the 'well-deserving' Deodato Graña.

Cibrian awakened to hear himself saying 'It is he who is alone and lonely'. Then he added, almost without knowing of the thought, 'For him no bells ring.'

The day of the ride to Cenote Perdida was dawning. He heard his batman stirring.

'Be quick with the coffee,' he shouted. But he did not confuse the servant by shouting what he said to himself. 'I need that coffee to oil oil the lock in the door of reason.' As the aroma of coffee comforted him he sank back into his hammock and said aloud, 'I wonder if I shall find her the same today as I thought she was last night. Good heavens, Felipe Cibrian you talk as if you are twenty years of age. No, at twenty one is certain she is wonderful by night and fabulous by day. Whereas I think her neither wonderful nor fabulous. She was charming, she had a sense of purpose and a serenity which gave repose to others. She was perceptive and quick enough to disarm hurt by a shrewd and well-pointed jest. No fool, in fact, intelligent even acute but not intimidating. Is she kind and gentle, kind and sympathetic, I wonder? Cibrian, up you get and give orders about your mule.'

The foreboding and distress of the dream had faded. He was now in high humour. When he reached Arevalo's house there were the mules waiting, saddled and in the charge of the corporal who had delivered the Commandante's message outside Karen Farr's house the evening before.

Arevalo met him at the door. 'Do come in, Major come in. Another cup of coffee?'

Cibrian declined. He greeted the ladies gaily. The morning shone and the promise of the day was glad. They were about to mount the mules when a maid appeared. Maria was urgently needed. A deputation of village women had arrived at the back door and were asking for her. She went and returned in a few minutes.

'You must go without me,' she said, 'or there will be nothing to eat at the dance tonight. Pigs broke into Mrs. Sanchez's kitchen last night and ate most of the food already prepared. She accuses another woman either of bewitching the pigs, or of deliberately opening the door of her kitchen to them. The catering arrangements are in danger of flying to pieces. I shall have to pour oil on troubled water. If I don't, the *chicleros* will get very little of the good things they are expecting and if they don't get them, there will be loud unpleasantness.'

She apologized at her desertion of the picnic, but gaily. She was laughing. In fact, she was delighted. She would have gone readily to see the dredging of the well. She had even suggested it. But here was something infinitely more amusing. She had here to quiet anger and resentment, disarm suspicion and with generous and ready tact rebuild dignity and value in the disgruntled and down-trodden. At the same time she would take charge of the catering arrangements without appearing to interfere with the hierarchy of the caterers. Provided her responsibilities to her immediate guests allowed it she would not have forgone this opportunity of being creatively busy even for the gift of a golden sleigh-bell.

'Besides,' she told herself, 'what will they see but dripping mud from a dark hole with perhaps a lump of something which in time will be cleaned off to become a bell?'

So the other three began the ride to the well in high spirits. Arevalo related to them how he had previously forbidden Maria to take part in the preparation of refreshments for the dance.

As Commandante, he had many sources of information and his sources were female as well as male. One source had, with every evidence of malignant glee, informed him of the terrible offence certain parties had taken when the archaeologists, without malice aforethought, had given other parties provisions with which to furnish the tables at the dance. So he had instructed Maria, much to her chagrin, not to accept appointment to the refreshment committee but to the decorations committee instead. No one had been gleeful about the decorations because it was a committee that had very little to do and was therefore almost totally innocuous. Maria would now be delighted not only to prove to him that she was of value in the situation that had arisen but also delighted to prove how right he had been in the first instance to forbid her entry into the situation. When even the corporal, who had kept within earshot, laughed at the husband's rueful summing up of the wife's triumph Arevalo closed the story by saying, 'Man is a child, a bemused infant when confronted with the paradox of a woman's mind.'

The corporal laughed again, certainly not understanding the word 'paradox' but understanding the sense of the summing up. He also understood the glance Cibrian shot at him and rode forward keeping a respectful distance ahead of the other three for the rest of the journey.

The path was often too narrow for three to ride abreast. Then Arevalo rode forward while, when the path would allow it, Cibrian and Candellaria rode side by side. There were times also when, perforce, she rode ahead and sometimes she rode behind but they were always close together as if they had earnest business to discuss. They talked sometimes seriously, sometimes gaily. Sometimes they were silent but without strain or effect. It was at the end of one such period of silence that Cibrian, looking towards her with a musing and abstracted gaze, found her smiling quizzically at him.

'Indeed,' he commented to the unspoken appreciation, 'what we have just been sharing was not so much silence as quiet, the quiet of the footfall on deep carpets and it gives the same feeling of security and comfort of,' he was suddenly shy, '"the familiar".' She did not reply but her slight smile of understanding warmed him.

Some few minutes later she began to speak on a subject which was so foreign to her and, indeed, to him that he reined in his mule to a stop.

'Oh no, no, you must not do that. Not without due warning and formal notice. You should not spring such a question on a defenceless man, any man, unawares. Ask me again slowly, and let me see if I heard you correctly.'

'You heard the question correctly and I know it sounds mad. It was your word "familiar" that made me think of it.' And she repeated her statement at greater length.

'She told me that from two years of hard labour she had got two pieces of information dealing with Maya astronomy and mathematics which were, she declared, one and the same subject to those ancients. One piece was an involved and laborious statement about astronomy. She said she was certain she was correct but could not prove it. The other was a simple thing so right ... not "correct" this time but "right" ... she was certain of its truth but she also couldn't prove it. She showed me the Maya sign for zero, for "nothing". The sign is said, apparently, by other archaeologists to represent a shell but she thinks that it is the sign of a closed eye. One closes one's eye on the familiar and lo! There is nothing to count. One experiences zero. She was not excited about it but I think she was rather pleased with herself. So now you know why I spring on you the question and ask why is zero important to enumeration. Why should the sign of a closing eye to the familiar be important?'

'Ah,' said Cibrian, 'I might have known. Mrs. Farr of course. Yes, from her one braces oneself to meet questions, or remarks, or replies, or even, sometimes, just a look that she gives you.

'But to answer your question. It is generally accepted that the invention of the symbol and the application of the idea of zero in mathematics are two of the profoundest achievements of the evolving and growing human mind comparable to the invention and application of the wheel to practical affairs. Why it is so magnificent an achievement is because it is a liberating idea. The application of the symbol of nothing heralded the inventions of a systematic approach to life. From the recognition of zero, of nothing, it became possible to start counting and indeed subtracting, add one, take away one and you have ... nothing. You see? Then the old Mayas went further, they made dealing with large numbers easier by inventing the idea of counting in twenties. I do not know what Mrs. Farr would think of my explanation but I hope I have enabled you to believe in the importance of zero. And as we are on the subject, I read somewhere that the Mayas made that leap in the dark. I mean the discovery of zero a thousand years, or at any rate many centuries, before the Hindus who were formerly thought to be the first to do it. One expects these things of the Hindus because they seem to have very early found a key to the postern gate of the arcane. Even so, they discovered zero when the foundations of civilization, as we know it, had been laid. The Mayas were and remained to the time of the Spanish conquest in the stone age.'

Candellaria shrugged, 'That makes at least some sense and it proves how little we understand even the most familiar of things. But then the most familiar to me of all things, that which one would think I know through and through, so accustomed am I to its vagaries, baffles me.'

'Oh, is that so? I had no idea you allowed the why and wherefore of things to perturb you. But then I have no idea of you, really. I seem to know you, as it were, by aerial survey, the extent of the boundaries, the general shape and contour of the personality and I am aware that there is much more than that and I am totally ignorant of it.'

With a sense of shock he became aware that he had made an extraordinary statement, an intrusion, a trespass to the edge of courtesy. 'And yet,' he said to himself, 'though I feel she has a right to resent it, I would never have found myself making such an extraordinary statement after so short an acquaintance with ... ' and he thought of his former friend of many months, she with the passion for Tchaikovsky.

Candellaria was silent, gazing pensively, but not sadly, down the long vista of the forest path.

'That is just what I was saying,' she murmured. 'You see that most familiar of all things to me, which baffles me, is me. The why, wherefore and whence of me, and why at times it may even be detached, me without myself.'

'*Querida*,' said he, the term of endearment was so spontaneous, so effortless and yet so proper in the sense of correct, that they accepted it as naturally as they accepted their friendship, 'you are of the tribe of women who are doubly damned. A man functions and the evidence is sweat. A woman functions and the evidence is sorrow. But for the woman who thinks as well ... she is beyond the comfort of sorrowing.'

Candellaria did not answer and they rode in silence for many minutes. When she spoke again it was to ask him something on an entirely different subject. She wanted to know how he, as an engineer, liked being exiled in this bush where there was nothing for an engineer to do.

'But you are mistaken,' he replied, 'an engineer always sees a million things to be done. It is true I am not doing an engineer's task now but, as for liking it, well, all I now do,' he paused, 'is to obey orders.'

She was quick to notice the pause.

'Are you still on the President's executive staff?'

'I am, as far as I know.'

'Yes,' she said, 'from day to day no one knows.'

'Does it ever strike you to pity him?,' Cibrian asked. He but vaguely remembered words, perhaps from his dream. 'He is so alone and lonely.'

It was characteristic of President Graña that so often he was spoken of merely as 'He'. A conversation might begin in mansion, or in counting-house, on a highway or in coffee-*finca*, in grog-shop or at the market with, 'I see *He* has gone to so and so' or, 'I hear *He* has done sò and so'. The context was instantly supplied. 'He' was like that.

'I do not know him well enough,' she replied. 'I have met him, of course. We were guests a few times at different houses of his and once on a fishing trip, but I don't know him. He was always so busy. He would be working when the rest of the world was sleeping. I did not think he needed my pity because he was so far removed from us. You know, he gave me a feeling that he had more than human understanding. For it was he who had occasion not to pity, but to sympathize with me. After that horrible affair, you know?' Cibrian nodded. She was referring to the assassination of her husband. He held himself taut.

'Now,' he said to himself, 'now, this is it. How much does she know – or suspect? How far does she feel the need of vengeance?'

To his surprise she continued placidly, musingly, 'He wrote me a letter, with his own hand. It was not a long letter though nothing I received at that time, or have ever read, and I have since read several classic authors on this particular theme, nothing was so appropriate, so tender, so respectful. He seemed to be bowing out of my chamber of sorrow stepping backward softly, hat in hand, murmuring words not of comfort to come from beyond the grave but words of one more instructed heroic mortal to another heroic soul. He had elevated me in the midst of sorrow. He had raised me up from the prostration of grief by an uplifting gesture. He had dried no tears but he had restored dignity to the imperishable but mortal me. I knew, then, of course, that he was a great man. What I now realize is that great men are great in many ways, not only in one way. In short, a great man must be, I suppose, a great soul.

'But you know Major you make me talk more than I usually do.'

Glancing round at him she was surprised to see Cibrian's eyes were narrowed and his countenance flushed. She looked hurriedly away not wishing to embarrass him.

'How sweet of him to be so affected,' she thought. 'He knows the story, of course, everyone knows it but to be so sympathetic shows what a nice nature he has.'

She was quite wrong. Cibrian had indeed, for a moment, been greatly affected but now he was not quite certain whether his feelings were dictated by rage at the innocent irony of her appreciation of the practised skill of the assassin or rage at the futile and ignominious position in which he found himself. He had to keep silence while he witnessed the, to him, revolting spectacle of a villain being named with a benediction and praise. He shuddered.

'Either I am too simple,' he thought, 'or I am too complex, too torn by conflicting forces to understand him. But what do I mean by "understand"? Do I mean by understanding to forgive him for those things which hurt my own particular and personal conscience. For, if he does not keep the particular and personal conscience of each of three million people, he at any rate gives them order, swift justice according to their lights and without barter or price. He also gives them great opportunities for education, health, security and a sense of possession of a dignified future. Yes, I boggle at the word "justice". My "justice" is not his and who am I to take to myself a private meaning of justice.'

The path was narrow enough now for him to drop back; they rode in single file. She pointed to a tree, tall and many branched which by the mass and spread of its foliage had caused the vegetation below it to be stunted, while the trees in its neighbourhood shot up, thin, elongated and gasping for their share of sunlight. Now it had shed its leaves while along the smaller branches to the very tips of its multitudinous twigs it was clothed with an enormous number of flowers of a soft, glowing, pinkish red. The sunlight of morning illumined the topmost branches where the glow appeared almost incandescent. Candellaria reined in her mule and Cibrian followed her example. They looked at each other in silence and turned again to gaze at the tree. The fast hurrying clouds of the upper air as they diffused the morning light, or allowed it free passage, made the fiery tree appear to pulsate as though irregular draughts were drawn up from the molten heart of earth itself by the roots of the tree.

'One should remove the shoes from one's feet at such a sight,' said a voice behind them. They had been overtaken by Dr. Cutbush and Karen and the Doctor had made the remark. Candellaria did not understand the allusion and Karen explained.

'Yes,' Candellaria agreed, 'it is holy ground, and not only the ground, the moment as well.'

They rode on to Cenote Perdida but it was now a party. The conversation, as far as the trail allowed it, became general. Cibrian was not sorry. He was glad of the lone companionship of Candellaria but she had suddenly become too disturbing. She disturbed not only his heart but his mind, his judgements and his loyalties. All these she did without once referring to any of the material or immaterial props of this security and he was quite certain she was unconscious of his perturbation.

They reached the Cenote in due course.

It seemed to Cutbush that at one moment they were on the beaten path, and at another moment, for no other reason but that Arevalo's corporal went thither, they turned into the thick bush. Cutbush could see no reason why they should have turned off just at that particular place and not at any of a thousand other places. There was no branching path, nor scarred tree, nor stone, not even a break in the bush.

'Of course,' thought Cutbush, 'it is not capricious madness that he should have gone just there. I look and I do not see, I listen and do not hear. The corporal is aware of everything in the bush while I am more lost and confused than he would be if he were suddenly to find himself in New York.'

The fact was that the Commandante had business elsewhere and he wanted to get on and return early enough to rest before the dance. So instead of taking the usual pathway to Cenote Perdida he had asked if it was possible to shorten the journey by striking directly through the bush. The corporal told him that it could be done with a considerable saving of time at this particular season of the year and the man rode on ahead, plying his machete and cutting a path through the bush. Soon they heard the creaking of a pulley and the whine of the rope through the block and came suddenly into a clearing. They had arrived at the long-forgotten well.

Gibberd, in the shade, was leaning against a tree. Miss Quinn, his secretary, artist and general 'girl Friday' was leading a mule to which was harnessed one end of the rope that passed through the pulley. The latter was suspended from a stout rope slung from two trees. Several labourers rubbed the mud through sieves. To Cibrian it looked a wet, messy, grubby scene. Gibberd wet, messy and just as grubby had a lump of what might have been mud or stone in his hand. He was murmuring to himself. As Cibrian drew nearer he recognized that it was not a murmur. Gibberd was humming to himself over and over again a few bars from the old Mexican song '*Adios, Mariquita Linda*'. Then he stopped his humming and thrust the muddy lump at Cutbush.

'Look, a bar of copal incense with the sacrificial blue on it still.

This is going to be good.'

After that he cheerfully greeted the rest of the company.

Cibrian felt a sensation almost of nausea. He was a cultivated man with a profound appreciation for, but little exact knowledge of, prehistory, or indeed of history. This painful grubbing for muddy lumps, this excitement at an ancient bar of incense, however, made him feel so insufficient that his insecurity was almost physical. He remembered how he had seen a motor-car assembly line in Detroit. First, there had been wonder, then pride at the prowess of man, then unease at the restricted and patterned movements of each particular worker. The unease grew to a sense of the obscene and he had hurried away. He loved to look at the finished product but the details of the execution, of the manufacture affected him as if they were morbid processes. So now the sight of Gibberd whom he knew as a gentle, selfless man, a man whose courtesy and fine-feeling for all other men, not excepting the humblest Indian load-carrier, was as well known as it was patent, revolted him. For Gibberd exemplified then the sweat, the muck, the toil, the aches and inconveniences, the patterned and restricted movements, not to speak of the occupational diseases and disappointments of so many who were as dedicated as he was.

'That is it,' said Cibrian to himself in a moment of self-insight, 'I am not myself dedicated to anything. Not even to myself. It is the knowledge of this lack, the acceptance of this vacuum, which weakens me.'

He took the lump of gum as someone handed it to him, looked at it, he hoped, intelligently and passed it on. The blue marks, he thought, must be of some salt of cobalt mixed in the substance of the gum. Then, as the excitement over Gibberd's discovery lost its first rapture, Cibrian looked around, 'Of all the places in the world,' he thought, 'the Petén forest is the worst in which to picnic.'

There were no open glades with springy turf; the grass was uneven where it was not frank bush and the ants were vicious.

The others were not looking upon the world with such jaundiced eyes. They persuaded Gibberd to wash his hands and Miss Quinn to unhitch the mule from the pulley. Its marchings and counter-marchings and the splashings from the well had made one part of the clearing unusable for their purpose but on the windward side of Cenote Perdida they made ready, even gaily made ready, to lunch. Cibrian, too, was gay, for as they arranged themselves reclining on their saddle-cloths spread on the earth, Candellaria, who was spreading her saddle-blanket said, 'It is quite big enough for us both'.

'Thank you,' he said and sat down.

It was at that juncture that Candellaria began to laugh, her laughter was so sudden, abandoned and whole-hearted that the others were astonised.

'So what's there to laugh about?' said Cutbush. 'Let us in on the joke; don't keep it all to yourself.'

'I am so sorry, friends, but you will agree the only thing to do is to laugh. You see, our lunch has gone.'

It was true. Maria, the good hostess, the exemplary housewife had handed the lunch to her husband packed in a knapsack. Arevalo the Captain and Commandante had handed the knapsack to the corporal. After the Commandante and his corporal had delivered the excursionists at the Cenote they had hurried on to their own particular destination and business and with them went the lunch.

In these circumstances Miss Quinn proved she was the perfect secretary. One of the labourers had shot an agouti that morning. It was fat and young. Miss Quinn suggested that the company should eat the sandwiches, brought by Dr. Cutbush and Karen, as hors-d'oeuvres while she arranged matters. In a few minutes she returned. She explained that the agouti, a kind of large rabbit, was being dealt with and she also produced a bottle of aguardiente. It belonged to the labourers and it was to be their priming for the dance and it had been loaned to Miss Quinn to be repaid in kind with compound interest at the dance. They toasted the appearance of Cenote Perdida in archaeological annals with a dose of aguardiente.

'I know this brand,' said Cutbush as he shuddered at the internal explosion of 'firewater.' 'It is the genuine Old Prometheus. Don't let any trickle into the well. It will set the incense blocks alight.'

Miss Quinn was not sorry that the dredging had been interrupted. She was, as was every one of the party except

Gibberd, exhausted by the strenuous work of the season. The dredging of this well was the last organized work that had been on their schedule and then everyone but Miss Quinn could relax. Gibberd never hurried, never relaxed, so Miss Quinn had to hurry and never had the opportunity to relax. Her work never ended. But the big very handsome blonde had herself as well organized as her work and she now organized the luncheon at which Gibberd so suddenly found himself acting as host. She diverted the labourers' tortillas and had the agouti baked in earth under a roaring log fire. Condiments were in the labourers' knapsacks and by the time the aguardiente had put the guests in a jovial fuddle the baked meat was served. It was a tremendous success. Coffee added the final and welcome touch.

They did not long delay at the well after lunch.

Miss Quinn ordered the labourers to dismantle the dredging gear before Gibberd could get going again and the apparatus was loaded on two pack animals.

'Don't forget the rope-ladder,' said Gibberd.

It had been prepared in the event that the dredging gear might have been fouled up in the well. The rope-ladder was tied on one of the pack animals. The mules of the guests were saddled. The whole party bade adieu to Cenote Perdida.

'Till next season,' sang Gibberd and Cutbush reassured his friend by a prompt, 'Yes, next season.'

Arevalo and his corporal overtook them on their way home. The shamefaced corporal, who had been responsible for the forgotten lunch, shuddered at meeting them but the high spirits of the Americans diverted Arevalo's wrath. Cibrian, alone, shot the corporal a look that made him break into a slight sweat. When they reached the Commandante's house they heard from Maria how soothingly she had applied unction to the troubled catering staff. So the dance, as far as food and drink were concerned, would certainly be a phenomenal success.

It was, in fact, long remembered and often spoken of. True, there were still a few *chicleros* in the more distant camps who had not yet come in but that, from the point of view of both hosts and guests, was advantageous. There were already so many men over and above the number of available women dancers that more men would be a nuisance. Men who were not occupied with dancing would as likely as not make a 'corner' of the food, or drink, to the embarrassment of those interested in more diverse pleasure. There were enough male dancers for even the most indefatigable lady to have a choice of partners for every dance. When the archaeologists had decided to join with the Chicle Company as hosts they had taken responsibility for decorations and music. They were able to get from Belize a couple of dozen collapsible Chinese lanterns and the loan of a portable gramophone. They bought nearly two dozen records mostly of famous Latin-American dance hits and, in addition, an assortment of those bright, cute and useless articles called 'favours'.

Many of the dance records did not survive transportation and Pedro's *marimberos* had neither time nor opportunity to learn more than a few new items from the records to add to their repertoire. But this was just as well, for each man, and there were eight of them, had to learn by ear his particular part of each number as well as that of his immediate neighbour to his right. Pedro at the extreme left could take any part but the other men were not as gifted as he was. Furthermore Pedro could be trusted not to get completely drunk until the last note of the last dance had been played. But it was expected that by a little after midnight, one, or perhaps two, of the players would be helpless and his comrades would have to take over his part as far as was possible. Late that afternoon, however, at a final rehearsal of the midnight waltz, which they had learned from one of the records chosen by Karen, Pedro told them that, on the word of the lady herself, for every two drinks each player did not take, a bottle would be put by for him. That being the case he, Pedro, then took the most fearful oaths binding himself to do so and so to whoever singly, or as a group, of his players forgot himself so far as to strike a fuddled note. Karen arriving just in time to hear the end of that declaration moved discreetly out of earshot and came back to reassure them that she had already secured, under lock and key, the drinks reserved for the *marimberos*. They, for their part, prepared to play the final practice of the midnight waltz and swore to her that they could play it with far greater appeal and tenderness than it was played on the brassily overladen record. Mrs. Farr walked away about thirty yards and signalled them to begin for the marimba is an instrument of the middle distance and the listener should not be too near. She came to them as they finished. 'My really sincere compliments. It is irresistible and played with far more feeling that it is on the record. It is a triumph. Well, *hasta tarde*!'

'*Hasta tarde*, Señora,' they replied.

For the senior members of the Chicle Company's staff the approaching fiesta was not one of unalloyed pleasure. Their organization had made the arrangements so often that it was now merely a routine. Every man knew what he had to do and everything was done in such a manner that their first obligation, the gathering and transport of chicle, should be interrupted as little as possible. The fact that there were still men in the bush and that some chicle had still be to be brought in, was nothing new. It had happened before. The warehouses were bulging with the season's gathering. The couple of days respite over the period of the dance would be useful to rest the mules. The business of the transport over the frontier of the chicle blocks would then begin. Each man knew what he had to do. The muleteers and *chicleros* might have a couple of days respite but there would be no such easing for the office workers. The morning after the dance they would be on duty even if Mr. Delfosse had not turned so irritatingly and suddenly punctilious. He seemed now to consider each man utterly incapable of managing the most insignificant detail. It had to be checked and double-checked by him. This ultra-fastidiousness was something foreign to Mr. Delfosse said all the employees who had been under his management for any length of time. There were one or two who had been with him for only a short time and they considered his present attitude and actions to be a logical development of his attitude and actions over the last few months.

PART SIX

THE LISTENERS

The dance hall was a large thatched booth. The posts of stout hardwood had no other function than to support the roof for there were no walls. The roof was renewed from time to time but no one renewed the floor. That was of cut stone blocks smoothly joined and evenly surfaced. Gibberd declared that the floor was laid by the Ancient Maya about the time when Constantine was proclaimed Emperor of Rome. Being an honest scholar, however, he confessed that other experts put the date some centuries later at the early middle period of the old Empire of the Mayas.

Whether their dancing-floor was put down when Constantine was Emperor or when Justinian held that office, however, mattered little to the dancers unless they happened to be archaeologists. The floor had been uncovered some few years before when the village of Shoonantonitch had had grafted on to it a chicle camp and had also become a way station for archaeologists on their journeys to Tikal or Uxactun, or others of the great ruined cities of the Early Empire, and to their latest find the ruins of Caracol, less than a mile away. The dance hall was illumined by two kerosene pressure lamps with the glare from them tempered by garlands of coloured streamers hung just far enough away from the lamps to escape charring. As the hours passed the pressure in the lamps declined and the glare gradually dimmed. Then the Chinese lanterns were lit and what had started as a carnival took on a more intimate flavour.

The lady guests were provided with benches placed on two sides of the hall. Strictly speaking every unmarried woman should have been accompanied by her duenna. But there were not many unmarried or unattached women and there were so many men that a duenna had to take her position very seriously to escape an invitation to the dance floor.

A number of smaller booths had been constructed nearby. One of these protected the marimbas, the others were refreshment booths. The archaeologists had had a booth constructed for their own use, a private box, looking onto the stage. This was so convenient as a point of vantage that when the Commandante and his wife arrived together with the widow Aycenena they were glad to accept Dr. Gibberd's invitation to share it. They were to go to a more private place, at Fuad's, for supper after the midnight waltz.

Pedro brandished his hammer, struck the first note, the other *marimberos* rolled out the national anthem; the entire company stood; the music ceased; the function began. For the first half hour few dancers took the floor. There was a bashfulness, a hesitation and a spurt of conversation when the music started which died down as the talkers watched the few dancers circle the floor. Even after Mr. Delfosse and Señora Arevalo had danced the affair seemed to hang fire. But no one was worried, or so it seemed to Cutbush, the women sat in the tempered glare of the pressure lamps, placidly, without sign of impatience. Elsewhere in the shadows, however, matters were going well. A couple of searing drinks of aguardiente would cause this, or that, *chiclero* to turn to face the dance floor.

The man would look long and carefully and make up his mind. Then he would take a strategic location in the outer shadows and wait for the music. At the first note he would rush towards the lady of his choice elbowing aside others who had made the same choice.

One hour after it began it was evident that this was going to be a dance of dances. Some men had already been persuaded to sleep it off in the darkness where Arevalo had posted a few of his gendarmes. As soon as a man was seen to be getting obstreperous he would be watched and, at an inconspicuous moment and place, he would be edged out of circulation and kept out by the gendarmes until he guaranteed good behaviour. Those too far gone to guarantee anything were handcuffed to a distant tree. The sergeant in charge had arranged that his men should be well fed at the refreshment booths very early in the proceedings and that each man should be issued with three bottles of beer. Other liquors were put by for their benefit to be issued to them when they were relieved of duty.

Sundry folk, who had deserved well at the hands of the archaeologists, were invited to the private box for drinks from their private cellar. Gibberd who had a head which no amount of liquor could befuddle did the honours. When he saw Fuad and his henchman Jaime Peat-Patterson in the crowd he called them over and Karen invited them to sit down. Jaime had asked for a soft drink and had then asked Señora Aycinena for his first dance. Afterwards he took her back to her seat and thanked her gracefully.

'You are a beautiful dancer Mr. Peat-Patterson,' Karen told him, 'you dance as if you and your partner were ... ' She addressed him formally, not familiarly, as she had when they had been Dr. Howard's guests in El Cayo.

'Absent-minded?' asked Jaime laughing.

'No, absent I would say rather than absent-minded,' she replied. 'You must have had considerable practice; I envy you that. At my school we were not taught dancing so I learnt to dance late.'

'I also only danced seriously when I was well on. That is, in my twenties,' he said. 'It was at the same period in which I learnt to play chess. I danced seriously and played chess for diversion. But I had excellent partners in both. I danced all the time with a girl from Tangier. Spanish was our only common language. That was in Alexandria.'

'But,' suggested Karen, 'she did not teach you to play chess as well?'

'No, no though she told me that there are often times and seasons in a woman's life when she welcomes, even doubly welcomes a man who only cares to dance. She told me that when she danced with me she was at rest, or rather, "in neutral". She said it was a time of recuperation for her self-esteem. I know this sounds priggish but I welcomed and respected her confidence. However, I was not able to help her when she really did need a friend. I could not stand between her and fate.'

'But he can still talk like an educated man,' thought Karen. 'He can still feel and think.' And she again thought of her days with him at the doctor's house.

Jaime continued, 'Sometimes for hours we would dance and then I would play chess. It was a life of forms and ceremonies, the formality of a few hours in the morning at the quartermaster's office, then the ceremonial of the dance in the afternoon, then the far more refined, the sustained circumstance of the chess board during the evening and night.

'However, there is nothing more tedious than an old soldier's warmed-over battles, especially if they do not tell of death but of living death. Then there comes over the company an unease which nothing can cure but the departure of the ex-soldier. As I see other people coming to enjoy your hospitality... Señora, Gentlemen, many thanks. Pedro is calling to me. We are old comrades in arms, at various bar-counters, on both sides of the frontier.'

Pedro, when Jaime joined him, told him, 'Amigo, there is a little thing, she is recently from Chetumal. I have told her man that you are quite all right. He can turn over his Micaela to you and go off with his bottle. I have guaranteed you with him. There she is wearing green shoes. She is a natural dancer but she has experience as well. For the sake of good music, my friend, let us see, at least, one couple who know dancing!' He gave a gentle pull at his bottle, flourished his hammer and tapped the marimba tenderly, possessively. Those who knew Pedro stopped talking, some got ready to dance. The music came beseechingly from the trembling hammers. Jaime approached Micaela and bowed. She rose unsmiling. After a few tentative paces the watching Karen saw Jaime's countenance change. Innocence seemed to wipe away the years from his ravaged face. He was aware of the outside world but it was an awareness that caused him neither hurt nor alarm. For in the arms of his partner he was protected by the music. Pedro saw them dancing and his heart warmed within him.

'Ah yes,' he sighed gratefully, his music deepening in feeling, responding to the warmth of the artist, 'Jaime, amigo, you understand, you are able to understand.' But he could not further clarify his ideas. Even when painfully sober such clarification was beyond him. He abandoned any further attempt to think. He was happy. His dog looked at his adored master and was happy in his own way.

The news of the murder of Modesto had not yet reached Pedro but it could not now be long delayed. It was surprising that some at least of the *chicleros* from Silva's camp had not arrived to take part in the fiesta but they would be here by tomorrow or the next day at the latest. The messenger whom Fuad had sent to bring a mule had brought the mule that evening. According to instruction the animal was put in the corral behind the certain house on the road to Pusilha and tethered in the corral. The messenger was now too busy getting drunk to think much of his unusual errand. Fuad helped his amnesia by encouraging him with a large and potent bottle. When the messenger recovered, the mule would be near the frontier carrying Silva, with Jaime as escort.

'Of course, my friend, he is practically a dead man,' Fuad had told his employee of Silva. He had also told Jaime of Silva's present whereabouts and of the plan for his escape. 'I must help him to escape, but you have no need to imperil your life defending him. You owe him nothing. Your companionship and aid is the last thing I can do for him. We are all doomed, some sooner, some later, but he has brought his doom on his head too soon. It was his sense of humour that did it. He thought it was whimsical. Others did not think it so funny. And one thing. Do not come back. You hear me, do not come back unless I send Fatima a letter to tell you to do so.'

Some hour or so before the midnight waltz a message had reached Fuad from Delfosse. The messenger said the manager had been taken ill suddenly. He had not been feeling well for some hours but had made a point of doing his duty by dancing the first dance with the Commandante's lady. Now he was in bed and he would be grateful if Fuad would take over the management of the party.

In the booth reserved as a private box by the archaeologists Cutbush had been doing the honours. He was an indifferent dancer though he liked dance music in its proper time and place. However, as he explained to Harkness, 'I wasn't caught young enough to be unselfconscious of my own ineptitude on the dance floor.' His life as boy and adolescent had been in an environment where pleasures such as dancing were not only a road to perdition but, what was much worse, they were considered a waste of time.

'Too late I now know that time spent in guiltless pleasure is never a waste of time. But tell me, what has happened to Delfosse? I had heard he was an enthusiastic dancer.'

Harkness replied that Delfosse had not been well for the last few days.

'He has been off his food and generally irritable. Of course the end of the season is always a bit trying and these super-conscientious fellows feel it most. He may of course have a touch of malaria.'

Señora Arevalo was beginning to be anxious. Her husband was a temperate man. It was not often he drank to excess and his wife knew that such excess only took place when he was very worried. Tonight he appeared to have much cause for worry. He was drinking far more than she had ever seen him drink before but the more he drank the less elated he appeared to become. She knew that at this rate he would soon begin to weep and then become violently sick. Any remonstrance on her part would only precipitate the weeping fit. Arevalo, however, had some care for his dignity and for hers. He had determined to get drunk but he preferred to finish the unsavoury part of the drinking in private. He was desperately worried and the attitude of Delfosse made his anxiety well nigh unbearable. As he swallowed successive glasses of alcohol he went over his various transactions again and again in his mind. There was nothing on paper. Nowhere could anything be found in writing which implicated the Commandante in any dealings which were to his financial benefit. The small matter which was causing him so much concern was on the Chicle Company's books as a loan to Commandante Arevalo to be returned as soon as the company had use for it. On a possible charge of duplicity he had arraigned himself before himself and had pleaded guilty. Therefore he drank to excess tonight at the same time that his care for his dignity as a responsible officer and his regard for his wife prompted him to provide a life-line, an 'Exit in Case of Emergency'. Earlier that evening he had approached Cibrian and asked him a favour.

'You are my superior officer, Major, and I would beg you to

order me home as soon as my wife should ask you to do so. You see, now and again, I take too much to drink and I do not like it. In such a crowd behaviour of that sort would be bad for our Service. So may I depend on you ... that is if you are not intending to enter the spirit, or spirits, of the party to such an extent as to ... '

'No, my friend,' laughed Cibrian, 'I shall take the minimum. I shall be if not cold sober, yet sober. So I will do as you ask. When you go, I will, of course, have to remain here so will you let your sergeant know that he is to report to me?'

While Arevalo danced and drank Maria's anxiety for him increased. Being a considerate husband he could not be aware of her anxiety without allaying it. She was to him an everlasting mystery. It was as easy to hurt her as to crush the petal of a rose. Yet, at the same time, it was as difficult to break her resolution when the welfare of the children, or his own welfare was concerned, as it was to bend a steel bar. So he told her not to be alarmed. There would be no disgusting scene. Cibrian would look after him. Maria did not spoil his boyish pride at his astuteness in arranging matters so as to satisfy all parties. 'Why spoil his pleasure by reminding him he is a man and should act like one?' she asked herself and replied to the question with a shrug and the words, 'Why indeed?'

When, a little later, she danced with Major Cibrian she though it politic to thank him for his promise to her husband.

'He is worried,' she said. 'He tells me all his affairs and it seems he finds that there is uncertainty in the air and uncertainty acts on him like a high fever.'

'Señora,' said Cibrian, 'worry is a contagious disease. I worry because I am here doing practically nothing. He worries when he has done well all that he is required to do. And have you noticed that Mr. Delfosse is so ill or so worried, that he has had to leave? Let's hope that all that ails him is a touch of malaria. Only our American friends seem to have no anxieties. You know of course that tomorrow will be the Professor's birthday? As a birthday greeting there will be a song and the singer is the astonishing Mrs. Farr. She is certainly a lady full of silence and surprises. She will be singing in duet with the Maestro of the marimba.'

Maria, however, was too full of her own particular problem of the moment, her husband, to be impressed by Cibrian's information and he thought, 'It is a good thing that this dance is held only once in the season, for in a small and isolated community the particular problem of each person, or group, would soon intrude into the fiesta and spoil its community spirit. At any rate for one performance the bite of each person's problem can be curbed by good manners.'

Then he began to think again of Candellaria. He saw her dancing with Harkness. He watched her move with approval. She seemed to dance with an easy, graceful reticence. Their eyes met, he smiled warmly.

'Yes. My God, yes,' he said to himself, 'I am in love again. Yes, that's it. *Jesús*.'

After the dance with Maria he conducted her back to the private box and then strolled out into the shadows.

'This is a problem,' he mused, 'but why a problem? She is by no means the first. So why a problem?' And the answer which came to him was, 'She is a problem because she is the widow of the notorious Aycinena, the man who thought too much. Whether she too is condemned I do not know. Perhaps she is even now on the proscribed list. If so where will any new lover be? If I had an affair with her, what then? That is supposing she were sufficiently interested. Thank heavens I did not meet her when we were, both of us, in France.'

Cibrian was an ambitious man and he knew he was an able man. His career could be ruined by an intrigue with the widow of a 'secret enemy of the people'.

'I must be careful,' he told himself, 'I don't know what Dato had in mind when he sent me here; but even he could not have foreseen that I would become so interested in the widow of Aycinena.' Then a horrible thought struck him, 'Mother of Heaven, is it possible he wanted to inform me of the danger her husband had become? So dangerous that he could not be dealt with openly. Have I been warned that such danger is like an infectious germ and that there may even be innocent "carriers"? And is Candellaria a "carrier", even if an innocent one?'

He struck a match and lit his cigarette and, to his own

surprise, Cibrian suddenly found himself overwhelmed by a flood of bitter resentment, a cankered anger directed against his respected Commander-in-Chief, the omnipotent Dato, President of the Republic.

It was a resentment that was not caused by the fact of the assassination. Cibrian could be shocked at the heartless engineering of the crime but he was of the age and class to argue that such things might be necessary, therefore excusable. He was not angered by the atrocious ethics of the profession of Government which depended, above all, on the ethics, practised and accepted of the governed. He had long ago decided that all citizens, in fact, all men could be divided into two classes. The first class was composed of those who could accept responsibility. The second was of the vast majority to whom responsibility was a burden, something as foreign and unwelcome as a wen on the nose. This was a dichotomy which transcended ethics or, more precisely, the ethics of man as citizen. Cibrian accepted every man as a man and brother but only in the sense that each man was his brother and he and every other individual man was a son of God. In his personal attitude to each man as a brother in the eyes of God, Cibrian set no limit to his obligations, nor questioned the reach of the highest ethics as applied to this relationship.

'When,' he thought, 'my corporal and myself are not in uniform, then I can think of him as Jorge Castillo, a man who by trade is a corporal in the army, but, more important than his trade, is the fact that he is above all things a man. Then, too, I am eager for him to think of me as Felipe Cibrian, by trade a major of engineers but more important than my trade is the fact that I am a man, his brother. But when we are both in uniform, we are no longer brothers before God. God is once removed. Every single complication of human relationship removes God by a step. The corporal and myself when we are in uniform have accepted, with reference to each other, a relationship which puts us beyond the reach of the ethics of brotherhood. So, in the State, when we are born into a certain environment of country, of history, of customs, we are conscripted into an army of citizens. We have thrust upon us a great multitude of relationships some of which carry responsibilities. Those of us who can carry responsibilities are the officer class. And are we not once removed but many times removed from God. So the ethics of man as brother does not apply in the army. Nor does it apply in the more complex army of conscripts called the state where the rules and regulations cannot be based on the love of one's neighbour. There are no neighbours in an army, at the best they are comrades, at the worst units. Neighbours, never.'

Thus the need of Dato Graña to act by a code of ethics which had in it no command that one should love one's neighbour did not shock Cibrian.

His sudden anger at the President was in part anger against himself. He was outraged that he should be left in doubt; that Graña had left him forever in doubt as to whether he, Cibrian, had been warned away from all things pertaining to Aycinena. He could not be certain that the proscription applied to the widow as it did to the thoughts of Aycinena. Was the woman as taboo as the ideas? A definite order he could have understood. The doubt was like a neurosis, an anxiety which produced a fretful anger. He took command of himself.

'He may treat me,' he thought, 'as a child. But I must not react by angry tantrum. That is the defence of the weak. I shall do as I think fit in my own eyes.'

And still thinking of the President he said aloud, 'God help him.' Adding, to himself, 'I wonder if for the last twenty years he has ever thought of anyone as man and brother!'

At that moment a group from the 'private box' passed him. Mrs. Farr was amongst them. On seeing him she detached herself from the party and came up to him.

'I thought you would like to know, Major, the answer to the question you asked me to find out,' she said.

Cibrian had not the faintest idea of what she was talking about. He looked at her. 'And this is another one,' he thought, 'she has never been able to think of anyone as man and brother. All people to her are seen flat, in profile, illumined only by intelligence. Graña at any rate apprehends in the round. He sees the past, the present, the future and the potential. That is why he is great, inhumanly great.'

'Señora,' he said, 'I am a bit distracted. I don't quite understand.'

'You asked me to find out from Pedro where the old man lived, the old man who spoke for those whose hearts were full but could find no words to ease their burden.'

'Ah yes, of course, so I did Señora. And is there such a person?'

'Yes, indeed, he lives in an isolated house, a ruin leading off the frontier road about a mile from here. The lower part of the house has been repaired and made habitable for him.' She did not tell him that she had known the answer to his question months ago. After all she had been asked a favour and she had complied.

'Ah, thank you very much indeed. You are very kind,' he replied. But Karen knew that he was still distracted. Her information had been received and stored away. It had no reference to the present.

'I hope,' she said, 'your distraction will not be so great as to keep you from the dance floor for the next piece. It is the midnight waltz. It is a piece I induced Pedro to learn. You will know it, I think.'

It was the nearest she could get to ask him to dance with her. He had already done so once and they had talked easily if disjointedly. But he had danced with all the ladies of the private box once, and then with the wives of notables of the village. He had been doing his duty correctly. He was not, now, on a second round needing to dance for duty's sake. His brooding in the shadows had not escaped her notice. She longed to know what the subject was that had had impact enough to make him smoke so feverishly and had, as she saw when he lit another cigarette, made his brows contract and his face tighten to a mask of furious concentration. Now, he was no longer angry, but absent. He looked at her politely but distantly. At the first note of the marimba she turned towards the dance floor. The other *marimberos* touched their keys and began to play the midnight waltz. Cibrian looked at her. They walked together a few paces, then he was quite certain. It was Tchaikovsky's 'Waltz of the Flowers'. He did not notice that she had also stopped and looked at him. His memories overwhelmed him and with those memories came the bitterness, the remorse that he had caused pain to another person. She who had loved him and with whom he had often danced the 'Waltz of the Flowers'. He looked at

Karen Farr without seeing her then looked around and about. He was seeking some means of blunting his memories or assuaging his pain, or some person to whom he could say, 'We were doomed both of us to that pain from the beginning of the first act. Who can create a third act which, if it is not trite, is happy? No one. We were foredoomed to bitterness, anguish, futility. And yet I would that I could do penance for us both or, by some acceptable propitiation, I could absolve her and take onto myself her sorrow and add it to mine.'

They walked towards the dance floor. He had said no word of invitation to the waltz, but their walk towards where other dancers were already taking the floor seemed the walk of a couple about to dance. Then she saw that he had seen Candellaria Aycinena and was looking at her as if he had only now recognized her as someone whom he had known long ago and he was walking towards her. Karen stepped aside into the kindly shadow of a tree and watched. He did not hurry but there was in his pace an inevitability and in the set of his countenance a purpose as if he were mesmerized.

Candellaria saw him coming and as by the compulsion of a similar mesmerism she rose from her chair and went towards him.

Karen was saved from herself by a voice which said, in English, 'Would you care to dance, Mrs. Farr; or do you find the music too old-fashioned?'

She accepted Jaime's invitation gladly because it came at a moment when she found herself most vulnerable.

'This is providential,' she said to herself, 'perhaps these sudden little ironic gifts of Providence are all the blessings I deserve. He may be a pedlar's lackey, a ragged husk but he is no more empty than I am.'

'You mentioned your dancing friend of your Alexandria days, what happened to her?' she asked.

She was not particularly interested but it was a conversational gambit on which they could chatter emptily through the dance and the encore. By then it would be tomorrow. Jaime, however, did not consider Karen as a person who chattered. He thought over the question and then he replied, 'She was not strong, or rather, she had only one source of strength and when everything else, including myself, failed her, when she was faced with a situation beyond her resources she ... she ...' He sought for the right words.

'She didn't kill herself?'

'Kill herself? No. That would have been no solution for her. She was a Catholic. No, she left the freedom of the life of a prostitute; for that is what it was no matter how we try to cover it up with terms like "café-dancer". She left a freedom that made her the property for the time being of any man who had the money and she became, in holy matrimony, the property of a man she feared and loathed. Her pimp, her boss. He told her that as she was becoming less profitable at the café she had better become respectable as his wife. I heard from her a few years ago. He was still alive, and there were then about half a dozen children.'

As he spoke a bitterness and horror of which he was quite unconscious surcharged his simple words. She glanced at him. His face was pale and the lines of dissipation and disgust had deepened. He looked at that moment what he believed himself to be, a prematurely aged, hopeless, helpless hulk. A wreck of a man.

'Well,' said Karen to herself, 'I am enjoying myself! Hurrah for the "Waltz of the Flowers." And it is no use trying to temper the wind to this mangy wether,' she thought. 'He is a romantic at heart and such people believe that their kind of love is the only heaven and the desecration of that particular kind of love the last degradation. If I were to suggest that out of that loveless union his friend might well have got a child, or children, who more than compensated for the stale bed he would think it a joke in poor taste.'

It was an effort on her part to bring his mood back from the past that she mentioned the music.

'He is really pouring it on, is friend Pedro. You used a phrase about some music we heard from the Doctor's gramophone at El Cayo. Was it "sounds that shine"? I have a vague memory of it, I think from school days. Where is it from, do you know?'

'Yes,' Jaime said, brightening at once, 'it is Swinburne.'

'Ah,' said she, 'Swinburne, of course – of course.' But he was already quoting the poet as if he was speaking to himself,

'The pulse of war, the passion of wonder.
The heavens that murmur, and the sounds that shine,
The stars that sing and the loves that thunder,
All these are over and no more mine.'

'Thank you,' said she, 'it is not only with music that there are "sounds that shine." And that passage you read at the Doctor's from the Bible, I was so struck by its pertinence that I wrote it down.'

'Oh that,' he interrupted, 'yes – but Swinburne again says it in but four shining lines,

'He weaves, and is clothed with derision,
Sows, and he shall not reap;
His life is a watch not a vision
Between a sleep and a sleep.'

Neither spoke again while they danced. She was looking over his shoulder when she saw Candellaria glance quickly into Cibrian's face and then sink her head until her forehead touched his shoulder. He seized the opportunity of a discreet shadow quickly to kiss her hair. They passed out of the line of her vision. Karen's philosophy of romantic love might have furnished her with compensatory values when she discussed the case of Jaime's café-dancer but no philosophy protected her at that moment. A quick sickening pain, a hollow sense of loss touched her as she saw Candellaria bow her head.

Karen did not lose step though, since her partner was an expert, even she did not know how suddenly he felt her droop and saw life drain from her face. They did not speak again until, the dance being over, he conducted her to the 'private box', and thanked her politely. She replied suitably. As he turned away she saw Fuad take him affectionately by the arm and speak to him for a long time.

Again the widow Aycinena and Major Cibrian met, as it were, by mutual compulsion at the edge of the dance floor. They danced in silence for a few moments then he said, 'I saw you from afar and then I knew I was looking for you.'

'You said once before,' she replied, 'that you had seen me from afar ... like a landscape seen from an aeroplane. Do you remember?'

'Ah yes,' he said, 'but the last time it was not a survey. It was a seeking, it was urgent, a compulsion.'

'I know, I know,' she said, 'and I met you. I had to meet you. I came to meet you. You had been so distracted, so troubled, you smoked so furiously. It troubled me too, your landscape, but it was shadowed by dark clouds from afar.'

'Now I know the why of the urgency, I know what I have been seeking,' he murmured.

She tried to divert his intensity by facetiousness. 'What? A country of happy endings?'

He persisted, 'Happy? Am I a child to ask first and last for happiness, the password for puberty?'

In a sense of distress, her effort at levity dissipated and she asked, 'What do you seek, then?'

'From you and with you, peace and replenishment. Peace for the heart and replenishment for the exhausted, the frittered, the belittled mind.'

She glanced quickly at him and leaned her forehead on his shoulder for a moment. 'Oh Felipe. Help me to dare to live. I need the courage of your love.'

'Courage is all I can bring you,' he said, 'but enough for us both!'

The music ended while they stood silent gazing at each other hand in hand and the other dancers applauded the musicians. Pedro and his men were pleased to play an encore. Felipe Cibrian and the other member of the cast of a comedy in three acts began again to play their roles to the accompaniment of music by Tchaikovsky.

Now the author of the comedy had changed the character of the lines for the male. Cibrian was not now so certain, he did not preen the caudal feathers so expertly. He was actually a trifle humble having discovered a situation in which courage is not enough.

As they left the dance floor Maria Arevalo came up to them and said, 'Now that we have danced the midnight waltz it means tomorrow has arrived. So we shall have the duet in honour of the Professor's birthday and then, after that, supper.'

The announcement was made to the crowd that for a few minutes the dancing would be suspended and a song would be sung. It was a song in honour of Dr. Gibberd, one of the hosts of the dance and as it was his birthday.

The song was an old favourite and the crowd was invited to sing the chorus.

Then Karen Farr and Pedro sang, '*Adios, Mariquita Linda*' and the crowd joined in the chorus. It was a terrific success. Pedro was overjoyed, triumphant. He had sung with a foreign lady, a singer of distinction. At last his value, his real talents had been given recognition by those who knew, those who could appreciate him. They had honoured his talents by using them to pay tribute to their friend. The party of the Commandante paid their compliments and added congratulations to Dr. Gibberd with Medina deputizing for Mr. Delfosse and speaking for all the employees of the Chicle Company.

Gibberd found himself the centre of a happy group. He had not had the faintest idea that he had won the affection of his staff and the respect and liking of the camp and the village. They seized the opportunity to wish him 'Happy Birthday'. Lavish as were the preparations for the dance there were now signs that liquid refreshments would soon be running low. Gibberd's health was drunk, repeated copiously, then copiously repeated. The sergeant suggested to Pedro that a little music might save some of the liquor for later hours. Pedro tapped his *marimberos* with his rubber hammer. The music of a rhumba crashed out. The dance began again, less inhibited now. The sergeant no longer extricated the drunks focusing only on the obstreperous and cutting them out from the crowd like a cowboy cutting out steer from a herd. One pressure lamp flickered out. The light of the other was not quite so bright. Soon the only illumination for the dance floor would be the Chinese lanterns. The rhumba came to an end, to be repeated as the crowd roared '*Pedro – maestro – otra vez, otra vez.*' Pedro obliged. Then the music ceased and Pedro called for his bottle, but before he drank he had an idea.

He would thank Señora Farr publicly for her encouragement of music and her appreciation of the arts. He approached the archaeologists' booth and began his speech but his ideas were too complex for his tongue. He thereupon appealed to Major

Cibrian as scholar, officer and gentleman to second the vote of thanks. Cibrian readily, if not willingly, spoke of the great appreciation the village and the camps and indeed all that section of Petén had of their American friends. It was hardly necessary for him to say more for the spontaneous outburst of good feeling at the mention of the birthday of their leader, Dr. Gibberd, was evidence enough. He would however re-echo the words of the Maestro of the marimba and express the gratification of the crowd at the delightful musical interlude Mrs. Farr had given them. There was loud applause for Dr. Gibberd, for Mrs. Farr and for Pedro, the Maestro.

Pedro was enchanted, he thanked the Major, waving his hammer at his musicians and strutted back to the marimba. His bottle was thrust at him. His large, foolish dog trotted proudly after him. He had eaten to the point of refusal, or almost, for during Pedro's speech Karen had given him something more to eat. He had caught it as she threw it and others in the crowd followed her lead. He was Pedro's dog and it was the day of days for Pedro's dog.

Cibrian finished his speech. He received the thanks of Dr. Gibberd. As for Karen, she smiled, she looked at him, then at Pedro and at the dog and said, 'I think he weighs about 40 kilos, don't you?'

Cibrian did not answer, nor did he swear. He accepted that he could expect anything from Mrs. Farr and why not an irrelevant anti-climax, or was it humour? If it were humour, why the bitter smile when she repeated, 'Yes, about 40.'

'I see Fuad is calling us into supper,' he said, 'shall we go in?'

Afterwards, about an hour after the rain ceased, the sergeant reported to Cibrian. He said that a man, who had just told Pedro something, had arrived late last night. He and another man were the first to have come in from the distant camp where Modesto Moreno, Pedro's friend, worked as a *chiclero*. The newcomer had enjoyed himself at the dance and it was not until the free-for-all after the song that he seemed to have drunk too much, too quickly. He may have been annoyed at Pedro's triumph, he may have wished merely to be the first with bad news. It may have been witless cruelty or cold malice. The sergeant did not know.

The whole thing started strangely when Pedro's dog commenced to bark with a distressingly hoarse sound and to run in crazy circles with the diameter of the circle becoming smaller as the way the dog ran became more jerky. Some of the crowd laughed. 'You have been feeding him the bottle, Pedro,' they cried, but Pedro was distressed. Then the dog stopped his jerky running and continuing his distressing barking he came slowly, jerkily and quietly to Pedro. There he sat down and began to scratch himself with alternate hindlegs, the scratching action becoming gradually less purposeful then slower and feebler. Finally, he settled near Pedro's feet and, as though his head could no longer support the eyes which were gazing into Pedro's face, it dropped to earth. As his master knelt by the dog a man approached. He spoke rapidly, quietly and insistently to Pedro. The latter sprang to his feet and grasped the man by the shirt.

'What is that? What is that?' he shouted.

Those nearby heard the man say, 'It is the truth. I tell you. They will say a snake bit him, but that is not so. He did it. He did it, I tell you.'

Pedro dropped his hands from the man and turned completely around. He appeared to be looking into the distance for something or someone to appear on the horizon. He raised a hand as if to shade his eyes the better to see into some incalculable distance before he turned again to find that the man who had brought the tidings was no longer there.

Then Pedro knelt and gathered the dying dog in his arms and remained kneeling, while the rain poured over them, alone on the dance floor. Great drops of water danced around them. Then, gradually, as if the music made by the rain had passed out of hearing the deluge had ceased and Pedro had begun to scream. He was mourning and it was not only for his dog. Another shower of rain had sluiced down across the Maya dance floor, and before what was left of the fiesta and the drinking could continue. By then, however, the women had taken advantage of the lull between the showers and had gone to their homes.

Those who had been Fuad's guests, both ladies and gentlemen, asked Jaime to tell him of their thanks for his gracious and copious hospitality. They regretted that he had had to leave on sudden urgent business so that they could not tell him personally but they quite understood that a man of affairs, so many affairs, would have sudden and imperative calls from those who needed his help, or guidance in an emergency.

They had left and Jaime had waited.

Fuad returned about an hour later. The dance hall was peopled only by a couple of sodden drunks, blissfully unconscious. Pedro was no longer there.

'This *is* a business,' said Fuad to Jaime, 'That damn, stupid fool did not remain where I put him on this night of all nights. Delfosse called me to tell me amongst other things that someone had entered his office. They must have had a key, for the door was not broken. Whoever they were they took some money he had in a drawer, not much, a couple of hundred dollars.

'But what is more disturbing is that they took a notebook from the drawer. It contained notes he had made on certain transactions. Nothing in it that was too bad but some facts might be difficult to explain. He did not say it but it is clear he meant "difficult" if Cibrian got further orders from Guatemala City to probe into the chicle business. Then something else came out. I suppose he had to talk to someone for his other affairs had crashed. He told me that his cousin and himself were in the same sort of business in Cuba. It was the same cousin who had been a rum-runner with Belize as his base. He, Delfosse, had put all his savings in it. It sounded to me like a casino. Then the bigger-boys from the States wanted to take over. They said the President of Cuba was about to give them the monopoly. But his cousin did not act fast enough and his business was closed by Presidential order. Penniless, he was booted out of Cuba. Delfosse said, pathetically, "For the second time '*El Gordo*' has escaped me. For the past three weeks I have been near madness, hoping against hope." He also said he had already resigned his post with the Company here and that signature Cibrian made him write across the pages of his office books means that he can no longer claim his private cut.

'I promised him I'd try to find his notebook if the thieves had not yet destroyed it. I would put out a whisper of a heavy reward for a quick return. I left him then and went to where I had left

Silva. I saw how that reprobate had crossed over the chicle blocks in my warehouse to Delfosse's office and how he had entered by a window looking towards the inside of the warehouse. But he was not where I had left him. I was afraid he might have broken into Mrs. Farr's house, too. But she came in just as I was about to leave. I could see her through her window. There was a black covered book on her table. She opened it, took up her pen as if to write in it but closed it. Then she opened the drawer of the table took out some paper and began to write. She showed no sign of agitation so I thought I must have been wrong but, as she wrote, it seemed to me tears fell on the paper. She wiped her eyes and started to write again. Then I left. Our problem is to find that bastard Silva and get him away before Pedro gets him or, worst of all, before Pedro connects him with us.

'I have no idea where he is at the moment but as Pedro, from what you tell me, won't be active till tomorrow, let us turn in and wrestle with it at breakfast. Good night.'

By early afternoon that same day Shoonantonitch yawned to tardy wakefulness and some purposeful activities seemed to start taking place. Amongst the first to be active were two messengers who rode in purposefully within half an hour of each other and with obvious relief dismounted. Each carried a small parcel, one for Fuad, the other for Cibrian. The parcels were in waterproof containers made specially for letters and other papers.

Fuad's letter was from Fatima. It was written in Arabic in her own hand. He read it carefully. Re-read it even more slowly then tore it up into very small scraps. Even then he did not seem to be satisfied with the destiny of the letter. He gathered up the scraps, poured a little kerosene oil on them in a frying pan and burned them. Even the smell of the kerosene seemed to him to linger too long and too significantly after he had ground the ashes to a spoonful of dust. Then he went to see Jaime.

Cibrian received several letters from his messenger. Some were official others were private. One, it seemed, was too private to be read more than twice for, like Fuad, he tore it up into small scraps and burned them.

Maria Arevalo awoke to a relaxed feeling of quiet content and relief and accomplishment. Near her, he who had given her so much concern the night before, slept peacefully. She was proud of his restraint, of his acceptance of a role when as Commandante he could never, never be less than in complete command of himself. She decided to make some coffee and, if Candellaria was awake, to take her some. So as not to awaken her husband she quietly got out of bed and left for the kitchen. In a few minutes she gently pushed open Candellaria's door with a cup of coffee in her hand. She stopped suddenly and almost screamed with fright.

Candellaria was awake for she was standing. It was the attitude in which she stood and the expression on her face which caused the shock. She was gazing into space or, perhaps, at a distant landscape. In her left hand she held a non-existent palette. In her right hand there was an equally insubstantial brush. She did not speak when Maria whispered 'Good Morning' but remained motionless like a figure in a display of waxworks.

Maria backed out of the room carefully and sped to her own bedroom where she shook her husband awake. He was about to speak when she put her hand over his mouth and told him what she had seen. He became alert and spoke his first thought, 'They say these people can have relapses.'

He had known as little as Maria about 'the nervous breakdown' which Candellaria was said to have had in France. He knew that she had been ill for 'some time' in a 'nursing home'. How long he could never find out without direct questioning but he had come after talking to Dr. Hastings in El Cayo, to certain conclusions which he had never told Maria. The Doctor had spoken of mental sickness and had told him, amongst other things that there were some patients who became like automatic dolls. It was a symptom called 'Catatonia'.

'I shall be with you in a minute,' he told his wife 'In the meantime tell the maid she is not to enter the room. Say the Señora has caught a chill and is feeling very poorly. Say anything but keep her out of the way.'

He dressed quickly and was about to join Maria when there

came an imperative message from Major Cibrian 'Would the Commandante come to his office at once; an urgent matter has come up.'

He peeped into Candellaria's room, saw what was to be seen and, despite the foreknowledge, he could not wipe the shock from his face before Maria saw it.

'Stay by her door,' he said, 'listen if there is any sound, but don't go in unless she calls you. I will be back as soon as I can.'

Not far away Fuad earnestly told Jaime, 'Something has come up. I received a letter from Fatima this morning. We *must* find Silva and you and he *must* start out tonight. Boot him over the frontier then go on to Fatima and wait there. Don't come back. *Don't come back*. If I want you to return I will send a message to her to give to you. As for Silva, I think I know where he hid amongst the blocks of chicle. You and he will have to leave here separately tonight then meet somewhere not far from here. Now let us try to find him.'

Karen decided when she woke late that morning to tread the remainder of the day delicately. She had some business to conclude with Miss Quinn and Gibberd but that was a matter of office routine. At some convenient time it would be arranged. She hoped she would not meet Cibrian, at least, not today and after that as fleetingly as possible before she left. As for Jaime another fleeting encounter would suffice.

However she remained much longer with Miss Quinn and Gibberd than she had anticipated because letters had arrived for Cutbush and Gibberd from the Nethersole Foundation as well as personal letters for all the members of the archaeological group.

In the meantime Fuad had retrieved Silva. The latter had found half a bottle of whisky in Delfosse's office which had been enough to keep him semi-comatose between a few blocks of chicle while Fuad hunted for him. He had been returned to his designated hiding place. From his window there he saw Karen leave her house after carefully locking her door. He could see the nearly full bottle of whisky that he had seen before and he remembered she had put something in it, some powder from a small glass tube which was in the drawer of her table. Then there was also the black book. There were things in the book which he had stolen from Delfosse which he could understand. He would have great fun later, say next year, when he would approach various people he knew with 'interesting' information. Perhaps La Farr's black book would also offer possibilities for other fun. He would try the bunch of keys which was amongst the loot from Delfosse's office. If she did not return by the time night fell and a key fitted the lock there were great possibilities for some fine sport.

Karen did not come back and one of his keys fitted the cheap lock she had on her door. He took the bottle of whisky. He also took the book and the glass tube of 'medicine'. He looked for money in the drawer; there was none. He grabbed a few bits of paper he found there which had writing on them and stuffed them and the glass tube into his pocket. Then he locked the door and returned through the chicle store and back to his hiding place to find Fuad waiting for him.

'Hand over everything,' said Fuad. 'A book. Good. Damn the whisky. What else, nothing? Where is that other book, Delfosse's book? Hand it to me. Good, now wait here. Any other damn fool move and I will call Pedro to you. I am fed to the brim with you.'

Fuad came back in about half an hour. He said, 'I will give Delfosse his book. Give me the bottle of whisky. Also I will take back La Farr's book. Hand me the key. You have spilt the whisky? How much was there? I have a bottle in my office. I will top it up and return it with her book. Wait here I will bring you food.'

Silva watched Fuad open Mrs. Farr's door, put the book on the table and the nearly filled bottle of whisky on the shelf. Then he quickly stepped back out of the room and locked the door. As Fuad left her house Silva felt in his pocket a glass tube and bits of paper.

Fuad was glad not to have had more than a few minutes with Mrs. Farr's black book. To his amazement he found she had written in Arabic. He was but an elementary scholar of that language. He could not appreciate any elegance or finesse of diction but he knew enough to see that it was not a business journal though the names of people he knew were mentioned. In the last few pages there was, for instance, the name of the Doctor of El Cayo and in English, the words, 'a wether who knew the most devasting poetry.' There were other things which he had no time to ponder. This was a woman for whom he had always had the most discreet respect. Now this proof of the breadth of her scholarship frightened him. 'With such a creature one never knows.' So the black book went back on Karen Farr's table. The bottle of whisky was also returned to its place.

Karen had supper with Miss Quinn and Gibberd and they arranged to visit the Priest's House that night when the evening star rose. Then a message came from Cibrian.

It was for Gibberd. Would he please see the Major immediately. It was a royal command so Gibberd had to go. In a few minutes he sent back word. He could not be with them for the rest of the evening.

Then Miss Quinn saw Jaime passing by. 'That's it,' she said. 'Let's ask him to play Gibberd's role. I can't go back to America without having heard this marvellous bit of old Maya cunning, no, not cunning, craft. He knows you better than he knows me, Karen, perhaps you could ask him?'

So Karen hurried after Jaime and asked him if he would be so good as to go with Miss Quinn and herself to the Priest's House there, when the evening star rose, to speak from the top floor of the House. They would be waiting below at the place where Cibrian had indicated.

Jaime was not sure if he could. He had something to see about. If it could be arranged he would be happy to go. He would return in less than half an hour to give her his answer.

Watching her as Karen stood talking to Jaime, Miss Quinn got an idea that her interest in Jaime might have been somewhat more personal than it had been at the beginning of the season; that, perhaps, it had had to do with the trip she had taken some weeks ago, to Belize, and especially after that. She had seen the same expression before on Karen's face, an expression fleeting and muted, when she had looked at Jaime. But Miss Quinn was nobody's fool. She held Karen in deep respect, in fact, in fear. 'She is someone with whom I should always be on good terms,' she admonished herself. 'God help anyone who arouses her animosity.'

Then Jaime returned. He told them he would be glad to go with them. In about an hour's time he would come for them. He would be leading his mule for he would prefer to go on after he had said his piece. But when the moon rose the walk back for them would be glorious. Nevertheless if they wanted him to come back with them he would do so because his errand was not pressing.

So it was arranged. Miss Quinn would hear the acoustic masterpiece, the sounds of wonder when Venus reached a certain mark and the moon a certain angle. 'By the way,' she said to Karen 'I had a note from Copius a couple of days ago. Yes, we got to be fairly friendly. He will not be coming back. In fact he will stay in Germany. He had told me he had two sisters, both married, with children there. His mother had gone to see them. It sounds odd to me but if he goes to Germany to work there the sisters and his mother would be allowed to leave for America. That is what some authority there let him know. So it is a swap. The information was in a letter waiting for him at the Company's office in Belize.'

To Fuad, Jaime's engagement to escort the ladies was a stroke of luck. 'Look,' he said 'we dress the bastard as a woman. He is small enough. We put him on the mule in a hat and scarf. He will be on the way before the moon comes up and if anybody sees him, even Pedro, the rider on the mule will be a lone woman riding quietly, doubtless to visit some sick relative. He will wait for you somewhere near the Priest's House but not too near lest anybody visiting the "Speaker" should see him. Then you go and speak your piece from the Priest's House and when that's done you join him and together set out for the frontier. You will then proceed to Fatima. You can give Silva the shotgun and the cartridges which you have been carrying. He will have the weapon tied to his saddle when he leaves here. His skirt will almost cover it. I have taken away all his pistol ammunition but left one bullet in the gun in case he meets Pedro. In his saddle-bags there will be food and cartridges. I have some women's clothes in stock and a shotgun and cartridges.'

So Silva was fitted out. At the last moment he begged for a bottle of whisky. Fuad gave it to him, a whole bottleful.

Gil Silva set out, his mule moodily pacing off into the darkness.

About an hour later Jaime met the two ladies as had been arranged. As the moon began to rise Jaime suggested that he ride rapidly ahead of them, get to the Priest's House and when they signalled, with their electric torches, he would reply with his own before starting to speak. They would not have to wait long for it took only ten minutes' riding to reach the Priest's House from where they would have to stand and wait. When they accepted this suggestion Jaime spurred his mule to a brisk trot.

Following a leisurely walk the two ladies reached the appointed place where Karen pointed out to Miss Quinn that from where they stood the Priest's House was, as the crow flies, about 300 yards. The building stood on a slight hillock above the plain amongst some trees. However, there was a ravine between where they stood and the House. It was not conspicuous and the path that was apparent to them, on their side invitingly so, did in fact lead down to the ravine but half-way down it had broken away and was dangerous to anyone who tried it.

Jaime would have had to ride about a quarter of a mile further on, go down a steep slope to the bottom of the ravine, then go up a matching slope and ride for another quarter mile to the Priest's House.

As they waited the two women, wrapped in their own thoughts, remained silent until Miss Quinn said, 'The star is just passing the bar of the window so we should see the flash of Jaime's torch at any moment.' But the silence dragged on without the expected signal until both women suddenly became rigid with shock as they heard the voice of Gil Silva as if from a room next door.

He said, 'Now, all together. You, Speaker or whatever your name is, take his head. Don't be a fool. Take your hand from his mouth and nose. Pedro take his legs. Now, all together, lift.'

And just as clearly they heard Pedro respond, 'Easy does it, careful of that arm there. You don't want to dislocate it do you? And give me that bottle. In fact, I had better keep it. You have had too much. To go and do such a damn silly thing. You must be out of your mind.' 'Jaime was a stupid fellow'. Came the response from Gil. 'So obstinate. I told him I had to finish the drink first.'

'Well, you are a fool. If you hadn't stopped for that drink I wouldn't have spotted you. This is damn good whisky. Here is to your last slow, very slow hour. But why did you shoot him. Or if you had to shoot, why not blow his head off? Why press the gun into his chest. There was hardly a sound. Why did you do it?' There was no mistaking Pedro's hoarse voice.

'Oh – playful like. You see it struck me as a sort of joke. He had to hide me away from you. But in order to do that he must come up on top of this old house and make a speech. In order that I should not spoil his speech by running away he wanted me to come up here with him, promising not to say a word. I promised to come up and not to say a word and offered him a drink. He wouldn't have it. So I thought it would be a damn good joke if I went off with his mule and in fact dressed him up like a woman as he had dressed me up. If he had had the drink we could have talked it over. But he was so damn obstinate. So I said, if Pedro is to kill me, why don't we go after Pedro first. But he would not see it like that. On no. Who the hell does he think he is? He can't come the gentleman on me. Damn it. I know where he comes from. I know his mother. She doesn't own the place any more but they still keep her as housekeeper or something and they say that when business is extra good and a customer is urgent enough and drunk enough they call her to attend to him provided she is still sober and that she is not there when he wakes up to see that she is as old as his mother and looks like his grandmother. Mind you I am not saying it was not a good whore house when she ran it. Pity she lost it. It's not as good now as in her time when Gaskin bought it for her and his chauffeur. But that chauffeur mortgaged it behind her back and ran away from her taking the nicest of the merchandise with him. After that chauffeur went the people who lent him the cash foreclosed on her but did not close the business.'

There was a loud clink of metal striking rock and Pedro expostulated again more loudly. 'You could have brained him by throwing that pistol at him. What is the matter with you, half wit?'

'Well, what was he looking like that at me for and moving his lips as if he were praying for me. They call him "Speaker", but he is too insolent to speak or pray for me. Anyway, let's have another drink. I had no more bullets in that gun. I looked.'

Karen and her companions sat their mules in stunned silence while the two men in the tower, forgetting its ancient Maya properties, filled the night with their evil conversation. Once or twice Karen shook her head as if to deny that she was hearing the terrible drama that was taking place. No one moved, however, because the ravine divided them from the ghastly scene which had taken place and was continuing to take place.

'Thanks,' Pedro's voice floated through the night to them. 'You know there is something about this drink. It does things to you. Even though I know you are *loco* and a murderer I can't get excited about killing you because that is what I have got to do, isn't it?'

'Sure, sure. But tell me first, what the hell are you doing up here with the, the ... Sh ... Shpeaker?'

'Speaker is an old frien' of mine, see? We, we do favours for each other. Señora Arevalo knew we were close so she asked me to let her know how things were with him. He would never ask but if I knew that his coffee was running low or his quinine tablets had finished, I would tell her and she would let me have the necessary. I would visit him and he would get it. And he would do me favours. For example, he was comfortable to sit with when one didn't want to talk. We would sit quiet for hours. I wanted to be quiet tonight, to mourn my old dog. But not by myself. He never has to know what is wrong to be sympathetic. Bit like the old dog himself. He was happy when I was happy sad when I was sad. So I came to sit with him tonight. Then, tomorrow I would be after you, after you for ever and ever, amen.'

'Sure, sure, I understand.'

The bottle clinked against something and Pedro asked, 'Where did you get this drink? Best whisky I ever had.'

'I got it from Señora Farr. Special. She put some medicine in it. I could see her from where I was hiding. The medicine was in a little glass tube. I got into her house, took the bottle, a black book she had on her table, a glass tube and some scraps of paper from the desk. Fuad was as frightened as hell. He put back the black book and another bottle of whisky. He didn't know about the bits of paper. *Saudé*. That's a strange one, La Farr. She would sit with the black book open before her for perhaps an hour then write for a minute or two, or perhaps shut it without writing, continuing to just sit. Sometimes she wrote but not in the book. Here are a couple of papers from her desk. One sounds like a funeral service. I could read it for you because you have to have a service before an execution.'

'That's good: read your own funeral service. Here take another drink and then begin. Here is Jaime's electric torch.'

'All right.' There was a pause then Gil spoke again, 'It's in English but you know enough to understand. "We were in El Cayo and the Doctor said something about the profession of medicine and the position of women in it and in other professions. His point was that the more successful women were in the professions, especially in the scientific professions, the more they found themselves in a sterile backwater deprived of the vitalizing responsibilities and heartbreaks of raising a family.

'"Then Jaime said that the finest statement he knew of the pride of endeavour and the disillusionment that women suffer was somewhere in one of the Prophets. He got up and took down a Bible from the Doctor's bookshelf and quickly turned over the pages 'Yes, here it is!' he said. Then he read:

'You said of yourself I shall be mistress forever.
You said I am and there is no other beside me.
You felt secure in your incantations.
Your knowledge and your wisdom led you astray.
And you said in your heart – I am, and there is no one beside me!
But evil shall come upon you, for which you cannot atone.
Disaster shall fall upon you, which you will not be able to expiate,
Let them save you who divide the heavens
And who gaze at the stars.
No coal for warming oneself is this
No fire to sit before.
Such to you are those with whom you have laboured,
Who have trafficked with you from your youth.
They wander about each in his own direction
And there is no one to save you.'

'"So he finished and I carefully thanked him and asked him to write out the passage. I told them I would read it over again later on. I was careful, very careful, cool and amiable for I could not let them know that I had heard the summing up and the sentence of the court. I could not let Jaime see that I had died. He had, unknowing, or perhaps uncaring, for he is far more subtle than he pretends to be, he had read my epitaph. I dared not look full at him. I died. I longed to touch him, this failing wreck, this lackey existing on the goodwill of a carrion crow, carrion that would buy or sell anything. I longed to touch, to embrace, to protect, to cherish this crow's peon. I longed to take him in my arms, to know him so that he should give me, that fulfilment, that warming of oneself from the fruits of one's own self, one's own body."'

There was a pause. Then Pedro said happily, in Spanish, 'If you say it is interesting it must be. All the English I have, I learnt on the docks in Belize.' But Gil was too excited about the fragments of paper he must have been holding because he started to speak again. 'All the writing here is in some sort of scribble I can't read. Perhaps it's Arabic or something. Now- ... wait ... here she goes back to English, Listen.'

'"It was the judgement of Paris. I dared not look at Cibrian. He had toasted the other three women as well. I dared not look at him but I had to. The music seemed to stagger and fall in time with my heart. Then it stopped. The music died away as I did for he spoke of me but had looked into her widow's eyes while he smiled. Then I heard them laughing, they were laughing at me, with me, for I also was laughing but at myself. Then I saw the dog, like me he was poisoned. My poison, the poison I had taken was the hope that Cibrian would look at me as he drank. The dog, with the other poison in him that I had given him, the Tontonec poison, walked with a spastic gait. It was an experiment. My heart also beat with a spastic gait, with a slow, straightened jointless effort and my breathing was even more witless and irksome."' He went back to Spanish, 'But enough of this. The first piece I read mentions this crow's peon's name so let's stuff it in his pocket. Like that. Good. Bottle's getting light. Then I'll tell you what. You have no gun, neither have I. So what about playing hide and seek amongst the trees with our machetes. You want to kill me. All right, it is no game for you unless I try to kill you. Yes? Good, now let's go and play tit for tat amongst the trees. We will go down the ladder and at the bottom we will each take our own road to the trees and the game is on. And, by the way, I have some more liquor in my bag on the mule. After the first round we will stop, have some drinks and start again. Right?'

Then after a couple of agonizing minutes while the listeners on the other side of the ravine seemed to have been turned to stone and following the sound of footsteps moving away another voice said, 'Jaime. Jaime can you hear me? Yes, I knew you had come out of your faint. That was why I put my hand over your mouth lest you should speak or groan. Yes they have gone. They are down there like children playing, walking stiffly, waving their machetes, jabbing at each other like puppets but not near enough to hurt each other. A slow motion puppet play and they laugh as they go through the motions.

'Now Jaime I must leave you here to go for help.'

Then they heard Jaime say, 'Water, water ... '

And the new voice reply, 'Here is water in the flask that fellow dropped. Drink my son, drink of Sister water, so useful, humble, precious and chaste.'

Jaime whispered, 'And Brother Sun.'

Then the listeners heard the voice intoning and Jaime responding.

'Most high omnipotent Good Lord,
To Thee be praise and glory, honour and blessing.
Be praised my Lord with all Thy creatures.'
To which Jaime replied,
'And most of all for Monsignor Brother Sun
Who makes the day for us and the light.
Be praised my Lord for Sister Moon and all the stars.
In heaven Thou hast made them precious, bright and fair.
Be praised My Lord for Sister water,
Useful, humble, precious and chaste
Be praised my Lord for our mother ... '

Then Jaime's voice broke and the Speaker remained silent until Jaime continued,

'Be praised my Lord for our mother, Sister Earth
'Who doth support and keep us.'

Then there was a silence until Jaime said strongly and with conviction,

'Be praised My Lord for Sister Death
From whom no man living can escape.
Happy they who find themselves within Thy Will
Because on them the second Death can work no harm.'

After that there was silence until they heard the voice say, 'He is gone God rest his soul. *Miserere – mei Deus secundem magnam misericordiam*. According to the multitude of Thy tender mercies blot out my transgressions. Wash me thoroughly from mine iniquity. And cleanse me from Sin. Against Thee only have I sinned and done evil in thy sight that Thou might be justified when Thou speaketh and be clear when Thou judgeth. For behold I was shaped in iniquity and in sin did my mother conceive me.'

PART SEVEN

THE CAVE OF THE VASE

Cutbush and Harkness met in the early afternoon as they had arranged at the archaeologist's office.

They had decided not to let the bad news of Jaime's seemingly pointless death when he was with the Speaker, or the fact that two drunken lunatics were chasing each other in the bush, with machetes and deadly intent, interfere with their plans. It was not because they were unfeeling but because they knew there was nothing either of them could do to mend the situation. Neither of them had been particularly close to Jaime and both of them were practical men of science who took the view of death that Samuel Butler had expressed in his notebooks. There he wrote, 'To die is to leave off dying and to do the thing once and for all.' It was an aphorism that was to come back and haunt Cutbush before long and make him wonder if the attitude it expressed was not a shade too glib.

'First Pedro's dog and now Jaime,' Harkness said as they set out, 'both victims, it seems, of alcoholic poisoning.'

'Are you sure it was alcohol that killed the dog and drove those other two to murder?' Cutbush asked as he climbed clumsily into his saddle.

Harkness ruefully confessed that he could not remember very clearly anything that happened after Mrs. Farr and Pedro sang. When Cutbush described the symptoms the dog showed and its manner of dying Harkness agreed that it might be a poison.

'Perhaps,' he said, 'some wit had been soaking cake or bread in aguardiente and thrown pieces to the dog. A sort of propitiatory libation or gift to the scapegoat. That stuff last night would kill any self-respecting dog. Only an animal lower in any scale of values than that dog could survive that drink. I know, I survived it but only just.' And he held his head gently with both hands.

'Why,' he complained, 'should I have been denied the blessing given to a dog?'

Cutbush kept a sympathetic silence for a while then asked, 'Is it true that you are not leaving at the end of the chicle season, that you will be here all during the dry weather?'

'Oh yes, it is true. You see I am not on the permanent staff of the Chicle Company. I worked down to the Petén plains from the mountains, the Alta Vera Paz. The Chicle Company was here or rather its immediate predecessor was. It paid them to have a botanist on their staff and it paid me to assuage the anxiety of tomorrow's bellyful. With that off my mind I have been able to do more in the last two years than I thought I would be able to do in five. My first few years in this part of the world were grim. At the end of that period I was in the hospital at Quetzaltenango, Guatemala, with pellagra. I was dying from malnutrition and overwork.

'That did not surprise me. I had accepted the risk with my eyes open but what worried me was that the notes I had made would never be published if I died there and then. Then my luck turned. A friend appeared. He arranged that copies of my notes be sent to him and to the Linnean Society in Stockholm. Then he established a fund. I could either eat out of the fund or publish the first two volumes with it. However, I had to promise that if I ate I had to eat enough and properly. At the end of seven years the fund would pass to the society to publish the first four volumes. He said that few men have more than one book in them and no man, with the exception of half-a-dozen in the whole history of the world, should write more than four books on any subject.'

'That, surely,' said Cutbush, 'was most generous of your friend but why pass the fund to the society? Why not pay you the money instead of a royalty and let the society pick up any income there might be?'

'Oh no, that idea would shock him. His attitude is, "Do you wish to do research on the fungi of Mid-America? Do you think it is a worthy task on which to spend the best years of your life? Very well, I will publish your results but you must realize you have spent your coin. If you live after your life's work is done then you must make shift for yourself."'

'My God,' said Cutbush, 'what a curious customer he must be. Surely it would have been better if he had made you the offer of a job, something in your line and thus provided for you?'

'As a matter of fact he did. It was a wonderful job, a wonderful idea. Unfortunately he is the sort of man it would be torture to fail. And I don't think I have in me that streak of uninhibited imagination which everyone recognizes as the touch of genius. What he offered was a job that needed a genius. If the genius was in good form he would bring enduring blessings to mankind and solve a problem which every gardener since Adam has bemoaned.'

'And the job which cried for the genius, what was it?' Cutbush asked.

Instead of replying directly Harkness told him, 'You see this friend of mine likes Victor Hugo and you will call to mind that remarkable passage about the sewers of Paris in *Les Misérables*. Well his idea was that I should investigate the breakdown processes of sewage. Sow it with fungi which I should discover. I should educate my fungi so that the sewage of the city would be denatured and made into fertilizer. In other words I should do to the sewage of Guatemala City, without offence to smell or sanitation, what the Chinese farmer does with village night soil.'

'Oh, to Guatemala City? So your friend is?'

'Yes,' replied Harkness, 'Deodato Graña.'

'But you know,' said Cutbush, 'that is a marvellous idea. I mean that is really germinal. Do you know any fungus that would do the trick?'

'No I don't but I am sure that it is only fungi that can do it. They are the answer to most biological difficulties. We have been using them ever since the first lump of wheat dough became accidentally contaminated with the yeast fungus and resulted in the light and porous loaf. But there are other uses for them now. Why only a year or two ago a chap named Fleming, in London, isolated a principle which he named penicillin. He extracted it from a very common fungus, *Penicillin notatum*, so common as to be a nuisance. Fleming found it destroyed the staphylococci of boils. It is a small beginning but do you know what that means? Why, that in a hundred years from now, no one will die of a germ disease. Pneumonia in the heart of Asia will kill as rarely as cholera now kills in London. But to return to Graña's idea. I am certain it is the next great advance in agriculture. Eventually, of course, the need will supply the urge to the solution. The need is getting more urgent by the day as the cities of the earth are getting larger and their sewage, or most of its bulk, goes into the unresponsive ocean. Hugo, as I have said, has a remarkable passage about it.'

After a few minutes' silence Cutbush asked, 'Do you know Deodato Graña well?'

'No,' replied Harkness, 'and I don't want to! My own little piddling private hell is enough for me. I doubt if anyone knows him well. But I do know that, to me, he is abnormal, a "sport". He differs from the run of the species. If he were a rose or a zinnia one would try to propagate him as a new variety, something rich, rare, strange ... and poisoned. Not poisonous, but poisoned or rather fated; loaded with its own perdition. Why he is so different that I don't even feel for him that resentment which one would naturally feel towards another person to whom one is immeasurably indebted; indebted beyond the bounds of repayment and outside the reach of words of thanks.'

For some obscure reason Cutbush had a feeling of acute discomfort. Harkness spoke with neither bitterness nor cynicism. Indeed, he spoke warmly and appreciatively of his friend. But that he a sane, literal scientist should, when speaking of Graña, employ terms like 'fated' and 'poisoned' seemed unnecessary.

To move the subject to a more commonplace level he asked, 'Is he much of a ladies' man? Is there a Madame President with or without concubines on the side? Or is there a presidential harem?'

'There is a Señora Graña. She is an invalid and lives in Paris or the Riviera, or so they say. I hear that he does not find women completely unnecessary but there are some curious tales about his mistresses. I have an idea though that he makes up such tales himself and propagates them. There is the story, for instance, of the woman who talked too much. She was European and had been discreet for a few months and then she talked too much. She was put on board a plane which landed at Puerto Barrios just as a steamer was leaving for her country. An official handed her a jewel box with a really generous lot of jewels. It was the gift of the regretful Dato. The official advised that as soon as the ship drew clear from the dock she should hand over the jewel box to the purser for safe-keeping and of course she should not forget to get her receipt for each separate item of jewellery. The official left the ship. The lady, not so dejected now, waved good-bye to him. As soon as the ship had cast off she took her jewel box to the purser. She wanted a receipt for each item. She wished to impress the world of the ship, that hot-bed of gossip in which she would live for the next three weeks, that she was not returning empty-handed from her exile in an outlandish country. She opened the box. It was empty. The three weeks at sea was a purgatory. When she reached her port of destination and disembarked naturally she did not declare any jewels to the Customs authorities. When the jewels were found in the false bottom of her trunk, the trunk like other articles was the gift of Dato, she was considerably embarrassed. The fine imposed and the cost of the defence were just about covered by the sale of the jewels. The defending lawyer called the next day to return the fee she had paid him. He had been briefed he explained to defend her by a friend of hers. This friend declared that she had all the charms and graces and abilities of Helen herself but she had one fault only, she talked too much.'

'She understood.'

'And then there is the tale about the song of "Blue Water". I do believe Dato wrote it himself or gave the order to a tame lyricist to write and keep mum. It was adapted to a rousing rhumba tune and was not played at public functions or on the radio but the whole country knew it and danced to it. It was a cautionary tale and Dato meant those who didn't see eye to eye with him to hear the song.

'It had a basis in actual fact. When his Penal Battalions were making the road from Coban over the Alta Vera Paz, which one day may reach the length and breadth of Petén, they ran into a belt of country which was notorious for its malaria. They had already passed through those valleys called "Valleys of the Blind" because of the numbers of people blinded there by onchocerciasis which is spread by those horrid little flies that lay their eggs in flowing water in the streams of the valleys.

Ferocious discipline had enforced the order for the battalion to keep away from running water because the insect which carries the infection does not fly from the water in which it lays its eggs. Not a man was blinded even if a few were infected. Malaria, however, called for a different technique and Dato did something quite characteristic. He sent the commander of the battalion a book! The commander knew his Dato. It was not a hint. It was a written order. For the book described the immobilization by malaria of the armies in Macedonia in 1918. Every man of the Penal Battalion thereupon had to take the quinine issued to him according to instructions. A supply of certain chemicals came from Dato when it was reported to him that quinine was being issued. So the men of the battalion were called upon to stand and deliver. If a man was taking his quinine according to instructions the urine showed a blue colouration with the chemical. So the road was built over impossible country and impossible conditions and Dato wrote a song. Malaria did not immobilize his army.'

'He seems to have a sense of humour and a pervasive power of persuasion,' said Cutbush.

'Pervasive is the word; he creates a pervasive uncertainty over the whole country. Uncertainty is not new but uncertainty that waits with certainty is Dato's technique as ruler,' replied Harkness.

'And is this uncertainty felt even in this nether end of his kingdom?' asked Cutbush.

Instead of replying directly Harkness enquired when the Foundation was expecting Fuad's mules. 'Tomorrow, or the day after,' was the answer.

'Yes,' said Harkness, 'and Fuad is so uncertain that you had to buy mules sight unseen to get out of Petén.'

'But this is ridiculous,' laughed Cutbush, 'do you mean Fuad's business with the mules was due to Dato's gift for creating uncertainty?'

'Well, what do you think made Fuad do the business of the mules in such a manner? Do you think he was holding you at gun point? I tell you, that's not Fuad's way of doing business. He is very sensitive to any hint of uncertainty that the wind may carry to him from Guatemala City.'

Cutbush, however, had his own ideas of Birbari. Harkness might have known the Syrian for years and on that knowledge be ready to give him all the virtues of an Archangel. But Cutbush had his own ideas.

He had millions of dollars at his disposal and he was more jealous of the expenditure of one cent of that money, now, than he had been of a hundred dollars at the time when, as a newly qualified doctor, he earned less than a hundred dollars a month. To him Fuad's operations were blackmail masquerading as business. There would be other seasons for the members of his expedition in Petén and he would see to it that there would be other transport arrangements.

Harkness reined in his mule and pointed.

'There is the tree,' he said.

They rode off the road for some little distance towards it.

'You see,' continued Harkness, 'it is now in full bloom.'

'My God,' said Cutbush.

There in a natural clearing was a tree with not a green leaf on it. It floated like a blood-red cupola above the sparse underbush which all but concealed its short, stout trunk.

'Now, we wait,' said Harkness, 'perhaps we shall be lucky, or perhaps we shall have to whistle for a little wind.' The trembling of the upper branches of the trees beyond the clearing told them they were lucky.

The petals of 'their' tree were gently ruffled and turned gently half over so that a white mark, getting whiter as it got higher, ran up the red magnificence.

'My God,' said Cutbush again.

'Yes,' said Harkness, 'I call it the "Tree of the Ray of Light". A trembling ray of light, a burning bush that is not consumed. Now, your place in Hawaii, you told me about, is it limestone or is it swampy? This tree would very probably grow in the climate you have there but if those two conditions are not met I would hesitate to say anything as to luxuriance of its growth.'

'Well,' replied Cutbush, 'there is a swamp but I am not sure about the limestone.'

'The best thing would be for me to collect some seeds from it in a few weeks' time and send them to you. I shall also send you all the botanical data necessary and you could consult the experts at the Honolulu Botanical Gardens.'

'That would be very kind. I shall be much obliged to you. Though is it not rather strange that this tree is so well established here because there are no swamps about? Yet it flourishes like,' he was about to say, 'a Syrian pedlar' but he stopped and said instead, 'a wicked man.'

Harkness then told him that they were not far from a group of shallow lagoons which for the greater part of the year contained water except at the height of the dry season when they would be emptied of every drop.

'As,' he continued 'we are now at the end of the wet season there is a lot of water in them yet and we are only half a mile from one of the most interesting things in all Petén. And it is almost entirely unknown. Few people have seen it in five hundred years. I discovered it and Gibberd has been there and says he will investigate it thoroughly one day. Every month, though, he finds something new and each new thing takes several years for him to work over so it will probably be forgotten. You have Stephen's *Travels in Central America* haven't you?'

Cutbush had read that classic of exploration and travel in the Maya country written about a hundred years ago.

'Then, you will remember that Stephen was taken down a deep hole in the limestone and along an underground path for, it seemed to him, a tremendous distance. At last he got to an underground lagoon. He said that the Mayas actually used the water from this lagoon during the dry season. One day I came across just such a sink hole. I thought the fungi growing down the shaft might be interesting so I rigged up my rope-ladder which as you see I always carry in the bush where it is as essential as my machete. About fifty or so feet from the top I saw a crack in the wall, stepped through it and went further in and came to a lagoon something like Stephen's but very much bigger. My torch was getting low so I hurried back. I went again some weeks later with a good supply of torches and a pot of black paint. I didn't have much difficulty in making my way back because the tunnel entrance from the lagoon end was clearly visible by the light of my torch. Nevertheless I marked the door with black paint. And my curiosity paid off. I found several broken vases and one in perfect shape and preservation, an absolutely perfect specimen of Tepeu ceramic ware. I sold it to the Guatemala Museum. They said it was Maya Old Empire and was made about the time when Charlemagne ruled France.'

'Can we see all that and return before dark?' asked Cutbush.

'If we start at once. Let us leave the mules tethered here. On our way I will cut branches of candlewood for torches. We leave the forest, pass between the lagoons, if the water has receded enough for us to see the path, then clamber down and up the sides of a deep narrow ravine. That is why the animals are of no use to us. If there is water across the path, or in that section of the ravine where we climb down, you won't see the underground lagoon this trip.'

Cutbush was intrigued by the prospect of seeing something which so few people had seen in so many centuries. 'What do you call your cave?' he asked.

'It has no name. Gibberd said there is no record of it in Maya writings nor in old Spanish recordings of the Maya, called Chillam Balam. Nor is there a whisper of it extant amongst the present-day Maya of Petén or Yucatan. So I called it the "Cave of the Vase", a name that has no authority but mine.'

They tethered the mules. Cutbush offered to carry the rope-ladder and followed Harkness watching the latter in practice as a bushman.

'You see both forest and trees, don't you?' he commented. 'You slide through the bush like a Mohican who is decidely not going to be the last of his tribe.'

'Yes,' said Harkness, 'like all craft it looks easy till you try it, then it seems unbelievably difficult. But one learns and one learns all the quicker if the need is imperative. I came to this part of the world from London streets and I had to learn bush craft the hard way. In those days I couldn't afford to pay for more than the most casual of help. So I learned, though I could have learned far more easily, quicker and more pleasantly if I could have paid for a teacher. This bush is notoriously difficult. It is a tropical rain forest which sounds so lush yet in the dry season, here, one can die of thirst quite easily. I had read, of course, the history of the Conquest of these parts and, when I came here from the barrier of mountains, I realized that the story of Father Avendano was unusual mainly in that he survived.

He tried to conquer the Mayas of Petén with the word of the Gospel. In fact he refused to work in territory which the soldiers of Spain held. He said they were too cruel to the Indians. He made no converts and finally had to flee for his life. Then he was lost in this bush for many days and when *in extremis* from hunger and thirst a ripe fruit, probably a sapodilla, fell within his reach. He was eventually found by friendly Indians and lived to tell the tale. The bush is the same now as it was in his day. Petén is nearly twice the area of the State of Massachussetts but has a total population of a few hundred. You must be a bushman to survive in it. If you are not, either be accompanied by a bushman or stay out. Now, you see that bump over there? It overlooks a shallow depression. On either side of that bump is a lagoon and between them, across the depression is, we hope, our path. At the height of the wet season the lagoons cover the depression, so there is no path. The sudden dry weather, however, might have exposed it for us. Then we reach a sort of ravine. It may be an old riverbed but more probably it was caused by a fault in the deeper strata below the limestone. After we cross that it is plain sailing.'

The distance they had to travel might not have been very far but Cutbush was beginning to be a bit apprehensive about the excursion.

Just as he was about to suggest that perhaps it would be better to call it off, to go another day, Harkness said, 'Ah, there it is; wait here for me,' and he dashed into the bush, machete at the ready. Cutbush heard him chopping furiously. In a few minutes he returned with a small bundle of sticks.

'Candlewood or torch-wood,' he explained, 'each stick will give a good light for about ten minutes though we shall not use them all. Here you take the sticks and give me the rope-ladder.'

They climbed the little hillock and descended to see what appeared to Cutbush to be an unbroken sheet of water many acres in extent. On closer observation he noticed a straggling line of stunted trees leading across the water. A partially submerged embankment on which the trees grew divided one lagoon from the other. They made their way along it by holding on to the bushes, or clambering over protruding roots. They reached a stretch of higher ground which suddenly fell away so unexpectedly that from a distance of a few hundred yards it was impossible to see the edge of the 'gulch'. Its depth was about twenty feet and the breadth about fifty feet. Its walls were steep and rocky and it seemed to run for a considerable distance but, as it curved away from them, Cutbush could not be certain that this was so.

'Throw the bundle of torches down, we'll pick them up at the bottom,' Harkness told him and released the ladder so that they could climb down it with Cutbush carefully testing each hand- and foot-hold as he descended. Nothing but the feeling that it was a childish thing to do prevented him declaring that he was not going a step further and was returning at once. It would have been to no purpose in any case because already Harkness had shouldered the rope-ladder and was climbing up the other side of the gulch where the hand- and foot-holds had already been cut into the wall showing that they were following the normal path between the lagoons and across the gulch. Cutbush gathered together his little bundle of sticks and climbed behind Harkness.

'When we are coming back we go by another path which takes us out on the other side of the lower lagoon. We could not come by that route because no torch-wood grows there. We are near the shaft of the cave now,' said Harkness. They had entered a thinly wooded patch of bush. 'Wait a moment, let me find the sink hole.' Like a retriever he padded backward and forward through the bush.

'Yes,' he shouted, 'this way and the rigging timber is still sound.'

He pointed to the trunk of a tree lying on the ground and began to cut away the low bush growing near the tree.

'My God!' said Cutbush for there was a hole in the ground with a wall that fell sheer away from the surface.

'Shakes you, doesn't it?' said Harkness. 'Think of going about your business in the bush and stepping into that?'

'Is there water in it?'

'No, it goes down for twenty feet or so below our door in the wall and then just stops, or so it seems, for I have never been down to the very bottom. You are wondering how it got here. I think it is a piece of Maya water-engineering. Don't ask me how they knew that they had to drive a shaft just here to meet the gallery. It may be they came the other way following the gallery to its least distance from the surface and then tunnelled upwards.

That would imply they came upon the cave and the pool from another approach which was so inconvenient they had to make this entrance. I felled this tree so that it should fall across the mouth. I call it my rigging-timber. We tie our ladder securely to it, stick a few torches in our belt, light one and we go down. Ready? I go first.'

Cutbush watched him descending.

'I wish to heaven I was out of this,' he said to himself.

He couldn't understand his reluctance now. He had been so keen half an hour ago. He shivered. He felt suddenly cold.

'Is it going to rain I wonder?' he thought.

Then he noticed the smoke from Harkness's torch rising quickly past him. Of course there would be a cold draught coming up from an intake maybe somewhere in the ravine, he thought.

He stepped gingerly on to the ladder. When he had taken a secure grip with one hand he picked up the lighted torch with the other. It was less unnerving than he had feared. For one thing he could see the light of Harkness's torch down below.

'Here we are,' said Harkness at last. 'Hand me your torch. Now hold my hand but don't let go the ladder till I have secured it.'

They had stepped off the ladder on to the floor of a small cave. In the wall of the cave, furthest from the shaft down which they had come, was an irregular opening. Harkness lit another torch and went through this aperture. It led into a long gallery the floor of which sloped downward sometimes steeply, sometimes gently. It seemed to Cutbush that they were walking forever in darkness which was held back almost physically by the smoky light of the torches. He seemed to be going down then up, turning this way and that. Sometimes the roof of the gallery came down so low that they had to crouch and at other times it was so high that it could only be seen with difficulty.

The walls of the gallery closed in on them sometimes and at other times it was some distance away.

It closed again then opened and Harkness said, 'Now, stop. Light another torch.'

By the suddenly increased illumination Cutbush peered about him. He was not a man normally given to the use of expletives so he had a very limited stock of them.

'Dear God!' he said for the third or fourth time in the last hour.

'Yes,' said Harkness. 'A forum, eh? A cathedral, a temple with the waters of the sacred well making the altar-pieces in the centre of the floor.'

They could discern that they had entered above the highest of a series of ledges cut in the stone. These ledges were so precise in alignment and elegant in the shape of the curve that it was clear they had been artificially fashioned. They were the pews of the cathedral, the benches of the forum. Several feet below the last rank of the ledges the floor was levelled off and gently sloped towards, in the middle, the surface of a pool of water.

'I think it may be shaped like an ellipse and we are at one end. I don't really know how big it is. I have never been round it. An underground amphitheatre with the water for a stage on which the final act would take place,' said Harkness. 'You know,' he continued, 'people who don't live in this land have no idea of the importance of water in the dry season. Many a man has gone off the track in this bush and died of thirst. When even lagoons miles wide dry up you wonder where all the water of the wet season goes. Think of a village or town dependent during a harsh dry spell on such a lagoon. Then it would be that a pool like this would come into the picture. It would be the last hope of the people. You must always remember that the civilization of those days was based entirely on the cultivation of maize. The regular alternation of rain and sunshine meant life. An unseasonable drought and there would be prayers for rain and propitiation in the sacred well.'

'Let us go,' said Cutbush, 'let us go. This needs lights and proper preparation. Let us go. It is cold.'

He hoped he kept the note of panic from his voice because for a moment he seemed to be witnessing the Maya ceremony of propitiation at the sacred well.

'Yes,' said Harkness, 'the past is close to us here. It is like cobwebs drawn across the face. I think this is the place, or at any rate in a place like this where one should try a bicycle.'

Cutbush hoped he had not heard correctly but he had no time to enquire.

He turned towards the entrance of the gallery but Harkness

was already preceding him. When at length he clambered off the rope-ladder and stepped out into the scrub on the surface of the ground he had to take a strong grip of himself to prevent a sob of relief bursting from his throat. He shivered as he moved away from the cold current of the shaft. It was bravado, sheer bravado, after he found he could open his mouth without his teeth chattering which made him say:

'Yes, that is quite a place. Did I hear you say something about a bicycle?'

Harkness was untying the rope-ladder. He nodded but did not reply until he had pulled it up, rolled it and shouldered it.

Then he said, 'Yes, let us go. That is the "Cave of the Vase". And "bicycle" was the word. An ugly word for an ugly contraption. But "*bicicleta*" is how Dato would say it. It is in the text of one of his sermons, the peg on which he hung one of his parables. Now we go back by a different route and leave these roads passing through that savannah to reach the gulch lower down.'

The afternoon sun was now and then obscured by dark clouds.

'We might have another shower,' said Cutbush.

'Yes, we might,' said Harkness, 'but it is unlikely. You do get sudden heavy showers now and then at this season but two in the same day is not usual.'

'What of this "bicycle"?' asked Cutbush a little later.

'Well, if you can stand another tale of Dato I will tell you why he considers a bicycle important and uses it as a text,' Harkness replied. He did not, however, begin the tale until they had reached the open savannah.

Cutbush was irritated. Something had made him uncertain of himself and of his world. He was a first-class psychiatrist. He believed he knew very nearly as much of the workings of the sick mind of mankind as any man living, but he had suffered bewilderment and, he hesitated, terror, yes, terror was the word. He had been bewildered and terrified by what he had seen in the light of smoky torches. That pool of water in the cave. His terror had been real, overwhelming and urgent. He did not understand why he had been so disturbed. He would have to think over the incident carefully but, in the meantime, until he was ready to examine the matter he preferred not to think about it at all. It was better to listen to Harkness than to think. Not that listening to Harkness was pure pleasure. The fellow was disturbing; his attitude to the things he accepted was not so much cynical as anarchic. He talked about Dato but perhaps the ideas he spoke of as Dato's were really his. He put them in the mouth of a mythical friend, yes, mythical.

Perhaps Harkness' acquaintance with the Dictator was of the slightest. It was known that Dato Graña was an exceptional man. He had to be to hold the position he had held for so many years. Perhaps the personality of this exceptional man had so intrigued Harkness that ideas, which were too bizarre for him to utter as his own, he spoke of as being those of his friend, Dato. After all Dato was short for Deodato 'God's Gift'. He was God's gift to an imaginative but weak man such as Harkness. Cutbush was on surer ground now. He had found no evidence whatsoever of any mental derangement in Harkness. There may be neurosis, yes, but the sane today may be unbalanced tomorrow. Then Harkness would probably display the delusion that he, Harkness, was a president-dictator named 'Dato'. Cutbush looked at Harkness hurrying on before him carrying the bulky rope-ladder.

The ethics of his profession were, however, real, very real to him in that he was an honest man.

'Good heavens,' he said to himself, 'but this is childish. I had no idea I was so upset. Fancy slapping a delusional insanity on this fellow because I was for a moment as frightened as a child in the dark. So that is what panic can do to you, friend Cutbush, pushing you to the brink of having delusions, yourself.'

'He is of course all over this country,' said Harkness suddenly and Cutbush knew that he was about to hear the story of Dato and his bicycle.

'You never know where or when the fellow may pop up. In his young days he knew this part of the country so, at present, he does not pop up here. No one can pop up in Petén. But they can in Coban. I was in a village there some few years ago hunting fungi as usual. I didn't stop at the village inn but at a house a little way outside the village. I had had my coffee and was about to saddle my mule when the local gendarme came panting up to me. He was pale with exhaustion, excitement and perhaps fright.

"Señor," he said and saluted, a gesture which he had not condescended to use to me for several weeks now, "the President desires the honour of your presence at breakfast at the inn."

'He helped me saddle the mule and quite unnecessarily held the stirrup as I mounted. He would have carried my bag of specimens but that I would not part with it. Dato had arrived some time during the night. By dawn he had had the local officials with their books before him. The various members of his staff had audited and examined the books and had gone off to check stores, examine public buildings and installations and so forth.

'The village was a smallish place though the centre of quite a productive coffee area. All this checking of Government property did not take long. The local functionaries returned with the inspecting staff and the report was satisfactory. In the meantime word had been sent to the citizenry that later that morning the President would be eager to receive any deputation they might care to send to him to discuss their local problems. I had a few minutes with him in private talking about my work so I was not the only guest at breakfast. However, he had the royal gift of making each guest feel that this function was for each individual's especial pleasure.

'After the meal he sat looking at the people hurrying about the village plaza. There was one young man who rode a bicycle round and round the plaza. It was clear he was proud of his machine. Indeed, it was a rare thing in those parts because they are so remote and mountainous with so few roads. We had finished the usual polite conversation with which such a gathering is weighted and Dato broke the silence. "It must be," he said, "three thousand years at least since the wheel was invented. Iron was forged long before that. Now of that bicycle there is nothing essential that could not have been invented three thousand years ago. But it took those thousands of years for man to discover that if he put his legs astride that contraption and pushed off, something inside him fused himself with the machine and they became one instrument, an instrument of rapid progression. With it he could defy the law of gravity and, with the expenditure of less muscular or bodily energy than in running, he was able to travel, on favourable roads at any rate, further and faster than a galloping horse. But the important thing is not this going further and faster and shaming the horse. The importance is in that this new method of progression is a personal achievement done by the fusible secrets and the energy of the human body with the body on an iron contraption. Now it seems to me that there are many roads open to man and he has so far tried to follow only a few. He has, for example, gone some interesting distance, through the arts, in the quest of beauty. But there are other roads. Some of them are too obviously forbidding, too crassly impossible as yet. Some break off at an abyss, some get lost in the heights of dizzy mountains, others seem to begin only where our imagination ends. And yet for each road I am sure there is a method of progression possible for that particular road only. I don't of course mean a literal bicycle but a method of progress which we could use now, if we searched for it. Think of the road which leads to the edge of the grave, an abyss if ever there was one. I am sure that a 'bicycle' exists with which we could span that one. It may be some philosophical discipline as simple in principle as a frame and two wheels. If we mount that discipline and push off with confidence we defy not so much the law of gravity but the crushing horror of the grave and we find ourselves sailing across the abyss ... to land where? But we would land, we would go and return and we would confound Charon, that one-way ferryman. But our journeys would not be for the sake of confusing and confounding but for liberation.

'"And think of our dormant faculties say, telepathy, in fact all parapsychology. They wait for a 'bicycle'. And there are other attributes of the body still to be discovered. Why, after all these millennia of sedulously cultivating and proving fertility have we only in the last twenty years known that for some certain days in the month a woman is not fertile? That is a 'bicycle', a means to an end. The healing abreaction of a psychoanalytic seance is a 'bicycle'. After many thousands of years it is a technique that is discovered in our lifetime. A healing discipline is mastered. The healer does not need incredible apparatus or the paraphernalia of chemistry and pharmacy. The sick man speaks. What could be simpler? He merely speaks of his dreams and, how positively childish, sometimes he just talks of what comes unbidden into his mind. And lo – he is healed! There are many such 'bicycles' that await the genius who will dare to mount. Freud mounted a 'bicycle' and pushed off! He put his problem in simple terms, simple for him, idiotic to his contemporaries. Perhaps we should all put our problems in the simplest of terms. Even the highest, the ineffable experience of the mystic; that experience which, in my opinion, is the son of Adam *in excelcis*; even that may be approachable on its appropriate bicycle. And we may even slip into the future. Past, present and future must be different aspects of Time."

'He turned to me,' said Harkness, 'in order to make the village worthies understand he meant this personally. He did not say, "Our friend here," but he said pointedly, "My friend here, who has shown us so much of the unrecognized wealth with which our country is blessed, told me of the experiments of a compatriot of his named Dunne, I think. This man has theories and tries to prove them by examining the structure of his dreams. He thinks that nothing dies, that past, present, and future co-exist in Time. Now that is an interesting 'bicycle'. He may not be able to ride it far but he has pushed off. Or to come back to mundane affairs. I am quite certain in time to come man will be able to fly as successfully as a bird. We have heard of those people who, if they will it, cannot be lifted off their feet. I last heard of it in a girl who was doing the trick on a vaudeville stage. How is it done? Something to do with gravity? I don't know. But if she could not be lifted because of a trick, the trick of gravity, may there not be another trick whereby she could be lifted by a little finger? Tricks may work both ways. And is she then as light as a feather? Well, birds wear more than one feather and they fly. But here comes the deputation. Gentlemen and friends, I thank you for your patience and courtesy to me while I mused aloud."

'With that we all went about our business. But now you get a glimpse of what I meant when I spoke of a "bicycle" in that cave. The place is full of the, shall I say, memories, prayers, petitions, exultations and agonies of mankind, and all these memories, agonies and so forth seem to have congealed. They have congealed into stalagmites and stalactites which we cannot see but against which certain aspects of our beings collide and recoil from in horror. Had we the appropriate "bicycle" we would not collide and recoil; we would be members of the audience of a drama, a sacramental drama. By our presence we would lend solemnity and credence to the rites. We would leave that cave not shuddering in panic but uplifted and purged by pity and terror as from a play by a Maya Sophocles.

'Of course what I have said sounds ridiculous but to the ancients a "bicycle", the thought of a bicycle, would have been ridiculous. A boy using his own puny muscles and riding a simple contraption of rubber and iron weighing ten kilos outruns and outstays the messenger of Marathon. Why? Because the boy has the power to learn a trick, the trick of using his own organs of balance. Yes, it *is* ridiculous. But so is the effect of that cave. I can tell you I felt a surge of panic the first time I saw the amphitheatre.'

Cutbush could not reply at once. He needed time for the shame and resentment at his own panic to subside. Then understanding came to his assistance. He had heard of places at which, whether by association or by a natural law, religious emotion was stored up ... at a temple, grave or grotto as if by an electric battery. Those who were capable of receiving the influence felt it. Others who, either by insensitivity induced by disbelief or natural lack or some other reason, were not capable of accepting the stimulus, felt nothing. Perhaps this Maya cave had that particular quality, the quality of the numinous. He did not know. All he knew was that he had a sensation, a feeling of overwhelming desolation and horror, followed by unreasoning panic. He no longer felt ashamed, but he was ashamed to find that he had harboured a resentment against Harkness. He examined this feeling, thinking, 'It is like a grudge. I do not feel as if he has deprived me of something but that he has accepted something of value which was offered to both of us. I did not recognize its value so I did not accept it.'

They walked on in silence until they reached the edge of the gulch. From where they stood Cutbush could see a rough path shelving down to the bottom. To get down would be easy but the opposite wall was steep without any visible path or hand-holds.

'Where do we climb out?' he asked.

'Oh, we go round the corner for some little distance before we find a good path out of it,' said Harkness, 'but it will be all to the good, we shan't be losing ground by coming this way.' As the gulch curved away at both ends this made matters no clearer to Cutbush.

'We go round the corner,' he thought, 'but which corner? Well, it doesn't matter. He knows this bush or he couldn't make his living out of it.'

'Well, here goes,' said Harkness as he threw the rolled-up rope-ladder down the rocky bank. The bundle bounced from rock to rock, loosening a small rock, which appeared to be the supporting stone for a part of the path, for a portion of it tore away and stone and earth plunged to the bottom. The dust rose but a strong current of air in the gulch dissipated it quickly.

'Just as well,' said Harkness, 'that shows where we should not put our foot if it was still there for us to put our foot on.'

His feeble schoolboy joke pleased Cutbush. The fellow was odd not mad but odd, sensitive. That's it, sensitive to personalities, other personalities, dead or alive.

'I wonder if he can tell how alive, or how far dead. I will ask his, some other time, if he can tell when an apparently living man is so dead to responsibility, or virtue, or ethics, so dead that in fact he is not living but only partly alive.'

He followed Harkness down the rocky slope. He was about ten feet from the top, when he put his foot on a smooth stone, slipped and was falling headlong to the rocky bottom of the gulch when he grasped at a bunch of grass growing in a crack in the wall. It saved him from falling but the sudden jerk had loosened the stone and it fell. He gingerly put a foot further down searching for a safe foothold when he heard a sobbing moan from Harkness. He twisted round and saw Harkness dancing what appeared to be a macabre dance. He was holding on to a rock above his head with both hands. His legs kicked and plunged and kicked again.

Then Cutbush saw the swift strike ... the flat head, the yellow jaw, the curving neck. The fer-de-lance struck again. It struck the legging of the struggling man. Harkness's hands slipped before the snake could strike again. As he fell Cutbush saw his face, the face of a doomed man, pale, withered, frozen in a mask of despair.

'Oh God,' said Cutbush, this time in a different tone of voice. He decided to jump. He released his hold, jumped and fell heavily near Harkness. Scrambling painfully to his feet he went to his companion.

'He didn't get you did he, he didn't get you?' he asked, desperately, but there was no answer. There was blood on a stone where Harkness had struck his head. The blood still flowed. Cutbush felt the man's pulse. It was of poor volume, rapid in rate but regular of rhythm. He looked along the gulch. On either side it curved away. The opposite wall was unclimbable.

'He is stunned as well as bitten perhaps, mercifully, stunned. Let's hope he stays stunned. But he can't stay here.'

Without thinking, Cutbush lifted Harkness. He had struggled up the rocky slope half-way up the same path by which they had come when he realized with a sick horror that he had just passed the crack in the rock from which the snake had struck.

He stopped, too weak with terror to advance further and too terrified to return. The weight of the unconscious man began to tell on him. He shuddered, took a sobbing breath and shuffled upwards again. After an agony of cold sweating fear, while he listened for the slightest movement behind him, he reached the edge and rolled Harkness over the top. Then he found that he himself could not climb the last three feet. He sat down on the path and shook as if in a violent malarial rigor. Then he vomited, suddenly and violently. His rigor subsided and he leaned against the rock. The cold sweating gradually ceased and the resurging confidence of his mind warmed his gelid body.

'Well, that's that,' he said some ten minutes later, as he crawled over the edge of the gulch and lay down beside Harkness as if to protect the latter's body from a biting wind. After a few minutes he yawned and sat up, fancying that he could now take a firm grip of himself. He felt Harkness's pulse. The volume was better now, the rate somewhat slower, the rhythm normal.

'He will come round soon now,' he said, and then in surprise he added, 'Why bless my soul. It just shows!'

He unbuttoned the left pocket of his shirt and took out a packet the size of his thumb.

It was carefully wrapped and sealed in tough waterproof paper. He tore this off to show the wooden tube within. From the tube he took out a glass syringe-ampoule. He fitted the hypodermic needle to the syringe and rolled up the left sleeve of

Harkness's shirt, plunging the needle in the flesh of the arm and pressing the plunger of the syringe. Relief flooded him. Certainty took charge of him. He was no longer petrified with horror, no longer shuddering with internal disintegration, or frozen by a chill-exuding moisture.

Then Harkness opened his eyes and looked at him, 'Hullo,' he said, 'what happened?' He paused, frowning. 'I remember, I slipped. No, the path broke away and I grabbed that ... ' A full picture of the scene flooded his mind. 'No,' he said 'No. Did it get me? I felt it strike my leg. Did it get me?'

He sat up suddenly and fell back at once with a groan.

'My head, my head,' he moaned. 'Is it bad?'

He felt his head and looked at his hands. They were smeared with his blood. 'That is from the fall, of course. If I try I can sit up again, slowly. Help me will you, please?'

He leaned against the rock, looked at the sky and said, 'It is getting late, it will be dark before we get back to camp. But they won't be anxious if they know you are with me. Now, let me see. That leg, I felt it strike me on the leg, but you notice I always wear high and heavy leggings.'

'I saw it strike at your thigh as you dangled from the rock,' said Cutbush. 'Do you feel any pain in the thigh?'

'No, nothing in the thigh. It is in the leg, below the knee. Unbuckle my leggings for me please and have a good look.'

Cutbush took off the leggings and pulled up the trouser leg.

Harkness twisted his leg around to look at his calf. There were the puncture marks of the fangs but the punctures were scarcely skin deep. They had only just broken through the skin.

'Well, thank heavens for that. The weight of the leather has saved me once again. This time the skin is hardly broken. They say it is a horrible death. The only consolation is if he gets you good and proper death follows in less than a couple of hours.'

A violent spasm shook his whole body. For the moment Cutbush thought the venom had entered Harkness's body by some other bite which he had not yet seen. But Harkness was apologizing as his teeth chattered.

'Awfully sorry,' he said. 'Reaction I suppose. I thought that awful creature had got me.'

His shivering ceased gradually then he started to sweat heavily.

'God, I am thirsty,' he said. 'But he didn't get me and I don't think those scratches are deep enough to do any harm. The skin is hardly broken. I saw him strike and again. I saw his yellow jaw, it was a *barba amarillo*, a fer-de-lance.'

'Yes,' said Cutbush, 'I don't know much about them but he had a yellow lower jaw with a neck about as thick as your wrist. And do you know what I did? I was so frightened that I carried you back up the track not knowing what I was doing. Then when I realized that I had passed his front door again I nearly died with fright. I was frozen stiff. A pillar of stone though I dared not look back.'

'Oh that would have been all right. He would not have been there,' said Harkness. 'You see he is as frightened of us as we are of him. He has gone and the path is safe for us as far as he is concerned. Of course there may be pals of his about but not likely. It is not the breeding season.'

'How do you feel now?' asked Cutbush.

'Not at all bad. Not really, a bit tight across the chest with aches and pains here and there,' replied Harkness cheerfully. 'The head is pretty bad of course but I shall soon be ready to travel. I will put on my leggings now.'

'Yes,' he said, a little later, looking at the fang marks again 'that was a good big chap. You can tell by the distance between the fangs. He must have had a lot of strength to perforate those leggings for the leather is not only extra heavy but extra tough. Anyhow hardly any venom could have got in because there is very little pain in the leg. But this tightening of the chest gives me some concern.'

'Then, if it is only a little venom that got in you are quite safe. You see, I gave you my shot of Bothrops atrox anti-venin in your arm there. That would protect you against even a heavy shot of venom. Think you can stand now?'

'Oh, did you, old man?' said Harkness and there was a strange bleak tone in his voice. 'Thank you. That was good of you. Have you got the syringe, or label showing strength and so forth?'

Cutbush looked around him and found the empty syringe ampoule.

'Here it is,' he said, wondering if Harkness had never heard of

Bothrops anti-venin before.

Harkness read the label and handed it back to Cutbush. He sighed and when he spoke his voice was muted and full of resignation.

'Quite right, old man, quite right. You did the correct thing. Thank you. Of course, that tightness across the chest. You did the correct thing.'

Cutbush was puzzled. Harkness said he felt better but made no attempt to rise, to continue their journey home.

'The blow on the head,' he thought, 'that's it. It is worse than it looks; he is still somewhat dazed, a bit gaga.'

Then Harkness begged a curious favour of him.

'Help me up a moment will you please? I want to sit on this side of the rock to look at the evening sun.'

Cutbush thought 'Yes it is getting late; it will dark, pitch black before we get home.' Then aloud, trying to keep the note of urgency, of expostulation out of his voice he said, 'How do you feel now? Think you can make it?'

Harkness smiled and was about to reply when he choked and coughed. He spat; spat carefully on the ground near him then leaned over and looked at the sputum long and carefully.

'The blow on the head. This is a business. I had better humour him' he said to himself.

He kneeled down and also looked at the sputum attentively. Harkness coughed, spat and looked at the sputum again, but casually, as if he had been satisfied by the first prolonged examination.

'Those clouds ... quite an effect ... the sunset. If this had happened in the forest we could not have seen it. I say, old man, you haven't such a thing on you as some Adrenalin, or aminophylline have you? No, of course not. There would hardly be any adrenalin in all Petén. Well it doesn't really matter. It probably would not have served any purpose.'

He coughed and spat again. But it was Cutbush who examined the sputum now with a sick foreboding. The coupling of the names of the drugs after examining the sputum and the faint memory of having seen just that type of sputum many years ago in medical school, frothy with a fine froth. It was like the froth at the nostrils of a recently drowned corpse.

'Look here, look here,' he almost shook Harkness so urgent was his anxiety, 'what's all this? What's all this? Let us go home. Do you think you can make it now? What's all this? It's the bump on the head. Epinephrin or Adrenalin as you call it would be the worst thing for you for that head. It would be the worst possible thing.'

He realized he was babbling and stopped speaking.

Harkness did not reply at once.

His breathing was a trifle short. Cutbush asked, 'Do you mean this oedema of the lungs is the result of an allergy?'

'Yes,' replied Harkness, 'it is allergic oedema of the lungs, my friend. I drown. I drown on dry land but, before I go under for the third time sitting against this rock, I must ask you not to take this too hard. After all, you were not to know that I am the exception to the rule, the one in a million. Don't take it too hard. Naturally, if you had the anti-venin, you had to use it. In a snake-infested country like this one ought to carry the anti-venin. It's only sensible.' He looked away into the distance and added, 'Those clouds are lovely.'

Despite the awful anxiety which oppressed him Cutbush turned to look critically at the sunset glow. But the clouds had not the same significance for him as for Harkness. He would see, if he chose to look, many more sunsets. This was not his last.

'Lookit' he said; he had dropped his voice and was whispering, 'you don't mean it, do you? I mean ... ' He could not put his anxiety into words.

Harkness turned his gaze from the clouds, looked at Cutbush and smiled. The latter stopped whispering and dropped his gaze.

'If it were so,' he thought, 'he is right. This is a drowning. His lungs will fill up like water rising in a flooded cellar. He will try to cough up this water, this transudate, fluid transudate pouring into his lungs from his blood and he knows, my God, he knows. I wonder if he wants to say anything.'

'You know,' he said in his most persuasive professional-cum-committee voice, 'we might be scaring the daylights out of ourselves. I declare anybody looking at us would think I am the sick man for you certainly don't look scared and I might be the fool scaring the daylights out of himself. This thing may not go too far. It is not all cases of pulmonary oedema that are necessarily fatal. So the only thing to do is give your constitution a chance and it will pull you through. You are as tough as hickory and still young. The shock from the blow would have lowered your recuperative powers early on but that shock has passed off. It will leave you with a hell of a headache later this evening but this lung business has a good chance of settling itself. So I don't see why we should begin to think of sunset and evening star and last will and testament, yet. The best thing to do is just to sit and sweat it out, right?'

Harkness did not reply for some time. Then, at last, he said, 'Yes, you are right.'

Cutbush was a trifle relieved, 'Even the dying fall for professional blarney,' he thought.

But Harkness went on speaking, slowly, 'You are right; I must speak of a last will and testament. I have nothing to leave anybody. My worldly goods couldn't bury me anywhere else but here where land is cheap. Have you paper and pencil on you?' Cutbush had an old envelope and a pencil, with a letter in it made up of several sheets of paper with writing only on one side.

Harkness began, 'If the worst comes to the worst, but why is it the "worst"? However I have no time now to quibble, please notify my mother, Mrs. Alexandria Harkness, 99c Emmanuel Villas, Palmers Green, London N.13. Say kind things, last thoughts, etc. Mothers are mothers they will believe anything "nice" about their children however completely out of character it sounds. Then notify my lawyers, Hernández Y. Pardo, 18 Calle Sandoval, Guatemala City. They have everything arranged re my notes, papers, publication of my books and so forth; they work for Dato.'

He was breathing more deeply now and the cough came more often and the sputum was more copious. It was clear that speaking exhausted him.

'Wife, or friends?' murmured Cutbush forgoing any more use of professional blarney.

'No, no wife; but something important. You haven't much paper left and this is so simple you will remember it. You may not know it but Señora Arevalo saved my life.' He spoke in short gasps; 'It was so silly an accident, a scratch on my foot but it developed into a vicious blood poisoning. Fortunately I was near

Shoonantonitch and reached it more dead than alive. But she, Lady Bountiful, took charge. She had received some tablets a couple of weeks before. They dosed me with them, two every four hours, day and night.

'I lost three or four days but by the fifth day I was better. Now this is where you come in. Here are my keys. You will see one for a security box is a bank with the name and address of the bank on it. In that box is another vase superior to the one I sold to the Guatemala Museum. I got it also from the "Cave of the Vase". They gave me 500 dollars for the one they bought. The one in the bank is worth several times as much. As a gesture of gratitude I gave Señora Arevalo a beautiful Mexican saddle made especially for her. But in the pommel of that saddle, in a waterproof metal tube, is a letter to the bank manager empowering her to open that box with this key and to possess the contents. She knows there is something in a bank, in some city, somewhere, which belongs to her if anything happens to me.

'I did not tell her any more for she would tell her husband and he would refuse Holy Communion from the Pope himself unless Dato specifically approved. The lawyers will write to my men friends. It is getting dark, soon you won't see to write. But I would like the little light left to us to write a letter to him, to President Graña.

'Say, "My friend, they say when a drowning man goes down for the third time he sees his past life pass before his eyes. The fates are kinder to me. I drown but I do not see that too long sequence of follies and attempts half-completed. Instead I see and I think of you. I shall not return thanks for encouragement, help and even for survival or for recognition of my efforts and the value of my work. I know gratitude embarrasses you; thanks bore you. No, I think of you as the man, the only human creature I have known, of whom I have not felt the same shame and disgust that I feel of myself.

'"In you, only, do I recognize validity for the hope that men are gods and that gods are the projection of what men can be. In one sense you are even greater than the gods of which we are, so far, aware for you are incapable of jealousy and you scorn revenge. As long as I am able to think of you in these terms the fate of man has lustre. However, I am, in one measure, not sorry to go before you do because then I shall never see and never have cause to mourn the pettiness of the strategems by which the jealous gods will cut you down to their level and to my level, the level of other men. When I say Hail and Farewell I ... "'

He was panting now. Cutbush could hear with each breath the moist rustling in the chest. A fit of coughing seized him. The sputum came up in copious mouthfuls. Cutbush bent closer to hear what he was saying.

'If you cut off a lizard's tail it twitches; dead, yet automatically alive. So if I seem to struggle it is a twitching of the tail. I read your medical textbooks on this subject and they talk about the anguished expression, the nostrils flecked with froth that is sometimes of a pinkish or slight-bloody tinge. If you see the anguished expression know it is but a twitching tail. I wouldn't give the gods the satisfaction of seeing me afraid. Perhaps a good drink of Karen Farr's "Sudden Glory" would be just the draught for such a situation as this. My sop soaked in vinegar and it would make one laugh. How good, to pass out laughing, to leave the very clay transfixed by a smile. By the way, tell the Farr the last specimen I gave Copius was not from Polyporus. It was from an entirely different species. I worked over the idea and brought in the resemblance of the stone paddle and, then, remembered some other tree with a similar type of epiphyte. However it does not matter now. Curious creature the Farr. If I hadn't been so taken up with fungi I would have tried to show her that even if she did start out on the wrong foot, she needn't continue to be out of step with herself for ever. But to get back to the letter "Hail – and Farewell!" Did I say that? Good, then write now. "One last favour, friend Dato! You can understand and you can cause to be delivered the message so that her husband need never hear of it. Tell Angelica Pinto of 38 Calle San Martin, Chichicastanango, that I die blessing her (and through her other women but don't tell her that) because she (and they) have given me such sustenance, such strength, such comfort, such loving-kindness that I think of her at the last because she gave as much as any and more than most but expected the least in return. She wanted, she expected nothing. Now, to you, my friend. I say Hail because ... "'

He coughed again. The sputum now came up easily without

the impulse of the cough to bring it up. He leaned a little sideways and the gasping breaths became agonizingly anxious. He leaned a little further sideways away from Cutbush. Then gradually, carefully lowered himself to the ground.

By the last light of evening Cutbush saw the fine froth at the nostrils. The wretchedly hungry gasping for air ceased several minutes before the pulse under Cutbush's fingers became imperceptible. The frothy liquid continued to pour out of his mouth and nostrils even after Cutbush removed his hand from the pulseless wrist. Harkness had been drowned, the mechanics designed to protect his body having betrayed him.

PART EIGHT

THIS IS THE WAY THE WORLD ENDS

Early on the morning of the same day which saw Harkness killed and Cutbush lost in the bush and the morning after Jaime's murder, Cibrian was at his desk when the courier arrived with the mail. It had come by the early morning aeroplane. The Major was in a relaxed mood.

He recalled like a benediction the thought of Candellaria. He promised himself later that day, at her convenience, other benedictions. Then the letter pouch was brought to him. There were not more than a dozen letters. A few were personal while the rest bore the official stamp.

The first personal letter that he opened and read caused him no obvious concern. The next made him somewhat thoughtful and he tore it into small pieces. The last came as a shock and he turned pale. 'No,' he whispered, 'there must be a mistake, not her, the people in Paris must have made a mistake. So, let us forget it.' And he tore that letter, also, into small pieces and put them with the other scraps of paper into an ashtray and set them all alight.

The paper seemed to him to burn lazily with an almost insolent torpor. 'No,' he repeated, 'It has to be a mistake.' Then he began the task of opening the official letters. As soon as he had read the first one he sprang to his feet and was about to rush out of his room to the outer office, where a gendarme was on duty, when he stopped abruptly. With forced calm he opened the other official letters and read them slowly. Then he rang the bell on his desk which summoned the gendarme.

'Go at once to the Commandante and say that I request his presence here as quickly as possible.' The gendarme saluted and set out at a brisk pace. He delivered the message emphasizing 'as quickly as possible' so that there could be no doubt, no hesitation in obeying it.

Arevalo arrived promptly. Cibrian greeted him quietly and said in a friendly tone, 'Here are your letters. I see from the envelope of this one that it is from your children's school in Guatemala City. You told me they are doing well. So I hope that it has nothing unusual in it. Please feel free to open any of your personal letters now. After that we have important things to discuss.' Arevalo thanked him, opened the envelope with the name of the school on it and glanced at it.

'No trouble there,' he said. He looked at the envelopes of the other four letters, chose one, opened it and read it quickly. Cibrian saw him frown. Then he put that letter in an inner pocket of his uniform. The others he put elsewhere in his jacket.

He looked at Cibrian who said, 'Now read that!' Arevalo scanned it quickly then re-read it. 'So it has come?' he said, 'That which I feared. Now begins a change of life, a change of values, the forgotten people of this forgotten land are about to be caught by their breeches and swung into the twentieth century. Of course it's all due to the airfields and the wireless installations. Now the chicle can be flown out but can the ordinary everyday necessities, say a reel of thread and the needles and the tablets of quinine, can the planes fly them in at the same cost as they now come from Belize by mule-back?'

'Yes,' said Cibrian, 'as of today the frontier is closed. Of course more gendarmerie will have to be sent to keep it closed. Now, as you say, begins a new period for this hitherto forgotten land. If things cost more, how will it be and how much will the aeroplane companies and the gasoline companies get? As for air-pilots, we know they will fly anything anywhere provided they can land. In this day and age, which they call the Depression, you can buy skilled men in every craft and trade. So they will be no problem. What money can't buy are the skills, the experience, the rectitude and the trust of his people which an administrator possesses. However, read this.' And he handed Arevalo another letter. The latter read it and said, 'This at any rate indicates some appreciation of the added difficulties of our position here. Isn't it just like "Him"? He says nothing then, when one thinks that one is a forgotten peon, he acts. Well, Maria will be pleased and I do not say I am not. So I am now Major Arevalo.'

'Yes, Major, and may Colonel Cibrian congratulate you? Yes, I also have been promoted. At my age, my friend, that is quite an achievement. It means of course that you and I between us have to keep the door locked and we must see to it that the closure of the frontier is a reality. We shall be getting more men and equipment and we will have to be ready to put the men to work.'

'Yes, Colonel. My heartiest congratulations. I may tell Maria, may I? Would it be too much to ask if I should hurry off to tell her now and return at once?'

'Yes, please go. Then, as soon as you return, we can go into the rest of these letters. They are routine, but, yes, please go.'

So Major Arevalo went to tell Maria. He hurried but his haste was prompted by anxiety as to their guest. The letter he had put in the inner pocket of his uniform also caused him anxiety. It was from the headmistress of the convent in Guatemala City where his daughter was at school. The girl had been irresponsible in her work and erratic in her conduct but seemed, now, to have decided to turn over a new leaf. There was no need for any anxiety about her, at least for the time being.

The report in the other letter with the name of the school on it where his son was a pupil was from the headmaster. It was on the whole an excellent report.

But he mentioned neither letter when he reached his house for his wife met his enquiring glance in a way which suggested there were serious problems to be faced.

'I touched her and led her to the bed to sit. She sat but did not speak. She drank the coffee when I put the cup in her hand. Then I took her nightgown off and helped her put on her clothes. She does not speak. She sits or stands as one puts hers to sit or stand.'

'Thank God,' said Arevalo to himself, 'she is not violent. Now what do we do? Dr. Cutbush is not here but he should return tonight. So tomorrow we shall know something positive. In the meantime Cibrian will hear. The maid has already guessed. By tonight the rumour will be about and if they see Cutbush here one might as well shout the bad news. If Cibrian asks I will tell him enough for him not to come to call on her. I will suggest, simply, that she is not fit to be seen.'

To Maria he said, 'I came to tell you a bit of good news. I had hoped we could have been together, alone together, to celebrate. Cibrian called me because despatches had arrived. They contained a lot of very important directions. And something else that I wanted to be the first to tell you. I have been promoted. I am now Major. And here are two letters about the children. They do not contain bad news, either.'

Maria embraced him. 'Praise be to the Good and Great who has kept us together, rewarded us with children and now rewards you in the eyes of all men. Dato has understood your worth. This should have been a day of rejoicing, of going to the altar to give thanks. That it cannot be is because in that room is a new burden. Cibrian is in love with her and she reciprocates his love.'

Arevalo said, 'I must return. Ask the maid to bring me a sandwich and coffee later. There is a lot to be done at the office. Oh heavens, I almost forgot. Dato has closed the frontier between us and the Colony as if we were at war. No one goes there from here and no one comes to us from there. First we have to call in all *chicleros* who are natives of Honduras, get them together and escort them over the frontier. I must go, there is so much to be done. You remain with her. The Doctor should be back tonight. Someone said Harkness had mentioned that they would be back tonight. Stay with her.'

He returned to Cibrian's office. They worked steadily through the afternoon for another bag of despatches had arrived. Technology had caught up with Petén. In a pause for refreshment while they sipped coffee they looked at the previous day's issue of a Guatemala newspaper.

The closing of the frontier was not mentioned but there were references to the obstinacy, the perfidy of the British about the Belize affair. Of course these references were nothing new. It was almost a daily diet for the newspaper readers. There was news however about the President. It was not blazoned in headlines but discreetly mentioned on the page given over to the marching and counter-marching of high society of Guatemala City.

The President had returned yesterday, it said, after spending two weeks in a private pavilion of one of the most prestigious of the medical institutions of America, the Osler Clinic of Chicago. The whole nation would rejoice to know that the eminent doctors had found him in excellent health and the only advice they had offered was that he should reduce the number of cigarettes which he smoked and also that he go on to a not-too-strenuous diet so as to lose some weight.

Although this appeared to be the latest news the fact that the President had gone to the Osler Clinic for his medical check-up was known to the 'inner circle' of the officers and the higher bureaucracy and, by diffusion, to a wider circle of interested citizens. Cibrian had known of it. Arevalo, of course, had not. These pilgrimages of Dato for medical assessment were not unusual but they were not on a regular schedule. He might go one year to Paris then the next to Rome. Two years later he might go to New York. One never knew when and where unless one had an ear in the inner circle. This was the second visit to the Osler Clinic. The first visit had been six months ago.

'Well,' said Arevalo, 'praise God for some good news. I mean about Dato. He will need all his strength and resolution to cope with this frontier business.'

So the two men worked through the afternoon together while messengers came and went. Some rode off rapidly and resolutely leading a mule laden with enough supplies to last the messenger a week or more, others were equipped for shorter journeys.

When Cibrian called a halt for coffee he said, 'Our ladies must be as busy as we are. I haven't seen either of them pass by our window for the whole day.'

He noticed the hesitation and the look of distress, almost a pleading for help on Arevalo's face.

'Oh, is it due to some family affair? If it is I am sorry I mentioned it,' said Cibrian.

It was the moment Arevalo had been waiting for. Cibrian would have to know before he heard the unhappy news from someone in the village.

'Yes,' he said. 'It is a family affair but one that won't be secret much longer. It is a terrible thing and sadly, Dr. Cutbush will not be back till tonight because it is a matter which is in his line his speciality.'

Cibrian turned gently away as if to put down his cup with excessive care. At the same time he looked at the ashtray on which he had earlier burned some scraps of paper as if he were looking in a crystal ball which featured some pre-recognition of events to come. He knew; he knew what would come next from Arevalo but he could make no move, give no lead, he had to wait while his heart shrank into a bitter knot; with hope and joy jellied to gall.

His friend had written in the letter he had destroyed 'Yes, I met her during my second tour of duty in Paris. She was interested in art as I was also. In fact, I had been continuing lessons which I had started on my first tour of duty in that city. We were not friends but met at the studio of my teacher occasionally. Then, not having seen her for some weeks, I asked our teacher if she had stopped taking lessons, which would not have surprised me for to me she was an accomplished artist, but he said, "Oh don't you know? She is a very sick woman. Fortunately she is under the care of Professor Menissier at his sanatorium." I did not want to appear to be too inquisitive then but by spreading appropriate pieces of silver I learnt that this was her second attack, the second time she had been in a mental hospital. The first had been in New York. Furthermore I learned that she was improving under the expert care of Professor Menissier. I never enquired again about her and officially her dossier did not need to come to my department at the Embassy.' The letter then went on about the gossip in Guatemala City and about Dato's visit to New York.

'It seems,' said Arevalo, 'as if Candellaria has had a nervous breakdown. She is abnormally quiet even docile, too docile.'

Cibrian said, with intense control of his voice, 'That is tragic news. I am sorry. It would perhaps be better for you to leave me. Your wife will have need of you, while I do not. All I have left to do today is to discuss matters with Gibberd as to how the closing of the frontier will affect his work and how he is going to square matters with the Archaeological Museum in Guatemala City.'

So Arevalo left the office while Cibrian remembered some words one of his English friends in Guatemala City had often used.

'This is the way the world ends.
This is the way the world ends.
Not with a bang but a whimper.'

'Yes,' he thought, 'I whimper. That is all I can do.'

The friend had told him the chant was the conclusion of a poem the writer had entitled 'The Hollow Men'. He remembered that he had read the poem at the insistence of his friends and had tried to understand it.

He had learned that 'whimper' may mean the cry of young animals like a young dog in pain, or frightened, or grieving, or lonely. There was a knock at the door. 'Yes, who is it?'

'Señor Colonel,' said the corporal, 'Señor Birbari would like to see you, if possible.' Fuad was standing right behind the man.

'Thank you, send Señor Birbari in.'

'*Colonel* Cibrian?' asked Fuad, entering. Cibrian bowed his head in acknowledgement. 'Oh, then good afternoon Señor Colonel and may I presume to offer my congratulations on the distinction "He" has seen fit to hand to you.'

'Thank you,' said Cibrian. 'Now I must warn you that I am extremely busy. If the matter about which you have come can wait for a more convenient moment, say tomorrow morning?' He did not give Fuad time to reply, but immediately continued, 'It can wait? Good. Tomorrow morning then at, say, ten o'clock?'

'Yes sir, Señor Colonel,' said Fuad and bowed in his turn. As he did so he noted that Cibrian's eyes were red and caught a glimpse of his hand in his lap holding a handkerchief.

'Mother of Heaven,' he thought, 'do the red eyes mean tears?'

Backing out slowly he said, 'Thank you again.'

In the office outside Fuad felt that his worst fears had been confirmed. The Colonel had received the same information he had. The rumour of the closure of the frontier was more than a rumour. 'One must walk very carefully,' he thought, 'and I must see Jaime to send another last message before he starts out for El Cayo with that misbegotten joker dressed as a woman.'

Cibrian remained all afternoon in his office. From the window he could see that only the maid left Arevalo's house and went back and as evening came left again for her own home. Then he sent a message to Gibberd who came. They had much to discuss, and Gibberd was cooperative, making many valuable suggestions.

'Of course you know that Cutbush will have to be consulted on all of this but I don't anticipate much or indeed any difficulty from him. He should be back at any time now. Indeed, I thought from what Harkness said they would be back before now,' said the Professor. He asked Cibrian, if there was nothing more urgent, that he be allowed to leave because he wanted to get an early report from Karen on her experiment at the Speaker's house and, he suggested, that if Colonel Cibrian had the time, he might accompany him. Cibrian agreed, glad of the distraction and hoping it would work on his agony of mind as an anodyne.

They were some way down the trail when they heard someone riding a mule at the gallop. It was Miss Quinn and she reined it in, shouting, 'You must come, you must come at once. Both of you. They killed him. They killed Jaime.'

'Who has killed whom?' Cibrian's tone of voice was icy and commanding.

'Some men – Pedro, I think is one of them.'

'Where?'

'At the Speaker's house.'

'Then you will lead us Señora and travel quickly.'

So they hurried and presently they heard a man's voice. He was intoning the 'Miserere', Karen Farr was kneeling beside Jaime's body and the chant came from an elderly man, with the look of an aesthete and a scar on his face who sat in a corner some way away from the dim light of a hurricane lamp.

Cibrian took in the scene in one quick glance; the dead man, the elderly Speaker, the two distraught women and made immediate decisions. 'I will send for the gendarmes,' he said. 'Gibberd, will you please escort the ladies. I will make arrangements with my men to bring Peat-Patterson's body back and for someone to care for the Speaker. I will also send men in pursuit of the murderers.'

The next day, on his way to see whether the grave diggers had reached the required depth, Fuad met Karen Farr. It was on his part a carefully contrived accident.

'Oh, Señora,' he told her, 'the Colonel said, after he had read them, that these papers had no relation either to the identity of the deceased nor to the cause of his death, therefore they are not necessary for evidence and can be disposed of. As they were found on his body the Colonel handed them to me, Jaime's friend, who stood by him in life and in death. Perhaps you can suggest what we should do with them?'

She took the two bits of paper and looked at them.

She read, 'I dared not look at him. I died. I longed to touch him, this failing wreck ... I longed to take him in my arms, to know him so that he should give that fulfilment, that warming of oneself from the fruits of one's own self, one's own body.'

'Thank you,' she told Fuad. 'I wrote that. Poor Jaime. Let it be his epitaph. And I will add this to it.'

She took a pen and wrote on the bottom of the page,

'Peace in thy hand.
Peace in thine eyes.
Peace on thy brow.
Flower of a moment in the eternal hour
Peace be with you now.'

She did not explain to Fuad that in one class in her school each girl had had to learn by heart certain poems by modern writers. She had learnt amongst others, Walter de la Mare's 'The Ghost' because she felt it was very short, had only three verses and meant little. Now by changing one word she had made it mean a great deal.

'And now, Señor,' Karen continued, 'we have the message written but there should be something more. A place for it. Ah, please lend me your knife. Thank you.'

A large cactus grew nearby. With a quick stroke she cut a large thorn from the cactus. Then it seemed to him, with the most devilish delicacy she pinned the pieces of paper together with the thorn and handed them to him. In the collection were all the quotations that Silva had read after he had killed Jaime topped by the epitaph she had just written.

'His memorial. I can ask nothing more from you, his friend, than that you place it in the proper place.'

With a gesture towards her chest she indicated where she felt it should go on Jaime's body. There were few times in his life that Fuad ever found himself at a loss for words. This was one of them so he offered a gesture as substitute. He took off his hat, bowed to her and walked slowly and purposefully to the grave. She did not wait to see him do what she knew he would do.

The grave was ready and the corpse was lowered gently and respectfully. None of the grave diggers thought it wise to ask about the paper and the cactus thorn put, at the last moment, on his chest.

The few, who helped the grave diggers to complete the duty of covering Jaime, included Medina.

The next morning came but with it came neither Cutbush nor Harkness.

On Miss Quinn's suggestion Gibberd sent to find Fuad. This was not difficult for he had to be near the centre of things, things about to happen or, things which would have to be delayed.

Fuad listened to Gibberd. 'Good,' he said, 'leave it to me. You will hear from me in about two hours.'

Fuad went to see Delfosse. They discussed the matter and the latter said, 'Thank heavens most of the *chicleros* are here, or hereabout. Let's call Medina.'

So the arrangements for the search for Cutbush and Harkness were put in the hands of the experts. Later that day it was reported to Cibrian that Pedro's mule had been found still tethered and also that Fuad had sent someone to recover Jaime's mule. Of Silva and his mule there was no evidence. Cibrian went over again in his mind what Miss Quinn had told him she and Karen Farr had heard, when the group of five had listened as the evening star rose to a certain angle and the moon shone on the quick and the dead, the sane and the lost.

Cibrian learnt of the arrangements being made for the search for Cutbush and Harkness.

Just before the first of the search parties left on their errand he announced that the murderers of Peat-Patterson were fugitives from justice and he personally offered a reward of two hundred dollars for each man, Pedro Lopez and Gil Silva, dead or alive though if dead, proof positive must be provided.

Night covered forest and plain and a rock against which lay a dead man and a living man who, for the first time in a career of achievement and distinction, knew uncertainty. He who had often dealt in certainty and competence with the sane and the insane but he now found himself with binnacle light obscured and navigation charts unserviceable. Death was nothing new in his experience having been part of his trade for many years. He had lived for long periods in hospitals, had seen the strong and the vigorous struck down in their prime and the lovely and the proud sentenced to a malodorous decomposition of personality while the body flourished like a lush repulsive excrescence and death was a welcome scavenger. The various reactions of the dying had interested him, at first, but his original interest had been dimmed because the reactions had to be supplied with drama by the living. 'As soon as Napoleon barks his shin against Charon's boat,' he had concluded, 'he says "Ouch" with the same note and accent of unbelief as the meanest of us.' But the death of Harkness affected him profoundly. It was not that he considered Harkness a Napoleon or even a very striking individual. He had met very many and known some intimately who had infinitely more intellectual drive and power than Harkness. Nor had the man been endowed with that disarming charm, that happy and accidental conglomerate of physical, mental and psychological attributes which give other people pleasure merely to be in their presence. Indeed Cutbush suddenly realized that Harkness was not important; certainly he had not been important to Harkness himself except, as he had once said, 'I am the instrument by which the gods mock me and, incidentally, themselves. That is my importance to myself!' He had not been important in respect of family ties; the delegation of the writing of the last letter to his mother was suggestive enough. His importance in science, if he had done sufficient work as yet to credit him with such a status, was so circumscribed and confined that perhaps not more than a score of savants scattered over the face of the earth would note his death with professional regret. Nor had he the instinctive courtesy which comes from an acute awareness of the value and dignity of each man. Nor did he give to each man, without hesitation, without thought or without the reflex compulsion of training in manners, a ready, equal and urbane acceptance. If Gibberd had died here, thought Cutbush, tomorrow there would hardly be a dry eye in this section of Petén. No one would weep for Harkness, none lament. 'I shall be his only mourner I think,' said Cutbush, 'and that partly because I killed him.' Harkness, however, had it seemed a faith in man's powers, an awareness of the potentiality of man here and now which was unusual and stimulating. He was a Boswell creating a greater Johnson or better, the art critic pointing out the mystery and mastery in the work of the artist, pointing out things of which the artist himself had so far not been aware.

He looked at his own handiwork after the critic had opened his eyes and did not say, 'I look upon my work and find it good.' Instead he exclaimed, 'What hath God wrought!'

Who was then the 'artist'? Not Deodato Graña, for Harkness had bewailed the pettiness of the stratagems that would fell that giant. The artist was a conception in the mind of Harkness, the artist was mankind: he was man, becoming more and more certain that he was not merely an instrument but a full orchestra. He had so many varieties of experiences that he could sample that the congenitally weak and inept would be confused at the wealth of choice. Like unto Buridan's ass they would destroy themselves by a negative compulsion; a hara-kari of the schizophrenic. Those however who had the power to place good and evil in their proper perspective in human affairs would be able to command the instruments of the full orchestra. At one moment a man, any man, might climb with the high-noted piccolo to the lovely solitude of the mystic, at another moment he might mutter with the bassoon of the daemonic, equally at home, utterly certain, quietly assured. Perhaps the only time man would feel a quiver of uncertainty, of awe, was when his full orchestra at concert pitch played in a majestic symphony of all his faculties. Then perhaps man would tremble slightly for did not the very heavens tremble slightly at that time vibrating in sympathy with the music. By his refusal to consider himself of importance Harkness had shed personality and accepted a tenuous individuality.

'In a prayer from the Rig Veda,' he had said, 'personality is one of the evils from which man prays to be delivered. I heard a lawyer say, more than once, for he was repetitive in his cups, that the idea of personality, that unique and precious attribute of western man, is nothing but a legal fiction dating from early Roman law. A man owned things, a man therefore possessed his soul, his mind, his body; this trinity, fused into one, was his personality, the goods and chattels of his selfness, the quintessence of his selfishness, the thing of itself. The most I wish to claim for myself is individuality, a separateness which is convenient. It allows me to work and move. It is but the licence plate on the motor car, a mark of identity. Personality implies the whole motor car, engine and fuel and, furthermore, a car that knows the road, even takes this road before it as it travels. Such colossal assurance is beyond me. No, my licence plate gives me elbow room to work and move, to utilize my time and my innate gifts. All this, however, has no overtones of godhead, of an everlasting me. That my personality and my soul could be everlasting is a bit of arrogance that is just funny.'

Nor did this quiet acceptance of his ultimate doom raise Harkness in Cutbush's estimation. For if a man is doomed it were better to die of a gradual suffocation than from the excruciating pains of snake bite. There had been no bone-breaking pain, no agonizing mangling of the body so that the reluctant moans break into the rending scream. Yet, the death of this almost negative man disturbed the positive, the successful, the dominant and purposive Cutbush more than any experience he could remember. That a response of allergy, the reaction of the body to an injection of horse-serum should take the form of dropsy of the lungs, was in the human being very, very rare. Cutbush had never before seen this type of dropsy from just this cause but he knew that theoretically it could occur. But Harkness by dying of it mocked in the only effectual way the ministrations and appurtenances of science and technology. Just for a moment, such was his perturbation, Cutbush gave thought for that school of so-called 'thinkers' which when they did get his attention gave him an intense irritation. He privately labelled them the 'poison-ivy' school.

He wondered for that moment whether by accident they might have stumbled on a nugget of truth. These people had had the imbecility to suggest that science in the form of industry which provided comfort, medicine which bade the sinking sun stay longer in the west and agronomy which grew several blades of grass where none grew before, that all these were not unmixed blessings. They questioned the blessing of industry which, with fatal compulsion at irregular intervals, had to dedicate the greater portion of its potential to making implements of destruction. They questioned the blessing of medicine which abolished infectious disease and left a population ageing into joyless decrepitude robbed of 'that last blessing of the old man, pneumonia'. They pointed out that to make several blades of grass grow where none grew before was, ultimately, to expand the desert. But even as he thought of this school of so-called 'thinkers' Cutbush dismissed them from his mind. They did not meet his problem. He had to face up to a deliberate and ironic jest of fate. That was his problem because he was the victim of the jest.

He had been the unwitting executioner, with the highest and most unselfish motive, of perhaps the only man in Petén who could have been killed by just this application of the most exquisitely finished product of science applied to the saving of life. He did not mind being the victim of a joke. He did mind if it were an ironic jest. Irony was something which touched him where he was defenceless. It could penetrate elsewhere than where he was protected by the pride of technical competence and by the assurance of unimpeachable motives. 'With a one in a million chance it had to be me,' he told himself and shivered. He began to feel cold. There was a cool wind blowing from the north. 'Of course it is still winter up there,' he thought, 'I should light a fire. I wonder if he has matches.' Cutbush did not smoke but Harkness did. Professionally hardened as he was he could not repress a shiver of distaste as he turned over the corpse. There was a book of matches in the breast pocket of the shirt. But the fluid which had welled up from the lungs and poured across the flat rock on which he lay had saturated the cloth. The matches were ruined. Cutbush wiped the sticky moisture from his hands and returned to the lee side of the rock deciding to try to sleep but that sought-for balm came only in short, disturbed naps.

Once he tried to warm himself by stamping his feet and swinging his arms but that awakened him too thoroughly. The cold was not an urgent numbing of will or limb. It was a persuasive cold that seemed to apologize for its intrusion, saying that the cold of a tropic night could not really be cold. It was a sneaking misery. Cutbush burrowed down trying to get between the rock and the earth. When he, at last, saw the few stars pale above him he almost cried with relief.

'Those clouds above us last evening had looked like rain.

Thank God it never fell.' He thought, 'Now the first thing is to protect Harkness from carrion hunters. But how?' They were some distance from the woods but the savannah grasses were nearby. He unbuckled the machete scabbard from Harkness's belt, cut sufficient grass with it, piled it over the corpse and weighted it with flat stones.

'That will do till I return later,' he decided. 'I could do with some coffee. The exercise cutting grass has made me thirsty and I must go for help. I must make for the mules. I hope they have not broken away from where they were tethered. I had better take the machete for I might meet that fellow.'

He meant he might meet the snake but he could not frame the word 'snake'.

When he came to the edge of the ravine and looked down the rocky path to the bottom, that path which he had twice trod, he decided that he could not pass down it again.

'I don't care,' he said aloud, 'I don't care. I will not, I cannot, go down there. Not that way again. No, no I must find some other path. There must be one somewhere else.'

With the machete scabbard attached to his belt he started walking along the edge of the ravine away from the direction in which they had come. He argued that if there had been a way on this side of the path Harkness would have taken it rather than come thus far; therefore he had to go on further to find another way back. He had travelled for over half a mile, without finding a safe path down the cliffside of the ravine when he looked back. The rock by which the corpse lay was no longer visible.

'Of course,' he thought, 'this big ditch turns and twists all over the place and there is another ditch joining it, in fact a whole delta of ditches. I must not go too far out of my way; it is too tiring walking under this sun on an empty stomach. I will try the next possible place I see.'

But it was not until he had walked much further that he saw a likely path down the cliff. He tried it, going carefully downward. It was not too difficult and then six feet from the botton it ended, so he decided to jump. His landing would have to be amongst loose stones. He jumped and fell heavily. The stiff machete scabbard with the machete in it hurt his side dreadfully.

'No bones broken,' he told himself, as he picked himself up, 'but I must be careful. Troubles come in battalions.'

The machete had fallen from the scabbard as he struggled to get up. He decided to unbuckle the scabbard – it was stiff and heavy and he was not accustomed to a heavy appendage flapping against his side but he decided, at the last moment, to carry the machete.

'Now,' he thought, 'I must retrace my steps up to that place,' he meant the place of the snake, 'and find the other path up which I must climb. But with these other ravines coming in from the left it means I shall have to climb down and up several of them. That would be all right if I knew the paths. If, however, I go up the first of them on my left and climb out on my left that should bring me by the lagoon. Once there I know my way for by following round the edge of the lagoon, keeping it on my left hand, I will come to the narrow isthmus between the two lagoons. That is practically home; besides I need water.'

He turned into the first ravine which entered from the left but its walls were as sheer as the other and he had to go a considerable distance before he discovered a possible path up the side. With great relief he made for it, gripping the machete purposefully. Even if he saw a snake he meant to go up the path for he was thirsty. He climbed out of the ravine and found himself not as he had hoped near the lagoon but in bush where the forest thinned to meet the savannah. He looked back at the ravine.

'Of course,' he thought, 'when I was walking along the bottom I didn't notice that it twists and turns like a worm. The lagoon must be up further on my right hand. If I strike through this bush, here, I ought to hit it in under an hour.'

His machete now came in useful and he used it continuously, sometimes to push aside the lower branch of a tree, sometimes to cut himself loose from an entangling liana. He walked briskly in what he thought of as the direction of the lagoon. Before too long, however, his walk became less brisk.

'I don't like this business,' he told himself. 'There is water in the lagoon but I don't seem to be getting anywhere near it. Now, let's take stock. First, I must find a place where I can see the sun.'

He looked at his watch and a faint chill of doubt and dread touched him. His watch pointed to a few minutes from mid-day.

'No wonder I am so thirsty. I had no idea I had gone so far. I think the best thing is to rest a little then push on.' The words passed through his mind as if they were on a piece of white tape. He sat down and leaned his back against a tree. Soon he began to nod and then he stretched out on the earth and slept soundly. When he awoke he looked at his watch again. He had slept for no more than a few minutes.

He got to his feet telling himself, 'Well, let's go, though a bottle of beer, no, a long glass of water would have been a welcome eye-opener'.

'The lagoon can't be far off now,' he said some time later; 'though this looks like real old chicle forest. This is a business'. His watch told him it was three o'clock and his thirst was really troubling him.

'Of course there are travellers' palms and other such plants I have heard of with water in them and there is that liana which Medina told me about,' he remembered. 'He said one could get nearly a pint of water from a couple of yards of the liana. But even if I stumbled over it I wouldn't know it. No wonder the people get out of the forests in the dry season. The lagoons dry up and the few rivers are at several days' journey from each other. So the villages must be near wells; now talking of wells.' Cutbush stopped suddenly and his machete dropped from his nerveless hand.

'This is stupid,' he muttered, 'I must pull myself together. This mental chewing of the cud must stop; for that way lies ... ' But he would not state what lay beyond being as he was an expert, world famous, on the subject.

'Curiously,' he told himself later, 'I am not hungry; but if I could see some sort of fruit ... ' There was no fruit to be seen. It was only when he could no longer see his way amongst the trees of the forest that he voiced the fearful words.

'I am lost. It is another night. I am lost and thirsty and soon I shall be cold as well'.

Later that night when the chill wakened him from his exhausted sleep he went over the position in his mind. Then he fell into an uneasy sleep to dream of a thin stream of water gushing from the flat rock on which he was sleeping.

In the dream the water was not inviting because it was covered with a fine foam. He immersed the tip of his finger in it and found that it was sticky. He woke shivering in a thin glow of light through the tree tops. He struggled to his feet and groaned at the stiffness of his legs.

'That is not only from sudden use, or lack of exercise,' he muttered, 'that pain is something else. However, enough trouble is enough. Now, where is the sun rising? If I could climb up far enough on one of the trees I could see the east.'

He looked carefully at those about him without finding one with convenient branches by which he could haul himself up, that was tall enough for a look-out station. He tried to climb a tall tree but the stiffness in his legs and the girth of the tree prevented him getting more than a few feet above ground. He decided to wait till the sunlight penetrated strongly enough for him to know from which direction the light came. Then he would start off with the sun on his left hand. He sat down to wait. Warmth crept into his veins like a strong liquor. He thawed out blissfully, then started walking his dappled shadow falling away from his right hand. He had walked for some distance before he realized he had forgotten the machete.

He had left it stuck into the tree by whose root he had slept. He had now been without water for many hours and during that time had been subjected to unusual and disturbing mental and physical stress. But he was not yet suffering because after that first creeping chill of doubt he had resolutely banished trepidation from his mind. He had no doubt that if he did not panic, and he did not intend to panic, he could satisfactorily rationalize his position in the forest. He would make a map in his mind and even if he had to take a spiral course he would sooner or later get to some recognizable point. Once he struck a road he knew that help would not be far off and he would have to walk no more than, perhaps, two days along that road before he came to a hut or a village if, that is, he did not meet anyone before. He had not reckoned on the distortion of his mental images by the deprivation of his body of water. He had started walking towards the south at seven o'clock in the morning and thought he had walked steadily for about three hours when it would be time to turn sharply to his right and follow his nose. Then he decided to look at his watch. It was a little more than an hour since he started. He had never before doubted its reliability. He listened to it. It was ticking with all its former precision and unconcern.

'Did I wind it last night?' he asked himself, 'I don't remember. Better do it now,' he said. So he wound his watch and continued to wind it until the spring snapped. It was then that something else snapped, or perhaps loosened. He felt his tongue suddenly large, dry, rasping and tender. He opened his mouth and blew gently but that made his throat ache. A dizziness came over him for a few moments.

'It isn't so much the loss of water; it is the enforced exercise in this infernal climate,' he muttered. 'But I must keep going, if I don't I am done.'

He put his useless watch in his pocket then took it out and threw it away.

'Useless,' he thought, 'useless, better travel light. Travel light; who travels light travels far but I have travelled too far. Too far, too far, too far from where? Travel light. I wonder if I am getting light in the mind. Rubbish, I have only to pull myself together. People have been without water for many days. What about people on rafts at sea from one birthday to the next? Bligh of the Bounty and all that. Bligh bringing plants in Bounty. Bounty in plants, water-bearing plants. Brumalia plants spread malaria in Trinidad. There are Brumalia here. I have seen them and Harkness agreed they were of the same genus. So all right let's look for Brumalia. Climb the tree when I see one and there you are; a pint of water in Brumalia; full of mosquito larvae but what of it? fattening; it's food and drink, dew of Brumalia. He on honey dew hath fed and drunk the wine, but steady, not too much of "Paradise". A trifle premature. Must not drink before the legal opening time.' For the next few minutes he walked with his gaze fixed high up peering at the upper branches of the tallest trees. He was searching for the epiphyte Brumalia. Then he tripped over a protruding root and fell heavily. He hit his head against a nearby tree and remained dazed and prostrate for some few minutes. 'I wonder,' he muttered as he lay there, 'what the name of the Abyssinian maid was who sang about milk of Paradise. Now, I have it, her name was Brumalia.' He struggled to his feet but, now, kept his gaze on the ground.

'Nose to ground,' he muttered, 'nose to ground, truffle hound, water diviner. And the waters were troubled. He troubled the waters. That fellow Harkness troubled the waters where I had drunk. By the waters of Complaisance I hung up my harp and drank my fill.'

After Jaime's funeral Karen, almost by accident, found herself near Fuad as the group of mourners dispersed. She was a lady that Fuad did not, in fact, particularly care for. He remembered a discussion with his wife about the two women who were with Dr. Gibberd's team. Fatima had entertained the ladies when they reached El Cayo and had admired the beautiful blonde Miss Quinn but had been captivated by Karen, praising her distinction, her poise, her charm which though not obvious and overworked could be so disarming, so generous 'it pleases you like the memory of an old song,' Fatima had said.

Fuad had been in a teasing mood. The Quinn he dismissed in a phrase, 'a lovely selfish bitch, with only one approach to her innards.' Karen had intimidated him. He had revenged his inadequacy by saying that he bet she could never forget herself enough one day to do so and so and he went into lush anatomical details. His wife had pungent things to say of his mind. He replied that the memory of old songs such as the memory Fatima had described could also be coupled with the memory of just such exploits as he had described.

Fatima laughed. And who was it, she wanted to know, had taught her those exploits?

Now he brought his attention back to this intimidating lady beside him. 'I bet she wants to talk about Jaime's death but nothing doing.' He would not discuss that matter with anyone until he was forced to do so in a court of law, though Pedro would never allow matters to reach that point. Karen, however, did not mention Jaime. She spoke of the closing of the frontier and of the weather.

Fuad was polite but non-committal even about the weather. It was after the weather, as a subject of conversation, had run dry that she mentioned the 'Speaker'.

'Aha,' thought Fuad 'here she blows!'

'Oh yes,' he said, 'I have known the old man for some years.'

Then he went on to tell what he knew, of what he had guessed and of the information he had collected from Chiapas, of the hints, legends and folk-tales which rendered his acquired information so baffling.

'The old man used to live with a family in Pusilha who had "inherited" him from another family. The latter family had returned to Mexico, to Campeche people said, to work chicle there. The "inheriting" family had scattered with the death of the old mother. So the "Speaker" lived alone in a broken-down hut that had belonged to one of the sons of the family. It was then that Señora Arevalo had had the Priest's House repaired for him and organized the charity of the village so that he would not starve. His health is poor. He has fits sometimes. He often forgets to finish what he is doing. In fact, he is very forgetful. It is no use, for example, to give him more than one cigar at a time. He will smoke one with great relish but forgets where he has put the others. He talks in a stuttering gabble but sometimes when he appears to be in the mood he can speak quite distinctly but slowly as if he has to count his words.'

'What does he talk about?' Karen asked.

'Oh, they say he will talk of the weather.'

'Why is he called the "Speaker"?'

'Oh, I suppose it is because when he speaks slowly he speaks so beautifully in a good accent not like the vernacular of Petén. His name on the books, the Government books of Petén, is "Gomez". But Gomez was the name of the Mexican family who first "possessed" him. That was the family who was said to have gone to Campeche.'

'Why did they go to Campeche?'

'One of the sons fell foul of someone in Petén, a chicle deal, or some such something. He was shot at and merely wounded but thought it wise to leave before another bullet got him. He went to Campeche and it is said did well there.'

Karen found it difficult to get information from Fuad. The latter was tired of her persistence. He was despondent about matters generally and he was really grieving for Jaime. Jaime who had been rescued and preserved by that economical housewife, his peerless Fatima.

Jaime the flotsam who had become his friend and confidant, his faithful henchman and court-jester, herald of Fatima, his wife, and the hero of his younger children. He had no doubt that Jaime had been killed in some tragic accident, some expostulation with the little humourist who must have suddenly decided to return and fight it out with Pedro, or the law, or anyone. And Jaime must have shown that to return would involve Fuad, as an accessory after the crime of the murder of Modesto Moreno, in that he had sheltered the fugitive Silva and provided means of escape. He did not believe that Silva would shoot Jaime, or anyone, deliberately except perhaps in imminent peril of his life. And Jaime was the last man to imperil the life of anyone. In war he was a killer, but in civil life he was the mildest, the most innocuous of creatures. No, it must have been an accident, one of those accidents, those things which added to other things, other little things, showed that the end of a chapter had come in Fuad's life for he, now, found the Petén distasteful. Colonel Cibrian was now the senior military officer in charge of that district of the Province yet Major Arevalo continued in charge of the civil administration.

This was, to Fuad, a bifurcation of responsibility which presaged a change in the method of government. It promised, Fuad believed, that the closing of the frontier was no bluff. Graña did not bluff. Obviously with so vast a territory dependent on supplies by aeroplane there would be an entirely new mode of life thrust on the Province. If the air lift was adequate, well and good, but it could be adequate only in capacity because nothing could be as cheap as mule transport. That it would, frequently, be inadequate in capacity and carrying power he had no doubt. Then there would be hardship for the people and exasperation for the chicle exporter. Also, whether adequate or not, it would strictly be a government business with a middle-man like himself frozen out for there would be no buying and selling with a profit each time. With any other administration the projected government monopoly of supply and of transport would have been a gold-mine. He would merely have had to get close, and the more lavish the 'lubrication', the closer the contact to the appropriate ministry. He would have had to grease certain palms and then he would have had his 'cut' from every pound of supplies brought in and every pound of chicle taken out. It would have been wonderful and would have continued until the people became exasperated and started the next revolution.

Under President Graña, however, there was no greasing of palms. He knew because he had tried it. A lowly clerk here or there would sell a little dribble of information for a few cents but nobody in the administration who was anybody and who could be useful to him would take a bribe. It had made things very difficult though he had managed and managed well. But not any more. Those days were over. He was weary of Petén. He would return to the Colony and become a model husband and father until his ideas matured on one or more of several new projects he had in mind. And here, in his thoughts, he paid tribute again to Fatima for knowing that with Jaime what you said sunk into a deep, deep hole because he never betrayed a secret or the smallest bit of information, even by accident.

He bade a courteous but firm adieu to Karen. He had, he said, a matter of consuming importance to think over. He had to decide what his attitude should be to Cibrian. In fact, he bitterly cursed himself for having acted so quickly in going to see the Colonel. Fortunately that man also had things on his mind for had he not been weeping and insisted on putting off the meeting? And since then had not other things happened?

PART NINE

EACH COLOUR OF THE RAINBOW SANG

Medina, at the request of Delfosse and Fuad, was given the responsibility of organizing the search for Cutbush and Harkness. He was given a free hand as far as men and material were concerned. Medina went away and returned with the Commissary Clerk. Yes, said the latter, within ten minutes he could begin to weigh, measure and pack provisions for eight days for each man. With extra assistance he could supply one hundred men within two hours. Delfosse dismissed him with orders to send for his extra assistance and stand by at his commissariat until further orders.

In the meantime Medina was drawing up the agreement. It was signed by Gibberd. All expense of providing equipment and provisions for a hundred *chicleros* was to be borne by the Nethersole Foundation with Gibberd acting as their agent. Each *chiclero* was to be paid five dollars per day while engaged on the search. A reward of two thousand dollars was to be paid to any-one who found Cutbush and delivered him alive; two hundred dollars to anyone who found him dead. Gibberd signed the document. Then he saw how Delfosse had earned his reputation. He seemed to know that vast forest as if it was a back-yard garden. In less than an hour groups of *chicleros* properly mounted and provisioned began to set out for the bush. Each group was personally checked and directed to their section by Delfosse. When they went to the location they were given they were to make camp and begin the search. A team of messengers relaying information from group to group and to headquarters would be constantly on the march reporting progress, or the lack of it. In two hours the last member of this properly organized and directed search party, each man a bushman of experience, had left to hunt for Cutbush and Gibberd was satisfied that all that could be done had been done.

'If you feel you must play some part,' said Medina to Gibberd, 'team up with the messengers. In that way you will hear any news first.'

Gibberd set out at once for the bush with the messengers with the result that he was already on his way when the first news arrived. The body of Harkness had been discovered by a *chiclero*, one of a group, and Medina decided to examine the body.

So he set out at once for the place, near the ravine, where the body of Harkness had been found. On arrival he examined the corpse carefully but learned nothing other than that death was not due to obvious violence though there were two small scratches on one leg and also a small wound on the scalp. He noticed that the machete and scabbard were missing. It was already late afternoon but Medina decided to take a chance. He looked this way and that then rode slowly along the bank of the ravine. He had ridden for about a mile and a half when he saw what he was looking for. There was a likely path down the side of the cliff. He threw the reins over the head of his mule so that the separated reins would trail on the ground. His mule had been trained. It was now more securely tethered than if it had been tied firmly by a rope. It was tethered in its brain and had been trained to stay in one place as long as the reins trailed and touched the ground at that place. Medina was half-way down the cliff when he saw the empty machete scabbard. His heart leapt.

'This is the trail,' he thought. 'That scabbard was dropped there after Harkness died. A living bushman would hardly ever abandon equipment and certainly not a machete scabbard. Cutbush dropped that. Therefore he did it after Harkness died. He passed this way. He came down into this ravine and doubtless climbed out but which of the many ravines did he climb?' That, he decided, would be either very easy, or very difficult to determine. Whichever it was it would require a team to cover the ground.

He returned to the group who had found Harkness and brought them to the place where he had found the machete scabbard. It was now too late to do any more that evening so they discussed plans for the morrow and made camp for the night.

Medina reconstructed his reading of the death of Harkness. He decided that Cutbush had climbed down the path and had fallen the last few feet.

His quarry had then climbed back up the path at the call of Harkness when the latter felt the seizure which was to prove fatal. After the death of Harkness, Cutbush had walked along the top of the ravine for about a mile and a half until he found another path. He climbed down this path to the bottom of the ravine and it was then he lost the machete scabbard. Cutbush would only climb down to the bottom of the ravine in order to cross it and climb up on the other side. But from which of the several tributary ravines had he climbed out? If they could discover that then they would be on sound ground. They would be following most positive evidence.

Early the next morning Medina divided his men into two groups at 'the path of the scabbard'. One group went down the ravine – the other group up. As they came to tributary ravines one man should go up each tributary and investigate it. But all were to return by early afternoon to the 'path of the scabbard' to report.

There was news from one of them when they met. One man reported that he had been up his ravine to a path where he found evidence that someone had recently used it.

He had climbed out of the ravine and beside this path he had seen that someone had used a machete to clear a passage through the bush. The person who wielded the machete was an amateur in its use. He had followed the traces left by the machete-wielder until low bush had given way to high forest where all traces were lost. His comrades and Medina heard this report with avid interest. It must be Cutbush. Then they all shouted with laughter except the man who had found and followed the tracks. It was clear to the others that he had returned to tell them of his discovery only because he had lost the trail. He was a very chagrined man. Had he been able to follow any traces not all the orders of Medina or of anyone else would have brought him back. The reward for the discovery of Cutbush alive was two thousand dollars. That was reason enough to disobey the orders of Lucifer himself.

They went up the ravine and out of it by the path to the passage through the bush. The evidence of the machete work was conclusive. It could only be the work of an amateur and therefore the work of Cutbush. Medina then suggested that each man put himself in the position of the wanderer and think what he would have done. It was clear that Cutbush would walk for several hours in the forest before he realized he was truly lost. Then he would stop and take stock of his position. He would argue that the essential fact of the layout of the district was that the road from the frontier to Shoonantonitch and the road from the latter village to Cenote Perdida met at an acute angle. Indeed for a part of their route the two roads were roughly parallel. Since he was on this side of the ravine and had not cut across either or both of these roads he would know that he had passed north of the junction at the acute angle. He would then decide to go south hoping to strike the junction but if he did not do so after a few hours he would then turn sharply right so as to cut across either road at a right angle. Once he struck a road he would keep to it. If he were not too far gone when he did meet the road he would be able to decide which way lay Shoonantonitch and set off in that direction.

The *chicleros* agreed that if Cutbush were not too frightened he would perhaps reason as Medina had done. They thereupon agreed on a procedure which Medina suggested in which every man would be on his own.

The party split up, each man to make a circle of differing diameter where all the circles would touch at the point on which they now stood. As soon as the man at the inmost circle was satisfied that he had searched sufficiently in his circle he would then invade the next circle. In such a manner, as the area of the search grew, the numbers of searchers would be increased. As for Medina, he did not tell them what he would do but he had faith in Cutbush's steadiness in a frightening situation. He had been quite sincere in the deductions which he had offered to the *chicleros* but he had no intention of working on a circumference. He would make for the junction of the roads, ride down the frontier road for two days on one diameter and then cut across the forest and strike the Cenote Perdida road and ride back to Shoonantonitch. He would therefore be back in camp by the sixth day of Cutbush's disappearance. If he had not been found by then he would be dead. Of course there was the chance that if Cutbush did emerge from the bush on to one of these roads his mental and physical condition might be such that he take the direction away from Shoonantonitch. In fact Medina was enough of a realist to accept the proposition that even were he in good physical and mental shape Cutbush could well set off in the wrong direction. Medina believed that given an even chance a man naturally chose the wrong road not five times out of ten but eight times out of ten.

Shortly past noon on the second day after he had held his council of *chicleros*, who thereafter searched circumferentially while he searched on the road, he turned aside from the frontier road and tethered his mule in the shade of a great ficus tree. He unsaddled the animal, rubbed it down and then prepared a meal for himself. He had decided that he would ride on for a few miles after re-saddling and then if he did not find any trace of Cutbush cut across the forest and make for the Cenote Perdida road. He finished his meal and strolled to where the road made a sharp curve about thirty yards from the ficus tree. He saw two men on the road, one bending over the other who lay prostrate, the man who was bending over had a gun in his hand. Medina thought he recognized Cutbush's hat on the road, an outrageous pseudo-sombrero that was unique in Petén. But the man who had been bending and was now standing up, still with the gun in his hand, was not Cutbush, he was a much shorter man. Medina quietly went back for his rifle and returned making a wide circle in the forest walking quickly but very quietly. He came out of the forest on to the road opposite the two men.

The man on the ground was Cutbush. The other man was still bending over him but now he was dropping water from a tin cup into Cutbush's mouth. Beside him lay a gun, a new shotgun. The man's clothes were new or very nearly new. His machete scabbard was new. He was bare-headed but near him was a straw sombrero. He was as bald as an egg. He looked up as Medina stepped on to the road. He looked into the barrel of the rifle levelled at him but made no motion and spoke no word until Medina took up the shotgun and asked, 'Is he alive?'

'Only just; he needs more water,' replied the bald man.

Medina saw now that he had only one eye. His left eye socket was empty while the right eye looked calmly at Medina from a countenance that seemed a hundred years old. His body, however, was not that of an old man. He held a water-bottle in one hand, the tin cup in the other.

'Then let us put him in the shade and give him some more,' said Medina.

Together they lifted him; Medina putting his right arm under the knees, the left arm still carrying the rifle. They laid him gently in the shade of a tree.

'Have you water,' asked the bald man, 'for this is all I have left?'

'I have water,' said Medina.

He bent down to examine Cutbush. He put the shotgun carefully to one side but still kept hold of the rifle. Cutbush was in a desperate condition. He was stuporous but still kept enough of his reflexes to be able to swallow if the water were trickled drop by drop on to his tongue.

'Have you any salt?' asked the bald man. 'A little salt in the water would do him good.'

'Yes,' replied Medina, 'at my camp, a little way from here. I will get it later.'

'Good,' said the other 'we shall have to carry him but two of us can't carry him any distance. In fact one of us had better go for help unless you have enough help at your camp so that we could start carrying him at once.'

'No,' said Medina, 'I haven't; one of us must go for help.'

The water in the tin cup was finished. The bald man said as he got up to fill it again from the water-bottle, 'Hold his head steady will you, please? We can't waste a drop.'

Medina kneeled down, carefully put the shotgun beside him and leaned the rifle against his thigh holding it lightly with one hand while with the other hand he steadied Cutbush's head. The bald man poured water into the tin cup but this time, instead of putting a few spoonfuls in it, he filled it to the brim. Then he bent down, putting the cup near Cutbush's mouth and suddenly throwing all the water in Medina's face at the same time kicking his rifle from his grasp. Almost before the rifle could fall he had leapt across Cutbush's prostrate body and grasped it. As he sprang back, levelling the rifle at Medina, the latter, who almost as quick and as resolute, grasped the shotgun and pointed it at him.

'The gun you hold is empty,' said the bald man. 'If your rifle is not don't move your hand to your pistol. I will pull the trigger if you move. Now, kneel and unbuckle your pistol belt with one hand and continue holding the gun with the other. Good. And drop the pistol belt and the shotgun because it is useless. Move on your knees towards me and stay there.'

He circled Medina with the rifle pointed steadily at him, took up the pistol belt with cartridges and pistol in it. Next he kicked the shotgun away.

'Now,' said he 'we go to your camp. Lead the way. I presume from what you said you are either alone or with a small party. Whether you are alone or not make no noise. I shall not hesitate to drop you at the first squeak. And I shan't kill you because a bullet in your spine won't kill you, not for a long time, perhaps many weeks. March!'

Medina had trained as a soldier. Victory and defeat were part of his trade. He had lost the upper hand temporarily with a man who was a complete stranger. He would not know that Cutbush alive was worth two thousand dollars and dead only two hundred. In any case nothing would be gained by being rash. He had seen men with bullets through the spine. He would be cautious until his time came. He turned and walked towards his camp.

'How far is it?' asked the bald man. Medina told him. They soon reached it.

'Now,' said the bald man to Medina, 'saddle your mule, fill up your water-bottle and hang it on the saddle. Lead the mule to the road and hand me the reins.' He mounted the animal.

'Now march ahead of me.' Medina preceded him along the road towards the spot where he had first seen the bald man bending over Cutbush.

'Now stop and hand me his hat. And let me tell you that what troubles him is not only thirst. When I first saw him I didn't know how far gone he was so I crept up to him and hit him on the head with the barrel of the gun.'

Medina picked up Cutbush's hat and handed it to the man.

'*Gracias*,' he said and, spurring the mule suddenly, he was off at a gallop down the road in the direction towards the frontier. Medina saw him go with relief. His going was obviously that of a man in a hurry with pressing business ahead, or behind. It is true that he had gone with his mule and his rifle, both very good of their kind. His pistol was good only to Medina because it had the habit of jamming unexpectedly. He knew the trick but anyone who didn't and had to use it urgently was going to be disappointed. The man had gone but he had left Cutbush and Medina decided to try to avenge himself on the robber by doing his best to keep Cutbush alive. His rage at being so coolly and decisively worsted spent itself. He went back to Cutbush. The latter had come out of his stupor. Medina fed him a little more water with a few grains of salt in it. He remained conscious for but a few minutes before his stupor returned. It was clear he was in a critical condition and he was muttering unintelligibly.

Now and again Medina was able to understand what he said, a few words in sequence, but for the most part it was a disjointed raving. As there was no question of travelling now Medina went to his camp and removed all his provisions to where Cutbush lay. It was obvious that if he were injudiciously handled he would die and that would mean a loss of eighteen hundred dollars.

Medina prepared to be nurse and physician. There was enough water for both for two days but he took no chances. He rationed himself severely. There was sufficient food. All that afternoon and evening he tended the sick man assiduously, feeding him water in small frequent doses when he could swallow. By early night the spells of delirium were less frequent. At about midnight Medina made a thin pap of wheat-flour, sweetened it with condensed milk and fed him a little. He promptly vomited the first few mouthfuls and collapsed in a faint. After a few minutes he recovered from the faint and in about half an hour he signed to Medina to try again. This time he did not vomit. Twice during the remainder of the night he signalled for more of the pap. Then he slept till well on into the morning. When he awoke he spoke rationally.

'Medina,' he said, 'how did you get here?'

Then he fell asleep again but to Medina's consternation the sleep gave way to stupor, the stupor of an agitated delirium. It was another trying day and night but next day a patrol of gendarmes newly relieved from their post on the frontier came along the road. Medina made certain that if the gendarmes could get Cutbush to Shoonantonitch alive he would double each man's pay for that month. It was a deal. They carried the Doctor in a hammock slung from poles. It was a slow business but the gendarmes wanted the money. They carried him all day and well into the night. Medina had made them understand that if he died he would give them nothing. When the fatigue of the journey seemed to be getting too much for the sick man they made camp. Next morning some *chicleros* arrived at their camp who told them the value of their prize. Fortunately Cutbush was now conscious enough to state that Medina had found him. No one could jump Medina's claim.

Although not stuporous, however, Cutbush was far from well. For one thing he would not be left alone. Not even the sound of company was enough. He had to see a friendly face and to hear a friendly voice. He begged Medina to stay by him. So Medina sat beside him and talked.

When sleep overcame Cutbush, Medina stopped talking and lay down in his own hammock. Several times that night his patient woke and nothing would comfort him but to hear Medina's voice beside him in the darkness. So Medina talked of this and that until he found it less fatiguing to speak of episodes from his own experience. He talked of his days as a cadet in the military academy at Chapultepec and of the troubles that preceded and followed the flight of the Dictator Diaz. As a young sub-lieutenant he first saw active service when he was in charge of a troop ordered to eradicate a nest of bandits. The bandits had been called insurgents a few months before and had fought as allies of the soldiers who now pursued them. Several times in those years he found himself either fighting or befriending the same people. Then he spoke of Tabasco and the Governor of the State who applied the anti-church laws with maniacal ferocity. He, Medina, as a soldier obeyed orders.

He was ordered to report to the Governor of Tabasco. He did so. He thereupon received further orders from the Governor. But even as a soldier he had thought, although he recognized that as a soldier he had no business to think, that the Governor used his armed forces in a way which was reprehensible. It not only troubled the conscience of many men in those forces who carried out his orders but, what was worse, it brought those forces into disrepute and public detestation. The glorious epic of the forces of the revolution were tarnished. Of course the conscience of a man under arms is residual but when it is troubled it can be as disturbing as trouble in that other residual organ, the appendix. That was why it had been so difficult for the soldiers to catch that fellow, Serrano. In fact it was so difficult that a special troop had to be created for that special purpose.

Serrano was a priest and, as such, a marked man in Tabasco in those days. He had been warned, had refused to take the hint and had been arrested. And then he had been released or rather rescued. And what made it most remarkable was that he was rescued by his own people, his own parishioners. Mark you, said Medina, they were people who had fought savagely for the revolution and had loyally upheld the Governor's most drastic actions. They had marched half the night and paddled canoes till dawn the next day through the atrocious swamps of their country to ambush the soldiers who had arrested Father Serrano. They had killed several of the soldiers and had left the sergeant in charge severely wounded.

They explained to the sergeant that they agreed about other priests and bishops, in fact they knew a couple of bishops, that they would have done readily just what, he the sergeant, had done to the bishop but this Father Serrano was different. It was not only because he was their priest. It was because he was different. And this man really was different, for as soon as he was unbound and ungagged he tended to the wounds of the sergeant then persuaded his rescuers to paddle hours out of their way to leave him at a place where medical attention was available.

It was fortunate for everyone concerned that the sergeant should have been no other than Rosendo Mendez, also called *Palo Seco*, 'Dry Stick'. He was a sergeant in the same regiment to which Medina had been posted as adjutant. There was no doubt about it the fellow knew his business. As a good sergeant he controlled his men, and as a good sergeant he made his officers know their place and that it was injudicious to overstep it. He had been, as a young man, one of the *Rurales* who had carried

Dictator Diaz's word throughout Mexico. At the revolution he was fortunate for an accident found him in hospital when his troop of *Rurales* became the hunted instead of the hunter. His accident had not been severe enough to keep him too long in hospital. By the time the avengers had finished with the rest of the troop, counted heads and received information about the one man in hospital, Mendez had disappeared leaving his uniform and taking a few peasant's garments. He went to another state and joined the revolution. But his escape seemed to be the last stroke of luck fortune had in store for him. Twice he changed sides just in time for the 'ins' with whom he had joined to become 'outs'. He seemed destined to be nothing more prosperous than a soldier and not even an officer. It soured him. When his regiment was posted to Tabasco he found work which was suited to his malignant and envious nature. With the full backing of the law he was able to take part in vicious and degrading assaults on those who were servants of the Church. When some officers and many men did as they did because they were so ordered, Sergeant Mendez did as he did because he was so ordered and overdid his orders because he loved such orders. His troop became notorious. He earned the nickname 'Palo Seco' by a particularly hideous exploit. A certain bishop was apprehended by this Sergeant Mendez and his men.

Unfortunately, the servants of the bishop resisted and some of the Sergeant's men were wounded. To make matters worse the bishop threatened his captor with the last ecclesiastical disfavour, he told the Sergeant he would be cut off from the blessings of the Communion, like a 'dry limb'. When, later in the argument the bishop begged for mercy, the Sergeant replied that he had no more mercy in him than a dry limb had sap. The bishop did not live long enough to ask for mercy again.

Much as the Sergeant enjoyed this part of his career as a soldier he knew that it really got him no further in the good graces of the 'ins' and it gave him an impossible name with the 'outs'. When Father Serrano was rescued from his troop and, to make the matter even more galling, when Father Serrano saved his life by giving him medical aid, 'Palo Seco' tasted the very dregs of bitterness. Nor did he die of his wounds so even that escape was denied him. But solace was at hand for him. The

Governor of the State had a special commission for him when he recovered. He was allowed to choose a dozen men for his troop with which to track down and apprehend Serrano. If resistance was offered or rescue attempted he was to use his judgement.

So 'Palo Seco' now had his personal and private army on a personal but not private mission. His officers, including Captain Medina, were glad to see him go. The Governor however was no fool. A mad bigot he might be but he did not intend a private army to roam over his state without some control. That was the way insurgent movements began. He knew, he had been an insurgent himself, more than once. He therefore kept a close record of the misdeeds of 'Palo Seco' and his men. The Sergeant in due course reported that Father Serrano had been executed while trying to escape. Then the Governor acted. Captain Medina was ordered to arrest Sergeant Mendez. The charge was that he had committed sundry misdemeanours, crimes and felonies not permitted by his special commission.

Medina related that he 'got' the Sergeant. It was a story in itself, but he 'got' him. However 'Palo Seco' escaped later and succeeded in fleeing from Tabasco. There were a variety of tales about the execution of Serrano. The most likely was that he was shot in the leg by one of the troop and limped towards the nearest place for refuge. It was the shop of the village blacksmith who had been too aware of events taking place in his vicinity to remain there. He fled but not too far. So 'Palo Seco' went to Serrano as he lay there his head resting on the threshold. To shoot him was too easy so he looked around. There was what appeared to be a nail but not a nail for a horse's shoe. It was too long. Or perhaps it was such a nail not yet cut down to its proper length. So 'Palo Seco' took the nail and a hammer and drove it into the skull into the temple that lay uppermost. With a couple of sharp taps the nail went into the skull. Then he called his men together and showed them his handiwork and marched them away though not before he had ordered the villagers to bury the body of the foul carcass in the blacksmith's shop. There were rumours later about that burial but they were never investigated officially. One rumour said that the blacksmith thought the corpse would be neater without a nail in its head so he drew it out.

Then came a revulsion of public feeling against such unnecessary brutality. The Governor was dismissed by the President but allowed to take enough to set himself up in a hotel business in California, in which respect he was lucky, for usually violence breeds violence.

A group was formed to take vengeance on those who, though they had merely obeyed the law, were accused of religious persecution. They organized a vendetta. They 'got' many. It is thought that they were behind the assassination of General Obregon. 'I learnt,' said Medina, 'that my name was on their lists but that was not what made me leave my country. I had once bitterly offended General Calles. That was why I was glad to get away from Mexico City to Tabasco. Soon he became prominent in the affairs of the revolutionary party and then President. With "Palo Seco" after me and a President who was biding his time I was in a hopeless position. No promotion, no safety, no chance of living in any sense, so I left. Yes "Palo Seco" was after me. He got religion, was converted and to wipe out his misdeeds became an "avenger". I learned my name was on his list to be "avenged". He had personal reasons not to love me. I had beaten him at his own game once but I could never do it again. Not in the face of the displeasure of Calles. I heard that, after he became an "avenger", Mendez claimed he was the "dry stick" saved from the burning and ... '

But Cutbush was asleep.

So Medina thought again of that bald man who had so effectively robbed him of mule and rifle and a temperamental pistol and Cutbush of his hat. It is true that he had left in the place of the hat a new straw sombrero but it was several sizes too small for Cutbush. The patrol of gendarmes had not seen this man on the frontier road. Medina could not remember having met him before. Then he thought of the two thousand dollars he would collect for finding Cutbush. It would come in very handy. It would more than make up for his loss on the season's chicle deal. The chicle was in the warehouse in Shoonantonitch. It was in the books as now being the property of the Company. That however was a foreshortening of the usual custom. Medina had bought or acquired the chicle using the Company's resources to transport it to their warehouse. It would have been sold to the

Company at a handsome profit. The payment would have been made by Delfosse who got his commission and everyone would have been happy. The chain of happiness would not have extended to the person from whom the chicle was first stolen or acquired but after that the profits were very agreeable.

Anyway Medina regarded Cutbush alive as a gift of the gods. Even if the bald man reappeared to claim the prize there were no witnesses to prove that it was he who had first found Cutbush, and Medina had let it appear that he had found Cutbush and then he had been held up and robbed by the bald man.

There was, however, another matter which gave Medina some concern. He knew that he had been a marked man and that his days in Petén were few. He had thought that with the news of the closing of the frontier all parties interested in chicle and its ramifications would be so dumbfounded that it had been safe for him to take part in the search for Cutbush. But now that he had come into money the dislike which had put a price on his head because of his chicle dealings would be reawakened. He determined not to move out of Shoonantonitch camp till he was setting forth for his final journey from Petén. His murder was not now necessary by way of chicle business but it might be acceptable to those who formerly disliked him and who envied him for winning the Cutbush lottery.

The next day Cutbush was taken to Shoonantonitch, his arrival coinciding with that of the many *chicleros* who had heard the news of Medina's good luck. It appeared to be a triumphant entry. They carried Cutbush to Gibberd's house and slung the hammock.

'Well, old man,' said Gibberd, 'you gave us one hell of a fright.'

'I am sorry, my friend,' murmured Cutbush 'and as for fright and hell remind me to tell you about them some time. I am now an authority. I don't remember even finding the road but that is where Medina said he found me. The fact is I don't remember anything till the day after I was found. He told me there was a bald man who robbed him of mule and gun and incidentally me of my hat, but I know nothing of that. My God I am weak, absolutely all in.'

Gibberd, thinking in terms of the order in time of events and of the loss of the hat, murmured, 'Perhaps you had sunstroke as well.' He had never heard of sunstroke in Guatemala but in his Cairo days it had been often referred to. He did not know anything of its physical or mental effects but he realized that Cutbush was not suffering only from the physical effects of his experience. There were mental repercussions.

Cutbush had been frightened and was frightened at his fright. He could not stand unaided and still he would not be left alone. Gibberd had helped him, however, with one word and Cutbush had already received healing. His complacency, his certainty in himself, would now reassert itself as soon as he could be transferred from the environment where he had suffered what Gibberd had called 'sunstroke'. But he was still in the midst of the makings of uncertainty. He was still a sick man.

'I can't sleep, I can't sleep,' he complained. It was not true; he slept a little and often but awoke with a start and looked timorously about him. By day and night sleeping and waking someone had to be with him. Yet he had recovered enough to ask to be shaved, bathed and made neat and tidy. His pulse raced, as he said, 'If I move an eyelid' and his condition was such that after speaking a few sentences his pulse rate increased.

'I am trying to remember,' he said, 'what I learnt about sunstroke in medical school. I believe I remember they said the after-effects may take some time to right themselves.'

'Well,' said Gibberd, 'Petén is not the place in which to let those after-effects have free play. We must get you out at once. And frontier or no frontier you are going. You are flying to Puerto Barrios. It is a shorter journey than to Guatemala City. Half an hour from Puerto Barrios is Quirigua Hospital. Dr. Moir there will know all about sunstroke.'

Gibberd had been to see Cibrian as soon as the latter had returned to Shoonantonitch. Cibrian, with Major Arevalo, had been at the new airfield awaiting the arrival of the first aeroplane carrying officials and technicians of the new air service. As soon as the necessary equipment was erected a regular service would start. At the airfield they met the officer commanding the Penal Battalion which had constructed the field. The aeroplane did not arrive at the hour expected. They waited hour after hour but it did come at last and made a safe landing. The officer of the Penal Battalion was overwhelmed with praise by the aviation experts. The field exceeded their highest expectations. The quarters and offices were adequate and would be rapidly improved as supplies were brought in. The radio-mechanics began at once to erect their instruments. The success of the air-service for this district in Petén was drunk and after these courtesies Cibrian prepared to return to Shoonantonitch. As they were riding away from the field the officer of the Penal Battalion who was also on his way to his headquarters rode by Cibrian's side.

It appeared to be the exchange of last-minute courtesies but after Cibrian heard the officer's information he had a sick perturbation of mind and heart. 'I received a "right hand" a couple of days ago,' said the officer. 'It was reported that a snake had bitten him. You knew him, of course. It was the right hand of Jacobo Carabajal.'

'So,' said Cibrian, 'God rest his soul, that is where he went to. We lost track of him. Oh, poor Jacobo. Thank you. I will keep this dark of course. Thank you.'

'Yes,' said the officer, 'he once mentioned you particularly. He told me that you understood what he meant to say when he designed his Privasion bridge.'

'Yes,' said Cibrian, 'I understood. At least I thought I understood.'

'Did you know he had lost an eye? Some months ago in an accident. He was cutting firewood for the camp. By the time the doctor got to him it was too late. It had to come out,' said the officer.

'Oh, oh! Thank God he is dead and thank you. Goodbye,' said Cibrian.

He was glad he was dead. It was better that the man who had been assistant professor when he, Cibrian, was a student at engineering school and who later had designed the bridge over the Privasion River should be dead rather than cut firewood for the Penal Battalion. Cibrian remembered him well and with the gratitude of a receptive pupil for a dynamic teacher. He had been a man of energy, of decision, and of talent. Cibrian remembered in his undergraduate days how Professor Carabajal who had just returned from a holiday in Europe was once invited by a student society of the engineering school to address them on impressions of his European tour. The address should have lasted at most an hour but it went on for almost three hours and it was not about Europe. Carabajal had spent his vacation in Switzerland and the adjacent parts of Italy and France. He held his audience enthralled as he described what he had seen and done. What he had seen were the marvels that the Swiss and Italian engineers had accomplished in bridge building with stressed concrete. 'They make concrete sing. Their bridges take off like a bird in rapture.' What he had done was to study each bridge that captured his imagination as a great constructive critic would have studied a work of art.

He measured and sketched, then photographed and his photographs included not only the bridge but the country it served. Cibrian did not know when or how he had fallen foul of President Graña but as he had had that misfortune it was better he were dead.

He returned to Shoonantonitch that night to hear that Cutbush had arrived. Gibberd came to see Cibrian next morning. He apologized for worrying the Colonel again about Cutbush but although by the greatest good fortune he had been found by Medina yet he was a critically ill man. Seeing that the frontier was closed did the Colonel think the evacuation of Cutbush by air could be arranged expeditiously? Someone would go with him of course ... Miss Quinn or Mrs. Farr ... because he, Gibberd, had to remain to see about the transport of the specimens.

Cibrian explained that with reference to the specimens he had received orders yesterday that an official of the Guatemala Museum of Archaeology would be arriving shortly to inspect them. Those pieces that he considered worthy to be placed in his museum would be acquired under the terms of the agreement under which all archaeologists were obliged to subscribe to before beginning work in Guatemala.

The Colonel thought that it would help all who had to do with the archaeological specimens if Miss Quinn remained to help Gibberd. Thus Gibberd understood that Mrs. Farr was unwelcome in Cibrian's territory. Why the sudden animus, he wondered? Time, he thought, might perhaps tell him.

Gibberd was not worried. He knew the officials of the museum. They respected his scholarship and they knew he respected their responsibilities. They would not acquire those pieces which he particularly wanted. With reference to the transport of Cutbush it seemed to Cibrian the idea of evacuation by air was an excellent one. As soon as matters could be agreed on he would send a message to the airfield so that amongst the first official messages sent by radio from the airfield would be one describing the position as it related to Cutbush and advising that he should be flown to Puerto Barrios which was a shorter journey than that to Guatemala City. Of course the Nethersole Foundation would pay for the charter of the plane. There was a 'favour', however, which Colonel Cibrian would beg of Dr. Gibberd.

The charter flight of the plane that was taking Cutbush was duly arranged. The Government, Cibrian explained, unhappily, gave him no funds for the aerial transport of invalids and he wanted Candellaria to travel with Cutbush at no expense to Cibrian or his Government. Gibberd immediately agreed whereupon Cibrian sent the necessary dispatches. The next day approval of the proposal was received from Guatemala City. As soon as it could be arranged a plane would arrive to take the sick persons and necessary attendants to Puerto Barrios. The cheque drawn on the funds of the Nethersole Foundation to cover the cost of the charter should be countersigned by Colonel Cibrian and sent to Guatemala City by the first plane flying to the capital after receipt of the dispatch. Cibrian was satisfied. At one stroke he would be getting rid of three of the disturbing elements in his domain. Then he heard something which gave him great concern. It was a story that Medina had been robbed of his mule and rifle by a bald man who he had never previously met. He sent for Medina and enquired whether the report was correct that he would soon be leaving Petén. He hoped it were so, he continued, because of a rumour that had reached him. The bad blood engendered in the past in the chicle business would, he explained, sometimes cause unhappy incidents. This rumour was one which he would like to stay a rumour. It would, he told the man in front of him, be a painful thing to have to hold an enquiry about the sudden death of so gallant a soldier as Captain

Medina. What he did not say was that, if a bald man with one eye was apprehended, it would be better for all concerned if Medina was not there to identify him.

Medina, being no fool, at once assured Cibrian that now he had received the cheque for the rescue of Cutbush he would be eager to get out.

Cibrian pointed out to Medina that there was an empty seat yet in Cutbush's plane for Puerto Barrios. Medina knew when an order was an order even when it looked like a gentle hint. He begged Colonel Cibrian permission to make a suggestion. Permission was graciously given by the superior officer. Medina begged to be allowed to leave in Cutbush's plane. Cibrian thought it was most humane of him and applauded his deep feeling. Yes, certainly Captain Medina could go in Cutbush's plane.

This having been settled Cibrian congratulated Medina on his good luck which he was sure was not luck but craft in finding Cutbush and he asked to be told the story. When it was done he asked Medina to tell him how he was robbed of his mule and his rifle. 'What did the man look like?' he asked.

Medina described him: 'A little man, bald as an egg who looked a hundred years old. And he had a big head. Cutbush's hat was not too big for him. Also he had lost his left eye. Another thing, he told me he had to hit Cutbush on the head with his gun but Cutbush did not know that. No one told him that he had been hit.'

Cibrian sighed and turned the conversation back to the charter flight of Cutbush's plane. It would be a good thing he suggested that Medina be very circumspect until the plane took off. The implication was that Medina might meet with sudden misfortune if he were too foot-loose. Medina vowed that he would keep himself to himself. Then Cibrian spoke in a different tone of voice, 'We shall be sending another patient on the plane with Cutbush. Would you be good enough to see that she is taken care of? Maria Arevalo, the Major's wife, is going with her. You could arrange transport by ambulance at the other end and be with her until the patient is delivered at Quirigua.' Medina, as one humane gentleman to another, agreed at once to this request.

He took leave of the Colonel. Cibrian watched him go. When

Medina left he looked over the reports of his gendarmes for the frontier road and frontier posts. There was no mention of a bald, one-eyed man.

For a moment he wondered whose was the right hand that had been delivered to the penal commander. Then with a shrug of his shoulder he dismissed the problem. Somewhere in the bush was a corpse with one hand missing. Until that corpse was found it did no good to anyone to wonder too much about that matter.

He thought it his duty to visit Dr. Cutbush to congratulate him on his miraculous escape and to assure him of the concern of his government over his unhappy illness. A servant admitted him at Gibberd's house, where Cutbush was convalescing, but Dr. Cutbush was asleep. Karen was sitting by his bedside writing. She quietly got up and came towards Cibrian. She explained that the sick man slept little, but often, and as often he woke in a panic and nothing would reassure him but the sight of someone he knew near him. They moved to the door of the outer room. 'As they say in English, he takes "forty winks" but often,' explained Karen. The word 'forty' reminded Cibrian of something. The idea was repellent but it persisted teasingly. The weight of a dog is not usually mentioned in polite conversation but the weight of a dog is of great importance in an experiment on a dog and the animal had died a short time after she had, twice, mentioned its weight.

It might be nothing, he thought, but the idea gave him a most uncomfortable feeling when he spoke to Karen. She, however, was asking him if he had any more information about the old man they called the 'Speaker'.

'I went to see him this morning. He appeared to be exhausted,' she continued. 'Indeed he said no more than a dozen words and those in his usual gabbling and disjointed articulation. He had packages of food in his house unopened and yet he ate heartily when the Corporal prepared coffee and a meal for him. He gave me the impression of being half-witted and yet we know his wits can be aroused to an appreciation of any specially significant moment. He seems to be an interesting example of a divided personality. I wonder if you have learned any more about him?'

The assumption Cibrian had made about Karen's part in the death of Pedro's dog made him take a jaundiced view of Mrs.

Farr's concern about the psychology of the 'Speaker'.

'Did you notice that he had been terribly hurt Señora? There were scars of dreadful wounds of the head. Is it not likely that when he gabbles it is as a result of those wounds? When he is deeply moved his earlier training triumphs over his disabilities. It may be the automatic reflex of the soldier wounded unto death but still obeying orders, it may be something more. I have not knelt in prayer spontaneously for more than twenty years but, as you must have noticed, I did do so that night when I heard the Miserere. I have seen men die and heard the last rites several times in those years and have knelt then as custom and manners. Jaime Peat-Patterson at his dying set a scene which changed the usual bitter, painful, and often degrading farce of the renunciation of life into something tragic and dramatic. There was the quite accidental circumstance that he knew and remembered the Hymn of St. Francis of Assisi and we, that is you and I, also knew it and acted as Chorus. At that moment that realization, of the littleness and awfulness of life, released in that old man the power to force one to one's knees as he made the triumphant assertion of what to him are the sources of mercy, of pity, of God's love. I have made no effort to try to find out who he was and I pray you do not worry him as if he were a rabbit on a dissection table. Maria will see to it that as long as he remains here he will receive such aid as he needs and can understand. He will not be allowed to suffer for want of food or shelter. We cannot aid him otherwise. Indeed he is above and beyond other aid. He has a fastness and a security which, though he is conscious of it only now and then, is enough. Partial and fleeting it may be to him, but of that I envy him. I have no such security. I hope you have Señora. Good evening.'

Cibrian's visit left Karen livid with rage. It was not only that he had warned her off pursuing the matter of the 'Speaker' but his attitude, from being that of a cavalier, one who whatever they spoke of reminded her by manner and tone that she was an attractive woman, had changed abruptly. There was now a biting harshness in his words. She was not to meddle with the 'Speaker'. The man was not to be harassed by her curiosity. What she had thought of as a most remarkable mystery of personality was to elude her study. And the firmness of his tone, the precision of his attitude to the 'Speaker', his decisive direction to her showed that Cibrian realized that there was a mystery and that, as it were, out of pity he preferred to remain in ignorance. That cloak of ignorance, of forgetting, which protected the 'Speaker' from the memories of pain would not be disturbed by any action of Cibrian. And he had forbidden Karen to touch that cloak.

It was in defiance, an unworthy paltry defiance she admitted it to herself, of Cibrian's order that she rode to the 'Speaker's' house the next morning. Cibrian could not spare a gendarme but a *chiclero* lounged in the shade of a tree hard by the Speaker's hut. As she approached he sprang to his feet.

'Señora,' he said, 'pardon me, but the Colonel ... '

She did not wait to hear more. She turned her mule quickly around and rode away. 'I must get away,' she said to herself. 'I shall try to get out on Cutbush's plane. I am doing no good to myself or anyone now. Anything I touch seems to misfire. I start with the best of intentions, the highest of motives but they do not suffice. The object of search is as far off and the search fizzles out in nerveless bitterness. I must get out and quickly.'

She did not confess to herself that the urgency was in part caused by Cibrian's change of attitude. But she did confess with a shock that she now found it uncomfortable to lose his friendly appreciation. Her ride in solitude made her feel more keenly how much more vulnerable she was now than say seven, or even three, years before.

But she did not ride all the way back to Shoonantonitch alone. She overtook a group of *chicleros* who were returning from the farther sections of the forest where they had been sent to search for Cutbush. They had won a prize of two hundred dollars for amongst them was Pedro, the *marimbero*, he of the dog that she had, accidentally in the interests of science, killed. At first sight he appeared most woebegone. He had lost much weight. He sat like a shapeless bundle on his mule. He was not the noisy, the usually vociferous Pedro. He seemed to have made a successful effort to contain himself, to cut his flamboyance and to contract into a hard centre all the remaining resources of strength and endurance. He had received the most shattering blow he could possibly have had in the death of Modesto but now he had just received an unexpected blessing. He explained this blessing to Karen when she rode up and joined the party.

She asked the *chicleros* if they would do her the favour of allowing her to have some private talk with Pedro. Of course, she explained, when they reached her house they would find a bottle or two of whisky or rum there for them to take away. So she was allowed to ride with Pedro and to ask him certain things.

'No, Señora, it was not the liquor. Look, I know rum, brandy, wine, whisky, I have had them all. It tasted like whisky but it was more, much more.

'For, consider ... can you imagine yourself four years old? Can you imagine lifting a stone to see how heavy the stone is then dropping it in fun on a man's head? Can you imagine playing with machetes like infants with little branches of trees, touching and pushing and prodding, knowing that one edge is sharp that the point is very sharp but not playing yet for point, or edge?

'And then the game got stale because the machetes began to sing. No, I mean to sound no, I mean ... not the machete. I dropped the machete. It was the rainbow. That was after he poured the rest of the powder into the other bottle of whisky and we started to drink again. It was not the rainbow one sees in the sky for the sky and the rainbow had come down to enwrap me. And each colour of the rainbow sang. Each had its appointed note. Then, when I was ready, came the chords but each chord had a taste. Yes, and then when you got to know the taste of the chord you could anticipate it for it had a smell, a fragrance and the slight note I heard with it led to the key in which I heard the music. Yes, it was music, the music of all that one can hear and see and feel and taste and smell and yet it was me, myself, above and into and beyond everything, but it was me, myself.

'Then I knew that neither sin nor sorrow were essentially me. That is that they came out of myself. Sin was like, yes, like the mildew on a loaf of bread, on it, but not of it.

'So, Señora, I ride back but I am indifferent to what happens to me. I know what I know. But why did I wake up? Because I did not have the final blessing, the little that is more than enough.'

He also told her that he had just been informed by some *chicleros*, who had come through the forest near Pusilha, that they had found the body of Gil Silva so they too had won a prize of two hundred dollars, 'dead or alive'. It was a blessing for, as he explained, 'It is true, he died horribly, Señora, but he is dead once and for all. I no longer need to seek him. I am rid of the need to kill him. I now have only to meet the law and to confess that matter of being an accessory after the event in the death of Jaime. But that is not a personal matter.

'The law deals quite rightly with mildew. It cannot do to me any worse than I do to myself when I think of him.'

Karen was not particularly interested in any more deaths, however horrible, but a remark of one of the *chicleros* galvanized her. 'What is that you say?' she asked quickly.

'Yes, Señora, he was lying stark naked in the bush. He had been mutilated before he was dead. He had bled after his right hand had been cut off. But he had not moved. He must have been senseless when it was cut off. And there was no injury, no blow to the head but rather as if he had been senseless.'

'But who cut off the hand?' she asked. She could not yet ask about the particular circumstances which the *chicleros* had mentioned. She would have to lead up to it or better let it come out in casual conversation again.

'Ah Señora. That is no mystery. The Penal Battalion has lost a man. One of them had escaped. To escape there is need of clothes and a right hand. So a small man took Gil Silva's clothes. His four comrades took Silva's hand and the escaping man's clothes back to their camp to the officer in charge of them. There is no mystery about that.'

'Yes,' said another. 'That is clear; but what is not clear is why a man, who is so senseless that his hand is cut off while he is still alive, should lie there and smile while he bleeds to death.'

Karen felt that if she spoke then she would shriek the words.

After a few moments and with a terrible effort of self-control she asked, 'Smile? Did you say he smiled?'

'*Si Señora*, the corpse smiled.'

'He may have been drunk,' she ventured.

Some of them laughed. 'We have been drunk, almost dead drunk, many times but we did not smile,' said one. Another added, 'It is true there was an empty bottle of "White Horse" whisky nearby. It is good whisky, Señora, very good but not that good.'

They thought her subsequent silence one of shocked horror. They were not far wrong. Near Shoonantonitch they met Fuad. Pedro told him the whole story of the discovery of the body of Gil Silva.

Fuad was decently sympathetic. 'God rest the dead,' he said aloud, adding to himself 'Even in death the little humorist had to have his laugh.' Though he did not understand why Gil Silva should have laughed just then. He did understand, however, why he had lost his right hand. Unless the escaping convict were recaptured and the man's equipment was traced to him his part of the affair would remain a closed book. 'God rest the dead,' he repeated and he understood, also, the gratitude and relief of Pedro that good fortune had spared him from the onerous duty of the pursuit and murder of the 'Little Rainbow'.

Mrs. Farr asked no more questions for no one could give the answers she required. She had now heard what had happened to the man who had taken the other doses of 'Sudden Glory'. But what did he feel? What sensation or emotions had Gil Silva felt? It was known that in life he had laughed and in death he had smiled. Perhaps he had known, felt, or experienced, more than Pedro had and he had decided not to wake up.

On her return to the camp she was informed that the aeroplane to take Cutbush would arrive in two days' time. So she went, at once, to Gibberd and insisted that she should accompany Cutbush because, she explained, Miss Quinn would be more valuable to him in view of the need, now, to open all the packages of archaeological finds and have them ready for the inspection by the officials from the Guatemala Museum. She would take Cutbush to the hospital at Quirigua. After that, she told him, her own programme would depend on certain ideas she was then pondering.

PART TEN

'... THE MAN WHO HAD COMMUNED WITH GOD'

Cibrian was a busy man. The arrangements for the evacuation of Cutbush and Medina and she for whom Maria and Medina would take responsibility were going smoothly. As for Gibberd, Cibrian had no doubts or hesitations. Gibberd was different, he was no problem. Gibberd could not be anything but reasonable, sympathetic, patient, understanding. He would wait for the official from Guatemala without impatience and in the meanwhile he would work like a beaver at his notes or his specimens while driving Miss Quinn to ever greater efforts.

But he would always have time, if Cibrian or the most unpretending *chiclero* passed by and bade him good-day, to reply with instant acceptance and return of the courtesy. He appeared to get as much pleasure as he gave from this contact and to return to his work, afterwards, refreshed. He understood that the officials had duties which they had to perform and that the duties might be different to the duties of an official in his own country. But Gibberd never gave the officials the impression that he considered the duties inconsequential and the manner of performing them somewhat baroque. Gibberd was different. '*Es un caballero*,' Arevalo said as he worked with Cibrian who agreed. 'A higher type of a citizen of the world,' he added. He had at that moment his hands full of the affairs of other alien citizens. Now that the majority of the *chicleros* who had searched for Cutbush had returned he could gather all of those who were citizens of British Honduras together and send them under escort to the frontier. This was not going to be easy for the escort, for one thing, because he could spare less than a dozen men for that purpose. For another, a *chiclero* was by training and habit an individualist. He would discontinue his journey when he felt like it and rest or eat or sleep and resume the journey as the mood moved him. Also those *chicleros* who came from the British side of the frontier considered themselves 'superior'. In what they were 'superior' they did not know but this irrational feeling of 'superiority' made them sometimes obey the directions of the gendarmes with reluctance or insulting slowness. These *chicleros* now began to realize, and it would not make them more co-operative with Cibrian's men, that if the frontier remained closed for the next and other seasons they would be reduced to penury. They would be like factory workers faced with a lockout. As for the remainder of the present year, if they saved their money and spent it only on basic necessities till the corn crop ripened they would not need to starve. They however presumed that immediately they reached home they would go into the forest to cut down and burn the bush on a selected site and to plant a milpa of corn. There was yet time if they didn't waste the favourable dry season and their money in drink. 'They are going to have a tough time,' Cibrian told Arevalo. 'It is going to be hard here but it will be worse for them. Here we still have chicle. There they have already bled out almost all they ever had. We won't need to have unemployment here. Over there they will find no work. In any case I shall be glad to get them across the border without a fuss. And in a few weeks we shall have everything in our section of Petén under proper control.'

Then Cibrian turned to his other responsibilities.

He had, on the morning when the body of Jaime had been brought to Shoonantonitch, summoned Fuad. They had met at Cibrian's office where the arrangements for the funeral had been quickly concluded and Fuad had told the Colonel that he could with all confidence leave such matters to him.

When he had been about to leave Cibrian had said, 'Now, another thing. Señora Arevalo is with Señora Candellaria now but she has many other duties to perform. Could you arrange for another woman to share her task with her? We have to wait to send her out by aeroplane but until then she must be guarded and protected against herself. And, by the way, any expenses involved in this will be paid by me. It is a personal transaction between the two of us. Until that plane takes off, you and I alone know how much it has cost. Understand? Good, then good-bye.'

Fuad had kept his eyes lowered as he listened. He had thought it wiser. Once he had looked up and then quickly looked down again. Cibrian's face was pale and his eyes moist.

As he was leaving Fuad had said, almost over his shoulder, 'That matter, about which I had an appointment with you, Señor Colonel is important but it can wait another day or two. It is, as I say, important but nothing that calls for immediate action.' Cibrian nodded and Fuad left.

Cibrian had spoken decisively, even harshly to Karen and had regretted the harshness as soon as he had spoken. Not only did it demean him but it would at once induce resistance and defiance. It was a bore, though he consoled himself with the thought that she would soon be gone.

He shook his head. Resistant or defiant she might be but she would not be allowed to molest the 'Speaker' who was written down on the official records of the district as Jose Gomez, a Mexican. Nor would she be allowed to counter his, Cibrian's, express orders.

The news that an aeroplane would be coming to take out Dr. Cutbush at noon the next day was welcome to all members of the Nethersole archaeological expedition. Gibberd was anxious that the sick man should get treatment as soon as possible. The patient had now recovered from the privation he had suffered and had rapidly overcome the more obvious effects of thirst, exposure and exhaustion. But his symptoms now were more complex. Though he appeared physically in good shape, he suffered from an extreme fatigue at the slightest effort. To put on his shoes wearied him, to walk twice around his room fatigued him to prostration. If he fell into an uneasy sleep he would wake suddenly and peer about him in terror. If he saw a friendly face he would be relieved. If the newcomer was unfamiliar his terror mounted until he struggled from the bed to the door and his anxiety for reassurance mounted until only the last discipline of self-respect prevented him from shrieking wildly.

The distinguished Dr. Cutbush, the magnificent exemplar of the success which his times and his contemporaries bestowed on one who had shrewd intelligence, great powers of application, a ready and deep appreciation of the qualities and limitations of other men, and superb administrative ability was now an ailing and frightened man.

Dr. Gibberd said the shock had unnerved him but that he would soon be all right. Miss Quinn dutifully agreed with a charming smile at Gibberd for his profound and sympathetic diagnosis and prognosis. Karen said nothing while a line from a poem of Burns ran through her mind. Cutbush was shaved, well groomed, neat, even the bedclothes seemed to lie in symmetrical folds but Karen was reminded of Burns's 'wee, sleekit, cowering beastie.' Gibberd was no fool. Out of earshot of Miss Quinn he continued the diagnosis, 'It seems as if the experience had stripped him clean, exposing some sensitive part of him.'

'Like a tooth stripped of enamel and dentine exposing the nerve?', suggested Karen.

But this was too drastic for the loyal Gibberd. 'Well, yes, but sunstroke, you know.' So Karen was more cautious. 'You remember the title of his book?' she asked. 'Do you? It was *Nociception as Destiny*.'

Gibberd changed the subject. 'Well it all seems that our plans are going to work out all right. The hospital at Quirigua is first class and less than an hour from Puerto Barrios. You can arrange matters there for him when you arrive. Miss Quinn and I can fix things here so that as soon as the museum officials have had their pick we can pack up. And now that the stuff will be going by plane to Barrios and not by mule to Belize this packing will be the final one. Maybe the air-service and the closing of the frontier will be a good thing for us archaeologists if for no one else. We had better arrange to leave here at dawn so as to reach the air-field with an hour or two to spare.' And then he added, 'When one had to travel by mule one had to allow oneself and the mule spare time. Now we can add "aeroplane" to make up an uncertain trinity.'

Karen knew the reference; an old man who had been of great assistance to Gibberd in his early days of exploration in British Honduras and had used a motor boat with a temperamental engine in his work, declaring solemnly to Gibberd that 'mule, motor-boat and woman are an uncertain trinity'.

She also understood Gibberd's reluctance to discuss Cutbush's illness and for his invoking 'sunstroke' as its cause.

He knew, and she knew, that sunstroke was highly improbable but Gibberd was his friend. Let those who could speak with neutral authority declare that the illness was a physical expression of a non-physical injury. Until such authority spoke, the illness was to Gibberd, 'sunstroke with unusual symptoms'. She did not know that Gibberd had run his fingers over Cutbush's skull and had found a place that was slightly swollen and tender. 'Can it be a skull fracture caused by a blow?' thought Gibberd. It was then that he took the word 'sunstroke' out of his hat.

They saw Miss Quinn coming towards them. The last mail allowed across the frontier had arrived and been distributed. Miss Quinn had collected their mail and now delivered it. Mrs. Farr went to her house and read her letters.

One letter she kept to the last. It had been posted in Portland, Oregon. Hislop Farr had written that he knew it would not ruffle her complaisance nor trouble her indifference to know that he was in tolerable health. And he knew also, that she would be delighted to learn that he had been rated eleventh in the nation-wide poll taken, to rank jazz-drummers, by the eminent musical journal, *Swing and Sway*.

He had not found the latest Thomas Mann novel to his liking. There was too much made of Goethe's failing for women. He was glad to report that the contacts which she had established for him in Mexico still supplied him, wherever the itinerant jazz-band took him, with that which made time so elastic. Could she wonder that sometimes in those wonderfully prolonged intervals of time he remembered her? But she would also wonder why, if every now and them, he did not abrade the texture of some particular interval by cursing her memory. He hoped she was 'in excellent health that will never fail you while you are able to appreciate time that he hoped for her would not be fictitiously, wonderfully or blissfully prolonged but would contract into a tight hard and bitter core, as tight and bitter as her heart.'

She read the letter a second time and then tore it into small pieces. At any rate he was not yet dead or in jail and was still in a job as a jazz-drummer. She did not think it would do any good to write to Mexico to cut off his supply of marijuana. He did not smoke it, he took the 'Tincture of Cannabis' which was made from marijuana, an alcoholic extract.

If she did cut off his supply he would then have to play his drums without the assistance of the drug. He would then no longer have the sensation that between one beat of the stick and the next stretched not a fiftieth part of a second, as the audience heard it, but a long time, perhaps minutes. And in that non-existent prolongation of the part of a second, he gloried in the feeling of god-like power that stayed time for his own especial benefit while he enjoyed the sounds of his music suspended, also for his own especial benefit, in non-existent time. He performed the miracle of Joshua for no such humdrum reason as the winning of a battle; he stayed time for pleasure, his own particular pleasure.

Six months ago he had boasted in his last letter that he was rated well amongst the outstanding drummers of his trade. Eleventh could not be called 'outstanding'. Of course he knew that she would make the obvious inference that he was slipping down in this particular trade. He knew what she would think because they knew one another well enough, after having lived together, husband and wife, for several years. And the reference to Thomas Mann's books would be well understood. It refreshed again for her the memory, never dormant, of a crime she had committed in those days for which there was no expiation.

When he had first heard Hislop Farr's extraordinarily exciting and baffling suite, 'Ishtacihuatle', Richard Strauss, the Olympian himself, had taken the trouble to say in reliable hearing – 'Why does he hide his talent behind the atonal scale?' But this suite and the two or three other pieces he had had played, particularly the 'Sinfonetta Isotopa,' first performed at Amsterdam, were setting-up exercises for the *magnum opus* on which he had worked for years. He had made many starts, none false, but none good enough and therefore all rejected. For weeks at a time he wrote not a bar of the opus. Once, early in their marriage, he did not touch it for six months but he looked at his manuscript every day. 'I can't force it,' he explained. 'No, you are not responsible for this long sabbath. I can't force it. It forces me, asleep or awake. It is there. Even in my moments of greatest abandon when I believe you love me, or rather when I believe you at last realize what love can be, even then I look over your shoulder and I see it. I look through the wall through the wood of the desk and I see it there because it is the best of me.

'In it, with humbleness and joy, I look at myself. At *myself*, at my best, my very best, those marks on that paper are me. I can't force it. It is greater than I shall ever be again. To have found you and to be those marks on that paper is perhaps too much for one man. In those two events too much has happened to me. That is why, sometimes, I am frightened. No, I can't force it.'

But when he worked at it his industry was ant-like. He would crouch over the desk day and night, writing, erasing and writing again or, perhaps, just crouching, pen in hand. Then perhaps he would tear up every page, the labour of many days, and wander away. In those days in Mexico there were several friends of theirs who were interested in the creative arts and one or two who actually did create something. There were also the camp-followers of this group. It refreshed his jolly and gregarious temperament to wander away to these friends after a bout of diligence. It was in that period that Karen had built the foundations of the renown she subsequently won in Zapotec archaeology. Her labours took her away from home sometimes for weeks at a time.

As she became more secure in her scholarship, more enthusiastic in her researches, more encouraged by the high appreciation of the authorities of the National Museum of Mexico her industry and application seemed to infect her husband. They laboured unceasingly. 'It isn't that it won't come now,' he said. 'I can't catch it fast enough. It is burning the pen and so it should. The nib glows. No, damn it, it is incandescent.' For no reason she could think of, then or now, she looked at him one day furiously writing and said, 'I say, do you know you have grown up?' He grunted, but made no reply. Much later, apropos of nothing, he said suddenly, 'But have you?' She did not refer to the subject again.

So Hislop Farr wrote his 'Dream of Hans Castorp'. It was an oratorio adapting the wonderful passage from Thomas Mann's *Magic Mountain* where Hans Castorp is lost in a snowstorm, falls asleep and dreams. He dreams first of a park – luxuriant green shade trees: 'Ah the trees, the trees. Oh living climate of the living ... ' The dream ends in horror after describing, as Hislop Farr put it, a whole library of 'Grecian Urns'. And Hans muses on his dream. 'There is both rhyme and reason. I have made a dream poem of humanity. Therein lies goodness and love of human kind ... Death is a great power. One takes off one's hat before him and goes weavingly on tip-toe. Reason stands simple before him, for reason is only virtue, while death is release, immensity, abandon, desire.'

Once he played for her on the piano a theme which appeared first to be a stately minuet but which changed and developed imperceptibly into a passage of sustained majesty that lifted the heart and the spirit up to a heightened experience. It was his prelude to the reading of the passage 'The mutual courteous regard these children of the sun showed to each other, a calm reciprocal reverence, veiled in smiles, manifest almost imperceptibly and yet possessing them all by the power of sense association and ingrained idea. A dignity, even a gravity, was held as it were in solution in their lightest mood, perceptible only as an ineffable spiritual influence, a high seriousness without austerity, a reasoned goodness conditioning every act.' He played the prelude to her several times before she began to understand what he meant to say. For the first time since she had known him she came to believe absolutely and was convinced at last almost against her will and past all doubts and perturbations that her husband had a true gift. How much, how deep was his gift she was not capable of understanding then. For his music was not easy even when he did not write in the atonal scale. 'You will not find it easy,' he told her. 'Nor will others, not for two or three generations. By then it will either be easy or it will not be known at all.' But she knew that he had no doubt that his music would be known and played. At about that time he had an offer to arrange the music and to conduct an opera company scheduled to tour Latin-America. He accepted the offer gladly.

'I don't mind going now,' he said. 'It is only for about three months and the little more I have to do on "The Dream" can wait. It is now but a matter of straightening out a few obscure passages and it is finished. There are one or two little things I can do. They have been flitting about in my mind and I had better pin them down and put them in place. One is a suite based on that story of yours from your archaeological find, "The Smile of the Totonac". Besides, I need the money.' Sometimes he was sensitive about living on her money. He went on his tour and returned.

Shortly after his return she had to go to Oaxaca on an

archaeological project on which she had been invited to assist.

The invitation was reckoned a great honour, for the project was sponsored by a famous German university. Karen was now accepted as an authority on the ancient culture of the Zapotec civilization. She came back unexpectedly distracted by a letter a 'kind' friend had written her. She accused him. He did not deny anything.

'What's all the fuss about? The woman was in the opera company. She followed me here. It was the easiest way to get rid of her. Nothing chastens a romantic woman so quickly as to find that the loved one is, after all, no better than good to average. She has gone, thank God. So what's all the fuss? It is of no more significance than a pinch of snuff, a good sneeze by two snuff-takers. Forget it, and I tell you what; I will come back with you to Oaxaca and help you dig up yours bits and pieces and watch you teach the Herr Professor something.' But she was impervious to reason, to confession, to penitence. Her anger and jealousy grew to horrible rancour. The next day he determined to work on his 'Dream'. The papers were not in the desk. She told him she had destroyed them. He was incredulous, 'No, no, no,' he wailed, 'do you know what you are saying? You didn't, you couldn't! Just because I took a pitifully foolish woman to bed for one night.' I am not and never was in love with her. Neither before nor after and certainly not after. Why she was even worse in bed than you are.'

She had rushed from the room into the kitchen. The papers were in the stove. She had meant to burn them, had struck the match but her spiteful hate had not yet mastered her completely. Now, after his last dreadful remark, she poured the kerosene oil on the manuscript. He smelled the oil and realized what was happening and that the papers were not yet burnt. 'Karen,' he shouted, 'for pity's sake. For your own sake, don't, don't, wait!' As he rushed into the kitchen she thrust in the lighted match. The flames reared with explosive eagerness. 'The Dream of Hans Castorp' was gone.

After that he tried alcohol. That did not help him much and it cost him his reputation as conductor and arranger. Then he tried mescal. That helped him immensely. He loved the play of lights and colours, but he had to eat. So he tried marijuana. He could get jobs as a musician and still use marijuana.

Karen sighed as she thought of him. 'He had not yet grown up completely. And as for me, I was still in swaddling clothes. A sneeze between a couple of snuff-takers! No, I never wish to see him again. It would serve no purpose. I could never undo the wreck of two lives. He is the albatross around my neck. To bed. I must be up early tomorrow. Gibberd is an early bird.'

But Gibberd could not come to the airfield with them. He had had a sharp attack of malaria during the night and the ague had been particularly violent. So, of course, Miss Quinn had to stay to look after him. Besides, Miss Quinn thought it was about time he was led to do a little serious thinking about himself. By the last mail she had heard that the wealthy gentleman who had paid such marked attention for so long to the former Mrs. Gibberd had been disencumbered of his spouse and was about to make his present arrangement legal. And Miss Quinn had decided that Gibberd should make some move in the same general direction. Not that there had been any kind of 'arrangement' so far but she wanted Gibberd to make up his mind before he heard of the marriage of his ex-wife and she wanted him to believe that he had made up his own mind all by himself.

Dr. Cutbush and Mrs. Farr set out for the airfield escorted by muleteers and servants.

Cutbush was conveyed in a hammock slung between two mules, one leading the other. Karen rode beside him when the path was wide enough. Otherwise she rode behind the hammock mules. They had set out early to get to the airfield without undue haste and bustle.

But Captain Medina and his charge had set out an hour earlier. The patient was in a hammock. Maria rode by the hammock when possible. Two *chicleros* led the mules of Candellaria's hammock keeping their eyes firmly fixed anywhere except on the hammock.

When Cutbush and Karen reached the airfield they saw their future travelling companion and the people necessary for that companion's comfort and safety. Medina had placed them at some distance, about one hundred yards from the shed which did duty as the airfield office. They were in another shed that was the remains of a shelter constructed for the builders of the airfield.

As Cutbush and his party rode past Medina's party Karen saw a sudden movement in that group. It was a movement which triggered off an organized and ruthless reprisal. Karen shuddered in horror at the necessity.

For clearly, if the patient was going to be obstreperous in a small aeroplane, then the patient had to be restrained and how more effectively than strapping her down to a plank. It would have been the plank on which Jaime's body would have had his last dignified resting place. Other people, however, had thought of other necessities and they were right.

Karen was revolted at what was being done to Candellaria but found it hard to feel pity. One can pity, she thought, the dumb animal, or the afflicted, the suffering and sane human but it is hard to pity the insane. Perhaps because their insanity lifts or, more probably, lowers them onto a different plane of suffering. How much, she wondered, are they aware of their suffering or, are they aware at all? Is suffering then only in the eyes of the beholder? Or perhaps they have escaped from this particular hell to a lesser, two-dimensional plane of suffering. 'I must ask Cutbush that,' she said to herself, 'he is a bit two-dimensional himself just now.'

Cibrian had decided to ride in the opposite direction as soon as he saw the hammock slung between the mules and the necessary attendants, with Medina in control, set out for the airfield. How far he would ride he had not decided. The sad procession passed out of sight but Cibrian had no opportunity to escape in the opposite direction. His corporal announced that Miss Quinn had arrived with a message from Dr. Gibberd. She apologized for so early an intrusion but Dr. Cutbush had suddenly thought of something.

Or rather he had remembered Harkness's dying words about his benefactress, Maria. He, Cutbush, was a wealthy man. He had, by sheer misfortune, killed Harkness. The man was cynical and harsh in his judgements of his fellow men but he had died nobly without recriminations. In his name, Cutbush would donate a handsome sum to Maria saying that it came in Harkness's name and that it was to be used at her discretion for the betterment of the lives of the people of Petén. He had given a cheque to Gibberd instructing him to add a donation from the Nethersole Foundation in recognition of the people of Petén's contribution to the work of the said Foundation. Gibberd was to pay the money through Cibrian to Maria so that the Government and Deodato would be aware of the transaction and be prepared to welcome the Foundation back at a later date.

The size of the sum mentioned on the cheque, when Gibberd handed it over, had surprised Cibrian and had filled the good Maria with the greatest delight she had ever experienced in her life.

Cibrian had undertaken that if there was any irregularity he would take the responsibility to see that it was taken in hand and controlled immediately.

So the matter was arranged. Cibrian returned to his office with the cheque to find Fuad waiting for him.

'Oh God,' thought Cibrian, 'he has come for his money already and she has hardly left.' But he was wrong. Fuad, noting his expression, sought to shorten any uneasy surmise.

'Señor Colonel, I am here because you only, I think, can begin matters in such a way that whoever comes after you cannot undo the memorial you have dedicated to the men whose lives have been lost serving the best interests of the people of Petén. I am thinking particularly of my old friend Jaime, but there have been others.'

'Memorial? What are you talking about?' asked Cibrian.

'Yes, Señor Colonel, you know the chicle warehouse of the Company? Almost touching it is my warehouse for chicle, storehouse for merchandise, my office and my sleeping quarters. Both of these buildings are roofed with sheet metal tiles. These two buildings, you may remember, had been roofless since the Jesuits were ordered out of Guatemala, then a Province of Spain, some two hundred years ago.

'The bigger building was the church and the smaller a school and living quarters for the Jesuit priest or priests. Yes, there was a school there then and there was no other school anywhere else in this district until Señora Arevalo arrived. She, as you know, began to teach the children in her own house then the villagers built a shed. But, Señor Colonel, that school must continue and teachers must be induced to come to this forgotten land. To cut it short, I wish to hand you as a representative of Government, my warehouse, office and living quarters as the memorial I have mentioned and that Señora Arevalo benefit from it for the school and for her everlasting approachability, her sympathy, always coupled to her energy, and above all her selflessness. I have sold everything in the warehouse. It will be emptied in a few weeks or earlier if you so desire.

Cibrian was so astounded at this speech and at the offer that he looked and continued to look at Fuad as if he were some rare specimen fit only for a zoo. Or so it seemed to Fuad.

At last Cibrian spoke. 'But does that mean that we shall lose you, that you will no longer have business here? Or is it that you will go elsewhere in Petén?'

'No, Señor Colonel, I have shares in the Chicle Company therefore I am interested in its welfare but family reasons force me to pull up my roots as a trader and chicle-contractor in Petén. I will return to the Colony.'

'But, Señor Birbari, this gift ... If you were to try to sell ... '

'Yes, I could sell my warehouse as easily as I have sold the contents. But some few of us, Señor, some few do certain things which to many of us seem the height of folly. Does it seem like folly to you that I should make this gesture? My wife, who is of the same kind of woman as Señora Arevalo, would approve and will approve, when I tell her. So, you accept Señor Colonel, on behalf of the people of this district the continuation of the school which the Jesuits founded and Maria Arevalo resuscitated? You accept? Thank you.'

Cibrian was overwhelmed. That such a thought, that such a deed should come from one who the world had told him would buy or sell anything, because he used money as he used breath, something that came in, and went out, but on the way, both ways, produced a benefit.

With an effort he pulled himself together. 'I need not say, Señor Birbari how much I, personally, appreciate your gift. As you say, the education of our people began with the Jesuits. Then, when they were forced to leave, education in this part of Petén went with them. Now, hardly has our great President rediscovered this province by bringing it into the twentieth century, than he finds two people, Señora Arevalo and yourself, prepared to bring education to these forgotten children. I am overwhelmed. I shall at once write to my superior officer in Guatemala City and ask him to let the President know. That, officially, I shall do at once. Unofficially, as man to man, I now thank you.' Cibrian stood up, came from behind his desk and shook hands. Fuad bowed over the handshake and thanked him.

Then, when he reseated himself he shuffled his hat in his hands and looked about the office as if he were trying to remember where, or what else it was he sought.

'Yes?' said Cibrian, 'Is there something else?'

'Señor Colonel,' said Fuad after a long pause, 'there is another matter of which I think you ought to be aware. It is known only to three people, no, two, for Jaime is no longer with us. It is known at the present time to two people but it concerns you and depending on what you do with your knowledge, well, that depends.'

'I don't quite understand. Has it anything to do with the gift of the school?'

'No. Let me put it this way,' said Fuad. 'Suppose you knew that our beloved President was in serious danger, you would react exactly as we all would, with horror, anger and a stiffening of the spine. Yes? Well now we all know that he has recently returned from a medical check up, no?'

Cibrian nodded, remembering that he had carefully burnt that letter as well as the other about the widow Aycinena. The scraps were in the ashtray. Now his attitude to Fuad was polite if casual.

'We were told, but of course you know what we were told about the President's health. We all believed it. Why shouldn't we? And we all thanked God! But suppose there was more about his health. Suppose ...

'Let me put it in a nutshell. I have a son. He is a doctor in a University Medical Research Centre in America. About two years ago, however, he was working as a trainee specialist in the X-ray Department of the Osler Clinic where Dato went.

'My son still has doctor friends at the Osler and a remark, in a letter from a friend, who knew of our Central American connections, about Dato alerted my son. He asked for more precise information.

'It was of course against the rules but doctors tell one another things which they do not tell the public. What I mean, Señor Colonel is this. Suppose we were told the whole truth about Dato's health? Suppose, oh but excuse me, I see through your window that Dr. Cutbush and Mrs. Farr are about to leave. I must go to say "good-bye" to her because it is the last time I shall see her. I go to wish her "good fortune" in the future because she was the only person who sent a wreath to Jaime's funeral, a wreath made of scraps of paper pierced by a thorn. Shall I return to continue our discussion? Yes? Then in no more than a few minutes I shall be back.'

Cibrian had decided he would not take part in the leave-taking. So he waited.

He looked at that ashtray and remembered that his friend had written of 'this rumour that someone had heard him cough. He had called for a document. It was being brought and as the officer came through the door he saw blood on the handkerchief. It was not more than a streak of blood but it was blood and he quickly hid it in his pocket. He works, as usual, twenty hours out of the twenty-four though, whether he is sitting or standing, he is breathing deeply and frequently as if he had run upstairs. This is the rumour so tear this up, burn it at once. I will write you no more on this subject. It is safer to wait until the whole world knows.'

When Fuad returned the first thing Cibrian said was, 'Were those pieces of paper found on his body?'

'Yes,' said Fuad, 'and she wrote four more lines, I don't know English poetry even though she told me what it was that she wrote. All I can remember are the last two lines.

"Flower of a moment in the eternal hour
Peace be with be now."'

Cibrian nodded then, apparently apropos of nothing, asked, 'Is it heart trouble?'

'No,' said Fuad, 'my son was able to get copies through a technician with whom he had worked in the department. I have photographs of those copies. They are in the Colony in the bank. I did not understand them but Jaime copied the words and asked the meaning from his friend the doctor at El Cayo, Dr. Hastings. He told him the diagnosis, in short, meant, "cancer of the lung too far gone for operation and X-ray treatment would be of dubious utility."'

'You are a British subject, aren't you?' asked Cibrian.

'Yes, Señor Colonel and my passport is perfectly in order. I have written to the British Embassy in Guatemala City to let them know that I shall be leaving Petén within a day or two. Certainly my plans do not include remaining here beyond the day after tomorrow.

'Now, Señor Colonel, you are as fully informed on the health of the President as I am. What you do next is up to you and your friends. But suppose, in say a year or less, the frontier is still closed. Then there would be the need for a new trail across the frontier, not to take out chicle but to bring in supplies which would be transported at half the cost of bringing them in by air. Also, of course, the transport of the goods from the frontier will give occupation to your people. Do you understand me, Señor?'

Cibrian looked levelly at the trader and replied 'Perfectly. I get certain papers and you get the contract for that trail, the sole contract?'

'Exactly, Señor. You will be able to contact me at my office in Belize when you need anything. But I shall not cross the frontier on that trail nor will my family live in El Cayo. I told you I was returning for family reasons. My two other sons will soon be leaving for further schooling abroad so my wife and I will go back to Belize.'

What he did not say was 'Don't try to kidnap any member of the family and smuggle them across the frontier to hold as a trump card after you and your friends have staged a *coup d'état* and there is a new President.' Cibrian nodded, following Fuad's line of thought exactly. He said, 'As soon as you have signed that paper donating your property as a memorial for Señora Arevalo you can begin to make preparations to leave by tomorrow morning's plane.'

'Agreed. So let us sign those papers. After that I shall say "good-bye". I have to leave Shoonantonitch for the bush and I may not return tonight.'

Cibrian, too, was eager to end his contact with Fuad, a man who really did sell everything including the tools of high treason. It was the second separation that he wanted to have done with as quickly as possible. 'She' had gone. 'He' should be hurried on his way. Was the price he was paying for a school and a trail to El Cayo too high, he wondered? Or was it very cheap? The disposal of an Olympian, of Dato, for a pittance. And what of the cost to his own conscience? Cibrian shrugged. Whatever action a man took he was never any more than an oarsman. Another, steered the boat. And who was he, a mere colonel, to march out against Fate?

Luncheon was served at the airfield to Cutbush and Mrs. Farr. Gibberd had arranged it. He had no faith in the schedule of aeroplanes. 'Under the best auspices they play havoc with time-tables,' he had said, 'and when the timetable is a virgin one they might get coy and not come at all. I will let the men take lunch and supper for the whole lot of us.' He was not there, but Cutbush and Mrs. Farr and the others of the party were grateful for his foresight. Mrs. Farr had a collapsible canvas chair put by Cutbush's hammock and after lunch she sat with him.

He was half-drowsy when she asked suddenly, 'When is a man mad?' He kept his eyes resolutely closed but she was not abashed. She continued, 'Can a man be made half-sane, half-mad by a nail which is driven through the head and comes out at the other side?' He still kept his eyes closed but almost against his will he asked, 'What part of the head?'

'Oh,' she replied, 'from side to side, just behind the forehead.'

He opened his eyes now, 'Here! What is this? Have you been reading of Moniz?'

'I don't know anything about Moniz but has it to do with madness or with nails?'

'Your madman sounds as if someone has done a Moniz on him,' he said. Then, as if regretting that he had opened his eyes, he closed them again wearily. But she went on resolutely, 'Tell me of Moniz.'

That he was glad to do. It was something which had come into psychiatry since he had left that subject. It seemed to him fearful and horrible, mutilating and blasphemous, but wonderfully it worked.

'You must realize, first of all,' he said, 'that mental hospitals all over the world are full of types of patients who make little or no progress towards recovery of their sanity. They live on and on in hospitals, sometimes for scores of years without responding to the most persistent, diverse and ingenious treatments. Now, it has long been known that the frontal lobes of the brain are the parts of that organ which intensify but do not originate emotion. Many types of chronic insanity are those showing variation in emotional tone. For example, profound melancholia, or the kind of patient who swings between depression and aggressive elation. Moniz, who is a Portuguese neurosurgeon, thought that the cutting of the fibres leading from the frontal lobes to other parts of the brain might normalize the emotional pattern and he tried it. He made a hole on one side of the skull and a similar hole on the opposite side. The holes were so placed that when he passed an instrument no thicker than a small nail through one and brought it out at the other he interrupted many of the fibres of the frontal lobe. And it worked. The aggressive fiend became tractable and the melancholic more equable. I mean, it works sometimes. Quite often these people actually leave the hospital and go back to what appears to be a normal life. But how normal they are we cannot judge yet. I mean, should a surgeon who has had a Moniz done on himself go back to operative surgery? Is an aeroplane pilot who has had this Moniz surgery done on him competent to take a plane full of passengers on a scheduled route in all weathers? We don't know. The time since Moniz started his leucotomy, some people now call it 'lobotomy', is too short to judge. But why all this about a nail through the brain?'

'I think I had better begin at the beginning,' she said. Then she told him of how Cibrian asked her to find out where someone known as 'The Speaker' lived. This someone, an old man, was said to give comfort to the afflicted by listening to their tale of woe and then speaking. And she described the scene at Jaime's death.

'I was a Catholic,' she continued, 'that is, I was brought up as a Catholic. I know the ritual. That old man spoke the rites for the dying from an afflicted memory. But he spoke it with authority. I am not so much struck by his knowledge of the "Hymn to Brother Sun" for it is so well known amongst people who are brought up as Catholics. Cibrian and I both knew it. But the rites for the dying and the dead were spoken, as I have said, with authority. I do not think he could be any but an ecclesiastic of some sort.'

'Well,' said Cutbush, 'that is very probable. You should hear

Medina sometime on his exploits when he hunted priests and nuns in Tabasco. And Tabasco is next door to Chiapas that is, next door but one to Petén. Ask Medina to tell you of his boy-friend, Sergeant "Palo Seco". I say, is your Speaker's name Serrano?'

'He has no name,' she replied. 'He is written as "Jose Gomez" in the official books of Petén. But Gomez is the name of the family who "acquired" him, no one knows how, and they brought him to Petén from Chiapas.

'Then another family inherited him from clan Gomez but family number two have gone back to Mexico. Now he is alone. But why Serrano?'

So Cutbush told her of that Father Serrano who was different from other priests, so different that his people rescued him once from 'Palo Seco'. Then they hid him for months while he was hunted. 'Finally,' concluded Cutbush, '"Palo Seco" got him. He shot him in the leg then drove a nail into his head as he lay on the ground. There were rumours of his death and more particularly of his burial. So your "Speaker" could well be Serrano.'

'If he is, it could well account for everything,' she agreed. 'Cibrian said it is, now, of no importance who he was. In a measure that it true, though he was missing a point that is very important,' Karen told Cutbush. 'He thought I was going to "psychoanalyse" the poor old man. Nothing was further from my thoughts. That old man had something. He had it before "Palo Seco" did a Moniz on him. He is the only person I have ever heard of in my life who has it. It is greater and different from genius and I know what genius can do and how genius can be made to suffer. But if this blessing is reached through suffering it is personal. No one suffers but that particular person. It is not a contagious suffering. But there's a contagious, shall I say, power that some people have to bring peace and release.'

Cutbush was tired and bored. He closed his eyes. Five minutes later he woke. 'What is this about genius? What do you know of genius?' he asked her.

So she told him. He had read Thomas Mann's *Magic Mountain.* He remembered what Hans dreamt after he was lost in the snow. When she told of the pouring of the kerosene oil on the manuscript of 'The Dream' he sat up in the hammock,

'No,' he said, 'no!'

'Yes. I threw in the lighted match.'

He fell back. 'The insensate bitch,' he gasped quietly to himself but she heard him. He broke the long silence that followed by asking, 'But he wrote it again, eh? He wrote it again?'

'No,' she replied, 'he never wrote a bar of music again. He told me oh, what's the use? He is now a jazz-drummer and a dope-fiend.'

'Jesus Christ,' said Cutbush. He looked at her sitting quietly composed, even in riding-kit after a long ride, looking neat, well groomed. A slight pallor had spread over her features when he had said, 'No, no.' It was gone now. Not by a twitch or a flicker did she betray the fact that she knew Cutbush regarded her with horror and loathing. He broke an uneasy silence by asking her apparently apropos of nothing 'Do you know anything of the plays of Euripedes?'

She did not reply directly but she said, 'You are right, of course. When I burnt that manuscript I killed my children as Medea did. But where I differ from Medea is that I wear that burning robe. I did not send it to the third party. It is for me the fire that is not quenched. Long after he dies, probably in prison, and as long as I have health and sanity enough to know what I did, that I murdered his, our, children, that fire will not be quenched.'

'Talking of Medea,' he said 'and children, did you have any?'

'No,' said she, 'I never had the privilege. A couple of years after we were married and no pregnancy came along, although everything seemed normal, we decided to have an investigation. Naturally the wife is blamed first and foremost. I had the most thorough investigations at a well-recommended clinic. No reason for my sterility could be found. Then the doctors learnt we had spent some time in the tropics and as a last resort they asked if we had ever suffered from any tropical disease. I hadn't. "As for myself," said my husband, "the worst thing that happened in the tropics was mumps. To us it was a painful joke for we knew mumps was world wide and not only tropical."

'"Aha," said the doctor, "and you had it where you never expected mumps to fall? That's why you said painful?"

'"Yes," my husband replied. "We were living in a village in

Yucatan. She was deep in her archaeology and I was writing music. The village suffered an epidemic of mumps and almost every child caught it. As for me it was no joke. They dignified it with a double-barrelled name, "bilateral orchitis," said my husband. You as a doctor know that I am childless because he waited until he was a man to have mumps in both his testicles. He was potent but sterile and unable to father a child.'

For the first time Cutbush looked straight at her and she shivered with rage, for he looked with pity as he murmured, 'Lonely spirits cry – to be remembered.' He looked up at the skies. They were empty. The plane was not in sight so no rescue was at hand for him. He took refuge from her by pretending to sleep. In fact, he did doze off for a few minutes. And Karen saw him pretending, as she thought, to be asleep and the horror and pity he had showed for her now left her unmoved. Suddenly, she found, she had lost interest in working for the Nethersole Foundation in Petén. She would not come back for a season or so, not while Colonel Cibrian would be in Shoonantonitch. But she knew what she would do. She had made up her mind. Archaeology could wait. It had been waiting for centuries. But what she had to do could not wait. Soon, it would be too late.

When Cutbush awoke she was not by his side. He looked around anxiously. She was to him a thing of horror but of compelling attraction and she was company. He saw her coming towards him. She had been to the radio room of the airport house and told him the news. The plane had left Barrios some time ago and, given fair weather, should be arriving in a few minutes.

'In a few minutes?' he said. 'Good. Oh, good.' He would soon be relieved of the need of talking to her. In the plane she would be there, but silent because there could be no conversation in a plane, not the kind of plane that would be on the chicle run. He did not want to get rid of her, yet. In fact, he couldn't get rid of her until he had learnt something. When he got her answer then he would probably pray for the plane to arrive. Then, he suddenly remembered he had a message for her.

'By the way,' he said, 'Harkness told me to tell you that the last specimen he gave Copius was not from Polyporus. He had had an idea. He said he had thought of something with reference to the "paddle-shaped" leaf of stone of the Totonacs.'

'If it was not from Polyporus what was it from?' she asked eagerly.

'I don't know; I don't believe he said,' he replied.

She heard this with relief. It had been a good idea. It was still a good idea. Sooner or later somebody would carry out the experiment, but it would not be her. And now Harkness had taken the clue with him. And she was not sorry. Others might wish to laugh at God and die in the same way that others cursed God and died. She would never do either one or the other, for she was already dead. Still it was a good idea and on the whole if one had to make some sort of gesture as one died it would be better to laugh than to curse.

'Yes,' continued Cutbush, 'and also he said something about you. He, er ... ' he stopped, confused, irritated and tired. She saw his confusion and laughed. He was astounded. She laughed gaily looking at him with merry eyes, 'Yes, what is the message from the dead and dying?'

'He said you were a curious creature and he thought of showing you that even if you did start out on the wrong foot there was no reason why you should continue to be out of step with yourself.'

She was still smiling. 'He chose the better part. It won't do him, or anybody, any good for me to say it. But, curiously enough, I respected him. He was as empty as myself but, unlike me, he was not criminal.'

'In fact, he has a couple of creditable paragraphs in my Journal,' she continued.

'Oh you write a Journal, do you?' he said. 'What is it, "Portrait of the Artist as a Young Woman" *à la* James Joyce?'

'It is not as banal as an account of day-to-day happenings. Nothing to me is more tedious than that kind of thing. I make notes, copy things that interest me from books or journals and add comments on the people I meet and my reflections on the day's, or week's, happenings. Then, when the mood fills me, I distil it all into Kafka-like acerbities. No, that is not the right word, epitaphs would be better.'

'Why Kafka? I have read some of his work, not much I admit. But "epitaphs", that suggests very, very finite conclusions,' said Cutbush.

'Yes,' said Karen, 'but when one deals with processes in which there can be no finite conclusions it's difficult. I said Kafka-like because he stated that no man can depict his experience of God, or even hope to know Him. All that can be known is the anguish of being eternally in search of Him.'

'Isn't it unwise to have so personal a document in such surroundings. I mean in a camp in a hut?'

'Yes', you have a point there but you know that I was at school in a French convent in Cairo for nearly ten years. There, of course, we learnt Arabic because it was more useful for us than, say, Latin. Then, after my father remarried, I began writing a diary in Arabic. At first I did it just to irritate my step-mother who spoke nothing but English. Then I continued for purposes of privacy especially after I married. It is a marvellously expressive language. The doctor at our school told another girl, a friend of mine who informed him she was going to university to study medicine, that he had to recite the Oath of Hippocrates when he graduated. Later in life he read the "Prayer of Maimonides". Hippocrates is kindergarten stuff compared to Maimonides, he told her. And don't forget he wrote in Arabic in mid-twelfth century. Also, when I am ready to publish it I can retranslate, redistil, add or subtract flavours and nuances and give the dregs their septic, lasting bitterness.'

'And you dared to say that Harkness was empty.' Cutbush sat up angrily in the hammock. 'He was far from empty,' he fumed. 'He had courage.'

'Courage keeps the vessel upright but does not fill it,' Karen told him.

'He had inflexible integrity.'

'Integrity keeps the vessel bright and shining. It does not fill it,' she returned.

'He was free from ... '

'Positive virtues, please,' she murmured. 'Tell me what he had, don't tell me what he did not have.'

To his horror Cutbush found himself groping wildly for something which Harkness had said, something to crush this viper. Tears of frustration and rage rose to his eyes. Finally, as a desperate lunge to escape from embarrassed shame he asked the question, that which he had wanted to learn from her before the plane should come,

'What is it,' he enquired, 'that that old man, "The Speaker" had? What is it?'

'Ah, that is different,' she said gravely. 'I am not speaking of saintliness, whatever that is. But to a few, a very few men and women and to some of that few after, but not necessarily because of, struggle and self-discipline, there has been bestowed the vision of God. Some have described it as overwhelming bliss accompanied by a change in degree and in kind of perception. Perception is then all pervading, exquisitely penetrating, illimitably expanded.'

'Yes,' said Cutbush and he grinned maliciously. 'That is how ecstasy is described in books of psychiatry.'

She ignored his remark and went on. 'It of course affects their lives, their conduct, their speech, their understanding of man and the destiny of man. Father Serrano was different long ago before the persecution. He was different or the villagers would not have rescued him. He would have used the discipline of the Church, of course, but only a few of all races, ages and faiths have reached, as he did, those lonely heights. However, heights as heights are not the important thing. What is important is that those who make that journey come back from it changed. Serrano was changed. He was different and the villagers of Tabasco realized he was different from other men of God.

'It is only of incidental interest to me that his sanity should have been shattered, his intelligence practically obliterated and, as you have just explained, his emotional content outraged by a nail through his brain. That would have interested me in the same way I am interested in any medical phenomenon, but it is an incidental interest. His supreme importance to me is that even when, after being barbarously mutilated the residues of his brain, his mind or his soul were still embued with understanding, with pity and the power to heal merely by listening and speaking. He could no longer preach, he could no longer hear confessions or give the sacraments; he was no more than a shell without either the physical strength or the mental grasp to plant corn to feed himself. He had not even enough eccentricity or character to enable small boys to hang a nickname on him and so to persecute. He was nothing and yet he was, at times, the man who had communed with God. It seems as if his experience had so endowed him that his body would have to be reduced to ashes before it lost its power to bless and to heal. These people, I mean these mystics, are not always or even necessarily healers.

'Serrano was a healer and his memory will probably not die. Medina and even "Palo Seco" may live forever because of him. For now that I know his name is known I know, too, what I shall do. I shall go to Tabasco and quietly enquire into the persecution and connect up the incidents leading to the shot and the nail through the brain. Then I shall go to Chiapas and finally follow his exodus to Petén. I am not a practising Catholic but the memory of so precious a soul should not perish. The Church has the patience, the skill and the experience. When I have found and given it the data, the Church can then enquire, write down and wait in its own good time to resuscitate the memory of such a one. He may yet be known to a wider audience, as he is known to some few women of Shoonantonitch, as the man who spoke for them and unpacked their hearts.'

It was not that Cutbush denied the supreme importance of the mystical experience. He had read of it, but had not met it in his own experience or in that of anyone he knew.

Cutbush nodded. 'There might be something in all that, like a homeopathy,' he said with condescension. 'There may be something which could, perhaps, be worth studying but, if there is, then it is a truth of so finite and so minute an import that one need not wait for an answer. "Truth what is truth?" asked jesting Pilate, and did not wait for an answer.'

Then an idea struck him. 'That is it,' he said to himself, 'that's it. I will give her a homeopathic dose of her own medicine, drat her.'

'Do you know what I would do if I were you?' he asked.

'Yes, what is it?' she asked. But at that moment she turned away shuddering. Some distance away she saw Medina and others bending over something on the ground something which fought and shrieked and kicked while they tied it more tightly to a plank.

So she did not hear Cutbush say mockingly, 'I think you ought to ponder on that business from the Bible, "Lord I believe. Help Thou my unbelief."'

As he said the words the plane roared in to a landing, 'Thank God,' said Cutbush, 'Swing low, Sweet Chariot'.

But she did hear him say, 'Tonight, tonight a long, long sleep. None of your barbiturates with sooty fringes, trailing the morning, but chloral hydrate. I shall ask the doctor for the good old chloral hydrate and a deep dark night and bright and sudden morning. Then I shall write those last letters that Harkness asked me to do just before he was drowned.'

The plane made a perfect three-point landing. Cutbush nodded in appreciation. 'Of course, he has to be good, flying that thing with no emergency landing fields, with one engine and such a terrain to come down to in case of trouble.'

He shuddered. He had been in that terrain. He had been fortunate. His physicians would have little difficulty in diagnozing the character and extent of the hurt and harm he had suffered from his adventure.

He did not know that their difficulty would be how to inform their patient as to the nature of his illness and that they would in the meantime libel the sun and call it sunstroke because he knew too much about the possibilities for those suffering from a fractured skull.

Soon the plane took off. It carried Candellaria who had sought security in her art and had instead found security on a plank to which she was securely tied. She had been secured by Medina, the man who always knew when it was time to get out and when to recognize that the tide of circumstances had set against him. Medina, to whom 'the expedient' meant not merely survival but the vigorous prosperity of rude health and moderate wealth.

Karen was now sitting beside the plank and Medina beside Cutbush. Earlier when Cutbush had told her that Medina knew about Serrano and 'Palo Seco' the idea struck her and she approached Medina and suggested that she should take charge of Candellaria because it looked better for all concerned if a woman was in charge of another woman while he, Medina, could sit by Cutbush. Medina was delighted.

Karen hoped that Medina, in return for her help with Candellaria would tell her more about Serrano, give her dates and names and any information he could remember even remotely connected with the time, the place, the people, the period.

She had no doubt that this was, for her, going to be a period 'like unto the dark night of the soul' which St. John of the Cross described. She could promise herself no bright and sudden morning. Yet there was a singular satisfaction in the particular labour which she had now set herself. She was a scholar. Her strength was the act of patient research, of quiet unhurried unravelling of the past. She had applied this art to a particular part of the history of the accomplishment of man. Now she intended to apply it to man's Future. For she had no doubt that only in some such way, by some such path as that by which the 'Speaker' had travelled could man escape from his particular dilemma, from between the daemonic drive of his intellectual prowess and the barborous, self-mutilating, self-pitying paroxysms of evil.

ZEE EDGELL
Beka Lamb

A delightful portrait of Belize, a tiny country in South America dominated by the Catholic Church, poverty, and a matriarchal society. Winner of the Fawcett Society Book Prize.

BERYL GILROY
Frangipani House

Set in Guyana, this is the story of an old woman sent to a rest home where she struggles to retain her dignity. Prize winner in the GLC Black Literature competition.

BESSIE HEAD
When Rain Clouds Gather

In a poverty-stricken village in Botswana, the pressures of tradition, the opposition of the local chief and the harsh climate threaten to bring tragedy to the community.

HAROLD SONNY LADOO
No Pain Like This Body

In vivid, unsentimental prose this powerful novel describes the life of a poor rice-growing family during the August rainy season; their struggle to cope with illness, a drunken and unpredictable father, and the violence of the elements.

ALEX LA GUMA
A Walk in the Night

Seven stories of decay, violence and poverty from the streets of Cape Town, and by one of South Africa's most impressive writers.

EARL LOVELACE
The Wine of Astonishment

'His writing is lyrical, reflecting Trinidadian speech habits as well as they have ever been reflected. This is an energetic, very unusual, above all, enlightening novel; the author's best yet.'

Financial Times

JOHN NAGENDA
The Seasons of Thomas Tebo

A pacy, vivid allegory of modern Uganda where an idyllic past stands in stark contrast to the tragic present.

NGŨGĨ WA THIONG'O
A Grain of Wheat

'With Mr Ngũgĩ, history is living tissue. He writes with poise from deep reserves, and the book adds cubits to his already considerable stature.'

The Guardian

NGŨGĨ WA THIONG'O
Petals of Blood

A compelling, passionate novel about the tragedy of corrupting power, set in post-independence Kenya.

SEMBENE OUSMANE
Black Docker

The leading Senegalese author and film maker draws on his own experiences and the problems of racism, prejudice and injustice to recreate the uneasy atmosphere of France in the 1950s.

RICHARD RIVE
Buckingham Palace: District Six

'Buckingham Palace' is a dingy row of five cottages in Cape Town's notorious District Six. The neighbourhood is enlivened by a bizarre and colourful cast of characters, including Mary, the brothel keeper, Katzen, the Jewish landlord and Zoot, the charismatic 'jive king' of the area.

GARTH ST OMER
The Lights on the Hill

The story of Stephenson as he stumbles through jobs and affairs is an elegant achievement in West Indian literature.

'One of the most genuinely daring works of fiction to come my way for a very long time.'

The Listener

MYRIAM WARNER-VIEYRA
Juletane

When Helene is packing up her belongings to move house, she comes upon an old diary, written by Juletane, a Caribbean girl, who turned to writing to escape from her traumatic marriage to a polygamous husband. A hauntingly powerful, feminist novel that spans the African and Caribbean literary traditions.